IAN M...

KIRINYA

The right of Ian McDonald to be identified as the author
of this work has been asserted by him in accordance with
the Copyright, Designs and Patents Act 1988.

This edition published in Great Britain in 1999 by
Millennium
An imprint of Victor Gollancz
Orion House, 5 Upper St Martin's Lane,
London WC2H 9EA

To receive information on the Millennium list, e-mail us at:
smy@orionbooks.co.uk

A CIP catalogue record for this book
is available from the British Library

ISBN 1 85798 876 0

Permission to quote from *A Shropshire Lad* by
A. E. Housman was granted by The Society of Authors
as the Literary Representative of the Estate of
A. E. Housman. Lines from 'Do not go gentle into that
good night' by Dylan Thomas, published by J. M. Dent,
by permission of David Higham Associates Ltd.

Printed in Great Britain by
Clays Ltd, St Ives plc

'The tree of man was never quiet'

A. E. Housman
A Shropshire Lad: XXXI

New Moon in Saturn

1

The dark was almost gone now. Morning clung to the horizon, a line of amber on ocean edge. As the woman watched, the line deepened, revealing interlaced fingers of cloud, darker on dark. Weather systems were moving far from land; ripples of indigo cloud spun out from the slow, vast spiral of the monsoon. The beach was a plane of sound; surf ponderous on the reef, running high on the fringe of the healing rains; pipe and flute of beach birds lighting and running a few quizzing steps and lifting again as easily as thought; the language of the breeze off the sea in the revenant palms and the tall, slim spires of the land corals. The music from the party ebbed and ran, now soft, now thudding.

In the place between the sown and the sand, the woman stopped and, lightly, fearfully, touched her hands to the baby slung between her breasts.

'Listen,' the woman said.

Impossible that the child should understand her, yet in the gaining light she saw her daughter fold up her face and fists to squeal; then relax, fall silent and still. In the same instant the wind from the ocean caught the music and blew it back in through the door of the bar. The woman and the child stood enfolded in presence. The moment stretched, the moment snapped.

'Nothing,' the woman said. She smiled for herself. 'You'll learn.'

She went on to the sand. There was light enough to make out the shapes of the scuttling crabs – but not enough to avoid them. They burst under her boots in crisp, kicking thrashes. The small white beach birds came sliding off the ocean wind to pick and tear at the agonized footprints.

'Look, there goes Mr Crab!' she told her daughter, who was now frowning because it felt good. 'And here comes Master Crab; will we get him? Yes!'

The baby gulped air. The birds lifted and settled to rip and heave with their orange beaks.

'Whoa Mrs Crabby!' the woman said, running fast after the big mother of a hen crab, as fast as a woman with a baby at her breasts may run in soft, tide-wet sand. Mrs Crabby hid herself beneath the lap of tide foam.

All but the brightest stars of the southern hemisphere had faded. The moon was still up, a day past new; the crescent moon of Africa, lying on its back, cradled by the open palms of the hand-trees. The moon held a star between its horns. The woman knew that a pair of binoculars could open up that big, soft star. It was a cylinder, passing through the same phases and occultations as the true moon. It was an artefact, a hollow world three hundred kilometres long, one hundred and fifty across its faces. It hung midway between earth and moon. Such truth put a catch in the breath and needle of cold in the sense of mystery.

'Hey,' Gaby McAslan said to the baby, who happened to have tilted her head back and turned her face to the moons. 'Wave a fist to Daddy.'

The anger was so sudden, so acid and smoking that she was paralysed for a moment. Crabs hurried around her feet. Only a moment: she walked on. Tidewater seeped out of the sand into her boot prints.

Second moon in the arms of the first. An auspice: a time of journeys undertaken, endeavours embarked upon, courses changed, lives turned to a different wind. Astrology was among

8

the least of human activities to have been transformed by the advent of the BDO.

They should rename it, Gaby thought. It's Big, it's undoubtedly an Object, but it is no longer Dumb. We just do not know what it is saying to us.

'Born with the BDO in Cancer,' Gaby whispered to her daughter. 'A journey begun. Death and rebirth.'

Saturn and the new mysteries unfolding among its satellites were below the western horizon. They would be partying with one eye on the monitors at the Mermaid Café. Gaby hoped she would not have to be there to see whatever happened out there. Her life had been tied to those far, cold moons by forces more subtle and powerful than astrology. Twelve years ago it had been a different shore, a different continent. Ireland. The Watchhouse. The Point. Home. A different person: the kid that had wished on a star and become Gaby McAslan, SkyNet television journalist. Gaby McAslan, exile. A different moon: Iapetus. She had gone out on to the Point that evening to be caressed by mystery, to be impregnated with sign and seal. From twelve years up with her child in her arms, she could look back at that gangly kid and see that she was not looking for a true sign, for that could have as easily pointed away from as to her heart's desire. She had looked only for confirmation of what was already certain. Iapetus had turned black; then Hyperion had vanished in a flash of energy, but it was decided somewhere surer than in the stars that she would become a network journalist.

'The older you get the more you learn, the more you learn the less certain you are, bub,' she told her daughter. Twelve years higher, might she look down astonished at the self-assurance of this thirty-year-old?

The upper limb of the sun was fountaining light out of the sea into the undersides of the clouds; staining them purple, crimson, black. The headland was still in shadow but highlights and glints lit Gaby's track up through the fan-cover. She went more cautiously than the gentle climb deserved. She feared slipping and crushing the baby. The way was well trodden; the headland was a popular viewpoint for the people of Turangalila. You could see twenty kays up and down the reef. On the clearest of

9

days you could make out the great breaches where the ships had passed through into the port of Mombasa. Now the only ships on the sea were the low, grey hulls of the quarantine fleet, pressed low on the horizon, afraid of infection. But the news from down the coast was of a great, vibrant culture growing from the stumps of dead Mombasa. The infection the quarantine ships feared was a disease of nations. It had killed Kenya, it was killing Tanzania by the minute, but the people of this coast were Africans before they were people of any nation. They were as fecund and inventive as the slow-breaking wave of alien life that was transforming their land, fifty metres every day.

But Mombasa is gone, Gaby thought. The Mombasa I knew in those final, frantic days of the nation formerly known as Kenya. I loved that nation, I loved that land, and the Chaga took it apart. I loved a man there, far away, and it took him. Everything I loved has been taken by the Chaga: the place I drew power from, the people I loved and tormented, the ambitions and abilities that defined me.

She paused on a steeper section of the slope.

'Woo. Still haven't got over having you, bub.'

Her daughter blinked at the sky. Tiny, tiny red living thing. Gaby continued up the path. The sun continued up the sky.

'You knocked me right out of condition, you know? If I'm going to play in the Kanamai game, I have to get back into serious training. Do some running, bit of swimming.' She paused again, out of breath.

The spine of the headland was thickly wooded in a mixture of alien and reconstructed terrestrial vegetation, but at the very tip it opened into a sun-burned nose of bare earth. Here Gaby set down the leather bag. She took her daughter to the edge. The headland tumbled in laps of coral rock to a low shelf where the sea ran dangerously. Over her shoulder the moons set; their brief conjunction broken.

Good, Gaby thought. I do not want you with your eyes full of moon. I do not want another life tied to the powers in the sky.

Gaby unlaced the papoose. Her two hands held her daughter up to the light.

'Serena,' she said, blocking out the sun with her child.

Gaby hesitated. She needed to say something elemental, but

the growing light of day embarrassed her little ritual. 'You are my Serena,' she said weakly. The baby kicked in her hands and she looked at her and suddenly saw that it would be the easiest thing in the world to open those hands. To let her fall. To let the waves slide the thing off the coral platform into the sea.

Serena kicked again. Gaby shook her daughter.

'You bitch!' she shouted. 'You little bitch! Do you know what you've done to me?'

Serena began to cry.

'Shut up, shut up, just shut up you little, fucking, bitch!' Gaby shook Serena to the rhythm of her rage but she could not shake silence into the baby. Serena screamed.

'It's because of you I'm here, because of you I can't go back, because of you they won't let me out. All. Because. Of. You.'

Do it. Be free. She's not perfect. She's not true. There are still tribes that expose the ones it touches and changes. Just open your hands. A fumble, a slip. It could happen. It would be dreadful, but only for a time. She's not perfect.

Gaby felt her hands tremble. Light filled her eyes. With a cry she snatched the baby girl out of the sun and pressed her close, enfolded her in her long, mahogany hair.

'Oh my wee thing, my wee thing; oh Jesus oh God, I'm sorry, I'm sorry, my wee thing.' She sank to the earth, rocked the screaming red blob, terrified by what the light had lit up within her. 'Oh Jesus, bub, oh Christ, I'm sorry, I'm sorry. I'm sorry. I'm sorry. What was I thinking?'

She remembered what she was thinking.

When the Chaga fell from the stars to spread across half the planet, it had changed more than geography. No one had ever seen the intelligence that had conceived and constructed the biological packages that had fallen for fifteen years – it was accepted now that the Chaga-makers were unrecognizable and unintelligible to human chauvinisms on life and intelligence – but their intentions could be surmised. Not conquest, not colonization – though the Chaga, converting all in its path to its matrix, was a particularly voracious imperialism – but discourse in the only way the Makers understood; through mutual evolution. Earth's southern hemisphere was a voice in a dialogue that crossed eight hundred light years and five hundred million years

11

to the complex fullerene clouds in the Scorpius loop. The Makers wrote their dialectics in human DNA.

Changed.

There was an irony to this.

In that other life, when she had been Gaby McAslan, East African Correspondent for SkyNet Satellite News, she had exposed that truth to the planet. Still a shudder when she thought of Unit 12, and what the United Nations had tried to hide in its labyrinth of levels and chambers. She had only escaped because friends in powerful places had pulled for her.

Thanks, Shepard, she thought at the place where the BDO had set. And I treated you like Satan's shit. But I do that. That's the way I am. And where were you the next time I ran up against the UN quarantine force and its long memory for grudges? You probably don't even know what happened, up there in that big tin can. You probably don't even know you have a daughter named Serena. You certainly will never know what they said about her, when they brought me out of decontam that time, when there was no one there, and they showed me the results of the tests and stamped the papers and gave me over to the troops.

Exiled.

They could not, or would not, say what the nature of the change would be. Only that the cluster of rapidly dividing cells in Gaby's womb would be a girl, and it had been touched by the alien.

Gaby closed her eyes as she touched her lips to the crown of Serena's soft skull.

'I'm sorry, I'm so sorry, my wee thing.'

She hooked Serena into the sling. Breast-warmth and heart-rhythm soothed her screams. Gaby unfastened the unitool. A twist of the shaft locked it into a short shovel. She dug until she hit cliff rock. She hoped the scrape would be deep enough to discourage scavengers.

The leather satchel had not leaked. There were still a few soft ice crystals on the afterbirth's liver-dark surface. Such an alien thing to keep inside you. Beautiful and repulsive, like something Chaga-grown. But she did not tip it into the hole, not yet. That would be to give part of herself to the land. She had always drawn her power from the land: her childhood expeditions to the hidden places of the Point; the wide places of Kenya, before the Chaga swept across them, now this promontory overlooking the sea. You gave yourself to the land and it let you put your roots down into it and suck its power and become definite. It made you a person. But she did not know if she wanted to be the person Turangalila would make her. To bury the afterbirth would be to bury Gaby McAslan. She was afraid she would not recognize the life that was reborn.

'Give me a sign,' she said. The sun stood three fingers above the ocean. Light filled up the land, casting new shadows and definitions with every second. The deep water was restless, all glitter and urgencies; the reef like knuckles of earth pulling back from the dissolving sea. The air was clean and cool and smelled of the big deep. That had always been the most evocative of smells to Gaby; restless and yearning. The elements were strong here, but they had no sign to give her.

The tide was high after moonset, lapping under the sagging shore palms. Turangalila's boats were beached high. Turangalila itself, blended with the canopy of pseudo-fungus and land corals, gave no indication of human presence on this coast. In the early gold the Chaga-growth and the coconut palms and occasional baobabs did not seem mutually hostile, but symbiotic products of an alternative evolution track, taken back in the pre-Cambrian.

Not such a fanciful notion, if the theories were true that this was merely the latest in a series of interventions in terrestrial evolution by the Chaga-makers.

The tide and the trees and boats hugging them and the settlement folded into them had no sign for Gaby McAslan.

She turned inland, to Africa, to the place where the ragged carpet of the coastal ecology lifted and tore into the stunning uplift of the Great Wall. There trees, or things that seemed like trees, rose sheer for a kilometre and a half before unfolding into a canopy of immense interlocking hexagons. The roof of the world. From here you could see that the Great Wall curved gradually inland to north and south. The formation was a curtain wall one hundred and fifty kilometres across. It occupied the whole of what had once been East Tsavo game reserve.

Beyond the Great Wall you could not see. From experience

she knew that it contained many landscapes and ecosystems nested like babushka dolls. But it was changing, adapting, moving towards humanity as humanity moved towards it. It was the evolutionary dialogue: the reconstructed palms, the neo-baobabs, the Chaga plants that were drifting towards terrestrial species, the animals that were creeping back through the coastal forests exploiting new ecological niches: symbiosis. Growing together.

The trees and the Great Wall and the landscapes hidden behind it and the creeping animals of the coast had no sign for Gaby McAslan.

Serena's fingers seized and tugged a coil of her hair.

'Ah! Shit!' Gaby said, and understood, and laughed, and tipped the quivering blood thing into the hole and quickly covered it with earth.

As Gaby went carefully back down the path to the beach she sang her daughter Motown soul classics that were old before Gaby had been born. The beach crabs were all down under the high water. The white birds that had pecked at the bloody footprints rested on the surface, top-heavy, as if the next gust might capsize them. The ribbons of dawn cloud had broken up into soft black beads, moving fast inshore under a strong wind running at a thousand metres. There would be rain on the coast before noon.

Gaby clambered over the slumped palm trunks, splashed through the sea-run around the thick red wrists of the hand-trees. She heard Hussein's radio before she saw him at his boat, pulled up under the wall of the dead hotel. He was tuned to one of the new stations beaming out of Malindi. It played morning music, bright, intricate guitar sounds and funk-Swahili DJ-babble. Hussein was scraping polyps from his hull. He liked his boat smooth and straight and lean and long. He was a tall, hairless Giriama with a streak of mission-widow Masai, and a devout Moslem in the way that all men who go on the sea are devout. They respect God, but not religion.

'Gaby. And Gaby's child.' He spoke hotel-English and hotel-German. Before the hotels were swept away he had run glass-bottom boats and snorkel tours to the reef. 'You know, my uncle's people used to fry it with onions and curry spices and eat it in chapattis.'

'That,' Gaby McAslan said, 'is disgusting. Is the Mermaid still open?'

'There was noise coming out of it when I went past half an hour ago.'

'You don't know if the Phoebe thing has happened yet?'

'Gaby, I sail boats.'

'Yeah, yeah. You're taking her out today?'

'Every day there are wetbacks and raft people want to come here, I go out.'

And they will have brought small handfuls of their treasures with them and you will ask for a something here, a something there, a token or favour to be repaid sometime never, Gaby thought. Not because you need these things – no one needs anything any more, but because freedom has a price. As if they have not already paid it to the freighter captains that put them over the side outside radar range, and pay again as they paddle and kick and swim past the blockade ships, and pay the sharks and the Portuguese men-o'-war, and pay the waves and the reef as they try to make it over into the lagoon. But they have not paid you.

'You are a God-damn pirate, Hussein,' Gaby said amicably.

'I like to think of myself as an immigration service. An underground railroad in the ocean.'

'I think the word is *submarine*,' Gaby said. Hussein fed syrup to the *putti-putti*. The biomotor burped and began to beat, pumping air. He adjusted the pulse, then disconnected the cell battery. 'But you be careful, right?' Gaby continued. 'One of these days those bastards are going to blow you right out of the water.'

'I am Captain Stealth, I sail under their guns and they cannot see me.'

'You put too much trust in that radar-transparent hull of yours. They may be Saudis, but they have eyes in their heads.'

'God's will, Gaby and Gaby's child.'

'Serena.'

'Ah. That is a good name for this country.'

'God's will, Hussein.'

Yes, Gaby thought as she went up the path that had once taken tourists to the beach and the glass-bottomed boats. That is

15

why you laughed on the headland when Serena gave you the sign you had not been expecting. God pulling your hair, hey, listen, after all those years of wanting and trying, you are an African. A white-skinned, green-eyed, red-haired African. And what makes you African is that you finally accept My will, whether you stay or go, whether you drop your baby from the cliff or bury your afterbirth in the earth. This is the world you have to live in, now, here. *Ismillah.* So laugh, because there is nothing you can do about it.

The path was not the most direct way to the Mermaid Café but the Chaga kept rearranging the shortcuts and the crumbled ruins of the hotel were treacherous. The empty swimming pool waited in there somewhere; a blue tiled pit trap. Gaby stepped through the place where the chain link fence had fallen under the weight of sulphur-yellow moulds into the tennis courts. The far service area had been colonized by bulbous blue and white growths like over-sized Chinese vases that exuded a strangely alluring musk. Clusters of minute orange crystals infecting the tramlines crunched like crab shells beneath Gaby's boots.

The carved mermaid was nailed to a palm behind the pile of scabrous machinery that had once chlorinated the pool. She had a sluttish leer and pointed along a track that meandered between palms and crown corals. The Mermaid Café was one of those unawares buildings that you are at before you realize. When you learned the trick of picking it out of the visual chaos of vegetation, what you saw was something ludicrously like an enormous straw sombrero propped up on short stilts. It was very much more alien and clever than that: its thatch was a fine solar fur that cooled the building in the heat of the day, warmed it by night, and generated electrical current in every fibre. When you ducked under the brim and your eyes adjusted to the bioluminescent shade that is best for contemplative drinking you saw that it was more like a tree than a hat, for a thick central trunk held up the roof. Branch-ribs ran down to the brim and became the strong, bone-like stilts. Tree-hat-hut.

The Mermaid Café smelled of warmth and things growing from deep soil, sweat and the urinous hum of spilled beer. Most of the tables were still full. There were some seats at the bar that circled the trunk. The main biolumes clinging under the canopy

16

were dull; the bar was lit by table lamps and television. The screens hanging from the central trunk were all full of stars.

'Gab!'

Sunpig was a short podgy white American woman of middle years. She wore more than one ring on each finger. Illustrated cards lay in various patterns across her table. They bore the wide eyes, seraphic faces and blessing hands of Ethiopic icons. Sunpig's work at Turangalila was to develop an uniquely Cha-African tarot. Everyone at Turangalila had a work; that was the dream of the place, the expression of the transforming potential of the Chaga into every field of human activity. Like most experimental artistic communities, these expressions tended to end up in the bar.

'I did it.'

'And?'

'There's an "and"?'

'Woman with child!' With a flick of his forefinger, Dr Scullabus directed his patrons to make way for Gaby. 'Sit.' She sat. 'Drink.' She drank the house beer set in front of her. The Doctor was tall, with bad skin but good jaw-length bleached dreads. Gaby liked Dr Scullabus hugely. He was that age when men like to give themselves names, but he had her respect. He had used the Chaga to remake himself. Before it came sweeping down the coast from the impact at Kilifi he had been a beach boy. He had worn good muscles, lycra shorts, no body hair, and fucked tourists and let them spend their money on him. When the tourists stopped coming, he fucked journalists and UN workers instead. He had never had any money so he lost nothing when the Chaga took the hotels away. His skills at getting what he wanted from people it could not change; they had earned him the Mermaid Café and his place behind the bar as supreme pontiff.

Gaby lay Serena on the bar. She blinked at the star-filled screens. It was hot under the sombrero; Gaby's shorts and vest stuck to her. But the beer was cold. She drank it down in one go. The Doctor brewed it himself but the bottles were many many times recycled, scavenged from the overgrown trash heaps of the lost hotels of his youth.

'You missed it, Gab.'

'Was it cosmic?'

'The man on the satellite news did not have any idea what he was talking about. You would have done it right, Gaby. You would have made us feel the size of the thing, and the bigness of space, and how far away it is, and how cold, and how wonderful.'

'Doc, it's no wonder you got so many rides.'

'It is true, Gaby. If you had been there, I am telling you, you would have given us such big awe that it would have made our balls go tight.'

'But I'm not.' Gaby rolled the much-washed beer bottle between her palms. 'I'm here. And this is another one on my endless account.'

Chaga-nomics. Quid pro quo: with Andre the Doctor would trade beer for a day's fishing beyond the reef; for a song from Harrison, for a reading from Sunpig, for a dinner from Marilynne, for a restyle of those dreads from Musta. But from Gaby McAslan, former SkyNet East Africa Correspondent, what has she to sell?

Gaby banged the empty bottle on the bar. Serena gave a small gurgle but thought sleep better. New beer was delivered. Gaby drank it down. Breakfast of champions.

Those amputees who suffered phantom pains in lost limbs, how long before the twinges faded? Ever?

She looked at the screens. Since the dark side of Iapetus had engulfed the bright and Hyperion had vanished, heralding the advent of the Chaga, a steady stream of space probes had been sent to Saturn's moons. The arrival of the Big Dumb Object, reconstituted from the fragments of Hyperion, in Earth orbit, had eclipsed the unmanned missions – why go to Saturn when Saturn has come to you? Then Phoebe had disappeared in a quantum black hole explosion, and the powers in the sky were moving again. Saturn satellite mission twenty-two, *Wagner*, had been retasked for a ring-side seat to whatever the Chaga-makers had willed for Phoebe.

It had arrived in the Phoebe Rift, two days after Serena's birth. It had unfolded its antennae, uncoiled its sensor booms like a luna moth hatching and seen slender arcs tens of kilometres long tumbling slowly in trans-lunar space. At three thirty-five GMT the will of the Chaga-makers had become manifest: the arcs joined. The processed images from the orbital telescopes had sketched a ring three and half thousand kilometres in diameter.

They had a name for this one too. The arcs had not even joined and they were calling it Éa. Enigmatic Artefact.

One minute to fly-by. *Wagner* would pass through the ring within one hundred kilometres of the inner surface. The terrestrial long-baseline interferometers could resolve with greater discrimination than the space telescopes: Éa was a thread, a hoop two kilometres wide by five hundred metres deep. *Wagner* would have to look hard to see anything.

Expert voices were opining that Éa did not account for all Phoebe's mass.

And suddenly there it was, swimming out of the dark as it caught the distant sun, like a bracelet of light. Somewhere, Gaby was aware that Serena was hungry. She slipped a tit out of her loose vest and picked up the grizzling child. *Wagner* swept through the hoop of light like a weasel through a wedding ring. Gaby glimpsed coiling white ridges, like twined intestines, valleys between bristling with stiff quills. Then stars. *Wagner* brought its rear camera booms to bear.

Every screen in the Mermaid Café went white.

'Hey, Scullabus!' someone shouted from the far side of the bar.

'My televisions are fine,' the Doctor said. 'Look.'

The probe cameras had pulled out and stopped down. Éa was a disc of white light. The dazzling screens threw unfamiliar shadows into the recesses of the Mermaid Café. Darkness. Where the light had been, precisely framed by the huge ring, was a moon.

Many of the Doctor's bottles that were more precious than what he sold in them hit the floor and shattered.

Not even the expert voices knew what to say.

The moon was a monster: rust-red, cratered and rayed. Dark *mares* were cracked and faulted like Japanese glaze. The satellite had a satellite. Hovering beyond the new moon's Roche limit was a curved disc eight hundred kilometres in diameter. Its radius curvature matched the moon: its dark side trailed floes and stalactites of frozen gas tens of kilometres long. Gaby found it impossible to resist the notion that the disc was pushing the moon.

Like its predecessor, this even bigger, dumber object was inbound. Simulations drew curves on the solar system. Its destination was not Earth. In twelve years Venus would have a moon, orbiting every twenty days.

Gaby grimaced; Serena was gumming hard. She probably needs winding, Gaby thought. The incongruity of that thought with the wonder stuff on the screens almost made her laugh aloud. All it was was one dead rock going to another, but this was a human child. That was mechanics. This was the future.

What a universe you're going to grow up in, kid.

The Crossing

2

Her name was Oksana Mikhailovna Telyanina. She had flown with the wild geese and swum with the salmon. She had run with the reindeer and stolen the eggs of eagles with the ermine. She had travelled on the wings of the wind and entered the spirits of the trees. She had become light, and the light beyond light that was the true illumination, of which all light was a shadow. She had dissolved into the waters like a drop of rain, she had been the blade of grass crushed by the hoof of the deer, and that deer that crushed it. And now all that remained were wisps of chemical ash in her bloodstream and she was a forty-something woman sitting in an oak tree. Bare-ass naked with the first frosts only days away. Nippled with goose-flesh, but the tits were still firm, by God. A tight fortysomething woman. Keeping in shape was an element of the greater spiritual exercise.

But you are cold and stiff and vertiginous from the mushrooms. And feeling old.

And unanswered. Two days until she flew south again, back to Africa, and her spirit was still unquiet.

'Tell me,' she had said to the wild geese and the salmon

swimming upstream to death. 'What should I do?' she had asked the reindeer and the ermine. 'Is this right?' she had questioned the wind and the trees. 'Are you listening?' she had asked the light and the water. 'Is there anyone there?' she said to the grass and the deer that trampled it. The geese and the salmon and the reindeer and the ermine and the wind and the trees and light and the water and the grass and the deer had answered fuck all.

It did not work any more. The spirit worlds were closed to her. She might as well have skulled-out on her living room carpet and read divinity into the swirling patterns of the Turkmenistani weavers. She would not have risked pneumonia and fractures from falling, stoned, out of a sacred oak.

The sky read imminent evening. She had been beyond for eight hours. Once she would have walked the branches of the world-tree for days on that much skag. It is a bad sign when it takes more and more to do less and less, she thought as she clambered down the steps cut in the trunk. She dressed quickly, bouncing up and down to shake heat into her body. There was chocolate in the backpack, and the hip flask with the last of the arak. She swigged from the flask as she took the shaman-path through the deepening twilit woods to the logging road. The stuff burned brave. For the first time she felt need of its reassurance. The spirits had closed their hands and eyes. Their protection was no longer assured. She unbuckled the strap on her bush-knife. The things that lived and killed in the dark were afoot, calling. She was glad to see the rusty Cossack 4x4 in the pull-in off the rutted road. Her hand lingered on the reindeer antlers fixed to the bull-bars. Once, an emblem of her uniqueness: look, here comes Oksana Telyanina, shamanka, now they were as embarrassing as an old school backpack covered in the names of pretty-boy bands. Fortysomething and you are still a teenager, Oksana Telyanina. You are on the downslope of your life and you still need these emblems and totems to tell you who you are.

She fished the magnet out of the glove box and pressed it to the scarred mound on her wrist. The diffusion pump control was tricky; confirmation of success was the purr of the processor as it leached the lingering traces of the trance drugs and arak out of her blood. Molecule by molecule it exposed the hollow in

22

her life. It was many-lobed, branching like a meltwater lake on tundra.

The slot of sky filling the narrow cut of the logging road grew dark. The autumn stars appeared, a great wheel turning above the Siberian taiga. Venus seemed to hover at the road's vanishing point: guide star into night.

It was an hour back to the highway, another two hours home. Stone cold and sober, Oksana turned the ignition.

Venus exploded: a white flare, hard and brilliant enough to cast the shadow of the steering wheel across Oksana's belly. She cried out with fear. She had destroyed a planet. Her power had run wild; the stars were falling through the twenty-seven heavens. The spirits in the forest would rise up and rend her soul for this. She flicked on the headlights; her wheels chewed dirt. The battered Cossack slewed on the needle-strewn surface. Eyes in the dark threw her headlight beams back at her.

Oksana floored the brakes. The 4x4 shuddered to a stop, antlers a rip of velvet from the trunk of a big larch.

On a dirt road in the middle of forty thousand square kilometres of wilderness, Oksana Mikhailovna Telyanina laughed hard at her presumption. The stars were not falling. She had seen two hundred billion tons of cometary ice enter Venus' atmosphere at one hundred kilometres per second and convert its mass into plasma.

She banged her hands on the wheel with delight. She understood why the spirits had been silent. They had long memories, in this triangle of land between the Stony and White Tungus rivers. They had felt the hammer of God fall. And that had been a few megatons, a few hundred square kilometres of felled trees, pointing *j'accuse* at the epicentre. The mother that hit Venus had another fifteen hundred sisters behind her. The scientific assessments appalled Oksana's shamanka spirit. The momentum transfer from the impacts – each enough to scour Earth as sterile as a gynaecological tool – would speed up the planet's rotation. The new dawn would break every forty-two hours, and a new moon would sail its nights.

Tectonics and carbon cycles: each impact blasted a hefty megatonnage of the planet's massive atmosphere into space. Tidal forces kept the inner fires burning, like Jupiter's sadomasochistic relationship with tormented, cracked Io, or Earth's moon with its mother mass.

Life, ultimately. That was what Oksana understood of the Chaga-makers. That was what she had seen in her years flying for the UN in the mutating Africa south of the equator: life exploding in a million new songs and dances. Big life. Great life. Before each spring must come a winter, be it the winter of ice or the winter of plasma fire. Or, she thought, hitting the radio tuner buttons at random until they settled on a pirate country and western station; ice and fire.

The new moon's companion object, the huge disc nicknamed Moondozer, had cast off when the red satellite was adjusted into its final orbit. Its course was a long, narrow loop that would return it to Venus in eighteen months in an orbit a scant one hundred kilometres above the cloud tops, ploughing through the nebula of ionized atmosphere. The theory was that Moondozer would use this gas ring as a seed bed to crash-cultivate fullerenes. For three hundred years a rain of Chaga-spores would fall upon Venus's cloud tops.

All worlds begin in ice and fire. The great cow licked the Ginnungagap from the universal ice. Out of the void the world tree had grown. The heavens declare shamanic truth.

'Moon-cow,' she announced to the great disc, speeding unseen on its outward course. 'I call you Moon-cow, life-licker.'

Half an hour down the highway she pulled in at a truck stop. She needed fuel for machine and body. Shamanic trances left her as hungry as a logger. The park was full of truck trains headed north with supplies for the outlying towns before winter closed in. The diner was full of loud drivers. They followed Oksana with their eyes as she took the loaded tray to the furthest table. Her expression said, leave me alone. Her Sibirsk jacket said, respect, boys. Her half-inch of blonde stubble and tattoos said, if you want to think I am a lesbian, that's all right. Her thirty centimetre hook-tipped hunting knife said, I can take the knob off your dick so fast . . .

The radio was tuned to the same country station she had half-listened to in the car. Oksana ate her heaps of food and helped her diffuser work on the last of the arak and the fungus with twelve glasses of tea. She paid the pile of chits the sexually

oppressed waitress had left on her table and felt the truckers'
eyes follow her back out into the car park.

She smelled coming winter in the dust of the last warm
autumn day. The night was immense. The truck stop was a frail
lantern hanging in the wilderness. A kind-of-pretty trucker boy
was standing in the middle of the lot, gazing ecstatically into the
sky.

'If you stare too long you can get lost in them,' she said. 'The
spirits of many shamans are still wandering out there; looking
for the path home.'

'That's your car, the one with antlers?' The boy's voice was
soft, high-pitched, feminine.

Cute, Oksana Telyanina thought. She said, 'How long have
you been following the way?'

'I'm just a beginner; I got some books out the travelling library,
optical-Roms, on-line newsgroups. Teach-yourself-shamanism.'

'I think we're condemned to be beginners all our lives,'
Oksana said.

The boy slowly turned his head, tracing an arc across the
night.

'You can't see it at home, too much light. Out here, it's
beautiful.'

Oksana blinked the café neons out of her eyes and saw what
it was that entranced this strange boy. A bridge of light hung in
the sky, soft as powder, growing in definition as her eyes
acclimatized to the dark. Intellect told her it was the mingled
tails of the comets that had come out of Éa, falling in towards
the sun. Instinct could not believe that. It was a star-bow slung
across heaven, the way of the spirits between the branches of the
world-tree.

The young man and the fortysomething woman stood silent
and watching for a timeless time. Then the orgasmic gasp of air-
brakes and the sudden headlight dazzle of a bus pulling into the
diner broke the enchantment.

'I really do like your antlers,' the boy said. 'Where are you
headed?'

'Back to Irkutsk. You?'

'South,' he said, and smiled.

South. Where the geese are flying, where the salmon are

swimming, where the reindeer are migrating, where the winds are blowing, where the rains are falling and the starbow is aiming; where the strange boy is travelling.

South, where you will be flying.

Are you answered, Oksana Mikhailovna?

All things may be host to the spirits.

She turned to thank the strange boy for his gift but the only other people in the car park were the bus passengers, eager for the light and warmth and companionship of the diner.

3

Samburu control knew better than to argue when Oksana brought her Antonov 72F straight in along terminum. Because it was run by the United Nations, staff changed all the time at Samburu. The new director would try to assert his authority but Oksana Telyanina kept bringing her rattling old transport in through the I-Zee.

'Hi, you in the back,' she said to her cargo, which today was two engineering advisors and several tons of military hardware. 'We're going to be landing at Samburu shortly, so fasten your seat-belts and you, yes, you, who's been smoking despite the fact that I don't allow it on my ship, this time you stop it. You on the right, you can see the Merti plain and the old East African highway. You on the left will have the best view of the Chaga you'll ever get. Thank you for flying Sibirsk, the official airline of the United Nations Aid Force in Africa, here's some music to get you down.'

She sat back in her seat and hit the button on the cell player with a well-practised tap of the boot. One hundred watts of Russian death-thrash rocked the little Antonov.

Aid Force. As fat a lie as 'engineering advisors'.

The icons and knotted leather talismans hung from the ceiling swayed as *Dostoinsuvo*, which was the name of the An72F transport, hit a thermal rising from the Nyambeni hills. From two thousand metres the frontier between worlds was sharp as a cut. The clear definition evaporated at ground level, where Earth and Chaga wrapped each other up in fractal coils; bush grass and hexagons of brightly coloured moss spiralling inwards. Up to a kilometre south of terminum thorn acacias and baobabs stood among the land corals, secure now that the northern march had halted and entrenched along a front roughly conterminous with the equator. The uplift of the Great Wall five kilometres in was a definitive boundary at ground level; from a height it melted into just another pattern in the many-coloured world-carpet. Terminum was not a line of division. It was a place of meeting. The hemispheres of the brain, the mind and the body, the gross and the subtle, the material and the spiritual.

The proximity alarm flashed. An I-Zee patrol was interrogating *Dostoinsuvo's* AI, querying course and manifest details. The interceptor appeared alongside, demorphing from savannah camouflage: a sin-black stealth, all fins and angularities. It carried Kenyan Air Force markings; from the side window Oksana could see the pilot was as blond and crew cut as she.

'Hold your missiles, Kansas boy,' she said to herself. 'You can trust me. Today.'

She waved to the young pilot, hand-jived to the cock-pit radio blare. The stealth rolled away and faded into invisibility. Arrogant bastard. The fucking things were inherently unstable. They only flew by constantly averting disaster. Crash their AIs and they would come fluttering out of the sky like camouflage confetti. Not like *Dostoinsuvo*; she was a real Africa plane. Not beautiful, with her high wings and tails and stubby body and big over-wing STOL turbofans. Not wicked, like the stealths, but she would go anywhere for you, do anything, forgive any sin against her. But you had to be an Africa pilot. She would not do it for an 'aeronautical advisor'. You had to have respect for ship and sky and soil. And spirit.

The memory came bright and sharp. She was three weeks qualified on jets, fresh off prop-busters on the oil-crew runs up country. Dmitri had called a meeting: unusual. Sibirsk's worker-shareholders gathered in Hangar Five, the one big enough to service the 142s. In came Bakhtin, accountant-hero; he had put together the buy-out package when Aeroflot came apart. He liked games. Aeroflot had let the plant go cheap, but held the landing slots in a death-grip and the bankers had their fists tight up the comrade-stakeholders' asses. Absolute silence. Then, the grin. No one had ever seen such a thing on his face before.

'Comrade shareholders, I have a deal!'

That big thing down in Africa, that no one knew what the hell was going on: the UN had accepted their tender. Sibirsk was cheap, it had the resources and it was desperate enough to move at once. But the collective was a democracy; this must be put to the vote.

On her left was an old Aeroflot supersonic man, flew that Tu144 all the way to Mars and back. On her right was a helicopter man, ran gunships in Chechnya for the Russians, then Hinds in Tunguska for the Siberians. In the middle, this kid, sharp, bright, excited as hell, twenty-three years old. And she stuck her hand up with the others and was counted.

She could not believe she had ever been that young. Twenty years flying down in Africa. Places, faces, cities and lovers, all drowned by the Chaga. Twenty years flying over it, around it, your coming and your going and your every act governed by it, but never once inside it. She thought, in that time, your one enduring relationship has been with this plane. Then she thought, even that has been rebuilt and modified and upgraded so many times that there is not one piece left of the *Dostoinsuvo* that first captured your heart. No, the one thing that has lasted, that has grown and developed like a relationship should, is the Chaga; and that affair remains unconsummated: sterile.

She looked south across the mottled crimsons and jade greens and yellow ochres. On this approach you could sometimes see the snows of Kirinyaga catch the sun and kindle, higher and whiter than you ever imagined. There was a fantastical city growing in its foothills; the satellite photographs gave hints of organic skyscrapers, graceful boulevards, garden villages, living factories. On night flights she had sometimes glimpsed patterns of lights deep in the Chaga.

Dostoinsuvo warned her that they were approaching the safe floor. Oksana switched to auto-land; the starboard wing dipped. The otherworld vanished underneath the fuselage. Samburu lay ahead, the old UNECTA base, immobile since terminum stabilized, white as spilled salt on the burned buff of the plains. The dark stain spreading behind it like a shadow.

They never grew smaller, the camps.

'I'll take this one myself,' Oksana told *Dostoinsuvo*. The stick came alive in her grip as she brought her little aeroplane down through the blue haze of wood smoke to the ground.

4

'How will I know him?' she had asked Ali from Cairo, in Damascus. Ali from Cairo, in Damascus, despite his Indian silk suits and his affectation of Ottoman opulence, was just another street boy lured like a moth by the pheromone of UN money. He was the smiling front of the UN-only club at the airport, and he knew all the Faces and some of the Names. Whatever you wanted, whatever you needed, whatever got you screaming like an animal, could not ruffle him. Nothing got round those tiny serial-killer shades.

'He will know you,' Ali from Cairo, in Damascus, said. 'This is where you are to go when you get to Samburu, and when.' He took a kiddy's magic slate from the inside pocket of his silk suit. Darker-on-dark were a level, a room number, and a time. 'You have it?' Oksana nodded. Ali from Cairo pulled the little cardboard tab that erased the message.

'He will tell you what to do, where to make the pick-up.'

'I said I'm not taking any passengers.'

'You do not give orders in this. There is a system. These people have been waiting a long time. Every day longer they must wait, the greater the risk of them being caught, and if they are caught, they will take the operation with them.'

'How many?'

'You will be told that at Samburu.' He poured chilled thimblefuls of vodka. The heat was peeling off the concrete in sheets.

Oksana held up her wrist. The strapping was already beginning to be absorbed.

'I don't have my protection any more.'

She could have watched the operation – they had taken the pump out under a local – but it had seemed too much like the amputation of part of herself. It felt like a betrayal of her body, though the faithful little pump would have been the thing that betrayed her, in the end. Those plastics and silicon osmotic gates, transforming, exploding in her wrist. She wondered briefly what the black medicals had done with it. Everything had a market price in Damascus.

Ali from Cairo pressed the tiny, iced glass on Oksana.

'Take it. I insist. A goodbye to a valued customer. I drink a toast to you because, personally, I think you will almost certainly die, and I will miss you. Luck.'

'Fuck you,' Oksana said. The glasses kissed. She swallowed the Stolichnaya down. White UN aircraft taxied and turned in the heat-dazzle. Ali from Cairo, in Damascus, smiled, but his shades betrayed nothing.

5

Samburu strip was theoretically the sovereign territory of the Kenyan government. Like everything over which the Kenyan government claimed jurisdiction, it was controlled by someone else. The UN ran the strip and the base and the camps; the whole I-Zee from Chisimaio on the Indian Ocean to Libreville on the Atlantic. The Chaga ran everything south. What the Kenyan government really ran was a requisitioned game lodge that was its Parliament House, and the ten shops, *matatu* garage, eatery, two churches, shebeen and graveyard that constituted Archer's Post; capital of the Republic of Kenya.

The Republic of Kenya's representative at Samburu base was Corrupt Carmine. Oksana liked her immensely. She had the baldest head, the biggest mouth, the most serious footwear and shades of any woman she had ever known. Her title was gross slander. She was not corrupt. She creamed. She taxed. She sorted things.

Her sawn-open Landrover was waiting at the stand as Oksana powered down the engines.

'You have them?' Corrupt Carmine asked as Oksana came down the tail ramp. Kenyan soldiers in desert camouflage moved to assist the engineering advisors with their engineering. None looked over seventeen. All had come from the camps. There was no shortage of willing recruits there. Oksana handed Corrupt Carmine the stack of video cells.

She shook her smooth black head at the cover of the topmost video. It showed a naked white woman with big hair pushing breasts that hung to her waist towards the lens.

'Why should they desire such a thing? That is not a woman.'

'White meat keeps them flying right.'

'The darker the meat, the richer the flavour, *m'zungu*. And they show them on CNN talking to their wives and children. Hey! You there! Get away!'

A group of men from the camp had seen the aircraft land and had come up the dust road to the perimeter wire. They hoped it might be unloading aid. They would be at the head of the mob when they opened the gates. Corrupt Carmine knew to move fast. Once word spread there would be a feeding frenzy. She pulled a big *rungu* out of her Landrover and ran over the wire.

'Go! There is nothing here for you!' She slammed the wire with the round head of the *rungu*. The men flinched back. Corrupt Carmine reversed the stick and jabbed it through the mesh. It caught one of the men in the ribs. He yelped, started to protest. Corrupt Carmine shouted him down.

'You know who I am. I know who you are. I know your faces. If you care for your friends, your families, you will do what I say.'

They muttered and lingered, not wanting to be seen bested by a woman – a government woman – but they went.

'You have to be harder than they are, or they will take you,' Corrupt Carmine said.

The boy soldiers had stopped work. One of the advisors was

consulting his PDU and pointing to the south west. Everyone was looking where he pointed. Corrupt Carmine took off her serious shades. Oksana unfocused her eyes, depolarizing the optomolecules bonded to her corneas.

High clear blue, dry season sky, hazing yellow with dust where it touched earth. A daytime star suddenly flared and faded.

One thousand four hundred and eighty-eight to go.

Corrupt Carmine drove Oksana the kilometre to Samburu base in the heat and the dust. Every time she came there were more portable cabins shoved up around the tractor units. Their cheapness and meanness disheartened her: each new shack was a declaration that Samburu base would never move again. The accommodation and research units piled ten storeys high on the tractor beds were getting shabby: paint peeled; gutters sagged; birds' nests clung to overhangs. The big blue UNECTA*frique* logo – a stylized Kilimanjaro bracketed by two crescents – was faded almost to invisibility.

Corporate money had built the mobile bases on the expectation of exploitable resources in the Chaga. What UNECTA found in there were half-living, half-machine systems of fullerene carbons that manipulated the world at the atomic level. They did not deal. They did not speak. They transformed. They could make anything out of anything. They were the death of western industrial capitalism. The industrials took what would not burn them – the organic circuitry, the cell memories, some pharmaceutical applications – and left the agency it had created to explore and exploit the Chaga to wither.

The prime function of the inderdiction zone slammed down along the equator was geopolitical, but it served the transnationals well as an embargo against a tsunami of cheap nanofactured goods from the south.

Oksana noticed scabs of rust on the tractor treads. For a thousand kilometres this unlikely collage of creeping skyscrapers linked together by swaying airbridges and power conduits had kept pace with the advancing Chaga, crossing plains and hills, fording rivers, felling forests in its path. Fifty metres every day. Here at the feet of the Nyambeni Hills, that march had ceased, and the base had halted and died. Better to have ended like the others, Oksana thought as the elevator platform rattled down its chain drive: trapped, lassoed by Chaga mosses, overgrown with corals and pseudo-fungi, absorbed into a new architecture. Better metamorphosis than the death of the spirit.

The elevator platform choked twice before hoisting Oksana up to level five. A Kenyan Army teenager checked her ID and base pass. They pick them young because they are malleable and they have absolutely no restraint, Oksana thought.

Room 517 was the old physical recreation centre. Treadmill, weight machine, exercise bike and yoga mat were squeezed into a three metre box. Someone had ripped out the sound system to sell on the black market. The jacuzzi still squatted on the balcony. Oksana peered in. Sin dry. A little pale scorpion scuttled down the drain at the touch of her shadow.

She remembered an evening here, in another land, with a cute American called Damon, and a few rolls of the killer skunk they used to grow in the roof gardens. A small celebration of a new moon in the sky. A lot of laughing, then. Almost fifteen years since the Big Dumb Object had gone into orbit between earth and moon.

Oksana leaned on the rail, looked across at the Chaga. No chemical communication from it on the wind today. It clung close to the ground under the haze, closed and secretive. Oksana passed time by thumbing through old body-building magazines. Someone had clipped out the faces of all the male models.

A fistle at the door.

Suddenly Oksana was inexplicably afraid.

Corrupt Carmine entered the gym.

It was like someone had replied to your anonymous small ad for leather sex and when you went to meet him you found it was your husband.

'Yes,' Corrupt Carmine said, anticipating any number of Oksana's questions. She unfolded a clasp knife. She seized Oksana's hand and made a small cut in the ball of her thumb. Oksana was still wincing, more in surprise than pain, as Corrupt Carmine took a cell memory from the pocket of her jeans and pressed the bloody thumb to it.

'It's imprinted,' she said. 'Only you can open it.'

'What's in it?'

'A course. Only activate it once you cross terminum. It also contains false cargo manifests, in case they try to interrogate your AI. You're carrying medical supplies. I have logged you a flight plan up to Kapoeta.'

'Sudan.'

'Yes. You will fly there tomorrow morning. The airstrip guards have been paid. The others will be waiting for you, they are coming in tonight, by surface transport.'

'I told Ali from Cairo no passengers.'

'We have to make the most of every chance we get. I should tell you, a helicopter patrol from Lake Baringo destroyed a truck convoy yesterday – blockade runners, almost certainly.'

'One of the stealths checked me out on the way in.'

'They are under orders to show scalps to justify their obscene expense.'

'"They".'

'What?'

'You said, "they".'

Corrupt Carmine looked at her as if she were a bright child who has said a cretinous thing. She tossed Oksana the tiny bloodstained sack of navigation fullerenes.

'Why, Carmine?'

'This is my country,' she said. Her shades glared. She held out a hand. 'Good luck, *m'zungu*.'

Oksana shook her hand and understood why the black woman was so hard on the refugees. They had all made the coward's choice and run from the Chaga. But it had given them a second chance: they did not have to remain camp people. There was a way, for the brave, for the visionary, but they kept making the coward's choice, day after day.

Yes, Oksana Mikhailovna, you can think that because you do not have a choice to make, now.

The half-healed scars on her wrist itched.

The wind shifted in the night, the strong, hot wind blowing out of the heart of the Chaga. It rang the chimes in the window of the cabin Oksana Telyanina had been given. It blew through the cramped room. It blew through Oksana's sleep, shattering it. The wind from the South smelled of spice and rot and secret sexual places and frankincense and oil. It smelled of night doubts and hopes. Knowing she would not sleep again that night, Oksana went to the window. The stars were bright and so close she could imagine their oppressive weight on her neck. Venus and the atrocities the Chaga-makers were working on her were below the horizon: both moons were high. The Big Dumb Object's soft green oval floated above the watch-fires of the camp. Tonight there was no sound of shooting from there.

Unearthly things fluted and sang in the dark Chaga. Oksana was suddenly certain that if she stayed in this room a moment longer she would fail. She pulled on clothes and ran along the narrow, staggering corridors to the refectory. The constant I-Zee patrols, the ceaseless movement of supplies and personnel made Samburu as insomniac as it had been when researchers sat up all night arguing exobiology and xenochemistry over the famously fine coffee. Oksana sacrificed all hope of sleep to three cups of black. Halfway down the second she began to feel the sexy warmth in the top of her womb she recognized as the glow of certainty and risk.

Outside, another day unfurled.

Half an hour before pre-flight checks she decided she must wash her hair. It dried as she walked under the huge morning to the field. It was too early for Corrupt Carmine to be about. Oksana climbed into her aeroplane, filed her flight plan, made her checks, and flew.

Bare dirt, a wind sock, a tin radio shack falling into disrepair – a solar-powered AI now ran Kapoeta field. Ground squirrel holes all over the strip, but no termite hills, no larger ungulates. *Dostoinsuvo* had put down at a thousand Kapoetas.

The land was bleached white; the sky the high, ionized blue of the hottest, driest days. No prayer of early rains. The acacias were dusty and weary. Oksana sat on the lip of the cargo ramp and draped her hands over her knees and watched the dust devils move across the scorched Sudanese plain. One of the gyres turned into a vehicle, fast approaching.

There were six of them, in a church minibus. Four men, two women, three black, three white. They did not expect the haste with which their driver dropped them and escaped back into the heat haze. They shrank from the sudden space around them.

'This is a UNECTA plane,' said the young Indian woman who stood next to the tall young black man. She had a local accent. She was suspicious.

'UNECTA is the only thing flies around here,' Oksana said.

'Apart from the interdiction force,' said the white man with the white woman. He sounded French.

The other white man, who looked like an American, said amicably, 'Russian?'

'Fuck no!' Oksana said. 'Siberian.'

It had been well meant. The other black man, whose folded prayer shawl identified him as an Ethiopic Jew, walked the length of the fuselage, examining the airframe. He ran his long fingers under the name stencilled beneath the cockpit window.

'What does this mean?'

'Dignity,' Oksana said and the word declared a truce and make them co-conspirators.

'They hit a truck convoy,' the Sudanese man said.

'Hind-Ds,' Oksana said; then, realizing that they did not share her vocabulary of aircraft names, explained, 'we are higher and faster than strike helicopters. They don't have my range, they can only stay over the Chaga for a limited time before infection sets in. We don't have to go back.'

She heard herself saying those last words and they did not feel right in her mouth. The American heard her uncertainty. He said, 'Missiles don't have to come back.'

'I have some counter-measure facility,' Oksana said.

'How much?' the Frenchwoman asked. She looked arty, and a smoker.

'Enough,' Oksana told her. Any more would only scare them and then none of them would do it. 'I have a flight plan, they will ask questions if I don't keep to it.'

They belted into the passenger pallet in the cargo hold. Everyone had a window seat. Oksana closed the ramp and powered up the engines. The Antonov taxied to the end of the strip, turned and was airborne in five hundred metres.

Dostoinsuvo boogied down to terminum to *My Fair Lady*. Oksana watched her passengers on the thumb-nail monitors. The French couple touched each other much. The African man and the Indian woman seemed very afraid, and whispered together. Oksana had the impression they were both doctors. The Ethiopian had reclined his seat and lay motionless, eyes closed, the fringe of his shawl gripped between his fingers. The American absently turned his Precious Object over and over in his hands. The thing he had chosen to take with him into the new world was a photograph of a child squinting in a brightly lit garden. The picture was sealed in a block of glass. Ali from Cairo, in Damascus, had explained to Oksana this new tradition of taking one essential thing from the former life into the next. After consideration, and reconsideration, she had selected the one thing that Chaga could not possibly manufacture and without which civilized life would not be possible: her Alessi espresso-maker. It was a classic; it had never failed her, but the coffee she found for it never quite matched its potential. Then Oleg had slipped her the little bag of brown powder out of his flight sack and she was addicted. Alien deep-space fullerenes did strange and good things to coffee. The stuff smuggled north across terminum went for cocaine prices. Chaga coffee tasted like it smelled. Thus: the Alessi. It could only express its potential in the South.

Dostoinsuvo levelled at eight thousand metres. Oksana unsealed the cell memory. Her thumb hesitated over its membrane. Panic was a sudden aerodynamic stall on her emotions. What are you contemplating, Oksana Mikhailovna Telyanina? Who are you, where do you think you are going?

She bit savagely at the tendons in the back of her traitor hand, tugged at the skin.

'Go!' she shouted. 'Go, go go!'

Her thumb came down on the cell. It read her flesh and opened to the ship's AI.

'These co-ordinates are south of terminum,' *Dostoinsuvo* said.

'Accept,' Oksana ordered. She banked her hand in the dataglove to starboard. *Dostoinsuvo* aimed itself at distant Kirinyaga. Terminum rose out of the heat-haze like a dark tide. Oksana had never approached it from this angle before, like a caravel off the coast of a new continent. *Dostoinsuvo* crossed the line between worlds. Chaga under both wings now.

'We're across terminum,' she told her passengers. 'We'll shortly be starting our descent towards Kirinya.'

She watched their reactions on the monitors. The American looked afraid and crossed himself. The French couple looked triumph and success at each other and clasped hands. The Sudanese doctors looked at the others to draw their response from them. They decided to smile nervously. The Ethiopian looked out of the window.

From Karamoja to the snows of Kirinyaga was four hundred and fifty kilometres. Under a hour's flying time. She would not take it low yet, though it afforded some safety from interdictors. *Dostoinsuvo* bucked, the icons jangled: turbulence rising off the Chaga. The virtuality visor drew strict tight course vectors across the coloured, chaotic canopy.

The alarm was like a coronary death. The visor threw visuals up on her peripheral vision: three stealths morphing out of camouflage into strike black. Ten thousand metres sunward, closing at six hundred kph.

'Combat systems!' Oksana ordered. 'Code: St Barbara and St Basil. Guesstimate weapons suites, times to firing range, give me tactical options.'

Jokes, Oksana Mikhailovna. Tough talk, bad movie dialogue.

'Highest estimate to optimal firing position, seventy-two seconds, lowest forty-three,' the AI said.

Mother of God.

'We are being hailed,' *Dostoinsuvo* announced.

Too high. Too fucking high. But too far out to canopy-cruise without your An72F coming apart around you.

'Attention Sibirsk aircraft,' the white pilot said. 'You have entered restricted airspace. Turn on to the heading I am transmitting over your data transfer frequency and exit this sector.'

Oksana willed herself along the long unwavering red line her datavisor laid over the alien rainforest. This is my answer, Kansas sky cowboys.

'The lead aircraft is attempting to effect control of the AI flight subsystem,' *Dostoinsuvo* said calmly.

'Fuckers!' Oksana Mikhailovna shouted. 'No one flies my fucking plane but me. Effect complete flight subsystem shut down.'

'Accepted,' the AI said.

Well then. Seat of the pants then. Africa flying, then. She clenched her fist in the dataglove and yelled all the way down to one thousand metres.

'Follow me if you've got the balls, white-boy sister-fuckers!'

'All three contacts are probing us with target acquisition radar,' *Dostoinsuvo* informed her.

'Initiate electronic counter-measures. And drop flares.'

'Guessimates of weapons suites assign a probability of eight per cent that the contacts are carrying heat-seeking missiles,' the computer said pedantically.

Three stealths up my ass and my own AI is arguing with me, Oksana thought.

'Deploy flares,' she ordered. The underwing eyeballs showed her hard white asterisks dropping slowly towards the tessellated red hexagons.

Oksana toggled the ceiling switch and watched the reactions as she told them what had happened. The French man squirmed in his seat. His wife tried to take his hand, to give and receive comfort. The Sudanese doctor's chest was heaving in terror; his Indian wife was numb, stiff with apprehension. The American clutched his precious thing more tightly. The Ethiopian Jew twisted a tassel on his shawl. He looked into the camera as if he knew that Oksana saw him.

'We're going to run for it,' Oksana told the strapped-in figures. 'They've got a safe operating time over the Chaga, but we're not going back, so it doesn't matter. I'm taking us down under their safe floor; out of range of their cannon.' Yes, she thought, but these are American aeronautical advisors; they are in love with technology. They will go for the missiles and the beauty of a missile kill. She had a plan for that, but she would not tell it to the people in the transport pallet. They were scared, but they were not yet scared for their lives.

'Enemy aircraft have engaged ECCM,' the AI said.

'Shit. Modulate our ECM and begin erratic manoeuvres. Hold tight,' she told the fearful faces in the cargo bay. 'We're E-M-ing.'

'Enemy aircraft have burned through our ECM and have acquired lock on,' *Dostoinsuvo* said calmly. 'Lead aircraft has launched missiles.'

'Jesus and Mary,' Oksana swore. The virtuality visor gave her battle truth, hard and fast. They were radar homers. There was no shaking them. They were accelerating at three gees. And the unbroken Chaga said, Oksana Mikhailovna Telyanina, you are not going to make it.

'Fifty seconds to impact.' *Dostoinsuvo* dispassionately counted down its own destruction. 'Forty seconds.' The red lines streaked towards Oksana's heart. They possessed the hypnotic elegance of all hunting things. Do not look at them, Oksana told herself. Do not be seduced by their eyes into the fatal passivity of the hunted.

'Open cargo bay door,' she ordered. Because the military arranged the seats the other way round from the civilians, they would be looking right at it, a slit of sky opening into an abyss of air and velocity.

'Brace positions,' Oksana shouted to the passengers. Do it quick. Do it now. Do it before they can think. 'Initiate drop sequence.'

'Twenty-five seconds to impact,' the AI said.

The *Drop Ready* sprite waved on her visor. She blinked it active and waited for the shift in trim that would tell her they were gone. Then she ordered, 'Initiate eject sequence.'

Oksana snatched the Alessi coffee-maker and hooked it to a

D-ring as the padded bars folded her in like fingers and the seat pushed back from the controls. The visor blanked as the cables tore free. A final glance at the monitors showed her the chute cluster open, the transport pallet turning slowly beneath it.

'Fifteen seconds to impact,' the AI said. The eject sequence count commenced. Oksana braced, grimaced. The roof panel blew, wind swirled the icons and talismans, and with an explosion and a yell and multiple gees redshifting her brain, Oksana Mikhailovna Telyanina was out, in the air, Baba-Yaga in her chair, hurtling over the endless forest. The gyros stabilized. The thruster burned out; the voiceless yell stomped down in her lungs roared out.

'Fuck fuck fuck fuck!' Oksana Mikhailovna screamed as she plummeted towards the canopy. The chutes slammed open. Deceleration tore at her. Oksana shifted into prana-yama breathing, battling black-out.

The light wind caught the canopy and turned it. Oksana saw the radar-seekers loop in on threads of smoke and join with the old Antonov in a beautiful conjugation of flame. White, gold, red: dark seeds fell out of the fast-fading labia of fire, drawing tails of smoke. Debris snowed down on the Chaga.

Stunned by the beauty of destruction, Oksana was gently spun away by the winds that were carrying her deeper into the alien. The passenger pallet drifted five kilometres north of her. It was as small and delicate as an aerial toy, put together and set in the sky, improbably flying. Oksana felt laughter tear up in her lungs. It was the big laugh of life, of relief and pride and excitement that it is alive. She laughed it at the drifting drop pallet, at the darting black deltas of the stealths, shimmering out of camouflage.

They heard her laugh. The second stealth pulled into a climb and dropped two black needles from under its wings.

'No!' Oksana Mikhailovna Telyanina yelled. She hurled every oath and curse she knew in her four tongues at the missiles, but words could not turn them back. Strapped into their seats on the transport pallet, the French couple and the Sudanese and his Indian wife, the scared American and the Ethiopic Jew saw the missiles arrowing in and knew that all they could do was watch the elegant approach of their own deaths.

The missiles joined with the pallet. They were proximity drones, designed to close and destroy the target in a hail of submunitions. The bomblets tore through the soft lives, tore them to pieces.

'No,' Oksana Telyanina whispered. 'Oh, no.'

The stealths that had used up their missiles turned back towards the north and faded into sky. But the third stealth did not make that fuck-you climb and fade. It turned and ran towards Oksana in her flying shamanka chair: speck to insect to howling demon.

He has missiles left, Oksana thought. But if he is really inflamed, if the videos I brought him of the women with stupidly big breasts faking love with each other have dehumanized him enough, he will go for the cannon. He will want to fuck me with his cannon. But even if you kill me, I will have beaten you, white boy. And you know this too.

The stealth howled down upon her. Oksana held its eye. It could not hold hers. The interdictor banked and climbed steeply. At the zenith it flashed its belly at her and merged with the big blue and was gone. Defeated.

To the north, the smoke blew away. Rags of shredded parachute fell twisting on the wind towards the Chaga. That same wind carried Oksana onwards, inwards, into exile.

8

After five days the breath waft of veil was a physical pain on her face. Oksana's relief to have the thing off, to be out and open, was both amusing and puzzling to the women from the village, who wore it from custom. She stood blinking and itching at the impromptu stop at the side of the coral road. The veil lay in Miswe's basket, but reality was still clouded. The veil was in her eye, in her spirit.

They had been unfailingly kind, the men and the women of

Oelende, as God allowed them. Had it been the men who found her, they could not have spoken to her, let alone bring her back to the village, but it was the boys, who had seen the air battle and the chutes come down, who came calling and whistling through the understorey in search of battle debris. They found a tattooed woman aviator, seemingly enthroned in flowers and crystals and flesh as the Chaga transfigured her ejector seat. Long glutinous drops of melted parachute hung from the fingers of the hand-tree that had caught and held her, like a palm-full of thick semen. She was as magical and terrible as an efreet to the boys of Oelende. She would not respond to their Swahili and good English. They could find no wounds. The places where radar-seeking fragmentation missiles tear through spirit leak no blood. Oksana Mikhailovna Telyanina was brought back to Oelende on a travois drawn by buffalo with command units grafted into their spines. On her arrival on the dancing floor at the heart of the village, two serious debates broke out: one political, the other theological. The boys had seen missile trails, an aircraft destroyed, but Oksana wore UNECTA fatigues: enemy uniform. Victim or victor, she could not go back now. It was that that resolved the political argument. The law of Islam dictated that hospitality must be shown to the exile and refugee. Oelende would help her. The theological argument was more vexed. The older men, who had much time for religious finessing, spent many happy sunlit hours in the square smoking and debating where to put her. The men's side was impossible; the boys would only be silly and immature and probably have their developments warped. An attempt to make Oksana an honorary man was dismissed as ingenious but impractical. The logical place would have been in the eunuchs' compound, but no one in Oelende had elected to that calling, even temporarily. The only place was among the women, in a household beyond reproach, and she must be veiled in the presence of men, even indoors. Thus Oksana Telyanina entered the side of Miswe, senior wife in the zenana of the household of Amin of the community of Oelende.

Oelende was a nation dedicated to the glorification of God. Among the last to be allowed through before the UN closed terminum was a small group of Sudanese Sufists. It differed from other Islamic sects in that it did not regard the Chaga as the sperm of Satan. It saw endless niches to live the life of faith. One hundred kilometres south-east of the Mt Elgon Gate, on the edge of the still-unsettled crystal monolith country, God's angels had spoken to the men in the whirling trance and told them this was the ordained place. The next morning the people of Oelende woke to find the ground lined with curving ridges and loops: the plan of their future settlement sketched on the moss. Molecule by molecule, the village raised itself out of the soil. It was shaped like a mind, a maze of curving walls and courtyards and rooms within rooms, complex and enfolding. Its veiled women and serious, happy children moved through its passages and alleys like memories; a glimpse into a compound might show you water trickling from a fountain, or an ox being hobbled, or a man, arms outstretched, spinning in the orbital ecstasy of God.

Like all Chaga settlements Oelende was self-sufficient. Its women and children could gather fifteen hundred varieties of foodstuff within ten minutes' walk of the village. Solar and biochemical arrays generated electricity; bucket-chains of nano-pumps siphoned ground-water into reservoirs and sumps. Buckies wove molecules in processor vats: from fabrics to vehicles, had God's people of Oelende desired vehicles.

All the contact Oelende needed with the corrupt world was the Babylon bus. Four times a week it went up and came down the coral road that wound past five hundred villages to Kirinya. It was for the Thursday run that Oksana and the women of Amin's house were waiting on the eroded verge. The road here passed through a landscape of massive-trunked trees, episcopal purple, that rose sheer two hundred metres before unfolding into a vault of interwoven spans and ribs. Birds chimed in the high canopy. Oksana sat down on the bare red soil. She breathed in the remembered musk of the Chaga, hoping the chemistry might burn away this veil over her senses and tell she was here, truly, really.

She looked down the road. She looked up the road. A sudden thought struck her.

'How am I going to pay? I don't have any money, I don't have anything, except this . . .' The Alessi coffee-maker sat canted on the uneven ground between her feet.

'Leon never refuses a passenger,' Miswe said. She was the only one of the Amin women who could freely speak with the stranger. 'You do not need money, he has no need of money.'

Amin's household had taken much convincing that Oksana wanted to go to Kirinya.

'A woman knows her own mind best,' Amin had said. 'There is the will of God, and then there is the will of a woman.'

'I do not think so,' Miswe said, pouring exquisite coffee into cha-plastic bowls. 'Wounds in the soul do not heal so quickly.'

'She may be white, and a Northerner, but she is not a child. And she is not your child.'

When the women had cut her out of her flying clothes, plastic seals and fastenings clogged with sulphur-yellow florets, and treated the cuts and abrasions of her drop through the roof of the world and put her to bed with a tranquillizer patch on her forehead to push the dreams down, Miswe had thought of this white alien as the daughter she had never birthed.

By the next noon Oksana was awake, eating the good-for-convalescents *ugali*, and slowly answering from beneath the *buibui* the concerned questions of the men. They clicked their tongues at the pursuit of the stealth interceptors, and clapped their hands at Oksana's attempts to outfly them, and were silent at the horror of the deaths of her passengers.

'All you did was choose another life,' Miswe said. 'For that, they send fighters to shoot you out of the sky.'

'They cannot accept that anything could be better than what they offer,' Oksana said. 'Because I say different, I am their enemy, you are their enemies, though they don't know you; your children are their enemies.'

'Must they have enemies?' asked one of the boys who had come to hear exciting things about war and fighting.

'They need an enemy to justify what they do in their own countries, so they can keep spending money on weapons, and keep everyone afraid,' Oksana said. 'When I was a girl, it was my country that was the big enemy. Then it was your faith that was going to take everyone's freedom away.' She saw the young men roll their heads in astonishment, but the older men rocked,

45

remembering. 'Yes, really. Now, it's one half of the planet against the other. The clever thing is that they have convinced everyone in the North that it's not they who are our enemies, but we who are their enemies. They really believe that we are a threat, that the National Liberation Armies are defending their people and their freedom. When my country was the big enemy, we could have destroyed their society. Now they only pick on enemies who can't fight back.'

'I have heard it on their radio stations,' one of the older men said. 'It is a very good lie, very big, very simple.'

'The very best ones are,' Oksana said.

The boy wanted to speak and ask more, but it was time for his Arabic lesson and Oksana had the impression that the men did not want him to be seduced by the snake glamour of war.

In the afternoon, when the shadows of the curving walls fell cool across the square, the men danced. From a high shuttered window in the *zenana* Oksana watched them spin, barefoot on the hot earth. Their loose robes flew out from them, their sleeves trailed. Their faces were rapturous, lost in the cloud of mystery. They cast long, elegant shadows, moving on the trodden earth.

The war is coming, she thought as the men whirled under the face of the divine. You are only fifty kilometres from the front line; they will not spare you because you dedicate yourselves to God. She tried to imagine that it was blood on the earth and not shadows. She felt nothing.

She was sitting alone in a sunlit courtyard filled with clambering, twining gourds when the troop of boys brought her the thing they had found. They were excited, but they remembered manners. They hovered in the gate until Oksana gave them permission to come in. She was not required to veil for them. They were too young to be inflamed by the sight of her face and cropped hair. There were five of them, under the leadership of Amin's son Hosnai. They were shy and beautiful. They set a metre-long something wrapped in fabric on the ground at her feet.

'We found it in the giant plantain gardens,' Hosnai said. His friends looked at each other, trying not to giggle. 'We thought you might like it.'

'Is this a horrible thing?' she said, knowing the enthusiasms of ten-year-old boys. 'Am I going to open it and be sick?'

46

'No, it is a thing for you,' Hosnai said. His affront was so honest that Oksana could not but unfold the cloth.

Lying on the rectangle of printed yellow fabric was an irregular chunk of aircraft fuselage, UN white. Three black Cyrillic letters, the last broken. She traced the ragged edge of the unfinished letter.

That night Oksana went to Miswe. She was in a room draped and ceilinged with the fine woven fabric of Oelende. She sat on a ledge by the window. Her eyes were closed, but her face moved as if in response to spirit voices.

'Miswe.'

The woman opened her eyes.

'I'm sorry, I was listening to the radio.'

'The radio?'

Miswe touched forefinger to forehead.

'Of course, you would not have, yet.'

'Miswe, I think I have to leave Oelende.'

'Yes. Was it Hosnai's gift?'

'I suppose so; he meant well. I heard Amin talked to him because he upset me, he shouldn't have done that, the poor kid was in tears. He wasn't to know.'

'It was only partly because he did not think that he might offend. It was mostly because he knows that he should not go that far from the village. There is word from Kilingiri that they are dropping mines on the forest gardens; a new kind of mine, that resists the Chaga.'

'Jesus and Mary.'

She sat on the window bench beside Miswe. The air was cool on the back of her neck; the warmth of the room leaked into the gathering dark. She had always loved the sexual stealth with which night took Africa. Thunder-growl silenced the night-singing creatures for a moment. Soon Hussein would sound the evening call to prayer from Oelende's fuller-domed mosque. Pattern of days: early blue, late thunder, five calls, five prayers, the swift dark.

'I had a friend once, a woman, back in the old Kenya days. I loved her a lot, but the first thing I did was lie to her. I met her in the bar in the old PanAfric hotel, and I pretended that I was this old, hardened, Africa-type who knew everything and

47

everyone. It was such a terrible lie, I had been in Kenya all of three weeks. I taught her this toast, when we used to drink, oh, what was it? Oh yes. Big cocks and vodka!' I loved her, but we lost each other. She got pregnant, and followed this story down across terminum into Tanzania. She didn't know that they wouldn't let her back; it had touched the baby. It was changed, she couldn't come back.

'The last time I heard from her she was at a place on the coast called Turangalila. We lost contact soon after the kid was born. She's probably moved on, but someone may know where she went.'

'You want to be with her.'

Oksana started.

'I hadn't thought of it like that, but yes, I do. But it's so long, the kid would be fifteen now. I don't know.'

'Fifteen years is not long. Time is different here, things do not change so much.'

'But we get older, we run out of time.'

'Let me ask you a question, Oksana. How old do I look?'

Oksana studied the woman's profile. She had the high cheek-bones and strong jaw of a Nilo-Hamitic, a timeless, sculptural race.

'Twenty-seven, twenty-eight?'

Miswe's composure broke into laughter. She slapped her hands on her thighs.

'God bless you, but my oldest son is already that age!'

Oksana knew that she was staring, that her mouth was open, that her eyes were wide. A sudden brief, bright flash outshone the biolumes: comet one hundred and eighteen hitting Venus.

'This is a thing you will discover,' Miswe said. 'Go to Turangalila, look for your friend, do not be afraid. You will find that it is all as you remember.'

But before Turangalila, Kirinya.

People from other communities scattered through the hinter-land were making their ways along the forest footpaths to the stop. The men greeted each other and sat down on the soil to talk and laugh. The women shifted their burdens and children and looked in the direction from which the bus would come. For a long time there was only road and tall trees. Then just as you thought nothing would happen again in the universe, the Babylon bus appeared at the vanishing point of the straight red road.

It was a rare vehicle. Oksana thought of the 1950s Streamliner that had dropped Cary Grant in the middle of the prairie in *North by North West*, and the testosterone lowriders of Mexico City, and the gaudy *jeepnis* of Manila, frosty with saints and spray-jobs. She thought also of rhinoceroses, and the iridescent horniness of African beetles. The thing looked like it had tusks, and a mane. It ran on ten wheels, two double sets. Overspill – material and human – perched on the roof. Lions'a'Zion and scriptural texts delivered day-glo Rastafarian exhortations. The Babylon bus was heir to a long and proud tradition of African public transport; the country buses, the old Peugeot services that would go anywhere for very little money, the ubiquitous, perilous minibus *matatus*, veering and honking through city traffic.

The bus pulled over in an agony of gear shifts. The men pushed to the front. The women took up their burdens. The bus could not possibly accept another passenger, but the people went up the steps, and in, somehow.

'Oksana.'

Miswe took Oksana's hand, pushed a gift into it.

'You will need this on your journey. Not everyone you meet will be as fair a trader as Leon.'

Oksana opened her hand. It held a gold hoop ear-ring, from which five smaller gold rings hung. To refuse a gift was a terrible insult.

Oksana looped the ring through her ear. The pull of heavy gold was warm and sensual. She wanted to embrace the women, but it was not in their vocabulary, so she thanked them and shook their hands and climbed up into the panting, fume-breathing Babylon bus.

'Eh, white meat!' said the driver, who had shoulder-length dreads and a pretty, scarred face and could only be Leon. 'You come sit up here with me, talk to me . . . I need the conversation of short-haired women. Where you for, *m'zungu*?'

'How far are you going?'

'All the way, woman.'

'Take me there.'

The door closed. The Babylon bus shivered, gears ground. It

drove off down the red coral road. It was only then that Oksana noticed the thing about Leon. From the groin down, he did not exist.

9

The Babylon bus drove south of east, following the old 104 that in other histories had run between Kampala and Nairobi.

It was a village on wheels. In its aisle and seats were gossip and wisdom and commerce. There was cooking and eating. There was singing and dancing and the healing of the sick. There was love and jealousy. There were frequent conceptions; there had been births. There were fights; sometimes deaths, by violence, more often by natural causes. There was crime and justice within two rows of each other.

The road led it through many landscapes. Purple chanterelles twenty metres tall curled their lips over the bus: silver, many-armed creatures flickered from cap to cap, too high and fast to be clearly seen. Expanses of hexagon-cover gave rise to startling micro-ecologies like clumps of grass, exact in every detail but magnified ten thousand times. The Babylon bus put its lights on to plunge into the darkness of the base of a tier forest; five distinct ecologies piled on top of each other. Light again, and the bus was grinding up hairpin bends as the road climbed a massive reef of land-coral as convoluted as a human brain. Sudden, stunning: Africa again; the green uplands remembered. A lone baobab stood in a valley: incongruous, it was not a tree of these cool, well-watered uplands. The incongruity made you look again, and then you saw with perspective, and were awed. The Chaga remembered with imagination: the baobab was a kilometre round its elephantine trunk. Its chubby grey branches rose fifteen hundred metres above the Nandi hills: the tree where man was born.

Everywhere, people. People in their villages that looked like termite nests, or woven baskets, or ceramic pots, or plastic domes. People sitting by the road, talking, trading, setting out their wares and ideas on its red earth verges; shading their eyes from the sun. People walking with their goods and their friends and their children. People moving in buses, and in over-loaded pick-ups, or little electric three wheeled buggies and biomotor mopeds. A ceramic wagon shaped like a huge wheeled gourd was drawn by a pair of dwarf elephants. A skinny youth rode one of the elephants, controlling them both by neural taps in the backs of their necks. He shooed away flies with a goat's tail whisk. A very tall man resolutely pushed a handcart laden so high with battered metal petrol cans that he could not see where he was going. A small crowd of little children followed him, teasing, hoping to steer him into a ditch. Black Buddhist monks begged from teenagers in repro Chanel and Lagerfeld scudding by on mopeds. Women in voluminous *kangas* printed with scenes of the founding of their nations haggled with Amharic priests shading themselves beneath white umbrellas. A man so wrapped in sheets of leather that he looked like a human turd sat beneath a fan-tree. Naked children hopped and shrieked as their mothers hosed off the dust of the red road. Old men perched on the lip of a water reservoir, fishing, spitting. A young woman sat in a chair under a canopy; two older women teased and waxed her hair to resemble the branches of a baobab. They hung the stiff locks with beads and tiny mirrors.

Oksana moved through this blood of life and felt nothing. She was the passenger, under glass, observing, never touching.

The nations got on, rode a time, got off. Sometimes, the differences in the Babylon bus's passengers were more than cultural. Here the road passed through the memory of a town. Before the Chaga it had been a place of some consequence; some of the ruined walls sprouting crystal clumps and floes of pseudo-fungus still stood over three storeys. Leon said it had once been Nakuru. The outskirts had been colonized by a nation of scavengers who slung gaudy cha-plastic sheets between the roofless walls and set out their finds on the road side. Old car engines, a set of windchimes, cases of empty Coke bottles, a battered recoilless rifle with a kilometre of ammunition. Downtown was a haunted place: shop names winked out from under eyebrows of purple coral. Translucent bubble-creatures tumbled through the vegetation-clogged side-streets, breaking around the prow of the Babylon bus. On the plinth beneath the old front wall that was all that remained of the Tipsi Café a figure squatting on a folding sling stool stuck up four thumbs. Four thumbs, four hands, four arms, no legs. A second set of arms and shoulders grew in place of hips. Oksana watched him stand on his lower hands as he folded the stool into a shiny yellow cha-plastic backpack. She had heard of but never seen this most radical of the Adapted. They were a sub-species evolved for space, for free-fall and ultra-violet; they caught buses in Nakuru because the North denied them their natural habitat.

The space-man was hairless and very muscular. He was dressed in a faded grey cotton leotard with Adidas stripes down the side. He had bracelets on all his wrists, his lower hands wore biker's gloves. His skin was blue-black. Oksana wanted to touch it. She felt that it was charged with an electricity that would sear away her inner veil. But she did not. She was afraid that, unveiled, the brightness and colour and smell of this new world would bleach her into translucency. The space-man and Leon shook hands, then in two thrilling leaps the space-man went up the side of the bus, clinging to the roof rack. Half an hour later there was a bang on the roof, Leon stopped in the middle of a forest of tree-sized cane. Ragged banners of moss hung like the pennons of a lost crusade. The space-man came hand over hand over hand down the bus, waved to Leon and cantered off into deep forest. Oksana never knew what his business had been with the ghosts of Nakuru, where he went with his bright yellow plastic backpack through the alien cane.

It was in the siesta time, when the bus was half empty and those passengers who remained had exhausted social commerce and slept, that the thing happened. Past Gilgil the red road parted from the line of Route 104 and struck due east across the valley of Nyandarua up into the cloud-covered volcanic ridges of the Aberdares. The Chaga had covered this high country in dense cloud forest; a green and dripping terrain of shadows and tall trees, humid and rank.

'We are not far from Gichichi,' Leon said to Oksana, who had sat beside him for the whole journey. 'I will take a break there, and get some fuel.'

Then the radio went silent. The lights went out. The engine died. Leon shifted gears, coasted the bus, tried to jump the ignition, but it would not relight. The Babylon bus came to a halt in the middle of the road.

'Oh shit,' Leon said. 'I cannot be that short on fuel.'

He pressed the starter button. There was a click that Oksana recognized as dead electrical system. They both knew that it was not a fuel thing.

'Hey, Leon, what's going on?'

'I don't know, something is up with the electricals.'

'Hah!' retorted a fat woman clutching a package wrapped in a *kanga*. 'I tell you, when it was the old RVP, they always got there, and on time too, you damn rude-boy! Nothing new is ever better.'

Then the soldiers came out of the forest and everyone knew what had stopped the Babylon bus.

They were like ghost soldiers; the spirits of the high cloud-forest walking. You could not see them until they crossed on to the road. The shatter-patterns of their clothing clashed with the colours of the highway. They were terrifyingly young. They carried appallingly powerful weapons. An army was on the move through the high, dark Chaga. An officer approached the bus. He wore a helmet that looked a little like a piece of clever hi-fi and a little like the shell of a disturbing insect, and was escorted by a female soldier carrying a heavy automatic weapon.

Nobody spoke on the Babylon bus, not even the voluble fat woman.

Leon opened the door, the officer climbed in. He took his helmet off.

'Where are you going?'

'The high road: Chehe, Castle Forest Station, Kianyaga.'

'Kairuthi?'

'I will be getting fuel at Gichichi.'

'That's all right. It's still safe there.'

'Are they at Kairuthi?'

The officer looked at Leon, at the place where his legs had

been, where now a gnarl of neural taps linked his spine to the control systems of his bus.

'They were.'

'KLA?'

'Yes. There is no Kairuthi any more. They are all over this country, but we will find them, and we will stop them. I apologize for interrupting your journey, when the damper field is shut off, your bus should restart easily. But you should be warned. Last week they attacked a *pujo* bus from Nanyuki at Naro Moru.'

'I had not heard; that close to Kirinya, eeh.'

'They are raiding into the Northern townships now. That *pujo*, they left no one alive.'

'Thank you. Who are you?'

'You should not know that, I think. Who were you?'

'Black Simbas.'

'That is a fine name. A very fine name. Hey, *m'zungu*!' The officer had noticed the Sibirsk patches on Oksana's flying jacket. 'This is what your people have done. Are you proud?'

'Not her people, brother,' Leon said gently.

Oksana did not hear the officer. She was watching the girl bodyguard. The soldier squatted on her heels, taking a brief respite from the advance. One hand rested on the knee of her combat pants; the other gripped her weapon for support. Oksana recognized it as a Ukrainian heavy assault piece. The girl had strong cheek-bones and a defiant jaw. Her eyes were soft and dark and animal. Her hair was a scrape of stubble, her skull long and finely moulded. Her breasts barely strained the cut-off cling top she wore. Her arms and cheeks and belly were patterned with scarifications.

The girl felt Oksana's gaze. She turned to see who was touching her with a look. Their eyes met. They held, then the officer stepped down from the bus and the girl got to her feet.

Oksana raised a hand: greeting, blessing, farewell.

The girl lifted a hand in response. She smiled. Then she shouldered her hideous weapon and jogged after the officer and was swallowed by the Chaga.

The veil was torn from top to bottom.

Not her people, brother. These are my people, this is my nation. I am not an exile. I belong.

Her fists were so tight her nails had drawn blood.

'Are you all right?' Leon asked.

'Yes.' No.

She realized she had stepped down on to the road.

'Hey, white meat, what are you doing, we should get out of here, it's not safe,' Leon shouted.

'Just a couple of minutes.'

Oksana walked away from the Babylon bus, down the unmarked centre of the road. She heard Leon roar the engine back to life behind her. She stopped, opened her senses to the Chaga. The spirits rushed through the rift in the veil. Her shaman soul kindled, and exploded. No drugs, no chemicals. Alien pheromones burned across her synapses. It was real. She was here. The monsoon of sensations drove her to her knees. Her breath came in shuddering gasps. She knelt, shaking with the beauty and the power, until after twenty minutes Leon unplugged himself and came running on his hands to ask the crazy white woman did she mind but he had this idea of getting himself and all his passengers to Kirinya, *tonight, intact,* if that was all right.

'Yes,' she whispered, forehead pressed to the dust-scented coral. 'It's all right. Everything's all right.'

10

The off-run on the bend of the road was the most spectacular place she had ever done a tattoo.

Past Gichichi the cloud forest dropped away and the road swung down to the Murang'a Valley in lazy loping loops across the outspread fingers of the Aberdares. The Chaga clung tenuously to this ridge-land; isolated parasol-trees; clumps of landcoral spilling down steep valley sides; lines of stubby green cylinders grasping the hill spine like tenacious fortified towns. Leon had pulled the Babylon bus on to the bare earth off-run.

'A break,' he said, and unplugged himself from the neural tap and handed himself down to the ground. 'This is such a great place, from here you can see for ever.' It was not for ever, but enough to fill eternity. The Murang'a valley was thirty kilometres wide below Gichichi; a carpet of colours and textures, the pattern of ecologies never repeating. Its eastern rim lifted in a long ridged escarpment. Afternoon cloud hid the heights, but Oksana knew that they rose up all the way to the snows of Kirinyaga. Kirinyaga, Kirinya. Mountain and city.

'I would like to be put under the earth here,' Leon said, unwrapping the dinner he had bought from a roadside vendor in Gichichi. 'I would like to look out at the land, and all the people, and their villages.'

When they had eaten, he finally settled his fare.

'The wolf's head?' Oksana asked.

'The wolf's head,' Leon said. 'Here.' Indicating the ball of his left shoulder.

'It'll be painful this close to the bone,' she warned. She was gentle with the needle and the dye, but it did hurt.

'Hey, careful with that,' Leon said.

'Sorry about that,' Oksana Mikhailovna said. Across the valley of Murang'a, the ragged hem of cloud caught and tore on the spines and pinnacles of the foothill forests.

'Back there, when we met that officer, you said you were in the Black Simbas. What unit?'

'Kariokor.'

When they gave you the gun and the combat boots and sent you to hold open the Simba Corridor, you would have been the same age as that warrior girl, Oksana thought. You could be Miswe's oldest child. You are some lost mother's lost son.

'I was there at the end, when Nairobi fell,' she said. 'I saw what your people were trying to do. It was an incredible thing, getting all those civilians up into the Chaga.'

'You saw nothing,' Leon said. 'You got into your UNECTA plane and you flew away. You thought that when Nairobi was gone, that was the end. It was only the beginning.'

'I heard it was bad.'

'You have no idea.'

'What happened?' Oksana asked. Leon knew what she meant.

'Anti-personnel mine. There were three of us in the patrol, it was up by Kitui. Malavai died instantly; I was not so lucky, I was just made half a man.'

'I'm sorry,' Oksana said.

'It was not your fault.'

'No, but it was my pension fund's fault.'

After a moment, Leon said, 'I do not think you will be collecting it now.'

'I owe you better payment than this,' Oksana said, resuming the careful mutilation of Leon's deep-honey skin.

'Hey, don't you know? The reason the North hates us so much is because we are its death. I tell you how: I give you a ride to Kirinya, you give me a tattoo I cannot get anywhere else and we are square. That is our economy. Things? Anyone can make things, anything you want. But a tattoo, like this? This is skill, this is art. Listen, you will need somewhere to stay in Kirinya. I know a hostel: the Mountain Lodge; it is quite close by the *pujo* station. It is good and warm and the food is excellent. Maybe the owner will like this tattoo so much he will want one too, and that would be more than enough credit to get down to the coast without having to touch the fine Islamic ladies' gold hanging from your ear.'

'There, finished,' she said. It was as good a *pleine aire* bus-stop dinner-break ink-and-needle tattoo as she had ever done. The blood was blackening into a crust. She waved flies away. 'It's going to itch like hell for a couple of days. This is probably wasted advice, but try not to pick the scabs. You know, you should really cover this is up, keep the flies off.'

'Hide my rare and valuable Russian tattoo?'

'Siberian,' Oksana corrected. Then she felt his climate change. She knew the play of men's muscles intimately enough to read a sudden shift in Leon's emotions from the play of his shoulder.

'Ah,' he said. 'Look.'

A new wind had blown up out of the valley, driving the clouds from the mountain slopes like merchants from a temple. Oksana saw that what she had thought were the foothills of Kirinyaga were mere footstools to the foothills. The cloud raced

57

back from the land, and the more of it was revealed, the higher and further it seemed to reach. The Chaga was a crazy quilt laid over the high country. Oksana discovered patterns in the seeming patternlessness. That cluster of tall oval cylinders; too regular. The pillars of that seeming termite city too tall, too structured. Those twin ivory horns; too graceful and symmetrical. That cantilevered out-thrust; wrong colour; those clustered whiteeggs on its summit: those could only be buildings. The slopes were as thick with cultures as a carpet with threads. Oksana's vision subtly linked separate elements together: this buttress to that dome; that mastaba to those spheres. By connections the city of Kirinya built itself out of its scattered towns and villages.

She knew from the satellite data that it ringed the mountain from which it had taken its name twenty kilometres deep. The thermal images showed a swirl of life and heat around the dark peak like the accretion disc around a black hole: twelve million people lived in the ring city. It grew from the mountain, nourished by mists and meltwater; its disorder was organic, intrinsic. It was not one thing, it was many. There was no Kirinya, in the way that there was no Los Angeles. Los Angeles was San Bernardino and Hollywood and Malibu and the Valley; more than the sum of its many 'burbs. Kirinya was Chehe, Castle Forest Station, Kianyaga; Embu and Meru and Nanyuki and thousands more; but here the whole was less than the identity of its components. Each district of Kirinya earned its particular name and nature; each was distinct, identifiable, a city within a city. You could never know all of it, for even if you went all the way round the mountain, through every district and township, when you came back some new society would have taken root there. World as city, city as world.

The clouds were almost gone now; rags of mist shredding on the pinnacles of Kirinya's highest steeples. Suddenly, thrillingly, the three peaks of Kirinyaga came clear; far and high and dazzling, white burning to gold in the low sun.

I know why you stop here, Leon, Oksana thought. You look at it, and you think, that a dog-soldier should have bought such a thing.

58

As if his spirit had chimed, Leon said, 'Come on, *m'zungu*, now I shall take you there.'

He heaved himself up on his hands. His fresh scabs burst. Blood trickled down his arm, over his hand, from his fingers on to the soil.

'Here, let me.' Oksana squatted down to lift and carry him to his bus. He snapped his teeth, tossed his dreadlocks at her.

'A woman does not carry Leon,' he said. 'Absolutely never a white woman.'

As he hand-walked to the bus he left a trail of bloody handprints on the red earth.

11

You cannot miss it, Joseph at the Mountain Lodge had said. Go through the arch, down the street, and you are in the middle of it.

After deep and dream-empty sleep in one of the Lodge's globular wooden rooms, followed by a huge breakfast, Oksana set off to find a *pujo* to the coast. As Leon the bus-driver had said, the price had been negotiable. Joseph was not the tattoo type, but he was more than happy with a *Sibirsk* patch off Oksana's flying jacket.

Street traders had come before dawn to set up their pitches in the shelter of the overhanging wooden buildings. They stood or they squatted or they sat on their chairs under the big live-skin umbrellas. A few had wares: fast food stands, skewers blackening on solar broilers; trays of cell memories with codes to Northern cable channels, or assembler instructions for home-made shoes, or electric kettles; some did the business there and then: hairdressers, beauticians, shoe shines, vehicle valets. Most had only their bodies and their talents: the cooks, the interior designers, the fortune tellers, the nanoware consultants, the hire-musicians, the professional poets, the personal trainers.

They saw Oksana's white face and they pushed themselves at her: you need a good custom car, new designs, like *nothing* out on the streets this season; that hair, woman, you need something doing with that; you look like you are no stranger to trouble, that's why you need me, advocate and mediator, I will solve it all in just two shakes; you're looking for the *pujo* station? Come along with me, I will take you right there, and by the way, my brother has this agency . . .

This one thing about Africa the Chaga could not change, she thought. Everyone is still trying to sell you one fucking thing or another.

The press of offers had disoriented her. A young woman was sitting on a stool in a beautifully worked live-wood doorway. The walls on either side of her shouted the word *Harambee!* – Let's Pull Together – sprayed in violent green. Oksana thought this woman looked unlikely to try to pitch her a medical services contract or a brilliant new party beer.

'Is this the right way for the *pujo* station?'

'It is. Just keep on straight.' The young woman rocked back on her chair, supporting herself against the intricately worked door post. She looked at Oksana and said, 'I've got room if you've got twenty minutes.'

Oksana Mikhailovna had been too many years in Africa not to know when she was being followed. She could not see them – you never can – but the shaved hair at the back of her neck told they knew she knew. She moved to the side of the street from which it would be harder for them to shepherd her their way. The *pujo* station would be the danger area; wide and open.

Suddenly, her skin told her they were in front of her. She stopped at a spice stall to sniff the paper packets of colour. *Harambee!* warned the tenement door behind the stall. Her peripheral vision registered two of them; men in white shirts and PVC pants, homing in like missiles from black stealth interceptors.

Oksana calculated the angles. If she went now, she could make it past them. She whirled; she collided with a very big woman in a *buibui*. The woman went down, bringing God's curses on the unmannerly white whore. Oksana threw apologies but the moment was lost. The two men had the street covered.

There was a way out. She knew they wanted her to take it. She knew she had to take it. The entry was so narrow she had to turn sideways to squeeze through, but in a few footsteps it had widened into a dark alley staggering between lowering tenements hung with yellow mosses and washing. The over-curving walls whispered *Harambee!* in fluorescent yellow. The alley probably coiled in on itself until she would be trapped in some courtyard, facing the white shirts. She hefted her coffee-maker. It was good and heavy and had sharp edges.

A glance behind her. White shone in a stray sun ray far down the entry. One glance away; but in that glance, they had appeared and were blocking the alley. Three boys in PVCs and cut-off T-shirts. They had dropped off a low balcony overhead.

She could not stop. She ran right into them. As they took her down, one drew a big, long knife out of nowhere. A fist tore the Oelende gold out of her ear-lobe. She swung her coffee pot. Metal struck jaw; a boy went down with blood for a face. Oksana fumbled with the clasp of her knife sheath. It was killing time now. The kid with the blade roared and leaped in the air, knife held high, tip hunting for her heart.

A streak of gold and black met him at the zenith of his kill-leap, and took him down in a spray of blood.

'Leave her,' a woman's voice commanded.

The third vinyl-boy froze in his crouch. His knife friend lay in the trash that the tenement people shat from their balconies. A leopard chewed his throat. He saw his friend that had gone down with the coffee-maker. A young woman with beaded braids dressed in leather shorts and knee boots was rolling the muzzle of a very big gun in his jaw blood. He ran.

Swearing and dizzy and trying to staunch the bleeding from her ear, Oksana got to her feet. Standing by was a young woman with enormous hair swept straight back dressed in a silky white body suit with black and yellow elbow and knee pads and biker gloves. An ebony panther rubbed against her legs. It bared yellowed ivory.

'Is it all right?' Cat-girl said.

Shorts-and-boots tossed the PVC-boy the hell out of her sight with a flick of her chin. She took the coffee-maker off Oksana

61

with the ease of a mercenary disarming a nun. She turned it over in her hands, wiped skin off it.

'It's all right.'

Cat-girl looked at the leopard. It quit its business and came to rub against her black thighs.

'You: you're coming to Mombi,' Cat-girl said to Oksana. She whirled and marched down the alley. The panther and the leopard fell in behind her.

12

He called himself Anansi, and he knew he was brilliant.

'Anansi, the spider, the trickster, the weaver,' he proclaimed himself.

Oksana already knew all about him from the fact that he wore flip-up shades indoors, and he smiled far too much. But he adored the coffee-maker. He could not keep his hands off it. He would lift it from his desk and play with it, then set it down again immediately.

'This is wonderful. Exquisite. We've had the juice squeezer for some time, but the coffee-maker completes the set. We can now offer them as a full service. You are sent by God, Oksana Mikhailovna.' This he said in liquid, accentless Russian. Anansi spoke eight languages flawlessly. He had designed the education buckies himself. From a deep live skin chair in the middle of the wooden floor Oksana watched, amused by his attempts to impress her.

Anansi the spider trapped beautiful artefacts. Anansi the weaver spun molecules. Anansi the trickster was a pirate, a faker, King Counterfeit in his office-nanofactory that resembled nothing more than an enormous head of albino broccoli growing from the squalid organic shanties of Kianyaga. But he was not the power here.

In the car Cat-girl and Shorts-and-boots had made it clear that it was the coffee-maker they had been there to save. The car was a new model Lexus. It had everything, it did everything. Shorts-and-boots drove it with reckless speed through the thronged, chaotic streets, but miraculously avoided hitting anything. Cat-girl sat in the middle of the back seat. Oksana sat on her left; the panther on her right. It flexed its claws, tearing wounds in the soft leather upholstery. The skin was alive; it healed within seconds. As a fake, the Lexus was better than the original. The leopard sat in the front next to Shorts-and-boots. Every time it licked its jowls, which it did often, its breath-stink of blood and throat-meat nauseated Oksana.

The reason Shorts-and-boots could drive so fast through the crowds so safely was that her sense of the present extended three minutes into the future. Cat-girl could ride in a car with two hunting cats and have them purr against her flesh because parts of her identity were grafted on to theirs.

Cat-girl was Lenana, Shorts-and-boots was Zul. Oksana was pleased to see that Mombi's girls had lost none of their street style. But their abilities had evolved drastically since the old Nairobi days, when attitude and guns had been enough to rule the townships. It was not sufficient to be poor, look good and shoot straight. Now for Mombi you had to look good, shoot straight and have HIV IV antibodies in your bloodstream. The disease was a Wooden Horse through the immune system, allowing Chaga-fullerenes to work their evolutionary changes on developed cells. The UN had known about the HIV-Chaga-spore vector for a long time; there were years of planning and work in their secret facility at Kajiado. It had housed hundreds of the infected; hundreds of adaptations and variants, hidden down in that huge underground labyrinth.

Gaby had blown that place open. It had been the story of her career, but big truths fall heavy. Unit 12 had cost her her lover, her job, her life in Kenya. But not her friend. I was there when it came apart, Oksana thought. I was there when you returned from exile, I was the one flew you to safety when Nairobi fell. And now I am here again.

Lenana and Zul were first generation. Plague daughters. Oksana tried to imagine how a human mind could stretch into a longer present than this sharp edge of *now*. There were theories about quantum effects being amplified by neural buckies into the classical structures of the brain. Non-locality; time-reversible wave-functions. Some were saying that it was the new physics of the mind; that the gas clouds eight hundred light years away in Rho Ophiuchi that were the home of the Chaga-makers were sentient; fullerenes tied together by quantum connectivity into immense intelligences. If that is what you believe, Oksana thought. But to me it is no different from saying *magic*.

One thing she could understand about Zul's long present. She had seen the attack before it happened. They had known she would be herded down that alley, that the PVC-boys would drop out of the sky, they were already there. And they had let that knife come within a whisper of her heart. You are nothing, Cat-girl and Shorts-and-boots' indifference said. You are just meat attached to a commodity.

Black panther and throat-leopard were coiled by the door of Anansi's office. Zul was not present, but Oksana did not doubt that she was watching through her identity-link. The black panther was licking its crotch. I wish I could do that, Oksana thought.

'You still look kind of shocky,' Anansi said. 'How is your ear?'

She had been given something that looked like the bottom half of a earwig that she really did not want clamped to her maimed lobe, but it had staunched the bleeding and erased the pain.

'It'll heal,' Oksana said.

'They really should not have let that happen,' Anansi said. 'Their orders are to protect investment opportunities. There is far too much of her pets in Lenana. Bitch!' This he directed to the black panther. The thing laid off crotch-sucking to curl a lip at him. Anansi opened an elegant cylindrical cabinet, took out two glasses and a bottle of Stolichnaya. 'Here.'

Oksana sniffed the thimble glass suspiciously.

'Better than the real thing, that's our selling point,' Anansi said. He downed the glass and hurled it against the curving white wall. The big cats started at the sound of breaking glass. 'Isn't that the tradition? It's nothing to nanofacture new ones.'

Oksana drank the vodka. It was exactly as he had said, smug bastard. It was Stolly as she remembered, but more. It was like the coffee that had found its way across terminum into the flight

64

bags of Sibirsk pilots: everything and then some. She was drinking the Platonic ideal of vodka.

She declined to smash the glass.

'Ah.' Anansi cocked his head to one side, as if listening to a distant whisper of his name. 'Mombi will see us now. Come with me, please?'

The hem of his white-worked *jellaba* whispered across the wood floor. Oksana followed. The hunting cats uncurled and padded a breath behind her.

The curving corridor opened into a gallery overlooking the nanofactory. Oksana saw a man carrying her Alessi coffee-maker to a device that looked like a cathedral organ fucking a whiskey distillery. The man slipped the coffee-maker through a sphincter. She did not like her precious object being subjected to something so colonic.

'Don't you worry about a thing,' Anansi said, noticing she had stopped to watch. 'We have to scan it in, program the processors. You'll get your pot back again.'

'Yes, but will it be the same one?'

Anansi was sincerely perplexed.

'Is that important?'

Such things as the quality of the scum, or the build-up of essential oils in the filter, could not be explained to someone with glasses like those.

'Do you do the coffee as well?'

'Oh no no no,' Anansi said. He leaned on the rail, propped one foot up on its toes. His feet were bare. He wore unforgivable toe-rings. He seemed very much enamoured with the business of the silent, sealed molecular processors. 'That's an organisation over in Uplands. We are officially at war with them. They took out some of our sub-contractors in Ngong; poisoned the limit-cycle catalators. They thought to scare people from working for us. We corrupted some of their programs. We'll probably get round to killing each other soon. But we're bigger and better organized. Vodka, malt whiskies, Chanel – that's very big in India at the moment. The liquids are the easiest to do, but we have a niche market in hard goods. Bangalore used to be our biggest market for Rolls Royces, but the police started to clamp down when every second shop-owner was cruising round in one. That's a pity, it was a genuine engineering challenge. We're mostly running small, high-value goods: big names, labels. Gucci, Cartier. If you go to Shanghai, ninety per cent of the Rolexs you see in the tax-free shops were made by us. Not even Rolex can tell our copies from their originals.'

'I suppose most of the big stuff sells on the home market.'

'Oh no no no, absolutely not. The domestic market is almost entirely bespoke. We are an information economy; processor programs, skills. Even those ignorant arboreals can make a car.'

'But how can it benefit you selling in Shanghai and Bangalore when their money isn't worth anything in this revolutionary economy you're so proud of?' Oksana asked.

'You will have an answer to that. Come now, Mombi should not be kept waiting.'

The door in the inner wall was circular, like an airlock, and marked with a green tree of life symbol.

'I warn you, it's a jungle in there,' Anansi said.

It was. Steam heat pulled sweat from every pore. Buckyball and terrestrial rainforest struggled like warring elementals. The air was saturated with perfumes and deep rotting. The shallow domed skylight gave dimension to the circular room: the sprawl of pseudo-fungi and lianas made it infinite. A Mombi-girl with a shaved head dressed in electric green exercise shorts and halter knelt on a stone contemplation stool at the head of the ceramic cobbled path that led into the interior.

'Rewa!' Anansi said. His tone was familiar, condescending and lecherous all at once.

Electric green Rewa slid her eyes off him like she would something decaying in an alley and on to Oksana. Oksana felt her hair prickle, her nipples tighten and withdraw. Rewa could see her spirit.

She unfolded from her contemplation stool.

The path was longer than it should have been. At the centre of the jungle was a pond of liquid mud. In the centre of the mud was the most obese woman Oksana had ever seen. She was waist-deep and naked, her tremendous dugs were lost in the honey-coloured mud. It was only by those planet-suckling breasts that Oksana knew this was a woman. Her chins fell fold upon fold, her eyes and tiny pert mouth were overrun by besieging fat. Her arms were thighs; fat, fat men's thighs. She was quite hairless; her neck spread like congealed lava.

The glossy mud smelled of come and cinnamon; it was a clever slurry of fullerene-impregnated living clays; nutrient and information-rich. It sensuously supported Mombi's obscene bulk. Beached, she would have suffocated under her own weight.

Oksana could not but think of hippopotamuses.

Rewa knelt at the side of the pool.

'You could think of her as a telepath, yes,' Rewa said. Her Swahili was soft, high, musical. 'Of course it is more sophisticated than that, but I find speech tiring and painful these days. You are most welcome, Oksana Mikhailovna Telyanina.'

'We've met before.' Oksana chose to direct her replies to the monstrosity in the pond.

'Yes,' Mombi said through Rewa's Area of Broca. 'The ladies' washroom of the Thorn Tree bar. You were assisting Gaby McAslan in an act of revenge involving shaving an enemy's head. My girls had ordered you out, I think we passed in the doorway.' Mombi shifted her weight, sent ripples across the surface of the mud. 'I was distressed to hear of the shooting down over Tinderet.'

'You know about that?'

'I hear everything. I know everything, and I remember it. I embody it. I become it.' Fingers surfaced, dripped mud, tapped the quivering breasts. 'Please do not make the mistake of thinking that this is indulgence. As I told your former friend on that occasion, information is life; in these times more than ever. Unfortunately, fat is a less efficient memory than neurons. It was a bad thing, at Tinderet.'

The temperature in the conservatorium fell sharply as clouds obscured the sun. The afternoon rains would soon fall.

'Thank you; it was bad thing, yes.'

'I have sustained my own losses recently. They are trying to close down my export routes. Last week one of my truck convoys was destroyed by ground attack helicopters at Rumuruti.'

'I heard.' But that is different, Oksana thought. That is things. These were lives, that had entrusted themselves to me. 'I saw

67

people die. They were shot out of the sky. They had no weapons, they were defenceless; and they shot them out of the sky.'

Mombi blinked her eyes, slowly, heavily.

'People died at Rumuruti. They were unarmed, unless you count Cartier handbags and Nike sports shoes as weapons.'

'Economic weapons,' Anansi said. 'She asked me what we buy one half so precious as the goods we sell, Mombi.'

Mombi laughed. Mud slopped on to the white ceramic cobbles. Rewa had not laughed; she said, 'Power. There is no commodity more valuable than that. Anyone who sells it for mere things earns the price they pay.'

'Blackmail?'

'Control. Some day – it may be never – I will have need of it and call upon my customers.'

'We fight the embargo on the fruits of our creativity and technology,' Anansi said. 'Every bottle of Chanel or Stolichnaya or Rolex watch we sell undermines the prestige of those companies. Their arrogance is unbelievable. The joke is that, to us, they are toys. Tinsel. Nothing. We could cure disease, extend human life indefinitely, give everyone the right to learn whatever they want to learn, give them the power to make any physical object as easily as they would grow a gourd, but because that would mean the end of their power and privilege, they let their people go sick and poor and ignorant and die young.'

'Anansi's cool is as engineered as everything else he produces,' Mombi said. Slabs of black fat heaved to a chuckle. 'But he is too young to wear it well, stir his passion a little and you see the preacher beneath. However, he is exceptionally good at what he does. Now business. What shall I pay you?'

'I beg your pardon?'

'Please listen when I am talking; every word I speak through Rewa destroys cells in her auxiliary nervous system. You have brought me a valuable commodity; now you must be paid for it. What do you want?'

'But you're giving it back to me.'

'Is that all you wish?'

'What's it worth?'

'What do you think it is worth?'

This is the continent that birthed humanity, and trading,

Oksana warned herself. And wove tales of djinns with wishes to grant, and clever trickster spiders. Ask well.

'A favour.'

'Certainly.'

'Whenever I need it. It may be never.'

'I have already agreed. That is the right price to ask. Already you are understanding our economy. Anansi, this woman wants to go to the coast. Please arrange transport for her. I think we can do better than *pujo* service. Now, I think that concludes our business to our mutual satisfaction. If you succeed in finding Gaby McAslan, convey Mombi's compliments and remember me to her. Tell her that Haran died by my own hands in his bolt-hole in Westlands after the destruction of the Cascade Club – she may not know this. Also, ask her: how long will she keep her spear hooded? Now, if you will excuse me, I have overtaxed myself.'

Rewa closed her eyes, rested her hands on her thighs. Mombi turned away and ponderously submerged herself in the mud. The thick slurry closed over her head. Not a bubble broke the surface. Sudden gloom in the indoor forest: the afternoon rains had come, thundering on the glass roof.

13

Anansi drove the fake-Lexus with all of Zul's disregard for consequence and none of her three minutes' foresight. Women swept children from under his wheels. Street boys jeered and threw garbage after him. Wheeled traffic veered and hooted and avoided disaster by skins of paint. Kirinya had not seen fit to reinvent the traffic signal. A beetle-shaped jitney Anansi had almost forced into a wall paralleled him for a kilometre, driver and passenger gesticulating and calling curses on Lexus drivers and all their seed. Though the rain was now a bombardment, Anansi flipped down his shades at them.

'They obviously don't recognize the car or they would have more respect,' he said to his rear-seat passenger. 'Unfortunately, I can't identify them, so they'll be spared an etiquette visit by the girls.'

Another thing Kirinya had not seen fit to reinvent was licence plates.

To avoid head-oning a bus, the Lexus grazed the length of a wall on which that word *Harambee!* had been sprayed in metre-high green letters.

'Oh Jesus Mary God!' Oksana exclaimed. It had not been this frightening with two Skystreak missiles coming down her jet-pipes. Questions would be a diversion. 'What does that on the wall mean?'

'Harambee? You speak Swahili.'

The fake-Lexus hit a pot-hole. Oksana hit the roof.

'I know what it says; what does it mean?'

'It seems that our cultural diversity and hybrid vigour are not enough for some; we must reinvent politics.'

'Harambee is a political party?'

'It considers itself as a forum rather than a traditional party. A consensus. It says that its purpose is not to govern, but to reflect and represent the diversity of its constituent societies. It makes much out of unity in diversity. If it is a consensus, then it is a market for talk, and it is impotent. If it is a party, we do not need such things here. Parties do not have a good tradition among our people. You know what the rump of the Kenyan National Party is doing up there. For forty years they told us, it is a bad thing to be tribal, and then the Chaga comes and we find that we like being tribal; in fact, it gives us a way we can live in our tribes, and still live together. No, I do not think we need this Harambee.'

His political analysis complete, Anansi hurled the fake-Lexus at a gap in the foot of a wall of fifty-metre root-buttresses Oksana knew could not take it. She gripped her coffee-maker, closed her eyes and thus missed the miracle by which Anansi passed his vehicle through the eye of the needle. Beyond was what she could only think of as a football-field airport.

The hard-top enclosed by curving palisades of the buttress-buildings was marked for soccer. There were goalposts at either end. What made it an airport was that a dirigible shaped like a classic Fifties-paranoia flying saucer hovered over the centre circle. The flying saucer was bright yellow and carried the invocation *God Speed!* spray-painted on its lower hull and *James Bond: the Killer!* on the upper. Ropes guyed it down to the goalpost cross-bars. Rain cascaded from its rim, a circular water-fall. Its two-man crew sheltered under the hull, half-watching a roll-screen television and sharing a home-rolled smoke. Anansi drove through the curtain of run-water into the rain shadow. The crew uncurled lazily to greet him with handshakes. Oksana got out, craned backwards to look through the window at the flight deck, peered into the fan ducts. The design was identical to the old Sibirsk logging dirigibles UNECTA had used as reconnaissance platforms over the Chaga, but the thrust and manoeuvring systems were radically reengineered.

'First class travel,' Anansi announced, as if he had woven this airship out of his own spider-silk. He might have. 'They will take you down to Mombasa, after that, you will have to find your own way to this Turangalila place. Fembe and Jonah have never heard of it.'

'It's supposed to be an experimental artists' community.'

'That explains it then. These things last as long as the first adultery. Here.' He took a short plastic rod from the sleeve of his *jellaba*. 'Lenana and Zul should not have let your gold be stolen. Mombi has invested her personal credit in this. It should last until you learn to shake hands.'

The crew-boys had already rolled up their afternoon kick-boxing and smokes and gone aboard. The one with Masai genes a generation back was seated at the controls. The fans spun up to lift speed. The other crewman beckoned impatiently from the top of the ramp.

'Go go go go,' Anansi said.

'I'm owed a favour, remember,' Oksana shouted down the ramp over the rising drone of the thrusters.

'Mombi knows,' Anansi shouted back as the ramp began to close. 'She never forgets.'

The shackle bolts opened automatically, the guy ropes fell to the rain-pooled ground. *God Speed!/James Bond: the Killer!* rose out of the palisade of organic towers, turned ponderously on its

71

axis and pushed lazily through the veils of rain towards the
south east. Within seconds the circle of dry ground and the
barefoot man in the white *jellaba* standing in it were soaked
through.

14

She came by sea with the full of the tide. She came in a long,
low *prau*, gunwales a-slop as its biomotor pushed it through the
chop. Beyond the reef the ocean was running high, white on
indigo, but the lagoon felt only murmurs, rumours of its trouble.
The water slid clear on the incoming tide; she could see the
shadows of the stealth-patterned bottom fish on the sand marl.
She dipped her hand in the water, fetched up ribbons of glutinous weed.

The boatmen who ran their hulls up on the white coral sand
under the encrusted hulk of the old Portuguese fort had all been
suspicious of city plastic, but Hammadi of the beautiful eyes was
hungry for a custom moped to impress a girl. He took Mombi's
rod in his hand, and squeezed it and closed his beautiful eyes,
and was hired.

Turangalila. The name was not familiar to Hammadi. Kikambala he knew; men lived there. Only men. Up north, beyond
Kikambala. Yes, he would take her up there. He would take her
all the way up to Old Malindi, if that was what she wanted.

Hammadi squatted in the stern and tended the syrup feed.
The biomotor burbled, the bow chewed water, the shells of dead
hotels slipped past, engulfed by the red and jade-green piled like
a second reef behind the selvage of sand. World-reef. Hints of
alien architectures reared piers and turrets and canopies above
the surface. Other ways of being human.

Oksana shaded her eyes, lest she be dazzled by sea-shimmer,
and lost.

'Kikambala!'

The *prau* swayed as Hammadi shifted position. Oksana gripped the sides and glanced round. He pointed to a cluster of cylinders roofed with solar thatch rising out of the tumble of coastal Chaga. One more headland – that headland – and it would be Turangalila.

Minutes away, Oksana thought for the first time about what she would find around that headland. She did not think about Turangalila the place – she knew she could live in any place. She thought of Gaby and her daughter and whoever she loved, if there was anyone she loved. They were as ignorant of what was coming as Kilimanjaro before the first hammer-blow from space. She was breaking uninvited into the world Gaby had been building for longer than they had been friends.

Of course Gaby would be glad to see her. Of course she would welcome Oksana into her home and life. Of course the years would roll back. Of course it would all be as it had been, then, when it was good.

Why?

Why should any of it be?

Why should they want her?

If they were there. If there were such a place as Turangalila any more; if it had not been absorbed back into the Chaga, a failed social experiment. She found herself half hoping that she would round that headland and find only land corals and pseudo-palms and sand.

It was only that half hope, half dread; that Turangalila was dead, that kept her from telling Hammadi to turn the boat round and take her back to Mombasa. There might be enough credit on Mombi's stick to build a life not founded on presumptions.

Hammadi's little boat rocked on the narrow green shallows between the fist of the headland and the reef. A swell caught the *prau* and carried it past the rocks.

Oksana saw land corals and pseudo-palms and sand; white coral sand, curving beyond her sight, all the way to Old Malindi. She also saw blue hulled boats pulled up on that white sand, and the curve of a thatched roof lifted above the parasols of land coral, and something that in the heat haze looked part mangrove, part stilt house stride out on root legs from the bowed palms across the sand into the lagoon.

Down by the sea house, a stick silhouette was performing an ugly dance on the thin strip of sand.

'Here,' Oksana heard herself tell Hammadi. The *prau* turned its bow to shore. The tide was high, Hammadi ran the boat up into the palms.

'Shall I wait?' he asked.

Oksana looked at the beached blue-hulled boats.

'No, thank you.'

The strong little biomotor pulled the *prau* off the soft sand. Hammadi spun it like a hunting needle, homed on the custom moped.

There were the bones of a decayed hotel among the palms and root buttresses of the hand-trees. Roomless walls, empty-windowed, watched Oksana and her coffee-maker walking up the hot sand. Paths fringed with knee-high biolanterns mean-dered into the opaque green. Patterns of foliage and root and vine became buildings, shrines, sculptures as she passed, then returned to forest when she glanced back. Oksana imagined ghost music.

She could see that the dancing stick figure was playing with a ball, keeping it up, up, up with feet and knees and chest and head.

The figure that was so skilful with the football was a white girl, in her teens. She was dressed in white shorts and a football shirt. The shirt was red with white and black trim. The girl's hair was red, and hung to the small of her back.

Oksana was on her knees on the hot sand. The coffee-maker fell from her fingers. She was shaking as if in the shamanka trance.

'Oh Jesus and Mary,' she pleaded. 'Oh Jesus and Mary and all the saints and spirits.' She was not ready for this. She glanced back, panic-stricken. Hammadi was out of sight beyond the headland.

The girl caught her ball and came over to look at the strange, distraught woman. Oksana looked up into the face of the icon. The girl's face was not beautiful, but it was strong. It would mature into handsomeness; people would look at it, then look again and say to themselves, *that is a good-looking woman*. Face, arms, legs were marled with freckles. Her eyes were sea-green.

74

'Gaby,' Oksana whispered.

'Gaby's up at the house. I'm Serena. Are you all right?' The girl spoke in English shaded with the edged accent of white Africans.

Oksana broke. Undammed fortysomething emotion mortified the girl. She looked at the sea, and looked at the land, and looked at the ground, then said, 'I suppose I'll have to take you. Come on.'

The girl led Oksana up a rope staircase and on to the pier. They walked out over the glittering water. The reef house was a cluster of interpenetrating wooden shells. Shallow open arches caught the ocean cool and circulated it through the vaulted interior. Oksana glimpsed live skin chairs, wooden stools, low tables, wide beds as Serena took her around the side to the sun platform. The boards were scarred with cigarette stub-outs. Wooden table, wooden steamer chairs. Candle lanterns. Empty bottles. A light gauze awning shaded a leopard-skin recliner. The fabric flapped, the wind was rising, turning to a new quarter.

A woman lay on the recliner, curled on her side, looking out to sea. She wore only an olive green thong. The skin of her back, her folded legs, was freckled. Her long, dark mahogany hair touched the deck.

'Gab,' the girl said to the basking figure. 'God, she's done one. Gab!'

The woman rolled on to her back.

Oksana touched hand to lips.

It was all right. Everything would be as she hoped. Nothing would be as she feared. Nothing had changed. This woman lying on leopard skin was the same Gaby McAslan she had hugged goodbye good luck on the strip at Tinga Tinga, when she went down into Tanzania. The bud of cells in her belly, that she had been so proud of, so scared of, had unfolded and blossomed into this beautiful, suspicious human female. Gaby had not become the other.

'Gaby,' Oksana said.

Gaby wrinkled her face and grunted as those woken from the sun grunt. Her eyes flickered open, screwed up against too much light.

'Hey, big cocks and vodka!' Oksana said.

Then Oksana noticed the circular patch stuck between Gaby's breasts. She looked again at the smooth skin and firm muscles and unstreaked hair of her friend and all the things she had trusted now became treacherous. To be perfectly preserved as if no time had passed since Tinga Tinga was to become utterly Other.

Gaby focused on the face between her and the sun.

'Oh Jesus!' she exclaimed. 'Get this fucking thing off me!' She tore away the infuser patch and tossed it across the deck. 'Oh Jesus Christ, it is you; fucking hell; oh God, Jim's going to be back in two days. It is you, though?' She sat up, peered into Oksana's face. 'It's this stuff, I dunno.'

Oksana saw contempt on Serena's face. Mothers should not wear fewer clothes than their daughters, she thought. But this was not right. None of it was right.

'Oh my God, my God, my God,' Gaby was saying. 'It is you, where did you come from, what are you doing here?'

'I'm sorry. I've presumed too much. I shouldn't have come like this.'

'No no no no, you stay. No you stay here. Oh shit . . . Jim. No, it's all right, I'll make it all right, you stay. With me . . .'

Gaby wandered towards the open arch of the house. She looked lost, distracted, as if she had put something down and then discovered that it was not where she thought she had left it.

Suddenly Oksana realized what the thing was that was so unright.

Gaby was stoned.

Serena was gone.

The building was called the Sea House by the women and occasional men who lived in it. It was a thing grown rather than made, and was very beautiful. It had been called from the bed of the lagoon by an architect-wizard who had passed down the coast ten years ago. He had heard that Turangalila was a crucible for the new arts of the Chaga; he wanted his architecture to take its place among them. He had grown the Sea House, and the big performance space and the labyrinth of the Spirit Hive where the dancers had lived in community for a time. He had created a pilgrimage of organic buildings: an Islamic school in Mombasa, a radio station in Zanzibar, a sacred place on the Isla Moçambica. The architectural footprints ended in an auditorium modelled on a human ear among the colonial wreckage of Laurenço Marques.

He had made his sea house at Turangalila well. He had built it like a ship, for he had seen the storms it would have to weather, outer and inner.There had to be a place that would float to the surface to which the survivors could cling. He had created this nautilus shell of living wood to shelter Serena. The girl could expand through its nested chambers protected from Gaby's emotional shipwrecks.

He had died in Laurenço Marques, killed by white mercenaries fighting for black South Africa against the southward spread of the Chaga.

Oksana fell in love with the Sea House immediately. She knew that she was that kind of emotional flotsam it had been designed to salvage, but she could hear the voices of the spirits in the air that blew through the louvres of the room she had been given at the top of the spiral of shells. The same spirits whispered in the walls of the curved rooms and the coiled corridors she explored. The house was much bigger inside than out. Oksana did not have a philosophical problem with the infundibular. The twenty-seven heavens folded out of each other in such a way, each infinity larger than the one which contained it. Sometimes the voices were so insistent, so almost human that she imagined that if she whirled quickly enough she would catch them like shadows on the walls, the black, twining, agonized figures of Makondé art.

Fish bones and fruit rinds on coral plates. The Alessi had fulfilled its potential with the Chaga coffee. Oksana watched it burn the last of the narcotic patch out of Gaby's bloodstream.

Muslin curtains, light as ghosts, drifted in the air flow. Gaby had lit the candles in the ocean room. The tide had turned and was running in again under the moons. Oksana could feel the lap of it against the wooden piers. The two women sprawled on coiled wicker sofas. They had talked their way into deep night. They had talked of the old stuff, of the Kenya days. Of their first meeting in the bar of the PanAfric Hotel, Gaby culture-shocked off the African night-flight. Oksana had told the secret she had confessed to the women of Oelende.

'I think I always guessed something like that,' Gaby had said, pouring another bottle of Dr Scullabus' good beer. They had talked of nights in the Elephant Bar where the Siberians drank and sang songs from the shows, and the football match when Team SkyNet, with its visiting Sibirsk left back, had fucked UNECTA United with that seventy-fifth-minute goal crossed by McAslan number 9 on to the head of centre-forward Tembo and into the net.

'Tembo; he was your camera-man. I flew him and his family down to Zanzibar.'

'He stayed there.'

'And that other one; the goalkeeper, the one you had the affair with.'

'Faraway. I've heard he's something in this Harambee organization. I don't know; I'm kind of out of things here.'

'And Shepard?'

'Shepard never came back to me.'

'I'm sorry.'

'Don't be.'

Oksana shivered, started. Something had whispered, an electric tingle inside her head; an almost name.

'You get to ignore it after a while,' Gaby said.

'You heard it too?'

'Everyone hears it.' Gaby got up abruptly and went to the

open arch on to the deck as if she had heard another voice, one Oksana was deaf to, out in the night. 'Hey, you fancy a swim? It's a beautiful night to swim.' She slid off the beaded waistcoat, unhitched the loose sarong and let it fall. She stepped out into the night. Oksana watched her cross the deck and descend the steps to the boat jetty. Something turned over in her heart. Thrilled at her abandon, she shrugged out of the too-big shorts and T-shirt she had been lent, padded across the living wood. Gaby looked at Oksana on the high deck, raised her arms and dived neatly into the water. She hardly disturbed the surface. The thing that had kicked Oksana's heart kicked again when she could not see where Gaby had come up. She hurried down the swaying wooden water steps, hesitated. Water was not her element. To a creature of forests and earth, the ocean was the avatar of death. Dissolution into anonymity; the annihilation of the mass.

'You've got to throw yourself in,' Gaby's voice called out of the darkness.

The boom of the surf on the reef was a felt thing, a tremor in the universe. Oksana breathed out the atavistic clutch of fear, and jumped. The water was blood-warm, black as the secret places of a body.

'Out here,' Gaby called again. Oksana saw her head and waving arm in the silver ribbon of the moon path. She was a long way from shore. Oksana swam clumsily towards her. Ribbon weed ran slick fingers over her body. I am far out of my depth, she thought. I could drown here.

Midway between shore and surf, Gaby and Oksana trod deep water. The full moon low in the east outshone the southern stars. The BDO was a lighthouse gleam on the edge of the world, the starbow of comets a wisp of phosphorescence.

'I need to warn you,' Gaby said. 'Don't get involved with me. Things aren't good with me; things haven't been good for a long time.' She looked back to the lights of the Sea House. They were far and small, a tiny constellation on the dark coast. 'Every day I do this. I swim out here, halfway to the reef. Some day maybe I'll make it all the way, and then the waves can pull me under and smash every bloody thing apart on the coral.'

The two women floated in the moonlight.

Oksana said, 'Gaby, Mombi told me to ask you something. She said, ask Gaby how long will she keep her spear hooded?'

Gaby was a long time answering.

'There is no spear.'

Oksana shivered as if a shark had passed close but not touching her, close enough to sense, and all the unright she had felt since Serena doing her tricks with the ball on the beach became anger.

'Fuck you, Gaby!'

'Yeah, fuck me,' Gaby said. 'Listen to me; I don't do it any more. There is nothing there, do you understand? There never was this fucking spear of destiny, or whatever kind of warrior Mombi thinks I am. All it ever was was ambition fooling me into thinking I had talent. You want something hard enough, you'll do whatever it takes to get it, but that's not talent. The worst thing you can do is to ever pretend that it's talent.'

'Gab . . .'

'Don't stop me, I don't want you to stop me. I need to pick this scab. I need it to bleed every so often so I don't fool myself like that again. I'm sorry it has to be you gets fucked over. I thought about you a lot; then, Jesus! here you are! I feel so fucking shabby about this; you come here, you see me just like I used to be, you think everything's going to be just how it was; Oksana and Gab together again, look out world. I'm sorry, I can't be that for you.'

'It wasn't because of you that I came, Gaby. Not entirely. I couldn't hear the spirits any more. I was ice inside. I was dying; I made the crossing because I wanted to hear the life speaking to me. I can hear it here, Gaby, I can feel it, it's like I had this shell, this thick shell, and it's been lifted off me, and I can feel the light on my flesh. It works here, Gaby. It's true.'

Gaby lay back, floated belly and breasts to the stars. 'What if I were to tell you every breath you've taken since coming here, everything you've eaten, every drop you've drunk, has been teeming with buckies, and that they've seeded themselves through your body? That they're in every part of you, every organ, every cell by now.'

'How could it not be?'

'What if I were to tell you that those buckies have been working on you, changing you, adapting you? Heightened sensory perception is part of it; that feeling you described, as if a shell had been lifted off you.'

The water felt very deep beneath Oksana's treading feet. Drowning, she thought. But even as she had fallen in her ejector seat towards the Chaga ceiling, she had been drowning alone and naked in a subtler sea of sentient transfiguring molecules.

'Am I sick?' she asked.

'Sick, no. Infected, yes. Okya, you can't get sick again. They've re-engineered your immune system. Nothing can touch you. Flu, malaria, HIV, Ebola, Dengue, nothing. Not even cancer. And there's another thing. Have you noticed that your piss and sweat smells weird?'

'I thought it was the change of diet. It still gives me the shits.'

'The buckies are scrubbing free radicals and toxins out of your cells. If you looked at your piss through an electron microscope, you'd see DNA fragments; they're snipping out the sequence that codes for aging hormones.'

'People here don't get older?'

'They get older. They just don't age. Look at me, Okya, I will be forty-five in October. In fifteen years my body has aged maybe two.'

Oksana said, 'I'm frightened.'

'Yeah. You should be. I was.' The wide African moon climbed the sky. Gaby said, 'There's more. Other buckies attach to the telomeres on your genes and prevent them shortening during cell division. Your cells can go on dividing and growing.'

'How long?'

'Indefinitely. No one has died yet from natural causes. Okya, you are amortal.'

'I cannot die?'

'I said a-mortal. If you got cramp out here, you would drown and the buckies couldn't save you. You can be killed. People are killed. Too many people. You're like a glass ornament. Fall over, and you smash. You're fragile.'

Oksana looked at Gaby's profile, dark in the moonslight,

lapped by water. She tried to project the memory of the warrior girl waiting on the road to Gichichi on to it. Only the young could be careless of a life that could see a million tomorrows. They do not think they can die whether that life is fifty years or five hundred years, so it means nothing to them. But the girl's scarred face would not fit over Gaby's, the image kept changing into Serena.

Oksana Mikhailovna Telyanina. Amortal. No shadow on the sun; no dark wings folding over the years to come. Time now is not her enemy; time is the lens through which history projects into your life. She could watch stone turn to sand, the mountain flow to the sea, the stars move in their courses, the rise and decline of civilizations, the future of humanity write itself on the universe.

Believe it, said the spirit voices.

She looked around, suddenly panic-stricken. She was alone, Gaby was nowhere to be seen; currents held her, taking her out to the reef where they would pull her down and shred her fragile eternal life on red coral.

'I'm here.' A moonlit arm raised from the water, closer than she had feared. 'Come on, let's go back. It's getting cold.' Gaby rolled on to her belly and stroked strongly in along the rippled moonpath. Oksana kicked and followed her, riding the tide in towards the guiding lights of the Sea House.

16

The candles in the drift glass lanterns had burned down to charred wicks. Lit cool green by the biolumes, Oksana stood before the big circular tidewood-framed mirror, examining her left wrist. Less than ten days since Ali from Cairo's black medicals had excised the diffusion pump, and the scar had faded to a line of pink flesh. She held up her arm so that its scar was reflected in the glass. She leaned forward to read the lines around her eyes and mouth.

Cat-curled on the wicker sofa, Gaby said, 'You'll lose between five and ten years in the next few months as the buckies clean out your system. And like you see, you heal fast. You can regenerate a finger, or an ear; I've heard of folk growing back hands after landmine blasts.'

Oksana touched a finger to her cheek, stretched skin over the line of high Slavic cheekbones.

'Now I know what the North is so afraid of.'

'No you don't. I'll tell you what really scares the shit out of them. Give me two six digit numbers.'

'286,542; 777,182,' Oksana said.

'Multiplied are 222,695,284,644,' Gaby said. 'Squared is 4.959319 ten to the 22nd. I can give you all twenty-three digits if you want. What date's your birthday?'

'Seventeenth October.'

'In 2093 that'll be on a Saturday. Happy birthday. You'll be one hundred and eight.'

'How . . .' Oksana began to ask.

Gaby said, 'You're supposed to lose a million neurons a day, and you never get them back. You do now. There are buckies in your head that recycle dead neurons. They rebuild them, reprogram them, connect them together. There's a second brain wiring itself up inside your head, making connections to your meatbrain, becoming sentient, a fullerene computer running in parallel with the meat computer you were born with.

'That number stuff is just party tricks, any kid can do it. What is useful is you only have to see something once, or read it, or hear it, and you can recall it exactly.'

Like Mombi in her bath of buckyball mud remembering a momentary exchange of glances outside a woman's toilet in a bar in a city now reduced to chemicals. How many exabits of worldly wisdom were stored in her slabs of fullerene-doped fat?

'That's only the start. By now the buckies'll have seeded your skull with fullerene carbon conductors. It's like nanotech trepanning; your brain is open to the universe.'

'Telepathy? You can read my mind, hear my thoughts?' It

seemed a monstrous violation, a groping of the soft flesh inside her head.

'God, no. Radio. They're sensitive to em-wavelengths.'

Miswe, sitting in the window of the *zenana*, eyes closed, face contemplative. 'I'm sorry, I was listening to the radio.' And her firstborn, older than his mother looked. 'Fifteen years is not long,' she had said. Her gnostic wisdom, which Oksana had thought nuggets of Sufi mysticism, had been nothing less than statements of technological truth.

Anansi, sly spider-man with flip-up shades, had said, we could cure disease, extend human life indefinitely, give everyone the right to learn whatever they want to learn, give them the power to make any physical object as easily as they would grow a gourd.

Oksana turned from the mirror. She thrust out her right hand to the woman on the sofa.

'Shake my hand, Gaby.'

Oksana looked into Gaby's green eyes as hand closed on hand.

'Ah!' Oksana snatched her hand away. 'I felt something, like the hair on the back of my neck.'

'We run an entire economy on the hair on the back of your neck.'

Oksana lifted Mombi's rod from the conversation table. She squeezed her hand around it. Something, a flutter in the back-brain, a bat-chitter of money?

'Let me try something.' Gaby quickly took Oksana's head between her hands. 'Listen.' Oksana found herself fascinated by the green eyes. They carried all the age her body refused. 'What do you hear?'

'Nothing,' Oksana said. 'Sea. Wind. You.'

'Don't force it. Open up, hear what's there to be heard, not what you want to hear. What do you hear?'

'Nothing,' Oksana said. 'I can't hear anything.'

Gaby's face was within centimetres of hers now. The two women turned in the centre of the ocean room; a close, intimate dance.

'Let it be what it wants to be. Hear what's there to be heard.'

'I don't hear anything!' Oksana shouted, and it was there, in

84

the back of the shout, an echo, spirit music. Drums, guitars; wavering, a candle flame of sound.

'What are you doing?' she whispered, wonderingly.

'Connecting your neural transducers to mine, amplifying the signal. I'm the antennae of your soul. I'm jump-starting your nervous system. What do you hear?'

'Music,' Oksana said. 'Dance music. And there's a voice, a man, he's speaking Swahili. He's saying something about ships.'

Gaby let loose a peal of laughter.

'You tuned to fucking Radio Free Kanamai! You're listening to King M'beki on the Night Patrol, broadcasting to the I-Force fleet.'

She took her hands away from Oksana's head.

'Still hear it?'

Oksana nodded, amazed. Then her expression changed to doubt, fear.

'How do I make it stop? Will it do this all the time?'

'Hey, no, Jesus, do you think any of us would be sane if you couldn't switch it off? It's all about burning in new neural pathways. Think it off. It may take a couple of goes.'

Gaby saw Oksana twitch her face, and again. The third time, her face relaxed.

'Gaby, thank you.'

'You don't need to thank me. It's yours by right.' The look on Gaby's face was complex, meaning hooded by the uncertain green biolight. She settled on the big wicker sofa and pulled her knees up to her chin and looked at the floor mats and the biolumes and the mirror and the darkness outside the window arches, at anything but Oksana Mikhailovna.

There was no sleep in the shell-room at the apex of the Sea House that night. Oksana lay staring at the ceiling ribs, mind staggering from monolithic truth to monolithic truth. But they were too big for her to put her hands around, or even to circle with her arms; too big even to try to climb, so she lay on the wide, low wicker bed and played with the new trick in her head. She hunted up and down the wavelengths, cruising the stations of the coast and the coded stutter of the I-force fleet out below the horizon and the soprano yammering of the spysats as they tumbled above the forbidden hemisphere.

Wearying of wonders, and finding that amortal, ever-young, omniscient, what she actually wanted was *sleep*. Oksana wandered downstairs in search of coconut milk or water. She found Gaby sprawled on the sofa, unconscious. Transconscious: the glossy disc of a pharmaceutical patch rocked gently in the hollow of her throat to the tide of her breathing.

17

It was party night at the Mermaid Café. It had been party night every night for the past fourteen years. Tonight the party was to celebrate the completion of panel eight of Sudha's tapestry sequence interpreting Afro-Indian mythology into post-Chaga symbology. The night before it had been the annual Turangalila millipede race. Tomorrow it would be the feast of St Michael and All Angels.

The Tokoloshe panel hung in the place of high honour behind Dr Scullabus's bar. The primeval forest demon presided over the drinking and the dancing and the dalliances. He had the four arms of Shiva; one carried a bust of Freud, one a child, one a buckyball, one a Kalashnikov. A host of fullerenes, landmines and fighter aircraft attended him. From her stool at the bar Oksana Mikhailovna concluded that the needlework was very fine.

'What happened to the other seven?' she asked the Doctor.

'There are no others. There only ever is one. When it has served its time, Sudha will unpick it and use the threads to make the next tapestry in the series. She says it is an allegory of our society; nothing is created, everything is transformed from one form into another.'

'She has little enough to do with her time,' Oksana said.

'Don't we all?' The doctor filled the painted ceramic cup with arak.

'Big cocks and vodka,' Oksana declared and downed it in one. She drifted with the currents of conversation.

'. . . cognitive search engines to surf the gnoosphere; believe it . . .'

'. . . shorts so tight you could tell his religion . . .'

'. . . I dunno, maybe spend a year down a long dirt road . . .'

'. . . no longer opera cycles, but cycles of opera cycles . . .'

'. . . this thing with thread and nipples . . .'

Oksana caught a highlight of glossy hair as she panned back across the faces. She took an arak to the table in the dark part of the bar.

'Hi. Can I get you something?'

'I've got, thanks.' A much-recycled bottle of Doctor's Remedy. Oksana did not ask if she minded if she sat.

'You don't like me, do you?'

Serena twisted her bottle, looked at the damp rings it left on the table top.

'I don't know you.'

'But you're suspicious of me.'

There was a game going on at the bar. It involved Sudha the tapestry woman standing on the counter and endeavouring to pick up a glass of absinthe in her teeth without touching anything.

'You think I'm going to hurt Gab,' Oksana said.

'I don't know. Do you think you're going to?'

'What would you do if I did?'

'This is a boring conversation,' Serena said. 'You are a boring woman. I'm bored here, I'm going.'

Serena surged up and ducked under the roof-lip into the night. Sudha fell off the bar. She hit the floor hard but she was too stoned to do anything but laugh. The tokoloshe looked down on its laughing creator.

Oksana caught up with Serena before she could lose herself in the tangle of paths around the Mermaid Café.

'Can I walk with you?'

'Whatever you like.'

'I don't know much about this place.'

'Don't try this let's get to know each other stuff, right? We don't have to know each other.'

'You're very defensive.'

'You ask stupid questions.'

'No, not about yourself. About Gab.'

'She doesn't need defending.'

'So why do you do it? Do you think she needs it?'

'Listen.' Serena was wisp and willow next to Oksana's tattooed work-out physique, but the Siberian woman felt physically intimidated by the girl's anger. Your mother's daughter in that respect, Oksana thought. 'You don't know nothing about Gab. You knew this ace reporter who blew the whistle on Unit 12, the one who stayed when Nairobi went down, the first one in to the Ten Thousand Tribes. Let me tell you something about my mother. My mother is a waster. My mother is a junkie. My mother does patches. Let me tell you something else about my mother. My mother hates me.'

'No.'

'Yes. She hates me. She hates me because I cost her everything. All those good times you remember, I was the reason they all stopped. I'm not perfect. I was touched by it; I'm changed. I'm not fucking human!'

Gale of red hair. Serena fled. Oksana ran after her: the girl was fast, the paths were unfamiliar. Gone.

'Serena!' Oksana shouted.

A small, half-suppressed cry. Serena was folded in the darkness beneath the pregnant belly of carved wooden mother-goddess, knees pressed to chest, cloaked in hair. A glitter of eyes: Oksana's heart stumbled. She did not see a tormented fifteen-year-old girl. She saw Gaby, the night she and Shepard destroyed each other. She had run him through with the spear of her anger, again and again and again, because she thought he had betrayed her. And then he had told her about the car crash. One of his sons was crippled from it, the other was dead. In an instant it had all toppled from triumph into catastrophe.

There had been one place and one person left for Gaby to go to when it all came apart.

She had sat like that, pulled in on herself. But the people in Unit 12 had cut her hair; carelessly hacked it away into a misshapen shag.

Oksana gently stroked Serena's hair.

'Don't you touch me!' Serena screamed. Her breath shuddered, she said, 'It's not fair, it's not fucking fair, I didn't want to be like this. She just doesn't understand it.'

'I'm sorry.'

'What have you to be sorry about?'

The girl's defences were adamant, bastion upon bastion. But Oksana could now see a way to slip through them.

'No, I think you're wrong there. I think your mother loves you very much. Listen to me, listen to what I've got to say here. She gave birth to you. She chose to do that.'

'What are you saying?'

'I'm saying: she didn't have to have you. When they told her in decontam that the foetus – you – had been changed, they gave her the option of aborting. It would have been the easiest thing in the world for Gab not to have kept you; everyone advised her not to; the UNECTA doctors, the folk at SkyNet, her friends. Even I told her not to have you. And she couldn't do it. She kept you. She chose between her career and you. She wanted you, Serena.'

Serena tipped her head back against the navel of the stone Venus. The tracks of her tears glistened in the dim biolight.

'We don't get any cleverer as we get older. We don't know any better, we just get stuck in the same ways of dealing with things, and not dealing. Gab's problems are her own, she made them, she's coping, or not coping – she never was any good at things like this – but you're not the cause of them. She doesn't hate you. You're all she has. She needs you.'

Serena shook her head.

'No. Not while she's got him.'

'Diamond Jim?'

Serena nodded, a banner of hair.

'You don't like him?'

'You'll see. More like, you'll not see. You'll fall for him like everyone does.'

Oksana breathed in the night musk, slowly exhaled.

'I'm not like everyone else. I see things no one else does. Trust me.'

Serena looked at her. Oksana shivered; something had arced in the sea-green eyes.

'Give me your knife.'

'What're you going to do with it?'

'It's all right, don't worry, I just need it for a second.'

Oksana unsnapped the sheath and offered Serena the handle. Serena took the blade and quickly drew the edge across the palm of her hand.

'Ah!' She grimaced. Blood filled her palm. 'Yours,' she said, gasping, taken by surprise by the pain. Oksana held out her hand. Serena slashed it open. It hurt hard. Palm pressed to palm. Blood mingled with blood.

'Maybe I can trust you, but maybe I can't. So I'm going to keep an eye on you. Wherever you go, whatever you do, I'll be there. I'll be watching. You hurt Gab and I will kill you with this knife.' She wiped the blade clean on the palm of her intact hand, returned the blade to Oksana.

Oksana marvelled at the almost immediate staunching of the blood. She could feel the edges of the wound drawing together, weaving biochemical nooses around each other.

A gust of wind shook the coast; in its wake came rain, sudden and hard and hot.

18

Diamond Jim came over the reef on the morning tide. He came from the south with flutes and presents. He had been playing a festival down on Pemba. The festival had ended two weeks ago but this thing had come together with a tabla player from Tanga and Ras Babamoyo *himself* and the music stations wanted sessions. The *putti putti* bumped against the jetty and Diamond Jim jumped ashore with his flute case in his hand and his presents in a tie-dye kit bag slung over his shoulder.

'What have you brought me, what have you brought me?' Gaby asked, child-eager.

'Well,' said Diamond Jim.

In his sack was a carved ebony box, Bible-sized, intricately tooled. The hinges were Arab brass. Inside were thirty narc patches wrapped in oiled paper.

'Fun from Moginçual,' Diamond Jim said.

He made her pay the boatwoman. He noticed Oksana at the top of the steps.

'Hello,' he said in a soft Australian accent. 'A guest. Great! You staying long? Jim.'

Oksana shook his hand. He was wire-thin but muscled enough, his skin burned by sun. His face was both wise and clever. There was a lot of silver in his ears. He wore his bleached walnut dreads clasped at the nape of his neck. Diamond Jim was dressed in a deep red sarong and a kingfisher-blue waistcoat worked with beads. He was low on body hair, a thing Oksana liked in men. Neither her old shaman senses or her new bucky-soul tweaked anything. But she did not like the way he went into the house. It assumed too many rights and liberties. She did not like the way he went straight to Gaby's bed. She sulked on the sun deck, tuning out the body-noises with the spirits of radio until Gaby came down smelling of sex, but even then it was not right, the thing they had was invaded. She could not get a word of good woman's talk out of Gaby. It took Diamond Jim twelve hours to sleep off whatever he had been doing in Pemba. The party that night at the Mermaid Café was a welcome home. It was a mother of a party. Players from twenty kilometres up and down the coast had come with their instruments to jam. The famous Kikambala drummers kept the back beat. They smiled to Diamond Jim. He nodded to them: respect. Turangalila put on its best to welcome him back. Diamond Jim moved among the people accepting their kisses and embraces, bestowing gifts from his bag. Wherever he went he seemed to invest with spirit. From her seat at the bar Oksana watched Gaby. Always on the edge, she thought. She listens, she smiles, she laughs, sometimes she says a word, but she is in shadow.

Half seen through smiling faces: Serena. A tall black girl was with her. Serena too was watching her mother and Diamond Jim. As if she knew that other eyes were on her, she turned and looked at Oksana. Oksana started: for an instant she had seen herself, seated by the bar, one finger resting on the lip of the painted arak cup.

Serena nodded slowly. She and the tall girl slipped away. She had said she would not stay under the same roof as Diamond Jim.

Diamond Jim drew out the chromium flute. The people gave him space. He closed his eyes, swayed his body to catch what the bass and drums were saying. He lifted his flute to his lips and made a new song. Diamond Jim played beautifully and democratically. Though the party was his, he did not demand the heart of the music. Sometimes the flute would soar in improvization over the rhythm; again it would nestle with the drummers or the bass while the guitar or the thumb-piano strutted their turns. Diamond Jim played music that demanded you dance. It made you suddenly notice that your foot was beating or your fingers were tapping on the side of your beer bottle. Gaby came through the jostle to haul Oksana off her stool and woman-dance, which is the tribal thing women do together for joy, that men cannot understand is not for them. Then there was a cheer as Malachi from Manarani came in with his accordion and Oksana found herself partnered with the Doctor himself who moved like water and was good to dance with and who told Oksana he really wanted to make *fiki-fiki* with her, which she knew was just man-shit to a fortysomething tattooed white woman but was nice to hear anyway. The party wore on, the drink wore down, the heat increased, the sweat flowed, the people faded. There were more bodies under the tables and on the bar than on the floor. In the end it was Diamond Jim and the guitar player trading long extemporizations and a lone guy from Kikambala tapping time on bongos.

Diamond Jim put up his flute.

'Time, people.'

He poked Gaby off the table on which she was curled, patch stuck on her forehead, mouth-breathing loudly. Oksana unfolded from Dr Scullabus, who had fallen asleep over her. They went back through the lamp-lit trees as dawn was rising out of the ocean. It had been the best night in the Mermaid Café since the last time Diamond Jim came back.

No one did much that day other than doze in the sun. Oksana

was started from sleep several times by the sensation that someone was standing behind her, close enough for her to feel the cool of a shadow. But Diamond Jim was in his hammock and Gaby was drawn up like a foetus on the wooden lounger, staring at the sea with one of the Fun from Mogínçual patches between her breasts.

There was a dinner that night, just for the people of the Sea House. Gaby prepared it. She wielded terrifyingly sharp knives for one so blurred from Mogínçual dope. The razor blades sliced vegetables and sashimied transmorphic fish. Oksana sat with Diamond Jim on floor cushions at the low livewood table in the social eating space. He poured fine wine and engaged Oksana in conversations about her adventures. He was a good conversationalist – Oksana answered all his questions, but a separate, non-vocal part of her observed Gaby's domestication with concern. It looked numb and slavish, a clause in a sexual contract. Doin' it for a man.

The sun went down. Gaby served the first course. She sat on the floor, eating with her fingers. She seemed distant, deliberately disconnected; the conversation belonged to Oksana and Diamond Jim.

'Another bottle of this, I think,' Diamond Jim said to Gaby as she silently took away the plates. To Oksana he continued, 'It is fucking serious shit, up there on the front line, and I wouldn't wish it for anyone, but sometimes I reckon we're a little too quiet and comfortable for our own good down here. I mean, Turangalila was meant to be an artists' community, and if art isn't dangerous, why bother? Art should be challenging; the whole reason I came here because I'd heard there was this place where they were finding new ways to express what it was all about living on this new planet of ours. These days, all Turangalila expresses is acid, booze and ass.'

'How long have you been here?'

'I came about three years ago, up through Mombasa from Zanzibar. The place was going belly-up even then; a lot of the best composers and writers had moved on inland to Kirinya. You know what it's like, you sort of get cast up by the high tide, and you're left on the beach until someone picks you up.'

Gaby poured the new wine and went back to plate up the next course.

'I might be moving on soonish, though,' Diamond Jim said casually. 'I mean, it's all getting a bit fucking political, this Harambee thing. Nations are falling over themselves to join; what is it they call themselves, the consensus? It was what I liked about this place, you make up the rules to suit yourself. I'm a natural-born anarchist, me.' A smile fluttered between him and Gaby. 'It was the reason I couldn't stay in Madagascar; politics. It wasn't just parties there, it was the whole state thing; laws and economies and flags and all that. Jesus, they even had fucking *police*. Fuck off, you know? We don't need that fascist groove thing. What is it they call themselves?'

'The Merina,' Gaby said.

'Yeah, the Merina. The. Definite article; when it starts getting to definite articles, all people of spirit have to get out. I tell you, first time I see fucking Harambee sprayed on a wall here, I'm on a boat out.'

'Madagascar?' Oksana asked.

'Place called Ambositra, up in the central highlands. Best place I ever was, until the Merina fucked it up. It was the music; I wanted to study Malagasy music; there's this fantastic tradition, goes back four, five hundred years, and no one in the west – the North, I mean – knows anything about it.'

'Is that why you made the crossing, because of the music?'

'Well, yeah, it seemed like a good idea at the time, but it always does, doesn't it? If I'd known ... I don't know. But Oz was so up its own fucking ass then; this was way before the Ooloru Event, there was this kind of unspoken assumption going round that it wouldn't touch Australia because we weren't properly southern hemisphere. We spoke English, you know? We were white. We were rich. And I think part of the reason I did go was to say fuck you to all that; you aren't God's little green acre, there are places better than you in the poor, black, alien parts of the planet. Of course now Oz is going with a whimper rather than a bang; back into the Dreamtime again.'

'New Zealand, now,' Gaby said. 'A biological package hit just south of Auckland last week.'

'Maybe I should go home, see what's happening,' Diamond Jim said. 'See if it's done any good.'

You can go home again, Oksana thought.

For desert Gaby served finger-sized green-skinned fruit. She showed Oksana how to pop the yellow flesh out of the husk. Chocolate. The unpromising looking things tasted of Swiss milk chocolate. Oksana gorged herself, then realized guiltily she had only left three.

'Sure they grow on trees round here,' Diamond Jim said.

There was coffee from the Alessi, and a particularly good liqueur Diamond Jim had brought back from the festival. The dinner things were cleared away and Diamond Jim fetched a flute; a bamboo *shakuhachi*. From the bedroom Gaby brought a small African guitar. She tucked her hair behind her ear and tuned to Diamond Jim's breathy notes. They played together. Warm with food and wine, Oksana observed how they made music. Gaby was an amateur, she had to concentrate on the chord changes and transitions. She always seemed half a beat behind Diamond Jim's soaring flute. It was pretty, but it was not a musical marriage, Oksana realized. He flew into improvisational landscapes where Gaby struggled to follow. Oksana saw a flicker of annoyance on his face as she missed a chord. He pushed the flute into higher, purer places. Gaby stopped playing. She laid the little African guitar on the floor. The *shakuhachi* climbed and spiralled and swooped in solitary brilliance. It was beautiful and transcendent and Oksana wished it would stop, stop now.

Gaby took a Mogincual patch from the carved ebony box on the table and pressed it to her heart. She curled up on the sofa. She sucked her thumb. Her eyes glazed. The flute played on, ascending into musics freer and more wonderful than Oksana had ever imagined.

Again, she shivered, invaded by an intangible presence. Oksana glanced over her shoulder. Nothing, of course.

Gaby's eyes closed.

Diamond Jim set down his *shakuhachi*. He looked at Oksana.

'So, then.'

'So?'

'You, me; her if you want.'

'What?'

'Look, we don't do this jealousy-possession thing. You won't be upsetting anyone, you won't be wrecking any homes or busting up any little marriages.'

'I think there's been a big misunderstanding here.'

'You've been looking for it all night. Don't deny it, Jesus, I can fucking smell it off you. Come on.'

Oksana got up from the table.

'I'm going to my room now, okay? I think the best way to look at this is that we've all had too much to drink and we say things we don't really mean, and in the morning we'll all have forgotten about it.'

She said these words crossing the social space and climbing the spiral staircase.

'Jesus, you've a lot to learn about living in this world,' Diamond Jim called from the sofa. 'You have to fit in, know what I mean?'

In the shell-shaped room Oksana sat on her bed and listened for a long time to the ocean on the reef. She felt it tremble up through the legs of the Sea House into her body. She thought about going downstairs and slamming the sole of her boot into Diamond Jim's mouth. She did not do that. Then she heard the *shakuhachi* and it melted her heart. That is how he does it, she thought. He picks that thing up, and puts it to his lips and he has total control over us. It drew her out of the bedroom on to the little balcony. She looked down on the scene in the living room.

Gaby was sprawled on her back on the sofa. Her legs were open. Diamond Jim sat at her feet, weaving a pattern in time with the notes from the *shakuhachi*. Gaby moved lethargically to the command of the bamboo flute. Her hips rotated. She rubbed a hand over her crotch. Oksana leaned against the wall, not wanting to look, unable to do anything but. The music drifted into silence. Diamond Jim pressed the saliva-wet mouthpiece of the flute to Gaby's crotch. He worked out the folds of her labia under the soft fabric of the thong. Gaby let free a little moan.

Oksana suppressed a little moan.

Voyeur.

She whirled. Oh God. There was someone in the house. There

was someone, right next to her. She almost cried out, she could feel the tangibility of the shadows cast by the biolights.

I'm going to keep an eye on you, Serena had said. Wherever you go, whatever you do, I'll be there. I'll be watching. The pressing of red palms, the exchange of blood: could Serena be hovering in the back of Oksana's soul like the angels of God? Watching the sexual humiliation of her own mother?

And the eyes through which she watched? What expectation had she of those?

Diamond Jim had worked Gaby's thong down to her ankles. He was pressing the tip of the flute on to her vagina, rubbing rhythmically against her clitoris. Oksana watched proud red flesh spread and fold. Gaby pushed her body towards the invading instrument. She ran her hands over her breasts.

Oksana could not look away.

Diamond Jim ripped the dead patch from Gaby's breast bone. He moved out of Oksana's view into the kitchen, returned with a fresh patch. He stuck it above the hypotenuse of Gaby's ginger pubes.

'Come on you bitch,' he said. 'Come on you cunt, you owe me.'

Gaby's eyes were wide. Her chest was heaving. She clawed at the new patch, Diamond Jim held her arms until her struggles subsided.

'No,' she moaned, 'no, no . . .'

He took a huge handful of hair and waistcoat.

'Oh Christ,' Gaby whimpered.

He dragged her off the sofa. The armholes of the beautiful beaded waistcoat had pulled tight under her shoulders, immobilizing Gaby. She twisted her body, but Diamond Jim was hideously strong in his slight frame. He hauled her on her back across the living room out on to the sun deck. Gaby twisted her body but she was too fucked to fight. Her protests had become a high-pitched keen that Oksana hated beyond anything she had ever heard.

If she went to the bedroom window she could see what would happen out on the sun deck. No, she said. An echo in her mind she was not sure was entirely hers insisted. Oksana willed apart the sheets of glassy cha-plastic.

Diamond Jim had dragged Gaby to the mooring posts. The carved demon heads leered: satisfaction, sacrifice at last.

He tied her hands to the landing lines. He pulled the ropes tight. Gaby gasped, crucified in the moonslight. He played her clitoris with the *shakuhachi*. He twisted, he improvized, he probed. Moistened with juice, the thing slipped far inside her. He rolled Gaby back on to the curve of her spine, spread her legs and tied ankles to hands. He began to beat her. He used the bamboo flute. He was utterly relentless and systematic about it. He beat her ass and thighs for ten minutes. Then he worked on to her breasts. When they were red with the prints of the bamboo cane, he did the soles of her feet, taking great time and care over each.

Gaby's shrieks coalesced into a child-like burble of pain and fear.

Then he started on her genitals.

Oksana fell to her knees. She closed her eyes but she could not shut out the cries. She clenched her fists as the screaming subsided into soft, stoned sobbing. I am going to kill him, she vowed. I am going to go down there and beat his head off the deck until it is pulp. But the echo in her head said, no. Wait. See it all.

Oksana tore at her cropped hair with shaman-fingernails but she could not refuse the wind in her head. She pressed her cheek against the glass, forced herself to look.

Diamond Jim was fucking Gaby. His penis was out and up and hard, but he was not fucking her with it. That he jerked off with his left hand. He was fucking Gaby with the flute.

Oksana knelt on the floor and quietly, elegantly, retched up the exquisite dinner Gaby had served to her.

Sun woke her, stunning her; she had not thought she could sleep. Low water, high sun. Diamond Jim was on the sun deck, basking in a steamer chair. Sun-dried vomit by Oksana's cheek was the only evidence that the dark had been no dream.

Oksana rushed through the shell-spiral to Gaby's room. Gaby lay on the big wicker bed. A sheet was twisted into a rope between her arms and thighs. Gaby's arms, shoulders, ribs, thighs, feet were livid with the marks of the bamboo. She pulled the knotted sheet closer to her and slipped her thumb into her mouth. Oksana whirled and marched down into the people room. The *shakuhachi* lay on the conversation table. She snatched it up and strode out on to the sun deck.

In a flicker of rage, Oksana was on top of Diamond Jim, knee on chest, ten centimetres of *shakuhachi* down his throat. His hands fluttered, his eyes bulged. Oksana gave him a fresh five centimetres of bamboo, just to let him know how easy and good it would be for her to kill him. He choked. He retched, he tried to tear the thing out of his gullet.

'You fucking little shit,' she hissed. 'You do not ever, ever do that to my friend.' She detubated Diamond Jim and stood back, wanting to hear what he could possibly have to say to her. He came out of the steamer chair in a kick aimed for Oksana's throat. Sibirsk had trained its pilots to fight, she caught the foot, twisted it, felled Diamond Jim. She rolled him on to his back and immobilized him. Her right fist gripped the *shakuhachi* like a dagger.

'Difference is, this bitch bites,' Oksana said.

'She needs me to do it,' Diamond Jim said.

'Fuck you.'

'If it wasn't me, it would be someone else. How do you fancy the job?'

'Fuck you.'

'She has to be punished for what's she done to herself. She can't live with the memory of what she lost.'

'Fuck you.'

'She wants it. She hates herself. She hates what she's become. You think you're doing her a favour, sailing in after all these years? Jesus woman, you just remind her of everything she can't have. If anyone's to blame for what happened last night, it's you.'

'You are a twisted bastard.'

'We'll see. Let's forgo the you're-out-of-here scene; I'll take it as read. But I tell you this, within six months, she'll be coming up on the morning tide.'

'Fuck you,' Oksana said. 'Fuck you to hell.'

'Do you imagine you can give her what she needs?'

'I love her.'

'Love isn't what she needs. What she needs I supply. There

are about twelve weeks of discs left. If she rations them, she might make them stretch to five months. But they'll run out in the end. She'll have two, maybe three days before the demons come.'

Oksana stood up. She stepped away from the recumbent man.

'Get up,' she said quietly. 'Go right now. Don't go to the house, don't get anything. Go. I ever see your face around here again, I will cut it off and leave it on the beach for the gulls.'

Oksana went into the Sea House. Diamond Jim did not follow her, nor did he call any parting comment after her. She did not see or hear where he went.

Oksana went to the bedroom. Gaby was awake. She knew what Oksana had done. She sat huddled in the middle of the wide bed, shrouded in the sheet. She hid herself from Oksana's eyes.

'Go away!' she shouted. 'Don't look at me, don't come near me, go away.'

Oksana sat in the living room looking at the sea, hiding from the sun. She hoped to hear a call, a cry, an animal need from the room upstairs. None came. In the kitchen space she unscrewed the Alessi, sluiced out last night's dregs, loaded it with fresh water and coffee. At every stage she fought the desire to throw the fucking thing into the lagoon. She tried to puzzle out how to work the storage cell hot-plate.

'There's a touch-panel to the left,' a voice behind her said.

Oksana spun. Her elbow sent the Alessi to the floor.

Serena bent down and picked up the coffee-maker. She set it on the hot-plate, stroked a mottled ridge of plastic. She was dressed in a print sarong and cropped T-shirt. She looked both very young and somehow lifetimes older than her mother. Oksana noticed a full tie-dye stuff-bag on the floor.

'Oh, I'm sorry, Serena. I'm so sorry.'

'I've seen it before.' The cold bitterness shocked Oksana. 'Is she upstairs?'

As Serena started up the curve of stairs, Oksana called, 'So: did I pass the test?'

'This time,' Serena said.

The Alessi gurgled and began to fill.

19

'She's an isopath,' Gaby said. She was with Oksana out in the boat, hunting on the reef at flow-tide. There were shells here, Chaga-changed, that, if you could pick them out of the dazzle of neo-coral, had meat in them that ate like the holiest thing you ever tasted. The sun was high; the surf low, growling at the atmospheric forces that held it down. Ribs of dark cloud fringed the oceanward horizon. Big rain was coming.

Oksana steered the long, narrow boat. Gaby lay in the front. Her hair was tied back and she held a glass-bottomed bucket in the water. Through this window in the sea she searched for the elusive shells. The weals had faded from her body with supernatural speed.

'She can share other people's identities. It's not like mind-reading, or empathy; there've never been any instances of that; it's more primitive; she sees, hears, smells what you smell. She gets behind the levers of your mind.'

'In Kirinya, one of Mombi's girls was linked to two leopards. She could control them.'

'Serena has animals – I call them familiars – she can control. There's a cat and a bird that I know of for certain. But she wouldn't take control of a human. I think the idea that she could be that powerful scares her. She's still coming to terms with what she can do.'

Oksana steered the boat along the dark water ribbon of a coral canyon. Gaby raised a hand. Oksana killed the engine. Gaby leaned over her viewing glass, circled her hand. Oksana dipped hands in the water, slowed the boat with outspread fingers. Gaby thrust an arm shoulder-deep. A wrench, and her hand came up grasping a mango-sized shell, fluted, painted with orange reticulations over purple. Gaby dropped the thing in the bottom of the boat. It slowly withdrew its translucent mantle. Naked shell gleamed.

'How far does it reach?'

'Wherever you go in the world, however far away you are, she can touch you. It's all something to do with non-locality and resonance.'

'Jesus and Mary.'

'She's not a voyeur. She won't spy on you. Let's try over there.'

Oksana started the biomotor. Gaby knelt in the bow and directed the boat towards a swirl of yellow coral close beneath the surface.

'But she did,' Oksana said. 'Spy on me.' She said carefully, 'then.'

'You let her.' Gaby had her bucket over the side and was scanning the coral head. 'At least she linked with you. Fuck all here. Right.' Gaby looked up at the sky, reading the barometrics. Slops of dark cloud were spilling over the edge of the high front in the east. 'Aye. It's not going to come yet. We'll try up by Kuruwetu. She doesn't trust me.'

Oksana throttled the motor up to a liquid burble. Coral carpet slipped past beneath the hull.

'She doesn't trust me, ' Oksana said. 'That's why she put the link into me.'

'Maybe, but she gave you the benefit of the doubt. I don't get that. I love her, but every time I look at her, I just see what a fuck-up I am as a mother. Don't try and tell me I did as well as anyone could in the circumstances; no, I didn't.'

'Fifteen years, and you still beat yourself up. Forgive yourself for once.'

Gaby turned around in the bows to squat on her heels, facing Oksana. Behind her the clouds were running in to shore, probing, exploring, advancing like Chaga.

'I let him harm her.'

'She said she'd seen.'

'No, that's not what I mean. Listen to me; I let him harm her. He helped her celebrate her fourteenth birthday. I was so fucked out of my head that I didn't even hear her screaming in her bedroom.'

'I should have killed him,' Oksana said. 'I should have cut the bastard in half.'

'And I kept him, Okya. I knew what he'd done, and I chose him over my own daughter. Mother of the year, yeah? And you tell me I still beat myself up too much.'

She lowered her spy-glass over the side, searching the waters of Kuruwetu for shells.

You are turning your face from me so you cannot see how I am looking at you, Oksana thought. Are you afraid that I will punish you, like you let that bastard do? Or is what really scares you that I might forgive you that?

By the time they returned to the Sea House jetty it was raining heavily. The sky was a plane of wet grey, but there were two shells in the water-logged bottom of the boat. Their reputation was not exaggerated. There were more of the chocolate fruit. After the meal Serena made her apologies and despite the weather went out: Team Turangalila practice night. In her fake Manchester United strip she was as drenched and windswept as a raft refugee before she reached the shore.

'This is no place for her really,' Gaby said. 'She never had anyone her own age to play with when she was growing up. Most of her friends are years older than her. Anyone she did get to know usually moved on.'

Tonight Gaby had lit the candles; the tiny spirit-flames guttered in the winds that eddied in under the eaves of the Sea House. She suddenly got up and went to a painted wooden tall-boy. She took a carved box from it and set it on the conversation table in front of Oksana.

'Hell, you might as well know it all. When I said that Shepard didn't come back to me, I told you half a truth.'

Gaby pressed the palm of her hand to the centre of the table. The grain of the wood flowed, then puckered into a mound. One half of the hemisphere turned translucent: a screen.

Oksana opened the box. It smelled of sandalwood and other, less familiar spices. Nested inside were folded sheets of paper, cell memories, thumb-nail photographs trapped in glass. She picked up one of the imprisoned photographs. It showed a tall, well-built man in his early forties. He had blue eyes, his head was blond-stubbled. The faded picture on his T-shirt seemed to show a nun with her habit pulled up doing something with her crotch. The man had his arm around a woman. The woman was a head and a half smaller than him. Her head had been shaved too, it was darkened by five-o'clock-shadow. Her T-shirt said *UNECTASpace: Team Green*. The man and the woman leaned together companionably. They had been photographed against landscape, the country rose up on either side of them, like a very steep valley.

Oksana knew that the valley went up all the way. The land curled over and joined in a circle. The photograph had been taken in one of the five chambers of the Big Dumb Object.

Oksana set the miniature on the table.

'Who is she?'

'Her? Sylvie. Sylvie Moracevik. She's from Quebec; French Canuck.' Gaby picked a cell memory out of the sandalwood box. 'Start with this one.' She touched the cell to the table-top; the wooden skin sucked it through. The screen lit. A gust of humid wind swirled the curtains, flickered the candles. Ghosts spoke from another world.

20

Audio recording: October 1 2014

Hi Gab. I'm not sure how this'll reach you – if it's going to reach you at all – you're probably down in Tanzania by now. I'll try routing it through Tinga Tinga.

I think it's day six up here; well, it's sleep six; a day on the BDO lasts a week; you don't actually sleep very well in constant daylight, you keep waking up suddenly, not quite knowing where you are. They should have recruited Icelanders and Lapps for this job. It's going to be real fun when we move into eclipse. It's about two days to sunset; we're in late afternoon. There are tremendous shafts of light pouring from the window slits. There's wispy cloud layer about fifteen kays up; enough to break up the light from the two and ten o'clock windows into rays and shafts. Absolute mother of God-shots. You can imagine angels sliding down them. The light from the six-o'clock window takes some getting used to; it looks like one of those Victorian paintings of the end of the world, where the earth splits open and rays of light shoot out of the abyss and all the sinners tumble in. I wish I could show this to you – all the video gear is tied up on mapping expeditions. I fear my powers of description are woefully inadequate – hell, you're the journalist, I'm only a soulless scientist. Supposedly. Why didn't they bring people who could actually communicate something of what it's like to be here, instead of button sorters and pin counters? On that very point, interesting story on this morning's supply tug from High Steel: CNN offered UNECTA*Space* fifteen million to get a reporter up here. Turned them down flat, of course, but it does get you imagining; how much would SkyNet pay to ship you and your old team up?

Okay okay, I can hear you fidgeting in your seat. You're saying, I'm not there, and I'm not going to get there, and the only way I'm going to know what it's like is if you tell me, Shepard.

Well, let me take you on a little tour of sweet home Green Base. We are five accommodation tents, a small mess and a Big Top which is our science unit. There're twenty-five of us here; to make the most of the continuous daylight, we run the same three-shift hot-bunking system we had on Unity and High Steel. As an old ex-Chaganaut, my job is to co-ordinate the exploration groups; the irony is that we don't so much need someone with experience of what Africa has become as someone with experience of what Africa was. What we've settled down into is reconstituted savannah; a big circle of it about sixty kays across. We spotted it immediately from the hub; it's easily the most prominent terrain feature in the first chamber. It's very like the old Ngorongoro crater; you can actually see the land curving upwards to clock and anti-clock – a little convention we've adopted: up, down, clock and anti-clock. Grass, acacias, baobabs, all kinds of animals, and I mean all kinds – what the Chaga-makers have done is fill this place with every savannah species from the last four million years. I'm talking about *Diceros* the size of *tanks*. Two days ago a herd of grazing *gompotheriidae* – monster four-tusked elephants from about three point five million years ago – moved in on Team Red 4 and mashed them flat. Come migration time we're going to have to get ourselves recoilless-rifle grade protection.

But it's good, Gab. It's what only you understood about me: that someone so intimately involved with the Chaga could hate what it was taking away. The land, the people, the beauty. That was the thing about the Mara, you remember? I said there was something I wanted to show you before it was gone for ever. And here it is again. And it's new, it's untouched, and it's all for me. My own private Africa. Hell of a toy to give a Kansas boy. But it's more; this one bubble of savannah in thirty thousand square kilometres of alien landscape, and beyond that are four more chambers. Whole dark continents to discover.

I feel like the fullerenes in every breath I take have laid this layer of conductors over my skin so that everything I see, everything I hear or touch or smell, triggers this tremendous response. I feel about five hundred per cent alive. Maybe it's that I now have time to process our time back in Florida before the launch – my God, it seems like about ten years ago. It was ... painful. When I saw you sitting there in the bar in the Starview Lodge ... I think I realized that what I had didn't compensate for what I'd lost. It wasn't what I'd been expecting: I was hoping you hadn't changed, I think I was so glad you had. It was grown-up – at last – and you were beautiful, and we laughed a hell of a lot. Never stopped laughing. I can hear you now, you're saying, don't try and be gallant, bastard. Okay, I won't. I'll just sign off instead. What I'll do now is see if I can get my hands on a stills camera, send you a few shots so at least you'll have something to look at while you listen to this embarrassing drivel.

Picture one. An establishing shot: white tents on a green plain. The tents range in size from two-man pup tents to a large marquee. Big hessian wrapped bales are piled beside the middle-sized tent; supplies, there has been a paradrop. The tents huddle close, the earth between them has already been trodden to dust.

Picture two. A group shot. Fifteen people, in two ranks, front rank kneeling. They are dressed in white fatigues; the logos on their breasts are too small to resolve. Only that their clothes are stained green with grass and red with dust makes them distinguishable from the white tent canvas against which they are posed. They are smiling; some are leering, or pulling faces. Both men and women are shaven-headed. They look strangely vulnerable, as if they are always aware of the alien shape of the landscape around them.

Picture three. Portrait. A black man and a white woman stand, arms around each other, under an acacia tree. They wear the dirty white fatigue pants and pale blue sleeveless T-shirts with *BDO: Another World Party!* on them. The man smiles well, he knows how to be photographed. The woman has her head tilted to one side, her mouth open as if to ask a question. The camera has caught her at a wrong moment.

Picture four. Landscape: telephoto. Looking south. In this photograph the cloud has broken; the south cap of the Chamber One is visible, eighty kilometres distant. Compressed by the lens, the land seems to rise vertically to the axis. Forests appear to cling to sheer cliff: the increasing curvature draws concentric rings of vegetation around the south pole. A wider angle lens would show that the land rises in a parabolic curve, steepest where gravity is slightest. The bulls-eye of the circles of forest is featureless; above the cloud belts the air is too dry to support heavy cover. For the first twelve kilometres out from the hub explorers scree-run through a plummet of tough lichens. Beneath lie cloud forests of giant fungi, balloon groves, coral gardens, stands of ferns and fronds. The south cap of the Big Dumb Object is the tallest mountain in the solar system. It has already been named Mt Improbable. There is a dark iris in the bulls-eye of Mt Improbable: the inner surface of the airlock is open. Behind it is a three-kilometre bubble in the outer skin of the BDO. Maximum zoom shows a mote in the eye: a tug pod cycling through, manoeuvring in to link with the pile of pods and domes perched on the lip of Mt Improbable that is Base Camp.

Picture five. Landscape: wide angle. Looking north. Chamber One is only fifty kilometres deep, though four hundred and seventy long; more of a ring than a cylinder. The twenty millimetre lens takes the landscape, spreads it wide, pushes out its perspectives. The north cap, a dark wall of blisters and craters, seems to swirl out of the heavy grey cloud like a black storm. No ascent here: the wall is absolute, one hundred and fifty kilometres vertical. No entry: the explorers who have reached the foot of the north wall have found no sign of any passage into the second chamber. Yet the perspectives of the wide angle lens create a sense of movement, something huge, fast approaching, rushing over the low hills and tree like the shield of God.

21

Shepard's private diary

The intimidation of the blank sheet of paper. Book one, page one, line one. Here you start.

I'm not a natural journal keeper. I don't like my soul leaving permanent stains. Writing this, I feel stark naked. You're to blame, you know, Gab. I read your diary. That smug bastard Russel Shuler had you down in that birthing chair in Unit 12, and I was reading everything you'd seen and experienced and felt on that crazy expedition into the Chaga. All your private thoughts, emotions, fears, confessions. Whose was the worse violation? I don't know. I tell myself I had to know how much you'd found out. I was covering my ass, of course. It wasn't a very big diary. It didn't cover very much ass.

Greatest of sins, reading another's diary. I read that other diary too; the one you were chasing when you went into the Chaga; the diary of that crazy woman you'd heard about the night of the Fourth of July party, the night Hyperion reappeared as the Big Dumb Object. That was an ass thing too, not covering, but buying.

What a fool I was. Imagining that you wouldn't wonder how I'd found it, why there were pages missing from it. What those pages were about. The things dick makes you do.

One thing that book said, you should never buy a diary,

always be given it. I can understand that. Sylvie's put a lot of work into this, and some cost. Sacrificed a bootlace to bind the pages. God knows where she got the silk print to cover it; everything that comes up is severely mass-rated.

It looks like it's diaries and ass again.

Scary, the way the vacuum of white paper pulls things out of you. Explosive decompression of the soul. Sylvie gave me a moment of pure wonder tonight, like that time in the Mara when I gave Gaby the lion cubs. These things have to be shared. Alone, they are illusion.

There's a memory I treasure from Africa, between sunset and night-rise when the day animals fall silent and the night creatures have yet to start their songs and for a moment, there is a huge silence. There is that same moment when the BDO passes into earth's shadow and night falls, but here, a whole world falls silent. It always was a crazy hour, you were never sure the world hadn't jammed in time. Half an hour before, half an hour later, I would have told Sylvie her suggestion of a walk was insane. Which it was, and dangerous. Some of those long-extinct felinids are night hunters. But she hit the mad moment dead right, and even though the Good Shepard in my head was saying, this is mad, bad and dangerous to contemplate, I went where she led. The Chaga-makers think of everything: the north pole casts a luminescent glow about equal to full moonlight. We're all tuned deep down in the wiring to that big light in the sky. Moonlight stroll in the Big Dumb Object: it could have been Africa again. It smelled like Africa again. If you didn't look too far, it looked like Africa again. I wanted it to be Africa again. But all this primevalness is pure Disney. This ancient savannah and the creatures that move upon it are the newest things in the solar system. I half-expect new-carpet smell, that my footprints will scuff up fluff, or find a plastic cover over the next acacia.

Sylvie took me to the six-o'clock window. Grand Canyon would be more accurate; thirty-five kays long, five wide, one and a half deep. That's a hell of a window. She took me a way I'd never been before, through dense groves of skeletal spires draped with feathers of moss. It was breathtaking in the silvery light from the pole. If Sylvie hadn't put her hand on my chest, I'd've walked right over the edge. We came on it that suddenly.

We were on the rim. In the moonlight the forests of the far side were like silver mist clinging to the earth. I glimpsed the distant glitter of falling water.

'No,' Sylvie said. 'You don't look out.'

I looked down into a canyon filled with stars.

It's right that we're allowed only a very few moments of awesome beauty in our space between the forceps and the stone. It's not that too much would leave us numb and cynical; we'd just be going around with our jaws stuck to our sternums all the time, high on sense-of-wonder. And we should be given time to turn it over, work it out, rub it in, let it change us.

I'm not sure how long I stood, looking at the lights below. It seemed like one of those things we've always known in our blood; that under it all is void and the world floats on a sea of stars.

This was cosmological foreplay. Sylvie's proposition: here, now, hot, wet. Sex, Shepard. And I didn't. I still had this red-haired, green-eyed, freckle-skinned woman curled up deep down in the heart of horniness.

22

Team Green 3: expedition log.
October 18: 19:08

Second day. Good progress: after ten kilometers of what can best be described as botanical plumbing, we're in an open terrain of tall – twenty, thirty meters – trumpet-like formations which seem to be composed of a kind of living polymer foam. Good walking country after the hack-and-slash of the tube and pipe ecosystem, but in the permanent daylight it's tempting to push on, another five, ten fifteen, kays, push yourself too far, too hard. Which is the purpose of this expedition; to investigate genetic modifications to the circadian rhythms of reconstructed terrestrial species. Certainly, all teams down on the ground have been reporting increasing stress and tensions as everyone's body clocks run wild. So: we stick to the twenty-four hour clock, and when Captain Shepard says make camp, we make camp, and when Captain Shepard says go night-night, we go push those zees.

We've made camp for tonight – the mind-set sticks – under a natural vault where six trumpet bells have grown together. It's raining; small waterfalls are running over the curled lips of the trumpets, but the canopy is rain-tight. Last of the rations; there's a paradrop scheduled for tomorrow. Most of our mass is research equipment; despite the low gravity, it's hard slog on foot. Conrad Feltz made a good comment; if the Chaga-makers can recreate four million years of African flora and fauna, not to mention fifty other planets'-worth, why can't we brew up some decent packhorses?

Why limit ourselves to the probable? Why not grow a fleet of ATVs, or even transport helicopters? I speculate this because the horns-of-plenty host an aerial species of what I can only describe as living rotor blades. They're small – no bigger than a dime – almost transparent; you only see them when they catch the light and shimmer like dragonflies. Mostly you hear them, a soft mosquito whine as they pass close to you. They hover and float like thistle-down. There isn't much more to them than five rotating petal-blades and a wisp of thorax carried beneath. Simple things, but they blithely flout our chauvinistic dogma that evolution can never produce wheels or bearings. Deep space fullerene clouds produce gyral forms preferentially, but these whirligigs must be a planetary species – their propulsion systems would be unworkable in vacuum. Speculation: these creatures have been touched by the Chaga-makers; how many million years ago did the Evolvers symbiose with their world? Question: and ours? And us?

October 19: 20:31

There is one body of water of any significance in the six-north tridant. It's an hourglass-shaped lake about three kays north-five of us, about two kilometers long, lying along a roughly north-south axis. It's called Lake Darwin; the hub telescopes have identified it as a refugium for several extinct semi-aquatic species, including a pygmy hippopotamus and a mother of a saurian sub-species that makes the contemporary croc look like a gecko. Navigation in Chamber One is so easy as to almost rob it of all sense of Great Unknown. Every part of the surface is observable from the hub. It's even taking the fun out of exozoology. They like to tell you what you're going to find before you find it.

Omniscience assumes it's omnipotence. Bad mistake. We radioed Hub the co-ordinates, the computers calculated the launch thrust on the drop pallet and Coriolis force, they'd allowed for local wind conditions; they had us on the scopes, they could see us waving it in as the 'chute cluster opened at two kays up, and they still managed to drop it right in the middle of Lake Darwin. Unanticipated micro-burst, was their excuse.

Enjoy, croc-mothers.

October 22: 13:05

I guess we always knew they had to be there. The Chaga-makers have reconstructed everything else, and if we've learned anything about them it's that they're drawn to intelligence like moths to a candle. Intelligence, and the potential for it.

Abigail's forage team stumbled on to them. For an exobotanist, she's an evil shot with the M15. In the absence of UNECTA*Space* rations, we've become enthusiastic big game hunters. We are not Team Green 3 any more. We are Shepard's Safari.

Abigail's hunting party went out due 9 after hub control reported a herd of hipparion moving six kays north-5. She wasn't the only one stalking them. Only the fact that the prevailing winds reverse at BDO-noon allowed her to get close enough to identify them. One molecule of humanity on the air, and they'd have left the hipparion standing. I heard the shot. Abigail dropped the lead hippy, and suddenly these small, brown bipedal figures were everywhere, fleeing through the grass towards a prominent Chaga-form the aerial surveyors had unimpressively named Elephant Turd Hill. When they got back we ran Jose's video footage through enhancement, but we'd already guessed what we were seeing. *Australopithecus Africanus.*

Coming face-to-face – almost literally – with our ancestors has sent shockwaves reverberating all the way to Mission Control. All other expeditions have been retasked, we're relocating to Elephant Turd Hill to establish a permanent research facility.

This is an expedition log, and not the place for personal opinion, but I must formally record my increasing misgivings over UNECTA*Space*'s response to this discovery. I'm setting down a complaint over the news black-out and the censorship imposed on our personal communications home, and I object strenuously to the increasing influence of the military in the research and exploration executive.

Well, that's it off my chest. For all the good it will do.

Finally, Rick Ianucci has a neat explanation for what the hominids were doing stalking the hipparion – as a species they're a couple of million years short of organized hunting. He reckons they were foraging for hallucinogenic *psylocybin* fungus growing in the hippy-shit. There's a theory that psychedelics were responsible for the neurological connectivity that gave rise to consciousness. The Ozzies were tripping themselves into sentience.

Hippy-shit, indeed.

October 23: 18:27

We have a winner in the Shepard's Safari Rename-Elephant-Turd-Hill contest. The prize – a personalized shower bath from the sex-object of your choice – goes to Paju for 'Red Fort'. It's official now – I insisted. One thing about the military, they like a good mouth-filling name.

The watch-station is five kays due south from Red Fort. We've dug in; the camp is a warren of trenches and canvassed-over pits – when the rains come it's going to turn into a WW1 offensive. Minimum impact is the color of the day. There were even fears that our hunting parties might frighten off the Ozzies. Hub paradropped us another pallet of supplies – on target, this time – and ordered us to suspend foraging.

Red Fort could be described as a series of Salvador Dali soft ziggurats melting into each other. The complex is circular, about a kay in diameter, the highest point is just under three hundred meters. And it is red; a pale rust. The colour and the way it rises sheer from the plain evokes comparisons with Ayres Rock, but it's not an extrusion of hull-material. Two similar structures have been charted at one hundred and twenty degrees left and right – uninhabited – and they are composed of a fine-grained porous polymer. They seem to play a role in the gas exchange system. Like its sisters, Red Fort is riddled with air-spaces and cavities, some large enough to shelter whole families of Ozzies.

(I must stop using this expression. I've already had to nip 'brownies' in the bud: I don't want edicts on palaeo-racism winging down from the hub.)

We've observed at least three *Australopithecus Africanus* social groups: Left Bastion, Esplanade and Castle Keep. We think there are at least three young in the Castle Keep group. The presumption is that they've moved to higher ground to protect the children.

I've watched the videos of them foraging away from Red Fort; how they communicate as they move across the plain, the way they watch for danger, their expressions as they comb the tall grass for seeds and grubs. More intimately, I've observed them through the main scope up on the ridge tops of Left Bastion; dancing, grooming, touching, holding each other. I can't deny that it's intelligence that gleams in those eyes and that guides their intimate touchings, but I can't believe it. It seems fake, somehow. In 2001 it had been men in monkey suits, and you knew that, it defeated the suspension of disbelief, because you knew that monkeys could never do those things with bones and stones. These seem like monkeys in man suits, like a man suit a monkey would make. Maybe it's because the BDO creates so casually; rather than these *quasi modos*, it could as easily have built McCook, Nebraska including the mall.

They impress me, I understand what they imply, but they have no connection with me. I don't feel awed or humbled, any more than I would by bonobo or a dolphin. They're playing at the game of humans. They're just an exercise in exo-anthropology.

Hub tells me that a team of engineers is on its way down Mt Improbable to help us accommodate our sudden population boom since Team Green 2 turned up at 01:30 this morning. I've told hub we don't need engineers – Rick's tunnel rats are digging and ditching like a besieging army before nightfall shuts us down – artificial lights would spook the 'Pithecenes – that's the official, politically inoffensive name. Between ourselves, we don't *want* engineers, but Hub commands, and they're on their way, and Marine Engineers don't turn back for no one, no siree.

Janis Ormand, my counterpart in Green 2, passes on a rumor that confirms my suspicions of systematic militarization. Word from the Hub is that the multi-national security force is gradually being replaced by US Army and Marines, and that six new tug-loads of soldiers are already in transit between Unity and High Steel. More worrying, Janis heard from her sources on Unity that US orbital weapons are being redeployed. That was five days ago, she hasn't heard anything from Unity since. She suspects the information blackout has reached there. I can almost believe her theory that the United States is preparing to pull a Grenada on the BDO. The EU is in no position to face down a *de facto* annexation; the Chinese aren't afraid of brinkmanship but without an effective space program, they're paper tigers.

This is paranoia, Shepard.

And we've lost Team Yellow 4. Joey Piacek's group was due in at fifteen hundred; when they went five hours overdue, we called Hub to hunt for them on the scopes. No joy; a rain front moved in over north-9. Our own equipment is watching 'Pithecenes watching the sky and fretting over the air pressure shifts. I've sent Abigail's hunters out to look for them – it's extremely unlikely that Joey's people have run into something catastrophic, but as those little brown pseudo-men up there on the red rocks prove, the BDO is full of surprises.

(supplemental: 23:00)

Very full of surprises. They are not alone. The 'Pithecenes, that is. Joey's absence is due to them running, about twenty kays north-11 of us, into another group of hominids. These were not foraging in hippy-shit. These had sticks and shaped pseudo-corals. These were hunting. They were not Australopithecenes. They were *Homo habilis*.

We've been upstaged.

October 25: 11:23

Well, we aren't getting our engineers. However, it seems that proto-humans are more noteworthy than terrestrially extinct hominids, so Janis is on the march again, our resources have been reallocated and Joey will get our daily airdrop of reconstituted shit. I should be piqued about this – you never get cured of Researcher's Blues – but perversely, I'm glad. The big light from the Hub is off me. We can run around our trenches and dug-outs and do what the hell we like.

This is paranoia, but I've just noticed that I've started to capitalize that word, 'Hub'.

(supplemental: 13:31)

No, this is not paranoia. This is worrying. I've just been recalled to the Hub. They won't say why, but they're sending a microlyte. It will be landing at twenty-two hundred.

I'm going to add a second capital. From now on it's The Hub.

(supplemental)

They're all over the goddam place. Team Red 12 has reported a primitive hominid society living in cloud-Chaga at the base of the Shield Wall. The Hub has tentatively identified them as Pre-*Australopithecus afarensis*, a semi-arboreal hominid species that died out in the early Pleistocene on Earth. There's a theory – they're almost as infectious as rumors, up here – that we'll find every human and prehuman-variant from the past eight million years up here, somewhere. With the exception of *Homo sapiens*. The Chaga-makers didn't need to Disneyfy them. They came of their own accord.

There's a lesson in this tin can, if we can just monkey it out.

(supplemental: 20:15)

I was wrong. You have to be human to say that. Gods and apes never apologize.

Jose's group brought him in. They found him under an *Acalypha* tree. He'd sustained a compound fracture of the left femur; a long stick, one end daubed in honey, told the story. He'd been there a considerable time; he was in deep shock and badly dehydrated. Flies had infested the wound; his colleagues had recognized a death sentence when they saw it and abandoned him. Jose's group had to drive off a troop of baboons closing in on easy meat.

They call him Sonny.

Our medical facilities are rudimentary, but we've cleaned up the infection, compressed the wound and restored his electrolytes. Without knowing the effects of anaesthesia on hominid neurology, we can't reset the leg. Untranquillized, the shock could kill him in his weakened condition. He's already feverish. I've informed The Hub. They're putting an army medic in the microlyte coming down for me, but I don't reckon he'll do any good.

I'm writing this by Sonny's bedside.

What do I see? It's a question of light and shadow. It's dim in this canvas-roofed circular earth dug-out; I look at the small figure on the bed and the biolantern highlights the ape-jaw, the animal slope of the forehead and the eyes are dull as stones. But I move the lantern a shade and the shadows shift and I see a child, a man in waiting.

Sonny fluctuates between shallow sleep and twitching, painful wakefulness. There's no need to restrain him, he's very weak, very afraid. You can see it in his eyes, the fear, and the knowledge. He knows he is going to die. He knows what death is. He knows it and he hates it, and that makes him human. No animal ever raged against the dying of the light. I am awed. I am humbled.

(final entry)

Sonny died at 21:15. Just before the end, he made a small noise and reached out his hand, looking for someone to cling to. I offered him my hand. After a moment's hesitation, he took it. His skin was dry and very warm. After a few seconds he exhaled and stopped breathing.

I know death. I've seen its many tricks and surprises. I've seen it take far too many people; far too many of whom I've cared about. Maybe that's why it no longer touches me as it once did.

They die and I'm shaken, but not moved. But the death of this foreshadow of a man has moved me like no other since that night the slip of paper slid out of the fax machine and told me my son had been killed.

The microlyte is on final approach. Its gossamer wing catches the light from the windows as it banks. It's flown a big slow helix down seventy-five kilometers of air. Now I can hear the bee drone of the engine. Just time to complete this entry, pack the book in my bag and go to meet the plane. And whatever it's taking me to.

23

(clandestine audio recording: UNECTA*Space* BDO Mission Executive, October 26 2014)

'You're looking, ah, attenuated, Shaw.'

'Tell me about it. Zero-gee. We're all on daily calcium supplements. They give me the shits. It's you guys down on the ground get the healthy exercise. So, did you do it with that Moracevik woman?'

'Jesus, Shaw, are you sure it's calcium they're feeding you?'

(Laughter)

'You're a fool if you didn't, Shepard. That's a hell of a flight, up from the floor.'

'You're telling me. Seventy-five kays of thin air and not a lot holding you up. So what've they hauled me up for?'

'I can tell you this, things are in, ah, a state of transition up here. They've recalled all division heads. They sent a tug to pull Chun Lizhi in off the outer shell. Cap'n on bridge.'

'Shepard.'

'Jimmy.'

'Okay, could we all try and float the same way up? Thanks. Okay, a few introductions. Some of you won't know my colleague here, Colonel Alice McKittrick. She's our new Joint Chief.

Alice, I don't think you've met Dr Evan Springer, Dr Jean Maturin, Dr M. Shepard.'

'Ah, the australopithecus man. What's the M for?'

'Mystery. Old joke. So, Colonel McKittrick, research is now a division of the military.'

'You're very direct, Dr Shepard.'

'Shepard, this is purely an administrational thing. I'm still running the research program. Alice represents Ground Control.'

'Okay. Okay, okay.'

'Thank you, now, can we get on? I'll not beat about the bush. We've found a way into the second chamber.'

(Background murmurings of surprise.)

'Here, have a look at these.'

'Jimmy, flip one up here, would you? Thanks.'

(Flap of floating paper.)

'Okay, this actually was Colonel McKittrick men's call, so by rights she should tell you what you're seeing. Alice.'

'Thanks Dr Iovine. As you can see, the survey team is rapelled into a crash web drilled into the face of the northern face. Observe the highlighted area, and the deformation.'

(Laughter.)

'Have you a comment, Dr Allenby?'

'Ah, no, I was just making a, ah, sexist comment. About it looking like, um, a woman's genitalia.'

'I think your expression was 'beaver'? This, ah, 'beaver', as Dr Allenby so colourfully describes it, expands markedly over the period of fifteen hours, as you can see in this sequence. Has everyone access to a photograph? Good. The portal, as we are now terming it, stabilized at eight hundred metres some six hours ago. We believe this to be the maximum diameter of the aperture. Our team has succeeded in penetrating the portal – Dr Allenby, your analogy was not at all helpful – and behind it is a spherical antechamber two kilometres in diameter, supporting a standard BDO atmospheric mix.'

'The same as the antechambers in the south cap.'

'We believe they are identical. Photoreconnaissance has identified a similar portal diametrically opposite the entry point.'

'You're sending an exploration party into the second chamber.'

'That is correct, Dr Shepard. On the basis of your experience we want you to head up Team Red.'

'First in.'

'That's correct.'

'Who do you need, Shepard?'

(pause)

'Jesus, Jimmy, you really are expecting me to give you answer right now.'

'We don't know how long the portal will remain navigable.'

'Okay; well, Evan, Jean here; Janis Ormand's good, if you can spare her. Shem Arne over at Dawkins – has Juliette Montalbani been cycled back to Unity yet? No? Good, her. Get Christo; and Hideoshi. Hector Moraes, Sylvie Moracevik, of course; Rick Poborsky is the best logistician I know.'

'If I could just stop you there, Dr Shepard. We have a logistician.'

'An army man?'

'An army woman. Lieutenant Sophie Bell. She is a highly experienced logistician and engineer.'

(pause)

'Is someone giving you orders, Jimmy?'

'Leave it, Shepard.'

'Jimmy, who is in control here?'

'Ground is, Shepard. Like it always was.'

'Jesus. How many soldiers, Colonel McKittrick?'

'The transfer pod holds twenty. We have eight UNECTA*Space* security personnel assigned to the first wave of the expeditionary force.'

'Security? What the hell from? Okay okay. But I have full command of this expedition.'

'Of course, Dr Shepard.'

24

Shepard's private diary

We were waiting in absolute darkness, and Dil was whispering the mantra of light. We seemed to have been waiting days, hovering at the exit vulva like a pollinating wasp inside a fig. In the darkness, it might have been. The pilot had shut off the floods to conserve battery power for the thrusters. Thirty cubic kilometers of air-space imploded around us: the skin of the antechamber enfolded the shell. We were a dragonfly fossilized in coal. All the sound in the world seemed to be Dil's murmur, and the creak of the pod shell as the air pressure outside increased. The antechamber was contracting, equalizing the pressure to the chamber beyond. Despite a swarm of insect analogies, my strongest sense was of being expelled from a dark, spasming womb.

If I'd known any mantras, I'd've chanted them.

The dragonfly simile is apt: the 'Inter-Chamber Transport Vehicle' – their name, my quotes – is a hair-raisingly rickety contraption; ducted fans, power cells, Canada Arms clasping our personnel pallet and the hardware pod. Two-man crew in a control bubble up front. Pure zero-gee engineering: a big diaphanous crazy bug, to which we are entrusting our lives over seventy-five kays of Big Drop.

The external pressure was up to one point two five atmospheres. High pressure, low gravity. We might have been in the dark, but we weren't going into this blind. Chun's wall-crawlers on the outer hull have been mapping the inner surface of Chamber Two through the slit windows. What surface there is to map. The interior is a continuous blanket of impenetrable Chaga. I mean, nothing moves down there. Chun's close-ups indicate at least eight different ecological tiers piled on top of and around each other. Seventy per cent of the surface is covered by tethered balloons floating three thousand meters above the next highest canopy layer. We're definitely not in Kansas any more. Or Kenya.

But what we were not prepared for, was the *sound*.

Chamber Two is an aviary for airborne species. And each of

them sounds its own chime or flute or rattle or yawp. None is anything that we recognize, but is this another world, or Earth as it might become – or even might have been, down a different evolutionary branch? New riddles here.

It's now four hours since our emergence into Chamber Two. We cling to the edge, afraid of the big blue yonder. They would swat us like a fly. The engineers are roped to the end-cap, inflating habitation bubbles. There's a problem; we hadn't thought the pressure would be so high, up here on the spin axis; the pressure inside the bubbles has to be a couple of per cent over even that to get the things to stay inflated. We're already feeling lethargic and headachy. Long-term, I don't know. The first people ever to suffer the bends at an altitude of seventy-five kilometers. There's another problem. The south wall drops sheer to the Chaga. Not even a helpful little ledge, as there was in Chamber One. You're absolutely not exploring this place on foot, bi-peds. The engineers are fixing the cluster of bubbles to the wall with a web of cables. Sweet home Chamber Two hangs immediately above the head of the portal. We've already christened the place 'Clit City'. I think the safest mental orientation is that you're lying with your back against good solid bed-rock looking up at an immense, dark ceiling. The walls of the world are decorated in Heironymous Bosch wallpaper. Watching the engineers drill and plug and inflate, a different sexual metaphor suggests itself: gluey translucent eggs squeezing from the oviposter of some frail insect. The military engineers move with the hard-wired efficiency of constructor ants; beautiful, yet disturbing because I know the orders they are obeying are not mine. And I can't trust that, in a crisis, they ever would obey mine.

They've laid cable through the antechamber to a transmitter on the north face of Chamber One: I got a call back from The Hub: e-mail from Shaw. Chun is gone. An order from Ground pulled him off the wall-crawler team. He's in an air-bag back to Unity, booked on the next HOTOL down. A Lieutenant Gary Hohrbach, of USAF Aerial Reconnaissance, now commands external mapping. Colonel Alice is flexing her biceps. Those faces looking in at us from the outside now belong to her. How soon before Indians, Indonesians, Europeans, *French-Canadians*, for Christ's sake, are as suspect as the Chinese?

I wish those fucking fliers out there would shut the hell up.

Chamber Two Team Red 1:
Exo-zoological video clips

The creature has the broken-backed profile of a whale, or a Portuguese Man-o'-war. Like that jellyfish, it is translucent; through its pale yellow skin great gas cells and compressor muscles can be seen pulsing and clenching. Tentacles hang forward of the mid-point of the belly, some almost the length of the animal itself. The zeppelin is four hundred metres long. Its tail flares into a rudder, though the creature prefers to sail on the strong winds beneath the fifty kilometre aerocline. The rudder is bright orange reticulated with green. Gill-slits in the rear pulse: manoeuvring jets. The front of the creature is an open maw, gulping in tons of plankton-loaded air.

The camera follows a single zeppelin as it moves from an aero-plankton-rich current of strato-cirrus towards a group of seven holding station above a clump of cumulus twenty kilometres below. Its translucent skin ripples as the gas cells contract like a fish's swim bladder, changing its relative density. The creature is attended by a number of much smaller objects that cluster around its rudder flukes and tentacle. The lens is not powerful enough to resolve detail of them. It is debatable whether they are parasites or offspring. The zeppelin turns into an air-stream; it rapidly descends towards the feeding group. As the newcomer enters the group, it strokes the upper surface of the closest zeppelin with its tentacles. Bands of crimson stripes run down its skin.

The balloon is at forty kilometres now. Its bag, pale green, shaped like a fifty-metre teardrop, strains against the coronet of plastic ribs that maintains its shape. It's near its ceiling, though some have hit sixty before exploding in a cloud of dusty spores. Long strands of purple hair trail from its lowest point, the dome of the bag is mottled with brown spots like a bald, freckled head.

Coriolis force has spun it a full hundred and twenty degrees around the interior of Chamber Two from the point at which it snapped the umbilical that anchored it to the Chaga canopy. The balloon scatters a flock of silvery fluttering creatures. They tuck their wings and dive in an instinctive panic reaction for cloud cover. The balloon billows, a sudden wind-shear catches it and whips it south. It does not resist. It cannot resist. It obeys the currents, without volition or sense. No sensory organs have been observed; the opinion in Clit City is that the things are dumb vegetable, though clusters of two or three, once four, balloons have been observed rising together, umbilical hair intertwined.

Forty-five kays now. The bag is painfully distended. An eddy: and it's gone; a cloud of dark pollen drifting like smoke, scraps of skin tumbling on the wind. Money changes hands in Clit City. There is a book on how high the balloons will go. This one was disappointingly average. Out in the air, predators slim and fast and brilliant as rapiers dive to seize the scraps of dead bag.

These they call kites. Great lozenges of transparent skin scoop in the permanent gales of the high-pressure lowlands. Kilometre-long cables tether them to shepherd's-crook anchorheads in the forest canopy. Though they are rooted, these are not vegetable.

The creatures are small, glittering translucent bubbles; tumbling blindly over the canopy-lands. The wave of bubbles blows through the grove of kites and suddenly the forest canopy lights up with flickering mirrors. Flight membranes warp and curl, the kites dive and dart. They envelop the bubble-beasts in wing: the kites plummet, aerodynamically dead. The jagged spires of the forest canopy reach to shred. The kites unfurl at the last moment; the wind snatches them high with a clap of billowing sail. The prey is firmly grasped by fingers at the base of the sail, wrapped in silk, digested by gut juices. In all these aerobatics, never once do the guy-lines cross. Entanglement is a death as certain as flying free.

They fly free only once. When the season comes, the males' skins become fluorescent; they hang in the night, bobbing lanterns, beckoning. The females come swooping in on their cables to twine and cluster and mate. Their sails yellow, the skin blisters. One day a higher wind snaps the cable like a thread and

124

they go spinning over the forests like leaves, sowing winged eggs from their sails. They die then, ribs broken, skin shredded, on the roof of the world. Gravity kills.

This species gave the namers of names in Clit City big difficulty. They were happy with 'glider', until one of the big thermal-riding wings shockingly dissolved into haze at the apex of its climb. 'Glider' became 'fog-flyer', even 'ectoplasm', until the cameras found another big wing slowly winding up the spiral of rising air towards the centre of the world. Seventy kays up, this too abruptly dissipated into air. Highest magnification revealed not dissolution, but disintegration: the glider had exploded into a flock of swooping sparrow-sized winglets. In a single hour the flock had dived down through what the big wing had taken three days to climb. Down in the lowlands the air curdled, motes glittered like mica dust: claw locked to claw, mandible to grasper, wing to wing. The big aerofoil stirred out of thick air, caught a thermal, began the slow looping climb towards its disintegration. Up, and down. It went up, and it came down.

There are the life-forms that are a problem because they are far away. Then there are the ones that are a problem because they are just too damn close. The helicopters are that kind of problem. There is much of the dragonfly in them: the iridescent colours, the stalk of a body, the flickering, irritated motion, the dumb inquisitiveness. What makes that a wrong name is their size – they are the length of a hand, their mode of flight – a rotating variable wing – and their idea of a good feed. They suck heat. Chamber Two dawn finds them congregated in their thousands around Clit City's power sources and airco exhausts. They can fold their rotors and creep through the very eye of a needle to find warmth. They have been found pulsing on computer heat-sinks. Researchers have been woken by an itch in the night to find dozens of them folded like fans in their armpits and groins.

The team has set up a powerful infra-red source a kay or so south of the base. Swarms of a million-plus mob its pure heat. The problem now is the noise: two million organic propellers swamp even the whooping and singing and bellowing from the big sky.

Of all the aerial species of Chamber Two, the helicopters are the most intensely studied, though it is study of the *how-do-we-get-rid-of-these-fuckers?* kind. A theory had been proposed that this is the foundation of all biology. Meant as a joke, it's starting to find serious adherents.

Shepard's private diary

Dark night. Big storm. Bigger even than the storm is the sound of the creatures, out there. They sing louder in the dark: the big winds disturb them. Disturb us all.

Things creep up on you in the dark. All the monsters of our deep nights – the werewolves, the vampires, the crawling and sucking things – grow out of the fears that come to us in the dark.

The biolume gives just enough light to turn the transparent wall of the bubble into a mirror. Beyond that: sounds. I can feel the bubble trembling: a womb, kicked from the outside in. Hot breath, little scrabbling legs; fidgeting mandibles.

Jesus, I'm spooking myself.

A dark mood for a dark time. Two dead: the Dragonfly destroyed. I didn't even know their names. They had ranks, they were engineers. I heard the woman called Charlie by her colleagues. The military are subdued – we're all subdued – but their way is to circle wagons and clean weapons. They won't talk to me. Jesus, they were bad deaths.

We aren't going into Chamber Three. Ever.

I didn't order the mapping expedition to the north pole. That was a military directive. Maybe it's a good thing for a bad reason. Had I been informed, I would have wanted to send some of our own people into the antechamber. And they would be dead. No, I like to think that, had I been informed, I would have waited until we had a few more clues about what's in there before rushing into a new frontier.

No windows in Chamber Three. Or Four, or Five. More games by the BDO-makers. But Chun's seismographic survey indicates that the shell is twice as thick around Chamber Three, and the shockwaves pass irregularly through whatever medium it contains. That should have warned us. It didn't. They took the

Dragonfly into the antechamber and the pressure went up. And up. And up. Until it levelled at a pressure equivalent to a hundred kilometers deep in the atmosphere of a gas giant.

We didn't know that until Dragonfly 2 went in to investigate the radio silence. They won't tell me what they found in there. I can imagine, but I think it's probably worse than that. They turn in on themselves and clean their guns and repeat the mantras they say to keep the dark things away.

The Hub managed to get some evidence from what was left of Dragonfly 1's systems. The gas mix in Chamber Three is not any gas giant. It's Saturn. And that means life, and another riddle. We are not alone in these worlds. But is that now, to come, or have we never been alone? Alice McKittrick and her new executive of stripes and stars shipped up from Unity have used the tragedy to take control of the whole operation.

It's really getting up out there.

More dark thoughts. Dil is gone. As I write, his tug should be docking at Unity. I protested the order – we need all the molecular biologists we can get – Colonel Alice's aide refused to hear anything I had to say.

The purges have begun.

Half an hour ago, Sylvie came to me. Seems my paranoid joke about French Canadians wasn't so far wide of the mark. She's to report to The Hub, ASAP. Meanwhile, all her passwords have been changed. For God's sake; she's a scientist, she is not some office clerk crashing the system as a final 'take this job and shove it' gesture.

I'm going back with her. A protest registered in person may make the point that we will not be pushed around by the army.

I'm doing it again. Going out on a limb. Putting my ass on the line; like I did for Gaby when they tried to vanish her into Unit 12. But here there's no T.P. Costello or Dr Dan Oloitip to tip off. And I don't trust that this time if it all fell on me, there would be a way back. They could bust me out of UNECTA completely. Gaby used to say she was tied to the Chaga; she could never escape it, it would always bring her back. It's the same for me, and I don't know what I would do if I could never go back to it again. But I know one thing for certain. I've become a BDO dissident. When you're floating in a womb of synthetic spider

127

silk anchored to a cliff-face seventy-five kays high in the middle of a storm, in the dark, it seems an entirely reasonable thing to do.

25

(clandestine audio recording: UNECTA*Space* BDO Mission Executive, November 12 2014)

'How many, Shaw?'

'About ten a day, for the past ten days. Maria Costas was shipped out an hour before you got in.'

'Maria Costas? From Cotopaxi?'

'You know any other Maria Costas's?'

'Jesus.'

'Basically, all non-North Americans are being purged.'

'Non-anglophone North Americans.'

'Yah. The Japanese and the EU are furious; they're talking about voting cuts in UNECTA's budget at the next UN plenary session. It's not a Security Council matter so the US can't veto it.'

'Insanity.'

'Total insanity. The military would just move into the funding vacuum. But they're pissed enough to do it; the French in particular. I've heard another rumour: there's a move to pull all the Space Monkeys in off the hull and ship them back to Unity. If French Canucks can't be trusted, how much less the Adapted?'

'I've heard rumours that they found something out there.'

'More than rumours, Shepard. They've found a way into the Fourth Chamber.'

'From the outside.'

'Without ever having to go anywhere near Chamber Three. There's more. They've been in. And word is, that's why Malice

128

Alice wants them gone. I've heard from more than one person that she's got some kind of goddam concentration camp out there, hanging on by its roots down in the Feynman mountains. There're two guys with guns for every poor bastard Space Monkey. Keeping them *incommunicado*.'

'What did they find?'

'Hey, I'm only a civ, you know? They don't tell us stuff like that. One thing I do know, they're outfitting an expedition to go in in the next couple of days.'

'Why wasn't I informed?'

'They're trying to keep this for themselves, Shepard. Trouble is, they don't have the experience. Malice Alice has admitted she will need, in her words, a "select, screened civilian specialist team". If you don't rock the boat about Sylvie, I'll have a word with Alice, maybe convince her you're screenable, selectable and specializable.'

'Shaw, that is a mother-fucker of a deal.'

'They all are these days. Shepard, Sylvie's out of here whatever you do. This way, maybe we get to find out the truth, whatever that is. By the way, you're taping this, aren't you?'

'Jesus, am I that transparent?'

'Nah, it's just amazing how quickly you develop a nose for paranoia up here. Shepard, this came in through High Steel.'

(sound of documents riffling)

'Christ, they've got me and Gaby at the Mara. Tsavo, down at Kikambala; fuck, this is her picking up my kids from Nairobi airport the time I was in-country on Fallen Angel.'

(pause)

'Oh my God, "In my opinion Dr Shepard's relationship with a member of the media significantly compromises the security of UNECTA operations in East Africa."!'

'I've read it all. It's enough for Malice Alice to bounce you clean off the Chamber Four expedition. In fact, it's enough for the Steel Bitch to bounce you right back to Kennedy. Except she's never going to read it.'

'You're futzing my security file.'

'I've futzed your security file. You're going out wide here, Shepard, I'm going out wide too, you know? I've made your file look pure as the Mormon Tabernacle Choir. Malice Alice will pass you as OK security-wise. It may fool her long enough for you to get into Chamber Four and find out exactly what the hell it is in there they're so scared of.'

'They're scared?'

'Military scare different from the rest of us, but you get to know the smell.'

'The Chaga-makers?'

'I don't know. But I do know it's only a matter of time before they bust all non-military personnel back down to earth.'

'Sylvie for whatever's in Chamber Four.'

'Yah.'

'Yah.'

Hi Gab.

While since I wrote. Not that I ever did actually put words on paper to you: fit the medium to the woman. But at heart I'm a diehard Gutenbergian: Africans have it right, cameras steal your soul, in that you can never bear it to a lens as you can to virgin paper.

Even more than my last communication to you, I don't know if you're ever going to see this. There are still a couple of folk I can trust back at The Hub; if they can get this material back down to the ground, then I know your dirty native inquisitiveness will bring you to it.

I don't know what you're being told about the situation up here. Censorship runs both ways. I suspect that as long as the news corporations get their pictures of happy smiling australopithecenes and cute little baby zeppelins, they don't much care who shot them. But it's as bad a scene as I've ever seen, and getting worse.

I'm at Feynman Station. Shaw wasn't kidding. They've got all the Space Monkeys in this cha-plastic air-bubble anchored beneath our accommodation pods, I can see them through the windows, these incredibly limber shapes moving behind the translucent skin. There are other silhouettes; larger, awkward, strangely uglier. Those are the guards. They're armed with tazers, in case the Monkeys try anything. They can't risk blowing a hole in the skin – we're in hard vac out here. Strange: it's the black marines who most despise the Space Monkeys.

130

They're shipping them out tonight. The transport pallet that brought us in is taking them back to The Hub. What happens then, no one will say. I don't like to think: they've been in, so they're never going to be safe. I think they know this.

Jesus, Gaby, I'm scared here. I have never felt this powerless, not even the Unit 12 thing. Now I think I can begin to imagine how it felt for you. And I think I also can begin to know why you did it.

The rumour is that there's a sentient species in there. A non-human sentient species. Like nothing we've ever imagined sentience to be. The alien.

The Chaga-makers? I don't know. But in two hours, we're going to meet them.

The entry point the Space Monkeys discovered is twenty minutes' flying due north of Feynman. It's a semi-permeable gas-exchange membrane – the BDO valves a lot of oxygen and water vapour from its interior – that gives access into what I can only describe as the object's vascular system. The Space Monkeys found capsule-like corpuscles – purpose other than as a transport system unknown – that took them through the skin to the interior. We'll be riding midget submarines through the BDO's arteries. It sounds bad, but it can't be as claustrophobic as the flight up here: hugged up in an air-bag clipped to a transport pallet while a USASF pilot practises terrain-following flying. When you get to Feynman – if you get to Feynman – then you have to relearn the gravity trick. This time, the centripetal force is not gluing you to the edge of the world. It's trying to throw you off into space. Down is up, up is down. This really is like those old jokes about Australians walking around the other way up. You don't look down. You don't look too far out either. Those mountains are stalactites. From claustrophobia to agoraphobia. But the Space Monkeys seem used to it. Another facet of their adaptation.

They're moving them out now. They're going quietly: there are fifteen of them; ten men, five women. One of the guards can see me watching through the pod window; he's waving at me to stop videoing. They're going very quietly. I've heard the Jews went quietly too.

The shuttle is leaving now, dropping away from Feynman.

Coriolis force whips it away like a top: the pilot's burning thrusters long and hard to bring him on to course. Bright jewels in the big night.

Gab, I'm really scared now.

(later)

The shit's gone down. Major league. Five minutes until we leave for the membrane, and word has come through. The Space Monkeys have hijacked the shuttle. We got some telemetry from the cockpit before they cut communications: they had it all planned. That's why they went so gently. Two of them cut open their airbags – in hard vacuum – went over the hull and fired the emergency release bolts on the control module. The crew are dead: the Monkeys dragged them out of their seats and let centrifugal force do the rest. Christ. That's a bad way to die. The shuttle has vanished. All ships and orbital weapons are on maximum alert but the Monkeys have gone to ground. There's a hell of a lot of chaotic terrain out there. Needles and haystacks.

The official line is that they can't stay out there for ever. I don't think so. They wouldn't have done this if they didn't trust that they could survive indefinitely. Outgassings, water, some kind of shelter, the infinite nano-processing capacity of the BDO: there is no reason at all why they couldn't build an entire society, out there on the skin. Feral Monkeys.

For us, the upshot is that at lift minus five, all bets are off. We're on indefinite hold while The Hub re-evaluates its position. The longer we hold, the more chance the Steel Bitch has of uncloaking our little conspiracy.

I have a bad feeling about this 're-evaluation'.

Just a moment, Gab. Something's come through. Lieutenant Charles's got a directive from Hub. I'm switching off the camera, I'll come back to you, let you know what happens. I promise. I will come back to you, Gaby.

Dr Shaw Wayt's personal video record

This is basically a coda to Shepard's records: I haven't got very long, they're expelling everyone whether they were involved or not. In the confusion, it may be easier to get this back down to Earth, where maybe you can tell the real story.

I've never met you; I know your name, Gaby; I know who you are, Shepard's told me a great deal about you; the fact is that circumstances are forcing me to trust you.

The facts are as follows. On November 16 the so-called Space Monkeys mutinied and stole a shuttle, killing the military crew. Colonel Alice McKittrick used this as an excuse to declare martial law and place both the BDO and UNECTA*Space* under her authority. The expedition into the fourth chamber has been postponed pending a re-appraisal, a euphemism for replacing all civilian personnel with military. Shepard refused to accept this; his decision was backed by myself, Jimmy Iovine and Monica Peres. The administrative council has been dissolved. Colonel McKittrick has issued a directive, backed by Ground Control, expelling all non-military staff from the Big Dumb Object. This is being enforced by marines. New teams are being flown up from Kennedy and Edwards. A total news black-out has been imposed: the official explanation is contamination by what they call a 'contagious cognitive meme'. A Chaga-spore that eats the mind. It's paper-thin, its purpose is to keep the Europeans and Japanese quiet until the US can present the coup – let's not mince words here, that's what this is, an interplanetary coup – as a *fait accompli*.

It is now November 18. Twenty-nine hours ago, Shepard, together with Hector Moraes, Trisha Aldred, Adeline Meissner, Jared Hunt, Elia Minkowski and David Pao, defied orders and went through the membrane into the fourth chamber. I've heard that a marine squad has been sent to secure their return 'with extreme prejudice'. Nothing has been heard from any of them since. I don't know if they are alive or dead, any of them. I don't even know if they made it through to the fourth chamber. I pray that they have. I pray that they're safe, that whatever it is in there that's scared Alice McKittrick and Ground Control into quarantining the Big Dumb Object can protect them.

Gaby – Jesus, it's weird talking to you directly, I've never met you, I don't even know who you are – Shepard's told me how you busted UNECTA once before. This is bigger than Unit 12, this is hijacking an entire world, Chrissakes!

133

Shit. That's my pager. They want to see me. I'm switching off now.

(snow)

26

The candles had ended their small lives hours before. In the deep dark, the screen radiated the brightest light. The last cell was excreted on to the carved table-top; the monitor dimmed and turned to wood and Oksana saw that the grey glow in the big room was that of dawn-edge. Wind and rain had passed over in the big dark; in their wake ragged lines of squall cloud furrowed the horizon.

Sudden coffee. Gaby had been watching all night.

'T.P. Costello,' Gaby said. Oksana curled beside her on the wicker sofa. 'It took him six months to get the disks and copy them to cell memories that the Chaga couldn't corrupt. In the early days, it was quite easy to smuggle stuff south through quarantine. I used to keep in contact more then as well. I had this idea that I'd be able to go back.'

'What happened to Shepard?'

'One of the last things I got from T.P. was a rumour from the marines that Shepard and the others made it all the way into Chamber Five.'

'What's in there?'

'No one knows. None of them ever came back.'

'I'm sorry, Gaby.'

'Why? It's not your fault. It's nothing to do with you. Do you imagine that somehow you could have prevented it?'

It was the old anger, the fast, poisonous, striking anger Oksana remembered from that Gaby-who-was, but she also remembered how it could thrash wild and flay things it did not intend, so she said gently, 'Hey.'

Gaby closed her eyes, turned the anger around.

134

'He said he would come back to me. He promised he would come back to me. He never did.'

'Did you really expect . . .'

'Of course not. But what I did expect was that, for even a moment, he might have hesitated. He might have thought about me, and doubted – just for an instant. You saw the video clip: he was looking at me, talking to me, did he ever once mention me? Did he ever once ask me to understand, or forgive him, did he ever once tell me that he loved me? No, it was all big shining bright mystery, and he just dived in headlong, without thinking once about how it might feel for me to have this man I loved – whose child I bore, you know? – to have him disappear. Gone. Not a word, nothing. Like he's dead, or stepped out of the universe. He never thought what his big truth might cost me.'

Oksana sipped the strong good coffee and the light was filling up the living room and she looked at this woman she loved in her old scabbed hurt and dark blood anger and she thought, you hypocritical bitch. I am thinking of the time when you came to me, that night you and Shepard turned on each other, and I gave you my sleepers and put you in my bed and slept next to you because I knew that when you woke you would need the warmth of a body you could trust: that time when you went after Big Truth without one thought about what that might cost the man you said you loved. What made it easy – what made it cheap – was that was the night God had chosen to smash down his wife and children, and so you never had to fight that fight as you should have, between a selfish woman and the man she betrayed. As you never will have to fight this one, between the man who went, and the woman who must remain.

Instead, she said, 'You never told him.'

'About Serena. No.'

'Does she know?'

'She's never talked to me about it. I've never talked to her. But she knows, who he is, what happened.'

'Has she seen this?'

'She knows where it is. Any time she wants, she can look at it.'

'But has she?'

'Never.'

Gaby left the wooden room that was beginning to click and creak in the strengthening sun. Oksana found her leaning on the deck rail, freckled arms folded on the grey wood, looking out to sea.

She watched the play of the muscles of Gaby's back. She read emotions moving under the skin. The sun rose clear of the curl and toss of the reef-surf. The sea was loud and white on the long ocean-following wind. The wind-chimes belled. Gaby closed her eyes against the power of the sun. 'It's going to be a beautiful day,' she said.

Fragile

27

The girl and the woman were out in the boat on the gleaming water of the lagoon. The little biomotor slept; the ebb lazily drew the boat towards the crash line of the reef. The females would wake it long before then. Their senses were tuned. They were hunting. This was how they hunted. The girl leaned over the side of the boat. Her right hand was in the water, her fingers were spread. The weed season was past, the water was so clear she could see the shadow of her hand and head on the rippled bottom marl. The sun beat on her bare back and she closed her eyes and sent her power out into the water. The lagoon fishes tasted her power and were drawn to it. It was not the pheromone thing by which fertile women seduce the Lord of the Fishes. It was the fullerene thing: a dissolving of self into sea. The fishes came and nibbled at her fingers. The girl laughed and wiggled them, the fishes scattered. Go, fish. Away. It is not you I am calling. The other female in the boat was broad and muscular. Her skin was burned brown, her grown-out crop of hair bleached pale. She stood in the bottom of the boat, balanced carefully so that the cool of her shadow would not fall into the water, or a shift of weight send warning ripples to the swimmers. She held the light spear ready. Her irises were polarized against the glare. She looked into the bright water, seeking the big fish.

It came slowly, but it came. The girl's power lured it out from its hole between the toes of the reef. The big fish did not know why it came, but the tingle of power around and through it drew it inexorably. It slid beneath the shell of the boat, circled in the deeper water, unable to throw the immaterial hook that reeled it in by slow spiral, turn upon turn, towards the surface. The girl held her breath as she watched it come up towards her. It was one mother of a fish. With a part of her mind, she stroked it in. Another part of her mind felt the woman's muscles tauten, the point of the fishing spear seek out the circling fish. The girl sang the fish up and up. Its cool flanks caressed her fingers. Now all was timing. She snatched her hand out of the water.

But the point of the spear did not come yelling down to pierce and burst the big fish in a thrash of scale and blood and wrench it up into the air.

Spell shattered, the big fish fled down into the deep water.

The girl looked up. The woman was staring in to shore. The girl got up and looked where the woman was looking.

The big flying saucer hovered just out of the reach of the tallest hand-trees. It was angel-white, sun dazzle-flashed from irregularities in its solar skin as it turned this way and that, hunting for a safe place to land. Its belly bore a large symbol: a bisected circle; upper half white, lower black. That same symbol had been appearing with increasing frequency carved on tree trunks, painted on walls, on the hulls of boats from down the coast, on the brave flags flown by the *pujos* and *matatus* from the tribes of Mombasa. It was the world-in-two-halves device of the Harambee.

The people of Turangalila were coming out of the trees on to the beach. They squinted up at the airship. Some shaded their eyes. Others shook fists, or made fuck-off gestures that the Harambee was not welcome in their Turangalila. The airship drifted towards the headland to the south of the nation. It drew the people after it. Out on the water the girl and the woman woke the biomotor and turned their small boat into the path of the airship.

The visitor drew the girl's mother on to the balcony of the Sea House. She watched the dirigible settle on to the dusty place where fifteen years ago she had almost sacrificed her infant daughter. The airship settled on its fans, red earth flew up. Land-anchors were dropped, gripped coral rock with molecular fingers. Oksana Telyanina ran the little boat up on to the beach. Serena splashed up through the shallows to join the others. The Harambee ship had put down a ramp. A man in elegant white was descending the steps. A second man in white followed him. They picked their way carefully down the headland path. To slip and clutch would destroy their dignity. The hems of their white *jellabas* were red with dust.

The men were on the beach now. The first one was very tall, very black, very elegant: Luo, maybe half-Masai. His head was completely hairless. Both he and the other man, who was smaller, but no less black – he had the features of a Kalenjin – wore very small circular dark glasses. An anachronism, or an affectation of the agents of the Harambee.

Serena noticed motion on the sun deck of the Sea House. Gaby was running wildly along the pier. She almost fell down the steps to the beach. The Turangalila people parted to let her through; she would have bowled them over like pins. She ran like a *mtege*, spirit-possessed, to the tall man. She leapt at him.

He caught her. He held her close as a child. Gaby wrapped her long legs and long arms and long hair around him. They spun around together, laughing. They fell over in the sand, the white woman on top of the black man. She straddled his chest, play punching him with soft fists.

'Oh Jesus oh God!' Gaby cried. 'It is you, it is you; Faraway!'

28

'Really,' the tall Luo said, 'if you must call me by that ludicrous name, at least grant me the dignity of my proper title. Mr Missionary Faraway.'

At the pomposity of which, everyone around the live-wood table burst into laughter, and Cimarron, with the linked spirits of the seventeen Elders of the Harambee Consensus in his head, fell backwards on his chair and cracked his skull against the decking. He had had very much of the Doctor's Prescription to drink at dinner.

'You'll always be Faraway to me,' Gaby said. 'Sorry, that's it, you're stuck with it. And Dr Dan . . .'

From their first meeting on the night flight to Nairobi, Gaby's life had been twined like creeper with the old Masai parliamentarian. That night at the ambassador's reception when Hyperion had returned, transformed, and she had fallen quietly in love, he had been there. He had been the one who rescued her from the Dantesque circles of Unit 12, brought her back from long exile when Nairobi fell. How had she imagined that she could escape the karmic coils that held her and him, her and Faraway, together?

'If you have worked for T.P. Costello, you can work for Dr Dan.'

'How is he taking the, um, changes?'

'Better than I would,' Faraway said. 'But then, my body is still firm, and good, and exceedingly well-hung.'

'And as full of shit. Faraway, I cannot believe that you, of all people, are working for the government.'

Cimarron laughed from the floor. It might have been his laugh. It might have been the laughs of any one of the Elders seeing through his eyes and listening through his ears. Sensing through his senses. Gaby wondered, if he got drunk, did the Elders become vicariously inebriated, rolling around the parqueted floors of the Great Boma in Kirinya?

'You are politically illiterate, Gaby McAslan,' Faraway said. 'In Kirinya every five-year-old knows that the Harambee is not a government.'

'Yeah yeah yeah,' Gaby said. 'It's a consensus. A representative body. A political agency.'

Cimarron mumbled.

'I think he said "Unity in diversity",' Oksana translated. 'I think it's time your friend went to bed.' She and Serena helped the isopath to his feet, steered him up the treacherous spiral staircase to the guest suites. Serena waved good night to mother and diplomat.

'Really, we could have stayed on the ship with the pilot,' Faraway said.

'No you couldn't.'

'No. You are right.' Faraway watched the two women manipulate Cimarron through the bedroom door, bubbling with giggles. Gaby noticed how his eyes lingered on Serena's thighs and flanks and arms.

'Faraway,' Gaby warned. She knew him of old. In all senses.

'Gaby. Please. She is very beautiful, but she is a kid. There is much of you in her, that is what I am noticing.'

'Too much.'

'May I ask, as it is obviously not me, who is her father?'

'Shepard.'

'Ah. Hm. I did not know that you and he had got together again.'

'Just before he left for the BDO. And you have a nerve, Mr Missionary Faraway. You were the one who left me for the fucked-up wreckage of Kenya.'

'I always said I would. From the first time I met you, but you did not believe me. But I also remember that you told me you did not love me.'

Distant lightning: a comet flash on Venus, low on the edge of the world.

'Hey,' Gaby said, chilled by an old, long wind from a neglected quarter. 'Enough about love. Tell me about your work: like, you've done pretty damn well for yourself; what are you now, some kind of ambassador?'

Faraway leaned back in his chair and peeled fruit. He slipped the *choka* out of its skin with unselfconscious sensuality. More than face or voice or words, his body-speak peeled back the years. From football to fucking, every move Faraway ever made

141

was beautiful. The buckies had kept him trim and tight. He still moved like an animal. Age had added gracefulness, wisdom and an aura of power that was almost pheromonal.

Faraway ate the *choka* in three bites. He licked the chocolately meat off his fingers.

'You are Irish, so you will appreciate irony.'

'Ironize me.'

'What Shepard did for UNECTA, I do for the Harambee. I am a vagrant diplomat, a roving portfolio. That is what a Missionary is. Until I was assigned to this mission, I had been working on the front line.'

'I've heard it's bad up there.'

In the same instant that a candle-flame flickered, Gaby thought she saw a colour of anger shade Faraway's face.

'The children have a dance there. It is a new dance. It is interesting that the same dance has appeared across many nations among the very young. It is like this.' Faraway got up, found space. Because of his grace, Gaby could not laugh at the dance, though it was ungainly: bird-like and pecking. Toe-forward, wait, slide back foot to front. Bend to the left, bend to the right. Other foot out, forward, down very gently, very gently, light as a hair kissing the earth before trusting it with the full weight of a body. Bend low, fingertips brushing sand from sand-blown boards. 'Do you know what these children are doing?'

'Oh my God. They're feeling for mines.'

He sat down. His eyes were hard and very far away.

'There are now five mines for every human up there. Five mines, ten grenades, twenty mortar rounds, fifty bullets. When I became Missionary, one of my first missions was to induct the Ambira Nation into the Harambee. They are my own people, Luo; they are a nation of economists and philosophers. They have a fine, small university. They have produced many fine policies and theories and thinkers. Last week I went back to Ambira. I had to walk two days to reach it, it is no longer safe to fly north of Nakuru. There was no university there any more, no economists, no philosophers, no fine thinkers. There were dead bodies in the streets and the buildings, all fat and swollen with rot. Men, women, children, old, young, animals. It was like they had all died where they stood or sat. The ones who had fled into the bush when they heard the helicopters told me: they used nerve gas. Two thousand people lived in Ambira. Those who are left could all stand on this sun deck of yours, Gaby. Ambira is dead. You see, they have a new strategy up North. They target Harambee nations, and they kill everyone. They destroy everything. They want to scare others from joining. The envoys from the Central African Confederacy and the Ogun say it is the same over in the Great Lakes and the West. They kill everyone. Our unity scares them, they will do anything to stop it; but who can stop them?'

'Jesus, Faraway.'

'Yes, Jesus, Gaby. The Armies of National Liberation are running wild. From Garissa to Labarene is a free-fire zone. This of course is their strategy, to create a large refugee population moving south into established nations and so destabilize the emergent consensi. We are trying to organize the local militias into a unified self-defence force, though armies are anathema to Harambee philosophy, and we must keep the local commanders disciplined or our negotiations are fucked up the ass.'

Gaby poured more Doctor's.

'You're going to tell me about these unfuckable negotiations, Faraway.'

'Of course. Because you know that I have not just called in for good old times and reminiscence. I tracked you to this shit-hole, Gaby, because I want something from you.'

'I don't deal in information any more.'

'I think you do. But I shall tell you anyway. For the past three months I have been part of a group engaged in secret negotiations with the UNHCR.'

'Christ.'

'Yes. I think that in the near future we can expect to see an initial release of refugees from the northern camps into the Chaga.'

'The NLAs will slaughter them.'

'Not if the UNHCR recognizes the Harambee first.'

'You can deliver that?'

'I would not have told you if I did not believe so. When did I ever bullshit you, Gab?'

All the time and never, Gaby thought. Ignited by Faraway's

vision, she found her imagination fleeing from years of control; chasing implications, shaping new world orders, hoping in futures. No. I cannot do that. I will die if I do that. She caught the flying thoughts. You charmed me, you old lover, you found my G-spot, that, if you tickle it, an old newswoman cries like a cat.

'What do you want, Faraway?'

'I remember several old answers to that question very well. What I really want is for you to come where I am going.'

'Where are you going?'

'Aldabra.'

'What's at Aldabra?'

'My mission.'

'For which they pulled you off the front line.'

'Yes.'

'I don't do it any more, you know. I don't do epochal events, Faraway. I don't do the end-of-the-world news.'

'I am not asking you to. I am asking that you come with me. Bring Serena. Bring your Russian friend.'

'Siberian.'

'Bring her. You need to get away from here. Before I came here, I had heard what you had become. I know about the drugs, Gaby.'

'Fuck you.'

'Yes. Fuck me. I am a bastard. You see, I looked in your eyes, I saw your soul when I showed you the mine-dancing, when I told you about the people who are dying. Maybe you do not do it any more, but it does it for you, I saw it, Gaby.'

'You're trying to seduce me.'

'Did I ever do anything else?'

Jesus, I should have loved you, Gaby thought. You are a good man, and all you have ever wanted was to love right. But you were the man who stayed, and Shepard was the man who left, and I was the woman in between who gave it all away.

'Seduction?' Oksana was coming down the stairs.

Faraway rocked back in his chair, made an expansive, man gesture. Gaby could not fight the smile.

'You as well?' Faraway said. 'It is a good thing my esteemed colleague has drunk himself into impotence, because tonight at

144

last I can achieve my long-cherished ambition to be the black meat in a white woman sandwich.'

Gaby threw *choka* skins at Mr Missionary. Oksana sat down.

'If I remember,' she said looking Faraway in the eyes, 'it was nothing exceptional. Purely functional.'

Faraway let out a yelp of laughter and clapped his hands softly.

'Jesus, you slut!' Gaby exclaimed. 'You and him?'

'Him and everyone,' Oksana said.

'Oh no, oh my God.'

'Ah yes!' Faraway said, pointing. 'I have it! The pilot's bar, what was it called? Yes, the Elephant Bar. One of the kick-boxing nights. You did that Serbian thing with rope. I have such a bad memory for faces. If you had shown me a different part of your anatomy, I would have remembered right away.'

Oksana laid her hands flat on the table. She was a little drunk, drunk enough to be spiritual. She held her hands perfectly parallel, perfectly steady. She said, 'That airship of yours.'

'What of it?'

'It flies.'

'Airships do this.'

'Do you remember anything else about that night?'

'You showed me your aircraft. You had a name for it. You loved it very much.'

'I need air.'

'Breathe deeply.'

'I need air around me. I need to fly again. I want to go to Aldabra with you.'

'Certainly,' Faraway said.

Gaby heard his respect. She said, half-joke, half-joy, 'You bastards. You utter complete bastards. When do we leave?'

'Whenever you are ready.'

'I'll need clothes.'

Faraway regarded Gaby in her informal undress entrepreneurially.

'I think you look fine.'

'Fine for you, Faraway. Not fine for an aide-de, whatever the hell it is, to a Missionary of the Harambee.'

29

The pilot's harness disturbed Gaby, but he assured her he was most comfortable hanging prostrate from the ceiling. Two-armer chairs were bad karma for Space-men, but Gaby was nonetheless disquieted by flesh strapped into black webbing. She knew where the image was rooted: in Russia, in the black end-days when she covered all those spastic, self-mutilating little wars. Her Moscow boss, the unhappiest man she had ever known, would, when he drank too much vodka, confess that the one thing that would make him happy would be Gaby swinging from his ceiling in just such a harness. Naked. For several weeks.

There was more to the shudder than old memories of a cold land.

Jim. Lately he had been sneaking too often down the back alleys of her head.

The pilot's name was Antinka, a name he had invented for himself. His ship was the *Kariokor*, a priority transport of the Harambee fleet, skipping across the ocean like a skimmed stone. He was a damn good pilot, the best in the Harambee diplomatic corps, but he had noticed that Gaby was nervy. For all her daughter's life, she had never been out of sight of home. *Kariokor* had whirled her up, the psychic umbilicus had stretched, broken, and she was a scared white woman alone over a huge blue drowning ocean.

Gaby hoped it was the old earth-root thing. She did not want to think it might be the patches.

Faraway was in the left gallery. *Kariokor*'s passenger areas formed a three-quarter-circle around the central lift and propulsion modules. The Missionary stood by the curving window, one hand resting on the plastic. Sea-watching. For the last half-hour *Kariokor* had been passing over the outlying reef-towns of the Aldabran nation. Fifteen years after the Kilimanjaro Event, a biological package had come down in shallow water eight kilometres west of the former British air-base on Aldabra in the Indian Ocean. Reef had run wild, sending mutant outcrops, half-mangrove, half-temple, rearing out of the sea. Thousands of nanotech atolls; self-contained ocean cities like organic oil-platforms. Deep under, brain corals mind-warped into transparent air-filled domes; forests of molecule-processing pseudo-fungi strained towards the surface and opened their parasol heads to the sun. And in the wombs of servicepersons and Indian Ocean fisherwomen the Chaga wove the race that would inherit this world: trans-human, semi-aquatic, amphibious.

Two races: the humans, and the great whales.

Kariokor passed over a community of sea-towns so close the islets had been roped together with walkways and bridges. Boats thronged the shady channels between villages. Faces looked up, brown people waved. Through the warm shallows, pale figures snaked with silky ease over the bright cha-coral carpet.

Gaby sat down beside Faraway at the window. She patted the floor. Faraway hitched his *jellaba* and sat cross-legged. He leaned against her.

'Ah, Gaby.'

She ran her hand over his head.

'Hey, you can do it.'

'I am not so sure. Look!'

A childhood spent by water had taught Gaby the trick of seeing subaquatically. The dapple of light and currents freckled, the freckles smeared into grey tears. Whales: pods, hundreds of individuals, moving slowly along the same flight line as the airship: south by south-east.

'I've never seen so many,' Gaby said.

The surface tore, a whale breached, breathed, dived down into the deeper blue.

'Eighty per cent of the Indian Ocean population in these waters. The Aldabrans tell us that eventually, every whale on the planet will pass through here.'

'Mecca for whales.'

'That is no joke. Yes. The whales come here, the Chaga talks to them. Now the Aldabran isopaths have worked out what it is saying to them.'

'And the Harambee wants to know.'

'My mission is to induct the Aldabran Nation into membership of the Harambee.'

Gaby could feel his apprehension through the fine, soft fabric he wore.

147

'This is a bit beyond your usual bailiwick.'

'Yes, it is outside our expansion strategy. However, we believe that a rival group is seeking the Aldabrans as clients.'

'Who?'

'The Merina.'

'That superstate in Madagascar?'

'Of course, the Harambee believes that its political philosophy of cultural diversity would serve the Aldabrans better than the centrist state of iMerina. You understand what is at stake.'

'This is the first confrontation between the emergent states – okay, okay, you're not a state, you're a consensus.'

'It is more than that, Gaby. If the Aldabrans are to be believed, they have a direct channel of communication with the Chaga itself. They are ambassadors; but which will they represent, old-style political conformity, or the Ten Thousand Tribes?'

'Themselves?' Gaby said softly, but a change in the pitch of the thrusters masked her word. Antinka was taking them down. Faraway said, 'Serena is spending a lot of time with Cimarron.'

'It's not what you think.'

'She is young.'

'She's curious about what it's like to have, seventeen?'

'Seventeen.'

'Other people in your head at the same time.'

'Why is this?'

'Because she is an isopath.'

'Au!' Faraway sat up, hands cupped to face. 'Of course! Of course; Gaby, you must forgive me, for all these years I had thought unworthily of you. When I heard about the drugs, I thought they were the reason. But of course, Serena.'

'They wouldn't let me, Faraway. They exiled me. It was like losing half my life; having half my body amputated: reduced to head, breasts, arms, that's all. Wave and smile and feed, but can't go anywhere. Can't do anything.'

'Au, Gaby.'

'Yeah, au, Faraway.'

Gaby grabbed for floor as *Kariokor* shifted attitude. She gasped, but not because of Antinka's piloting.

The object that had come into view around the edge of the window bulkhead was enormous. Gaby guessed that the part of it above water was ten kilometres across, the submarine form many times that. The superstructure rose from the water on tens of thousand of stilt legs. Bone pale, warped as mangrove finger-roots, they seemed too delicate to bear the structures piled on top. Gaby counted fifteen levels: domes, crystalline minarets, coral spires, layer upon layer: ziggurats and pagodas. She thought of sacred cities sacrificed to jungles, drowned Lyonesses, fossilized leviathans.

The submerged part was a maze of channels, convoluted as a human brain. Gaby pressed her hands to the window for a clearer view: whales, swimming one after the other down the pseudo-coral canals towards the central island. She saw a whale breach among the white stilt-roots that upheld the island-temple.

She realized her mouth was open.

'It speaks to the whales,' Faraway said answering the unsaid question.

'What does it say to them that it won't say to us?' Gaby asked.

'That is what we will find out. The Aldabrans have hinted that they have learned something from the object.'

'Which is a little prick-tease to get them into the club.'

The whale-temple slipped out of view as Antinka used all four of his hands to bring the airship in to Aldabra. *Kariokor* came in low over a flotilla of three ocean-going catamarans, cutting hexagrams across the sea. They were beautiful white ships, with tall hyper-critical sails, but when he saw them Faraway leapt to his feet and pressed his face to the window. He beat a fist against the cha-plastic.

'No!'

The full white sails each carried the symbol of a green open hand.

Gaby understood.

'The Merina.'

'Yes. Now we are going to have to fight.'

The iMerina ships passed out of sight beneath the hull.

149

30

Sari was eighteen, had much English Air Force in her blood, and was patently a spy. The Aldabran Chamber had assigned her to the non-diplomatic guests as attaché. Her job was to show the visitors miracles and wonders, and every night report on them to a man in an office. Gaby liked her little spy. She was helpful, friendly, funny, ingenuous as a puppy. Gaby also knew that if the need arose, she could play Sari like a flute.

Like all her race, she was hairless, scalp tattooed with society signifiers. Her skin was fuzzed with fine, downy scales that increased the oxygen absorption area when she breathed water. She had a nap, like velvet. When amused or bemused she would unconsciously blink down her transparent third eyelids. A layer of insulating fat softened her contours. Her be-ringed fingers and toes were gently webbed.

The alien ambassadors seduced her. Gaby was touched when the girl asked if she could brush Gaby's red hair. As she brushed, she sang lovely songs that Gaby remembered from her father's record collection; Harry Belafonte calypsos. Gaby hesitated before granting Sari hair-brushing privileges with Serena. As well as being an enthusiastic spy, Sari was also blatantly and evangelically bisexual.

The Merina fleet had arrived in Nemo's crab-claw inner harbour four hours after *Kariokor* had set down on a local market-place. All Faraway's political tendrils had been blocked by Pierre, his Aldabran attaché. He could learn nothing of his enemies.

'They want to observe our reactions when we meet,' Faraway mused. 'They are smart, these fish-people, but they have a lot to learn about diplomacy.'

The Harambee party had been lodged in a cluster of elegant, airy waterside coral chambers known as the White Suites. Gaby suspected they had been custom-built for the summit. From her Gaudi-esque coral balcony she could see the iMerina fleet riding at the glass anchor buoys. The ambassador had declined Aldabra's hospitality and remained secluded aboard ship.

Sari had thrown herself into the preparations for the official reception with more enthusiasm than panache. Gaby had to politely tell her to fuck off before she ruined the evening dress Sudha had nanofactured for her. It was only when she saw how the girl helped Oksana adjust her Siberian Ice-Queen gown that Gaby guessed the subtext. Loving the alien.

The summit hall was a short drive into virgin canopy-Chaga. It was a great sphere of woven wood; its nested chambers were decorated with intricate painted reliefs of Indian mythology. Gaby caught the same new-birthed smell exuded by the White Suite. Architecture was easy with cha-tech. Every making thing was easy: the merit lay in the talent that designed the making.

Gaby navigated the fringes of the party, keeping within recognition but outside conversation range. The champagne was well faked. Faraway and Cimarron formed the centres of two knots of Aldabran politicians. The beautiful brocaded white robe accentuated Faraway's Luo height. Gaby admired him from a distance, then steered into the heart of the party. The Aldabrans parted before her. She lightly laid her hand to Faraway's back. He flinched.

'Serena says you don't need to be an isopath to read you, honey.' She took his drink off him, downed it herself. 'Don't do any more.'

Mme A.O. Rananatsoa of the Merina brought with her to the party five aides, including an isopath, and six children, all her own. She was tall, slender, pale-skinned, fine-featured, aristocratic, a Merina of the iMerina, that ancient race of Malagasy lords. Accordingly, she was not allowed to speak her own name; an equally elegant, aristocratic aide introduced the Envoy to Gaby. Her eldest child, a twenty-year-old daughter, could have been sister to Mme A.O. Rananatsoa. Her youngest, a tumbling small boy, spent the evening hiding from his attaché under tables. Prepared to hate her on sight, Gaby found Rana, as she liked to be informally known, witty, generous, and a sister mother in a man's world. Within two glasses Gaby had agreed to her suggestion that maybe it would be good for all the unofficial delegates – friends, partners, ex-lovers, children, ex-lover's children – to enjoy the activities the Aldabrans had planned for them as one group. Sari said, the whale havens, they must see the whale havens. It was the only thing that got the youngest Rananatsoa out from under the table.

'She is going to tear my balls off and eat them for breakfast,' Faraway said as party currents brought him and Gaby into momentary passage.

'I rather liked her,' Gaby said, snaffling a moving drink.

'You were supposed to,' Faraway said. 'How many of those have you had?'

'Only six. Not including yours.'

'Gaby.'

'You wouldn't want me shaking.'

That came in the night, in the billowing, white-draped room full of moon and sea. Shaking, and the sicks. Serena came in to ask was she all right, was there anything she could do? Gaby shook her head, cupping water into her mouth – no, nothing. The true answer was yes, get me a fistful of euph patches, daughter.

It went. It went.

She woke with her face in a ray of sunshine and the sounds of morning coitus coming from the adjacent suite.

'Paedophile,' Gaby said. Oksana grinned. Sari pulled the pure white sheet over her head.

'She makes me feel as young as I look,' Oksana said.

'What if Serena was linked in, eh? What about that?'

'What about it? You know, if you don't get some action soon, Gab, it's going to heal up down there.'

Sari had regained her bounce by the time they met at the harbour to take the boats to the whale havens. Oksana made her apologies at the jetty: water was not her element. The little fast skiffs took the rest looping out of the harbour through a labyrinth of islets and sea-towns into deep water. Gaby discerned submarine shapes, darker on dark. Whales. Eotippe, the Rananatsoa attaché, steered his boat over the moving pod. Sari followed. The whales swam on. They swam like fishes. They did not surface.

Something marvellous here.

The suits were cool. It was not the sensual crawl of oxygen-absorption cha-plastic over her skin that spooked Gaby. It was when the breather-suit tried to worm tendrils down her throat

152

that she panicked. Drowning in clear air. Sari rushed to shut the suit down. Gaby lay in the bottom of the boat staring at the sky. When they had all gone over the side, she asked Eotippe to take her back to Nemo. Afraid and feeling very old, she found a bar. She placed one from her stash of Moginçual patches between her breasts, sank back in a hammock-chair and went to heaven.

Three metres down in the Indian Ocean, Sari tied Serena's hair up in plastic so it would not get in her face. She showed her guests how to swim like an Aldabran, with the whole body, like a fish. Then she kicked for deep water. The four older Rananat-soas came after. Streaming red hair like a water-comet, Serena followed the sea-girl. Sari swam naked: her skin-scales had puffed up like soft fur. Serena envied her freedom. A world all to yourself, infinite, three-dimensional; a place where you could be what you wanted to be. You could hide and seek yourself in this clear blue water.

When she had seen her mother spasming in fear in the bottom of the boat, Serena had almost panicked too. But then she saw the whales in the water, and the others her own age who had been able to do this, and she broke the panic and opened her lungs to the breather-suit. Now, flexing down deep towards the slow arcing shapes of the whales, she was glad Gaby had freaked. This was hers; the excitement, the adventure, the dazzle of new people and peoples. Hers alone.

Sari led the arrowhead of swimmers in over the pod: five big blues, moving lazily along a cold current. Serena saw now how the whales swam without surfacing. Long banners of transparent cha-plastic trailed from tail flukes, flippers, the hinge of each jaw. Oxygen transfer membranes: the whales wore their own breather-suits.

Sari led the visitors closer. A sudden prickle on Serena's face – her only un-suited skin. The water swarmed with just-visible, darting motes. Animals, machines? Both. Buckies. She held her hand out. The intelligent chemicals flocked to it, surrounded it in a fuzz of activity, then dispersed. Serena thought she saw a ribbon of motion, like an eddy, loop from her hand to the eye of the whale.

She felt another thing: an unease at the bottom of her consciousness, as if someone were looking over her shoulder. She had felt that from Cimarron; now this whale was touching the fringe of her isopathic sense. Through her Change she understood that the whales knew she was here, and approved.

The sound was so uncanny that Serena thought for a moment it must be in her imagination. Then she saw that Sari was singing. The treble twittering whistle seemed too like a bird for this deep water, but the whales recognized it. The whales responded.

The water seethed with buckies. Motes swarmed together, linked, locked, built themselves into larger and more complex structures. Nano to micro to macro: the buckies wove with dazzling speed.

Serena arched back as the grasper reached towards her. Fingers opened: the eye at the base of the tentacle swivelled on to her. Sari nodded: Serena tentatively reached out her hand. She felt a laugh of relief as the fingers closed gently around hers, the plastic in her lungs sealed it in. The construct was in fact too kooky to be frightening; an amalgam squid/spider/crab/Korean car-manufacturing robot. It shook hands gravely, then rippled fins, spun propellers and darted off to offer the same gesture to the oldest Michelle Rananatsoa. As the children clustered around the thing, five more came torpedoing up from underneath the whale. Serena had no doubt that they were under the whale's direct control, that, with a wish, it could remake the remotes into anything it desired.

A memory, an understanding. Deep ocean storms had driven the whales close to Africa; they had gone with all the others up on to the viewpoint to watch them breaching and sounding out beyond the reef. She had been small, because Sunpig had been there: she had watched the weird woman go down on her knees at the sight of the great whales.

'Why?' she had asked.

'They're what we should be. They're the true intelligence of the planet. They're the smart ones.' She remembered Sunpig's exact words, and her reply: 'But if they're smart, why don't they have any hands?'

They had hands now. Billions of fullerene fingers, sea-weaving. Like magic: thought into object. Like Oksana had tried to teach her about shamanism; the power of the song over the physical world. Like the shamen of Finno-Ugaric legend, the whales could sing the substance of the world into their chosen form.

The squidlings darted away, morphing into the deep blue. Strange shapes, peculiar evolutions: the whales playing with their shaping powers. Serena shivered; the sea-cold was beginning to penetrate her skin-suit. Sari pointed towards the surface. The humans kicked upwards, the whales swam on: Serena thought she saw, on the very edge of visibility, the constructs dissolve back into the free-swimming nimbus of buckies. As she rose towards the plane of rippled light, a new thought came to her: perhaps whales had no hands because they had chosen to give them up. Perhaps they built toys to show their disdain for things made with hands.

She thrust towards the light.

31

The fire drew him along the dark beach. He looks tired, Gaby thought. He looks like he has had a hard-fighting day. He went down on the sand like something hunted and felled.

'I'm sorry I'm late,' Faraway said. 'They threw a reception on one of their ships. I left as early as was polite.'

Gaby said, 'Take your clothes off.'

'I'm sorry?'

'There's no one around, well, except maybe Sari, spying. Take your clothes off.'

She was already pulling up his white *jellaba*. He surrendered quietly.

'Now lie face down under that palm.'

Jesus, you still look good, Gaby thought as she watched Faraway suspiciously lower himself to the sand. It's all solid and tight under that close-fitting black skin of yours. Too tight: too hard. But I can make you feel good.

Hanging most of her weight from the slumped palm trunk, she paced out Faraway's body. Toes, ball of foot, heel felt out the knots and spasms.

'You are an evil evil woman,' Faraway said, twisting his mouth out of the soft sand.

Gaby thought; it is far far too long since anyone called me that. Her feet worked out the tensions. She could feel Faraway melting under her soles. She twisted the ball of her big toe in the back of his neck. He gasped, then relaxed.

'So?' Gaby asked.

'We did our best. They respect our ideology, but . . .'

'But.' She worked the ball of her foot into the base of his spine.

'Eight years ago a joint Iranian-Indian fleet attacked these islands. Ships shelled the outlying communities, aircraft dropped napalm on the inner sea-villages. The Chamber told me that when their missiles were spent, the aircraft came in low and used their cannon on the refugee boats.'

'Jesus.'

'Yes, but the Harambee cannot guarantee that that will never happen again. How can we? The Merina, however . . .'

'Over. On your back, negro.'

As she trod out his length, Gaby was careful not to catch and hold his look. Why? Because what you might see there would scare you. So: you are pressing the soles of your feet over the naked body of a wonderful man who once was your lover: what do you expect? Why are you doing this, Gaby McAslan, unless it is to see that smoke in his eyes? Do you hate him, that you would tease him like that?

He felt the hesitation in her muscles.

'Gaby.'

'Yes?'

'I have something I have to say to you.'

Oh no. Don't, Faraway. Please.

'Gaby, I want you to work with me. The Harambee needs someone to tell the truth about it. Gaby, you make the world listen. You tell me it's gone, it's died; I don't believe that. I don't believe that can ever die, any more than your hand can die on your arm, or your heart can die inside you. It is not part of you; it is you; if it dies, you die. Gaby, I am taking another big risk on this mission: I have persuaded the Harambee that you would be a valuable asset, and that you can be trusted. I have trusted you with much. I hope you will repay that. Gaby, I am an out-of-his-depth diplomat lying on a beach completely naked in the middle of the night, I have very little else to lose.'

It would have been better, kinder, if he had told her he had been crazy for her all these years. The beach fire hissed and flared blue; sand on driftwood fusing to glass.

'Shit, Faraway.'

An answering flare from beneath the horizon; a brief glow on the edge of the world from beyond the world. The punishment of Venus.

32

The Harambee mission to Aldabra failed the next day. Gaby could read it in Faraway's muscles when she knelt beside him as he lay face down in the soft sand by the firelight.

'Fuck,' she said gently.

'Yes, fuck indeed. Madame Rana outmanoeuvred me at every turn. In view of its unique culture, Aldabra will enjoy the status of Protectorate of iMerina. Whatever this wonderful thing they have learned from the whales, now we will never know it. A full directorate has already sailed from Ambilobe to supervise the unification, together with a flotilla of gunboats for the protection of the vulnerable outer islets.'

'They say.'

'Yes. I think they will find that gunboats do not sail out as easily as they sail in.'

'I'm sorry, Faraway.'

'It remains to be seen what the Elders will make of my performance.' The shrug was deep and angry. 'I should be at an official celebration in the conference centre right now.'

'I know; Oksana and Serena have gone.'

'Quite frankly, I do not want to. I am sure this must look undiplomatic, but right now I do not feel very diplomatic.'

'Neither do I. Turn over.'

He obeyed, as always. He stayed her hand as it moved down over his belly.

'Now, if I could introduce the Elders to our new spin-doctor . . .'

He yelped. Gaby had bitten him gently on the navel.

'I need time, Faraway.'

'Well, we will be another day here winding up the mission and negotiating for a permanent Harambee representative to the new Protectorate.'

'That should be long enough.'

'For what?'

'I've been following a few leads.'

'You are irrepressible.'

Maybe I am, she thought. Maybe you were right, and it is like a biology, or a perversion, that you can never escape while you live, that beats you on.

Fireworks were blasting the sky apart now; dozens fountaining up into thousands of falling stars, celebrating the new nation. Gaby remembered another night, with fireworks, the night she had fallen in love and a dead moon came back, alchemized into Big Dumb Object.

'Leads to what?' Faraway asked.

'Watch the fucking fireworks,' Gaby McAslan said.

33

Boatpersons, Gaby had found, were generally a discreet species. Melisa steered, and did not ask what business took her alien passenger across water in the night.

The biomotor was as hushed as a heartbeat; the dark water broke smoothly around the blunt bow. A cloud front had moved in before dusk, but the sea was full of stars: the reflected lights of the islet communities and the night-fisher boats. Glancing back past Melisa, Gaby could no longer distinguish the lights of the White Suites from those of the capital. She wondered how far Oksana had got into the thing with the tattoo needles that, she had assured Gaby, would keep Sari occupied all night. The lights rippled on the water. Gaby clutched the carved wooden box tighter. All of a sudden she was afraid. All of a sudden these were not the lights of island habitats and ocean cities. These were the lights of home; old home: Ireland: the Point, on a humid summer night with the August stars ascendant and the lights of the towns across the lough and the ferries in the roadstead twinkling. She was wound back more than half a life to the night she stood on the edge of the land looking out to sea for that sign she could steer her life by; light ships, guide stars.

She had never imagined the lights in the sky would take her so far. Into another world.

Be here, be now. You have work to do, Gaby McAslan. Melisa threaded her boat through the inter-island channels, around concealed shallows and reefs. The engine pulse dropped to a murmur. Gaby sensed herself ghosting in towards an unseen landing. Lights loomed over her, she caught brief laughter, then the boat bumped against a jetty.

'This is you,' Melisa said.

The lantern came on when the boat was gone. Gaby suspected its bearer had been standing there in the dark all along, watching.

'Come with me please.' Man's voice. But not the man she had arranged to meet. The biolume was hooded; it said follow, no more. As she climbed the steep path, Gaby smelled flowers, green growing things, mould. There were farms on the backs of many of these villages. The guide steered her away from the cliff-side apartments, the lighted windows and the voices and the music.

'Here.'

Here being a door in a blister of coral rock.

'Here?'

'It is easy, just follow the stairs down. There is a hand rail.'

Beyond the door, the spiral stairwell was lit by biolumes.

'Okay then, down,' she said. Twenty turns down she came to another door. She opened it and stepped into wonder.

The room was a transparent teardrop suspended like a jewelled bauble over the ocean. An earring worn by the coral islet, Gaby thought. Biolume domes gently lit the live-wood surfaces, the soft furnishings and upholstery, but did not out-glare the lights out in the night. Constanz was waiting in a sling-chair. He was barefoot, dressed in soft fabric, loose pants, a sleeveless shirt. His scalp bore his people's device; a stylized whale motif. Runs of ornamentation scrolled down either side of his nose. In the low light his skin had the soft brush of suede. His face said thirty, fortysomething. Gaby knew he was only a few years older than Serena. Like Serena, he was an isopath, and it was slowly charring his soul.

'This is a beautiful room,' Gaby said truthfully.

'It is, yes, I spend much time here,' Constanz said. He sounded tired. 'In our society, there are very few places where you can be solitary. We have a national horror of being alone. May I see this?'

He nodded at Gaby's wooden casket. She gave it to him. He glanced in.

'Sit down then,' Constanz said. Gaby sat in the sling facing him. She crossed her legs, ankle over knee, like a man; a posture she knew vaguely intimidated men when struck by a woman.

'Have you seen the Diamond Reef?'

'Yes, we flew in over it. It's impressive.'

'Yes, it is. Do you know what it is?'

'Suppose you tell me.'

'It's a computer.'

'Yes, we have similar constructs at home; like crystal inselbergs.'

'No, I don't think you have anything like this. This computer is powered by whales.'

Gaby hoped the dim lighting concealed her boggle.

'It uses whale song as its primary processing language. Being analogue rather than digital, it can do computations impossible for digital computers.'

'Whales are computing?'

'In a sense, yes.'

Obvious question: 'What?'

'I have to go back a bit here. You are aware of what we call the Sea-forts; the communications platforms?'

'I was there when Foa Mulaku emerged. I heard the thing scream at the BDO.'

'They are more than just transmitters to the BDO. They, eavesdrop?, is that the word? They listen, they record, they relay it to the whales on the migration cycle; by the time the whales reach Aldabra, they've processed the information into song-code.'

It's not Diamond Reef, Gaby thought, the whole Indian Ocean is one enormous slow computer.

'Go on.'

'They're constructing a map of history. Human history.'

'I don't understand.'

'It's a fractal,' Constanz said, struggling for language. 'Like a curve in partial dimensions. It looks like ... I can't describe it. It's sharp, but it has soft folds, like feathers, but the feathers cut, you know? And the deeper you go into it, the more it opens up, and it's the same at every level. Everything repeats. It fits a pattern. That's what seems to be the important thing to them. Everything is song to them, everything is language. How can I explain this?' He was sitting forward in his seat now, his hands were animated. His face was years younger. 'It's like, for them, when they use their sonar, they don't hear a word, they see a sound picture of the thing they are probing. They see it in their minds; to them, the word is the same as the thing.'

He calls the whales 'them', Gaby thought. As if they are people, and not aliens.

'You're linked with them.'

'Two Elders in the Disturbed-bottom-foraging-great-squid-current pod. That's a very rough translation, you understand. In my mind . . .'

'I understand. To the whales, language is what it describes.'

'Yes, it is literal reality. So if human history has a language-like structure, if it's a song . . .'

'Then they can change the song.'

'And change human history.'

161

And there's still more, Gaby thought, sitting very still in the jewel-like room, encircled by lights.

'This curve, this map, it only fits if it's generated from a specific point in time,' Constanz said. 'Any other point, it's just random; there is only this pattern if there is this singularity. By singularity I mean, a time – a place – from which all of history is generated. Everything we will do, everything we have done, spreads out from this point outside historical time.'

'This is some kind of, ah, God-like event, outside time, that breaks all the rules of cause and effect. Like creation.'

'Or the end of the world.'

'The whales have mapped this, ah, alpha-and-omega point using the Diamond Reef analogue computer.'

'That's right.'

'So, just when is the end of the world as we know it?'

'The end of the world, as we know it, was on December 18 2014 at eighteen-fifteen, GMT.'

Gaby should have laughed. The world ends, creation begins, halfway through the early evening news, and it doesn't even make the first edit. Nobody notices. All of history is compressed to a singularity, and we go on with whatever we are doing, walking our dogs, hating our jobs, hurting our lovers, making our deals, damaging our children. A soft apocalypse.

Her old school sixth-year centre had been on the top floor, overlooking a building site – very popular in the summer – and a Jehovah's Witness Church. Halfway through Gaby's final year, the world had ended. The Witnesses telegraphed their punch; for several weeks before Armageddon they had been stashing groceries against the tribulation, mostly baked beans and toilet paper. They seemed nice people. They drove nice cars. Gaby had wondered why, when all gross things were to be tried by fire. She wasn't quite sure when the world actually ended; she felt nothing, the believers in their upper room went on as before, untried by fire. There they sat with their beans on toast and their clean arses, looking at the schoolgirls looking at the construction guys with no shirts on, thinking, *don't you know, you're all dead?* After three days they came down and got into their nice cars and drove off. There had been a lot of toilet paper left over.

But she could not laugh at this little armageddon as she had at the Witnesses with their calendars and dates. Their date had been wrong. The Aldabrans' was not.

'You gave this to the Merina.'

'Yes,' said Constanz. 'That is all I gave them. Now, if you please.'

'Sure,' Gaby said, distracted. Constanz did not take the box greedily, but Gaby knew that when she was gone, he would rip out the crumpled silk and the waxed paper just to get to a disk, a fucking disk, press the fucking thing to his heart and get away from the aliens in his head that made him very very old.

He started when Gaby rested her hand on his for an instant before leaving.

'Thanks.'

Constanz grimaced. You think you are a traitor, Gaby thought. You are now. While you were a tribesman, while you were just Constanz the cetacean researcher of the Aldabran nation, you were just bribable, and everyone is. But now you are a citizen of the Merina Protectorate of Aldabra, and with that come secrets and betrayals and guilts. And traitors. She closed the door on the beautiful room.

34

It was the last night that Gaby would build her fire down by the sea. In the morning *Kariokor* was to fly back to the mainland. There was a problem at Lossogonoi, on the Masai Plains south of Kilimanjaro, that required a Missionary. But tonight Gaby read tired satisfaction in Faraway's back. He had saved the Harambee Mission in the final quarter. In the old SkyNet days he had always been a better goalkeeper than he looked. In the early autumn fogs of the Great Boma, the Elders were debating the significance of the message from out of the sea.

'The date is still a puzzle,' Faraway said. He rolled on to his front. He knew the tricks now. 'The Elders have been running correlations, but have so far failed to find anything meaningful.'

It was a huge, star-bright night. The wind was low, the surf muted. The fire had collapsed down to red coals crusted with flakes of white ash whirled up by the wind.

Gaby took her hands off him, sat on the sand, knees pulled up to her chest.

'You know what I told you about the stuff T.P. Costello sent me from Shepard? Well, there was more.'

'From Shepard?'

'No, no. From the Space People. The ones who went AWOL out on the hull. They call themselves the Big Sky Nation now, they've got some kind of set-up up there. They've been communicating with Earth using spare channels on the Iridium comsat necklace – as far as I know, they still are. There are people up North who listen to them, circulate the information. They report that Shepard's renegades obtained access to the fifth chamber, and entered it.'

'When was this?'

'December 18th 2014.'

'What time?'

'Seventeen ten, GMT.'

Seven waves broke softly before Faraway spoke.

'They went into the fifth chamber, and an hour later, the world ended.'

'They encountered a singularity.'

'A literal black hole?'

'It's possible. It might even be the same one they used to destroy Hyperion to construct the BDO. There seems to be virtually no limit to what the Chaga-makers can do. If it was . . .'

'Then they are certainly dead. I'm sorry, Gaby.'

'Since I talked to Constanz I've been through this, through it and through it. What I think – what I like to think, what I hope – is that it's a metaphysical singularity; some kind of consciousness event horizon. What scares me is that they somehow generated a singularity.'

'You haven't heard anything since.'

The moon was floating on the edge of the sea, huge and red

and fake. The BDO was in occlusion. Gaby was glad of that. Suddenly, she pulled off her shirt, stepped out of her pants. No little spying Sari tonight. She was in disgrace. Sleeping with the targets was a cardinal sin. Let alone a still-scabby wolf's head tattoo on the left tit.

Gaby lay down and pressed her skin to Faraway's, flank to flank, the length of her long body. She rested her palm on the flat muscles of his belly.

Faraway did not respond. Instead, he said, 'Because we look like we were then, because we feel that way, we imagine that we are, but we are not. We're old, time has passed. We are not what we used to be.' He sat up, touched Gaby gently on the hip. 'Gaby, this will sound strange to you, but there is someone. We have been together for three years now and she seems to love me – I cannot imagine why. I would not hurt her, Gaby. I think maybe we should put our clothes on and be professional. I still have to get an answer to my question.'

He dived into his *jellaba*.

'Hey, Faraway, as turn-downs go, that was one of the nicer I've had.'

'Thank you. You deserve no less. I may be old, Gaby, but I am still the greatest guy you will ever meet.'

She laughed against her will. After he had gone, she sat by the fire until it all fell into white ashes and wisped away on the rising wind.

35

Enticed by rumours of early rains over Serengeti, the elephants were walking west. If the elephants walked, so did Fwa Nation, its people, its homes, its villages. Now on the fifteenth day of the progress, Townships Seven through Fifteen were stalled on the bare high plain of Tarangire facing four hundred Loolma-

lasin Masai armed with cattle, attitude, spears and repro-shop
AK47s.

There is a theory that human history is the dying echo of a
primeval war between farmers and nomads. The theory breaks
down when the farmers, their farms, their settlements, are as
nomadic as the pastoralists. Inspired by the juggernauts of the
old mobile UNECTA bases heaving themselves over the savan-
nahs, the Fwa villages rode on the backs of enormous walking
machines. They moved with the speed of seasons, shuffling
forward a kilometre a day along the elephant migration routes.
Now their migration had run into another.

The Fwa were elephant people.

The Loolmalasin were cow people.

The Missionary of the Harambee was here to stop them killing
each other.

'It is of course disgraceful that two member Nations should be
on the verge of war,' Faraway said, sipping his very cold beer
under the parasol on the viewing deck of Sub-Ship One. Gaby
polarized her eyes to pick Township Twelve, two kilometres
distant across the bleached savannah, out of the glare. In the
deep shadow beneath the ecosystem-plate, the transport lifted a
shoe, shuffled it forward, set it down. Dust eddied up and blew
away. She thought of old educational TV about open-cast min-
ing, and behemoth walking draglines. She thought of legends of
star-swimming turtles bearing worlds on their shells. Gaby knew
all about one tradition demanding the right to walk through
another tradition's territory.

'Shouldn't you be doing something, negotiating, facilitating,
empowering, whatever?' Gaby said. Faraway contemplated, and
ordered, another beer. Sub-One was maintained as a game lodge.
Its usual place was forward of the main advance, among the
elephant herds; it had been pulled back into the Samba Line, as
the Fwa called their migration. Up front, isolated, it would
certainly have been burned by the Loolmalasin. There were
rumours that the Masai had killed elephants that had strayed
into their grazing.

'I merely represent moral authority,' Faraway said. 'This really
is most excellent beer. No, they are quite capable of resolving
this dispute themselves. And they will, now that they know

166

their parents are watching. Meanwhile I shall enjoy some deserved R&R. Relax, no one has died yet, and you are all on the Harambee's ticket. This is a fine place, we have just come at a not especially propitious time.'

Very fine, Gaby thought, and specially propitious for what you want, which is a positive answer to the question you asked me that first night on the beach. Because it is easy for me to be seduced here; it's old Africa again, it is the high plains and the animals moving upon them, and the huge sky and the people reduced to atoms of sentience, it's all the things I loved and thought were lost, and you know that.

It was Tsavo West again; that time when her notion for Shepard had become a wonderful ache. Like the UNECTAfrique researchers, the Fwa were a Nation of many nations: black, white, Asian. Beautiful hybrid children ran between the pot-shaped houses and through the factory-farms. A US zoological research group had been marooned here in the crazy time when Tanzania disintegrated; evolved by the Chaga, work had become life had become faith. The polymer houses were decorated with elephants. Men aspired to the virility of bulls; women prayed against the tortuous pregnancies of cows. Their multi-racial children wore elephant amulets and charms. Every township carried its shrine to Ganesh. The mobile habitats walked like elephants. They made many handshakes from the visitors who came to see their elephants. Gaby appreciated their sense of identity and purpose. It was yet another reminder of that lost Africa. Part of Faraway's diplomatic seduction.

But Shepard took me out to show me something wonderful, Gaby thought. Can you do that?

The ATV driver had warned Serena that she would be covered in bruises if she insisted on standing up. He drove very fast. He was right, her ribs, hips, breast bone would be blue in the morning, but the sense of speed was transcendent to one whose fastest mode of transport was the chug of a lagoon pirogue. Plumes and banners: her hair, the cracking Harambee flag conferring diplomatic protection on the tourists, the dust boiling back from the wheels, breaking into spiral devils skittering across the plain. Serena waved to Gaby. The second car was close enough for her to be able to make out her mother mouthing *sit down*. Faraway was laughing.

The two Fwa ATVs split around a termite city that had become infected with ten-metre red quills. Gaby and Faraway took the riskier route to the north herd; Serena and Oksana went west. One car per herd. Elephants were to be respected: too much human curiosity demeaned them. The driver hit a rut at eighty; Serena was almost catapulted over the roll bars. Oksana grabbed her by the thighs, hauled her down.

'Jesus and Mary, are you all right?'

Her exhilarated expression was the answer.

It was more than pure speed; out here space itself was thrilling. Sea was big, the skies that hung over it infinite; but out on the ocean you were always a visitor, floating between alien dimensions. This land you could be part of. You moved through it, not over it. So it was joy to be jolted and bruised and hurt, because it was the land telling her it existed. It was real.

The buggy struck a ridge, bounced four wheels in the air, and Serena's perceptions inverted. She was real. She existed. After the hormonal battles of puberty comes the neurochemical crusade of selfhood. It is a work of years to make a soul. In the space between the ATV leaving the ground and coming down with a bang of suspension, Serena saw how small and tight her big, sunlit world had been. Here was a huge world to grow into, and she knew she could, fill up every space and fold of it with her emerging self. You can have it all, this land was saying; you can go as far and as fast as you like across it and every moment you will find something new, something you did not know before. This is a place you can learn to be you.

I don't want to go back, Serena thought. Her knuckles were white on the padded grip bars. I want to keep going for ever. I want to find my nation.

The driver dropped gears to go down the side of a wooded river cut. Shadows and tall trees. The driver was pointing at something. Oksana nodded, tugged Serena's pant leg.

'The monkeys!' she yelled.

'What about them?'

A white bearded male left off ferociously masturbating on a

pseudo-fungus frond to chitter at the invaders. It bared teeth, and raised a startling sail of veined black skin from its spine.

'Photosynthetic,' the Fwa driver shouted.

On the far side of the river the land closed in. The ATV moved cautiously through heavy stands of parasol fungus and coral fingers interspersed with stretches of hexagon cover and cha-grass.

'They've been around here for the past two days,' the driver announced. 'There's a gourd grove up at Endabash, they've been storing up water for the rest of the journey.' Five minutes later he slowed the ATV to a creep. Oksana climbed up beside Serena.

'I wish I had binoculars,' she said.

'You won't need them,' the driver answered. 'Believe me.'

He steered around a copse of wine-glass shaped trees. They were bull-bar-to-toe with an elephant.

'Jesus and Mary,' said Oksana.

'Wow,' said Serena.

Then they saw the thing about it, which was more than big, grey, ears, tusks, elephant. Its trunk was two trunks, two long, flexible arms terminating in four-fingered hands.

Nostrils in the back of each wrist flared. The elephant reached, seized the rim of one of the goblet-trees, bent it down. Water slopped from the bowl. One arm held the tree down, the other scooped handfuls of water into the elephant's mouth. The elephant drank the tree dry, then let it spring back and sauntered into the deep cover.

'God,' said Oksana.

'Cool,' said Serena.

They came on more in a clearing in heavy frond cover. There were nine; two bulls, five females, two calves. The cows hid the calves among their bodies. Serena wanted Dal the driver to push forward to see the calves better, but he stayed on the edge of cover, engine turning, ready to sprint. The bulls were edgy, defensive. The smaller, leaner male brandished a thick frond spine in one hand.

'You don't want to know how far they can throw one of those things,' Dal said.

They encountered the third group of elephant moving across open bushland towards a great wall of crimson pseudo-fungus as sheer and sudden as if the horizon were burning. This was a migration herd; fifty head. Dal took the ATV in alongside, just outside threat range of the bulls. Serena was enchanted by the babies, then noticed a more remarkable thing. Some of the cows were towing branches laden with big orange squash-fruit. Others had water gourds slung over their necks by the ropy tendrils.

'They're carrying their food with them,' she said. 'Like an army on the march.'

Dal took the buggy in across the head of the procession. The leader was a young male – none of this sub-species was over twenty. Serena thought he led with a confident swagger. With reason; in his left hand he carried a smouldering tree branch.

Fire. In a grasping hand.

Serena had grown up with the tenet that the Chaga-makers nurtured intelligence, but until she had seen the elephants with fire, until she had touched the thing the whales had spun out of their thoughts, it had never carried any emotional weight. Dal had stopped the ATV ahead of the migration; Serena could look the big male in the eyes. He owned the future. The true journey was not across Lossogonoi after the rains. The migration he led was through time. A thousand generations were following him. The ones at the rear of that procession could only be glimpsed. Their forms and abilities were obscure, perhaps unrecognizable to their forebears, but the earth shook to their tread.

Dal moved the ATV off. The spell was broken, but the great plain and the sky over it no longer felt accepting and exhilarating to Serena. She had been reduced to a speck, a louse on the skin of Africa, young, mindless, ignorant of what she was. You think you have come so far, done so well, and then you see the way ahead and you have not even begun to begin. The procession is long. She had chilled herself with a deep, cold stare at her own immortality.

Dal had been right. By the time the ATV drew up beside Sub-One's left foot, the bruises were beginning to purple on Serena's forearms and ribs.

36

Faraway's charge burst the cabin door like dry wattle.

Gaby was on her knees on the floor, like a dying dog. Her hair hung over her face. Her body jerked, she was dry-retching, gasping.

'No!' she screamed. 'Go away! Go away, don't do this to me!'

Faraway was on his knees beside her. Gaby lashed at him with a weak fist; a fresh spasm wrenched her.

'It hurts! It hurts. Make it stop.'

Sub-One had been roused. The narrow wooden companion-ways were filled with concerned faces. Serena was in the doorway.

'Get out of here!' Faraway roared at her. Serena fled in tears. Gaby was on her knees, head down, cheek pressed to floor, arms outstretched. Her fingers scrabbled at the wooden boards. She was keening, long, high-pitched inhuman shrieks. The incongruous eroticism of Gaby's pose revolted Faraway. He snatched her to him. He could not look at her like a rutting animal. He folded her tight in his arms. Every cry he tightened his grip, as if he could squeeze the demons out of her, like sweat, or burst boils.

When the spasms passed he brought her water.

'More.'

Gaby gulped down ten cups of water.

'I ache,' she said, puzzled, as if betrayed by her body. 'It hurts to move. It hurts to breathe. Oh Jesus, this is scary.'

'You are all right,' Faraway said.

'No I'm not. I haven't been in a long time.' She twitched. Faraway pulled her close. 'Oh Jesus; it never hurt like this before. You shouldn't have shouted at Serena. She knows what to do.'

'She should not have to.'

Silence for a time.

Gaby shivered, then said, 'I thought it was a good trade; all the fucking things for the information.'

'So that was how you bribed Constanz.'

'Ah, shit . . . I thought maybe, one big, bad night, and I'd be out of it. Out the far side. Clear. Jesus, right now, if you were a patch user, I'd kill you for one. And if you didn't have one, I'd cut out your liver and eat it. It builds up in the liver, did you know that?' Her muscles clenched. The shaking began. Gaby barely pressed the words out through chattering teeth. 'Fuck . . . If I didn't want to die so much, I'd be amazed at the things my body is doing to me.'

'You don't want to die.'

'Trust me in this: I'm forty-five; if I only had about thirty, forty years left, maybe I could handle that, but to feel like this, be like this, indefinitely . . .' She cried out as cramp stretched her tendons like violin strings. 'Water . . .'

She downed less than half of the six cups Faraway brought her. 'Sorry, sorry,' she would whisper as she slopped water over him. The shakes passed. Faraway laid Gaby out on the bed.

'Faraway.'

'What?'

'That question you asked me on the beach?'

'Yes.'

'I think you have your answer now.'

'Gaby.'

'I can't. I'm not. Just . . . just don't ever talk about this to me again.'

Faraway sat on the edge of the bed looking at his reflection in the dark window. After a time he heard a sigh and turned round to see that Gaby had curled up into a foetus. Her thumb was in her mouth. Her breath was short and fast. Faraway combed her hair back from her face. Her eyes rolled wildly under their lids. Staring at terrible things.

Staring at terrible things. Faraway challenged his reflection until it surrendered with the approaching dawn. Grey light filled the little wooden room. The hulls of the townships were masses of darker darkness. They rested in the night to feed: ground-penetrating tendrils beneath Sub-One's belly siphoned up minerals and organic material to convert to fuel.

'Hey.'

'How long have you been awake?'

Gaby was curled on her side, facing Faraway.

'A while. Looks like it's going to be a lovely day.'

'Yes, I think so,' Faraway said. 'How do you feel?'

'Like a warthog shat in my head. Stupid. Embarrassed. Guilty as all fuck. I'm sorry, Faraway.'

'It's all right.'

'No it's not. I think I said that last night, didn't I?'

'You said something else, about working with me.'

'I remember I said don't ever talk about that to me again.'

'You did. I'm sorry.'

In the growing light, substance separated from shadow. People were abroad on the plain, engineers checking the motility units; surveyors charting the day's march of the Fwa nation. Giraffe moved through light bush; in silhouette they seemed like vowels from an organic alphabet. Zebra grazed, nose to earth. A kilometre east, Township One slowly raised its vast front left boot. It took a step. Back left lifted, slid forward. By steady five metre paces, the townships followed the rains.

Silent fans gave no warning of approach. Suddenly the airship was half the sky of the man and woman in the little cabin. It hung fifty metres off Sub-One's prow. Its passenger could be clearly seen standing by the port window: a black man in a white robe.

Cimarron.

'No,' Faraway said. 'You should not be here, so soon. What has happened?'

Kariokor lifted, revealing the Harambee roundel on its belly. It came in for landing on Sub-One. Faraway leaned back, stretched tight muscles in his neck.

'There is a Luo proverb,' he said. 'Never judge a day by its dawn.'

37

The morning Corrupt Carmine died she shaved and oiled her head. She put on her most attitudeful footwear and a red polymer box jacket she loved very much. Then she cleaned her large white teeth, slid her serious shades up her nose and went to collect her sawn-off Landrover from the car pool, where Useless Moses was supposed to have fixed the sticking front brake. He had not. It made a whistling grating noise as she drove down the dirt road from Samburu base to the airfield. The flight crews and the aeronautical advisors gave her sympathetic looks as she drew up to collect the ministerial briefcase she was to take to Marsabit. Today her route would incur a lengthy detour, south-east to Kinna, down on the edge of terminum. In old Kenya it had been a game lodge; now years of disuse and decay were returning it to soil. She often drove out of her way to this place. In its collapsing dining room she conducted the secret meetings between the UNHCR and the Missionaries of the Harambee.

Corrupt Carmine had been a Harambee agent for three years.

On the day she died she did not go to Kinna. She did not get through the gate on to the Marsabit road. Today there were soldiers on the wire gate, and a KLA hummer parked right across the road. Corrupt Carmine stood up in her Landrover and tried to bluff the soldiers out of her way, then joke them. They did not move. It was then that she knew that they knew.

They slashed her tyres with bayonets.

She tried to run then, but footwear that is good for attitude is bad for running. The boy soldiers brought her down on the main runway like hunting dogs. They yipped and howled in anticipation. The aircrews and advisors turned away.

By the time the soldiers had brought her to the hummer they had stripped her down to her boots and her shades. They spread-eagled her across the hood of the vehicle, they tied her open with tow hawser. They tied her face up. They wanted her to see what they were doing. There were twenty soldiers. Each took five minutes to rape her, each had two turns. The second time some of the soldiers wanted to try new things, like bottles and gun muzzles and bayonets. There was a big cheer when the guard dog was brought up.

When the boys and men and dog had all taken their turns, the soldiers took Corrupt Carmine round to the back of the hummer. They bound her hands with hawser, then ran a length to the tow bar on the back of the vehicle. A thirteen-year-old in purple

174

combat gear took her shades. They were too big for his pinched face. They left her her boots. She would need them.

The US military hummer as supplied to the Kenyan National Liberation Army has fifteen forward gears. This enables it to drive long distances over rough terrain at low speeds that would shred the gear-boxes of civilian 4x4s. They took Corrupt Carmine out along the Losesia road. Twelve kph. A comfortable jog. After five kays she was still running so they went cross-country. They took her through acacia scrub. After three more kays they saw she was no longer upright, so they increased speed to thirty. After half an hour they hit the East African Highway. It was good, fast road that went straight back to Samburu, so they pushed the hummer up to its maximum eighty-five.

An hour after setting out the hummer returned to Samburu. At the end of the steel hawser was half a woman. Serious boots, feet, shins, legs, did not exist. A bloody stump of spine, abraded to sharp point, protruded from a lower abdomen glistening with black flies. The soldiers unhitched what remained of Corrupt Carmine and took it to the camp. There they hung her by her wrists from the wire. The people who lived there needed an example. As a final touch, the kid in purple combats was ordered to give Corrupt Carmine back her shades. He set them on her face, but in the absence of a nose they kept falling off, so after five tries he decided God was telling him something, and kept the glasses himself.

Antinka had completed the preflight checks. The fans were powered up. *Kariokor* was ready to cast off from the roof gardens of Sub-One. His lower left hand hovered over the sensor ready to retract the loading ramp and seal the belly doors. Then the mad *m'zungu* woman with the tattoos came running through the rum-cane waving her arms and shouting.

Fans dropped to idle. Faraway met Oksana at the foot of the ramp, in the shadow of the curving hull.

'Faraway, take me with you.'

'Why?'

Cinemascoped on her eyelids, Oksana saw Corrupt Carmine the last morning *Dostoinsuvo* flew into Samburu, sunlit and grinning in disbelief at the tits of the Hungarian porno women.

She saw the girl warrior on the Gichichi road, the wave, the smile before she disappeared into deep forest. She thought, if you were an isopath, you would see what I am seeing, you would feel what I am feeling, and that would answer you.

Oksana said, 'Carmine was my friend.'

'There is no place for personal feeling in the diplomatic service,' Faraway said.

'Like you and Gaby?' Oksana said.

'What could you do?' Faraway said after a time.

'I could fly,' Oksana said. 'I'm a fucking soldier, I can't make things up on my own, I need orders. I need it like it was in the UNECTA days. Someone tells me what to do, go here, do that, take that there, bring that back, I do it. No questions, no hesitations, no complaints, it's done. Jesus and Mary, you need couriers, you need someone to run errands for you.'

'Can you fly one of these?'

'No.'

'What can you fly?'

'Aeroplanes.' Proper, God-honest, heavy-lifting, brute force aerodynamics aeroplanes. Turbo-powered, fuel-swigging, noisy, brash, busting aeroplanes. That you could take up and put down and would love you and do anything for you. That would drop you out of the sky if you ever fucked with them, that were always dangerous that way, and so exciting, because it was a love affair based on lust, not trust.

'If we had fixed-wing aircraft, I could certainly use you.'

'Is that a promise?'

Faraway considered a moment.

'Yes, it is.'

'An aeroplane will be provided.'

Faraway was much amused.

'But I will need you to take me to Kirinya.'

'That is reasonable. How long do you need to pack?'

Oksana held up a small leather backsack.

'Right. Then we go to Kirinya.'

The ramp was closing even as Oksana sprinted up it.

38

The proposition was so outrageous that Anansi flipped up the dark lenses over his glassless glasses to scrutinize its finer points.

The café balcony clung to the curved face of the tenement like a cummerbund around a full belly. It overlooked the intersection of the main roads from Kanja and Nembure. Throngs of people passed through the junction and paused to talk and trade news and change *matatus* and shop and eat or drink from the many stalls. Oksana Mikhailovna thought, it is good to have a city around me again; lost among people, their voices, their smells, their public pettinesses. The *maître d'* in his impeccable white shirt had cleared a couple from the table in the corner for Anansi and his guest. Whispers and nods quelled complaints. Coffee came at once, with crisp almond fingers.

Anansi the spinner bent over the scroll of sketches weighed down at the corners with empty espresso cups and the repro Alessi coffee-maker. He smiled wryly.

'When I said that Mombi owed you a favour, I hadn't imagined that you meant an aircraft.'

'Is my credit no good in this town?' Oksana said.

'Mombi never welshes,' Anansi said in his immaculate Russian. 'As you know, manufacturing costs are never a problem, though I think we will need to build this thing *in situ*. The difficulty is that it presents certain, ah, design challenges.'

'Surely you're man enough for them,' Oksana teased.

'Please,' Anansi said. He had grown a small belly in the months since Oksana had last seen him. Business was huge now that they had won the coffee war. Only five Uplanders had been killed, and they had all been members of the rival family, thus legitimate targets. The new war was with a group running buckyware out of Kirinya over the front line. Mombi had already lost control over several processor packages. The Runners enjoyed heavy protection. Destroying them would be troublesome.

Everywhere is war, Oksana thought, aspirant dog-soldier of the Harambee.

'You do want it exactly like this.' Anansi sipped his coffee.

'As much as possible.' High tail, high-wing, engines over wing. Big empty belly, carry anything, anywhere, like a mother. *Dostoinsuvo* reborn.

'I can see there being a problem with the VTOL capacity. We wouldn't have access to Ukrainian aeronautical engineering designs. I doubt even the old Nairobi university databases would carry that information. I'll have to go to Nawa to get it out of the North, and she will cost.'

'How much?'

Anansi held out his hand. Oksana took it. She felt her eyes widen at the feel of the wealth in Anansi's buckybrain; contrasted with her own poverty.

'Hm,' Anansi said. He stirred his coffee with his almond crisp. 'I understand you are trained in Siberian shamanism. This is something that interests me very much; the similarities and differences between African and Siberian shamanism. The idea of a universal spiritual language intrigues me. Would you be prepared to discuss this with me, here, for an hour a day, until the aircraft is made?'

'This is your price?'

'I will shake Nawa, and you will give me an hour of your time.'

'Shamanism.'

'Yes.'

'No subtext, no ulterior motive, no fucking me about?'

Anansi flipped up his dark lenses.

'Would I?'

Yes, she thought, but not that way.

The first fake Lexus took Lenana and her new partner L'Oriente to the sports ground in Kiamutugu where Oksana had flown away on *God Speed!/James Bond: the Killer!* Zul had been an early casualty in the war against the Runners. Foreknowledge of the future could not save her from an assassin who was a brother precognitive. Zul and her killer had hunted and hidden through the moiré pattern of intersecting predictions until he stepped out of the least probable of futures and gutted her from sternum to clit. L'Oriente dressed in black rubber catsuits and was fast. Very fast. Neural accelerators pumped her reaction speed to five times human norm. She and Lenana went to every door. Favours were called in. Manners enforced. The big cats were most effective at that. Goalposts were taken down, footballs confiscated, children told, politely but unrefusably, to play down someone else's street while the hardware team set up its things that looked like diseased tree stumps in the centre circle and watched them spin their cocoon.

The second Lexus took Anansi and Oksana Telyanina to Nawa the ware-woman. She lived in a courtyard garden with fountains and blue tiles and formal plantings in Moorish style. Nawa was a tall, wire-thin Galla in her late twenties. Her short cropped hair was bleached white. Her cheeks were pocked by childhood diseases. She sat at a tiled table among flowering shrubs and served mint tea while her visitors explained what they required of her. Then she shook Anansi's hand and went to do her work. As she rose from the table Oksana saw what the bushes had concealed: the thick, flesh-coloured umbilicus hooked into the base of her spine by a gnarl of neural taps.

Her orthobody crouched on its muscular, corpse-blue chicken-legs in a bower of climbing roses and japonica. As Nawa stepped out of her silk dress, it opened to receive her. Lips of flesh sealed, the neural implants plugged her into Planet Net. The symbiont took a step forward on its clawed feet. Oksana thought of the shuffling townships of the Fwa nation. She thought of the hut of Baba Yaga loping through the forest on chicken legs, hunting children. She could not look at Nawa's scarred, pretty face cowled in folds of red flesh.

The ware-woman closed her eyes.

'We can go now,' Anansi said. 'She is out there.'

Nawa had the schematics down from Kiev before Oksana was back at her cheap guest house. The Lexus squeezed a cell memory from its nervous system. While slipping it into the breast pocket of his *jellaba*, Anansi almost managed to martyr most of a religious procession toting a black madonna around its parish. Oksana had forgotten his formidable driving.

'Now I evolve paradigms and then let them kill each other,' Anansi said. 'We should have a fit survivor by morning. Remember, first discourse, eleven o'clock. The *maître d'* is holding a table.'

But what they talked about the first session was what Anansi was doing that could build a vertical take-off repro Antonov transport aircraft out of soil and shit. 'In diamond,' he added. 'It's cheaper. And safer.'

It was a Darwinian thing. Anansi spun codes into fullerenes, machine DNA, replicated them, mutated them, set them down in an arena. Design solutions the size of molecules fought and fucked and traded and cannibalized each other until the one that most efficiently fitted the parameters survived.

'The design parameters are the environment,' Anansi said. 'The population evolves to fit it. Normally, that would be it, I'd let the things loose in a reactor, but complex machinery is more a symbiosis of parts: this is just the airframe, I'll have to generate separate blastulas for the control and power systems and graft them on to the skeleton.'

'You're not a engineer, you're a gynaecologist,' Oksana said.

'And a gardener as well, a pruner and grafter of nanocarbon bonsai, if we're going to martyr metaphors. Now, could we talk about this idea of the world-tree?'

'You eat too many of those almond roll things,' Oksana said.

Anansi had told Oksana that there would be nothing to see for several days, activity was on the atomic level, but she took a mopedcab over to Kiamutugu that evening. The minders – two short-contract local boys over-enamoured with the big guns they had been given – nodded her in. She pressed hands and face to the two-metre sphere of semeny liquid in the centre of the web of beam and girders and imagined she could see the seethe and heave of reproducing buckies.

'The characteristic of the world-tree is that it is constantly renewed,' Oksana told Anansi at their next meeting. There was political unrest in the streets; a group of men carrying home-painted Harambee banners were noisily confronting a second, bannerless group. 'It is eternal return; souls are born on its branches like fruit; the place of the dead is beneath its roots, they are drawn up through the roots and reborn. Our lives are written on its leaves, when a leaf falls, a man dies. Its branches hold up the sky – the twenty-seven heavens, though the worlds are only close in the sense that different branches of a tree are close because they grow from the same trunk.'

'I think this is a universal truth,' Anansi said. 'The tree is the abode of the spirit, of God; man was born from the baobab. The tree is the family tree of humanity.'

'I climb trees,' Oksana said. 'For me, it is flying into the spirit realms.'

'Ah! Flying,' Anansi said.

The altercation below passed off without *rungus* and broken heads, but much name calling.

Anansi took Oksana to the womb-factory. He had programmed a magnifier into the egg wall.

'There, see?'

At last she did; a tiny curl of translucent gristle, smaller than flea shit, fizzing at the edges with fullerene activity.

'My aeroplane,' she said.

'This drug-flight,' Anansi said at the next session. 'Tell me about it.'

There were protesters on the streets again, today only the Harambee men.

'Ecstasy trance and spirit possession is common to all human religions, but to me, it's a symbol, a metaphor. To me the spirits are internal states, aspects of my personality, sub-consciousnesses.'

'Ah, so you're a Freudian shaman.'

'No, I'm a linguistic shaman. The altered states of consciousness remain unconscious, preconscious, because they have no language structure – or whatever structure they have, it is not logical, language-like. It's like, in a dream, identities are not fixed; you can have a different face, your best friend looks like someone else, everyday words have totally different, but quite consistent meanings. A different logic – I know there is wisdom in there, and very great power, if we can tap it. Shamanic flight is the flight within, to these altered states of consciousness, the drug trance is the language it speaks.'

When she next went to look at her baby, it had grown from shit to spider, a glistening, wiggling thing, all legs and wires, embedded in jelly.

'It will fly,' Anansi said.

There was little shamanism discussed the next day because Chehe was celebrating its new status as a member of the Harambee. Anansi viewed with disdain the children's choirs, the drummers and dancers, the firecrackers thrown at old women and dogs.

'They give away their freedom, and they throw a party. I cannot understand why people need to belong to things.'

'I can,' Oksana said.

Mopeds and power scooters circled the intersection, blaring horns. Pillion passengers waved Harambee banners. The back-seat riders were all female, Oksana noticed.

'Kipchobe, I trust you have nothing to do with this madness.' Anansi snapped into Swahili to speak to the *maître d'*.

'Absolutely not. This café will remain a Harambee-free zone.'

'Then I shall remain a customer.'

Oksana could not understand how the Café Lucky could exempt itself from the political will of its neighbourhood, like one tree in a monsoon asking not to be rained upon.

'It is not so hard for Africans,' Anansi said, back in Russian. 'First and foremost, you are your nation, your people, and you are that wherever you go, whoever you are among. Non-geographical states come naturally to us.'

That afternoon Oksana checked out of her cheap, dismal rooming house and used the last of her handshakes to put a deposit down on an apartment in the block by the football field. It was only partly that she wanted to be near the birth, feel the thing growing, gestating, knitting itself together in its sac of fluids. Anansi's casual accusation had stung her; she did need to belong. She did need people around her, solitude annihilated her. She had to have a tribe.

The people of Kiamutugu were politely suspicious of this potentially child-eating *m'zungu* woman, *with no man*, moving on to their corridor, but the first morning there was fruit wrapped in newspaper outside her door, and a bottle of roof-top beer that night. It was well to keep on-side of Mombi's friends.

By now *Dostoinsuvo Surrexit* had grown to a cross of nanofac-tured carbon the size of a hand, a diamond hawk hovering in its shell. Over the coming days the cocoon would expand until it filled most of the courtyard. Within, the nanobird would send out ribs and spars, building the skeleton of an airframe; fuselage, wings, tails; struts and riggers. Anansi had already evolved the buckies for the control system – the AI would link directly with her auxbrain through bone phoresis. Fly-by-mind. He brought them in a sealed aluminium container to the next session: they would be introduced to the foetal aircraft that day. In his workshop, the propulsion units were struggling for survival against the harsh judgements of Nawa's stolen design data.

'Perfect language is the ultimate goal of shamanism,' Oksana Telyanina said at her customary table on the balcony of the Café Lucky.

'Define perfect language.'

'Language that describes its object so completely and precisely that to change a sentence, a word, even a letter, changes objective reality.'

'The power of word over matter.'

'And mind. And spirit. Objective reality.'

Anansi twirled his almond crisp between his fingers. Oksana had noticed that he did this when thinking creatively.

'Shamanism and nanotechnology are sisters, I think. Buckies move the atoms around, but it is language, my programming of the fullerene codons, that tells the buckies how to shape reality.'

'There is a Northland myth,' Oksana said. 'Variants can be found from the Bering Straits to the Baltic.

'It's of a device, the Sampo, like a magical mill; one side generated corn, another salt, the third money. It brought prosperity to the Northland. Through its power, people could survive the winter.'

'A useful device,' Anansi said. 'Though a money mill would not be good for inflation. There is a similar Nandi legend: of a magic forge that could make anything so that the Nandi people grew extremely powerful, but the crocodile grew jealous and cursed it only to make water, so the forge is now at the bottom of Lake Victoria, which is why the Nile continues to flow. But your point is taken.'

As she walked through the alleys of Kiamutugu, Oksana found Northland in her head. Its seasons – she pined for climate, rather than the weather that persisted here. Its deep cold winters, that turned humans in on each other for companionship, warmth, touch. Its sudden, savage springs, its brief burn of summer, yelling out of the earth, its haunted autumns. Its emptiness – it appalled some, that beyond this tree-line ridge was another, and another, and hundred, a thousand, who knew? Not her. She felt assured that no one had ever walked that way to tell. No one ever would. She found herself squatting on red earth verge beneath a sign for Dr Alimantando, Painless and Kind Dentist, with tears in her eyes.

Her tenancy deposit gave her foraging rights in the roof farm. Hearing voices between the meat-yams and milk-gourds, she discovered a rooftop volleyball match. Team Blue was one short. They had to ask her twice before she could believe that her neighbours really wanted her to play for them. She was very bad. They still managed to win.

The buckyball womb was now a twenty-metre sphere overgrown with a web of white creepers. If you peered through the translucent shell, you could just make out something like the skeleton of an aeroplane. Oksana thought of it as reverse decomposition: out of the soil came ribs and wires, bones and spars. Already they were being nerved and sinewed with control circuits and hydraulics. Anansi was too proud to say, but Oksana knew that this was the pinnacle of his career.

Across the street from the Lucky, outside the Excellent Laundry and Pressing Service, the local proctors were bagging up the bodies from the night's kill. Mombi's filthy little war was escalating: a tip-off that the Runners were making deals over the goose-ironed shirts brought down Lenana and L'Oriente and half a dozen other of Mombi's killer fetish mutant babes with their heavy ordinance.

'Tell me, Kipchobe,' Anansi said as the *maître d'* poured from the Alessi. 'Does your wife do your shirts?'

'No, sir.'

'I think it would be a good thing for her to start.'

The kids were irrepressible. They accosted her in the dirty little forecourt; Team Kiamutugu, with subs: fifteen seven-to-fourteen-year-olds in repro strip with a battered ball and a statement: excuse me but our parents want to know just when we're getting our football field back, because they're demented with us banging balls off people's front doors. The hoods with the guns just looked at them. What they really wanted to know was, what have you got in there, *m'zungu*? She took them to see.

184

The cocoon was now at its fullest, a swollen egg thirty-five metres across; penalty spot to penalty spot. She showed them the trick of looking inside: *see*? The aerofoil skin was going down now, section by section, the froth of buckies locking carbon atoms together into sheets of diamond polymer.

Yes, an aeroplane. No, those wings don't flap. And it doesn't float. How will it get out? Straight up. How? Jet power, kid. Newton's third law.

'Will it burst?' the smallest footballer asked. Oksana looked at the encircling tenement, the washing hanging from the balconies, the old men doing nothing, the pregnant thing throbbing with birth juice.

'You never know your luck,' she said.

It was a good bar. It was dark. It was smoky. It had a radio, no television. It was close enough to walk home from drunk. The brew was good. Kipsang the barkeep would let you run up a tab on the promise of Harambee money. Its clients were mostly men: they might think a *m'zungu* woman drinking on her own improper, but they would never say so. It was a bar of companionable silence, which was a man thing Oksana appreciated.

For the first time since crossing terminum she felt she could stop being a special person and dissolve into the anonymity of the mass. Just being, with other people.

It was good, not having to care. Gaby, Oksana thought, I love you, but it's too much to have to care about you. And Serena: a daughter should not be parent to her mother. You deserve better, kid. You deserve a whole big fucking brightly lit world, for you to keep up in the air, like a football.

Two, maybe three days, Anansi had said. Then she would fly. In her own plane. Fitted to her like a skin. She could not slip the feeling that this was a Faustian gift. Some day, it would cost her everything. But this was the payback. This was the favour returned. This was how the economy worked. No more difficult to build an aeroplane than a half litre of beer. Molecules, moving, falling into place. Just things. Value was a human commodity: Nawa's running the Green Net, Anansi the spinner; Oksana Mikhailovna Telyanina, who knew how to fly.

For the final session Oksana could have had any table she wanted at the Café Lucky. But it was tradition now that they take the corner overlooking the square. She could distinguish occasional pecks of gunfire as Mombi's mercenaries flushed out the last knots of Runner resistance.

'Aren't you taking a bit of a risk?' she asked Anansi. The *maître d'* had already apologized several times for the lack of almond rolls today: 'The security situation, sir.'

'Personally, no. I'm a resource, not a target. But I do question Mombi's wisdom in escalating the conflict. There are other parties involved.'

An armed *pickni* entered the square. 'Flage skin made it and its boy-soldier gun-crew indistinct. They quartered the street, acquiring targets.

'What other parties?'

'The Black Simbas.'

'What do you mean?'

'Black Simba dog-soldiers have been augmenting the Runners.'

'As mercenaries?'

'Our initial thought, but no. We've interrogated prisoners; it seems that the Runners are part of a larger Black Simba strategy.'

'To smuggle Southern bucky technology into the North? The people who fought to build all this? That's insane.'

'So it seems. Unfortunately, our prisoners were not highly placed enough to be party to this strategy. In fact, when we told them what they were fighting for, just before they died, they were most surprised.'

Just before they died. The platoon was gathering in the street beneath. Stragglers emerged from the warren of alleys back of Kanja Road. Some dragged weapons. Others dragged looted things. Some of their bags moved like they held body parts.

'I think I have it,' Anansi said. 'Shamanism and the power of language over reality. Nanotechnology is the language of matter. It is a language-like system; look at it another way, language is a nanotechnology-like system: phonemes make up word make up phrases make up sentences make up everything that exists.'

'And what doesn't exist, what we can imagine. And what can never exist.'

The people were returning to the street. The traders unfolded their stalls; the food merchants fired up their braziers, the barbers set up their chairs.

'So, am I a shaman now?' Anansi asked.

'In a few years you might begin to begin to understand,' she said.

Anansi smiled.

'I thought it might be something like that. But I'll have to find that way myself.'

'We're finished?'

'Today, the egg hatches.'

The people of Kiamutugu had turned out to watch the birth. It had grown in the midst of them, it was as much their baby as Oksana's.

The web of supporting ribs had dissolved in Oksana's short absence. The egg stood alone, a soft translucent bubble wobbling in the wind. Oksana noticed the football kids, up on a high balcony. Maybe it will burst for you, she thought.

Anansi checked birth signs on a palm monitor.

He gripped the command bud tight. The big bubble shivered. Ripples ran over it. There was a high-pitched farting whine and a very bad smell.

The *waMutugu* grimaced.

A little liquid leaked from the bubble's underskirts. It convulsed, seemed to shrink in on itself, draw tight.

The *waMutugu* were transfixed.

The skin split silently. The bubble sagged, but the tears raced over it faster than it could collapse. It fell apart into rags and ribbons. Oksana stepped back to avoid a falling scarf of skin, and a gush of plasticy-smelling liquid. Then she saw not the bursting bubble, but the thing it contained.

'Oh Jesus and Mary,' she said. She clapped her hands to her mouth. 'Jesus and Mary and all the saints.'

The Darwinian wars of the design solutions had taken the AN72F she had loved and turned it into something other. The thing that stood before her on the football field said, that was an Africa plane: I am a Chaga plane. I will fly for you. I will take you anywhere you want, I can do anything you ask, but you must respect me, because I am very, very beautiful.

If you took a hawk and turned it to diamond, it would be the plane. If you took an angel and grafted engines under its wings and fed it steel and fuel until it turned into a machine, it would be this plane.

It was one evil bitch-hawk-angel of an aircraft.

Streamers of birth-skin strewn across it wings and tail dissolved into liquid.

The crowded balconies were applauding and whistling.

Anansi raised an eyebrow.

'Can I?' Oksana said.

'It's yours,' Anansi said.

The hatch opened to her touch. The crew cabin smelled of new, treacly plastic. She avoided the pools and runs of fluid on the floor and wall panels. Oksana touched the sinuous curves of the instrument panels. Liquid: a Dali flight deck, melting, tactile. She started as the pilot seat moulded itself to her contours. The manual control panels reached towards her, arranged themselves in the most comfortable configuration. She reached out to touch them, then gasped, a little panicked, as a transparent green cowl unfolded from the back of the seat, sent its buckies crawling over her scalp, feeling for their partners within. System icons blinked up behind her eyes. *Ready to go*, the aircraft whispered in her skull. *Ready to fly*.

'Excuse me . . .'

Oksana blinked back the control hood. The chair uncaressed her. Anansi was at the hatch.

'May I come aboard, captain?'

'You made it,' Oksana said. 'I see you filled the tanks.'

'What use is an aeroplane with no fuel?' Anansi said. She saw how he looked around the flight deck.

'You didn't know how it was going to turn out, did you?'

'It was an experiment. Usually, my brief is for form, not function. Appearance is everything. Evolving a design solution for fitness of function was something new.' He paused. 'Is it all right?'

She pulled Anansi to her and hugged the proud, shy man. He hated it.

'I'm going to take you on the maiden flight.'

'Good God no,' Anansi said. 'Birds fly, men dream.'

Some men dream birds, Oksana thought. They went back into the cargo hold. Strange cargos. Rare passengers.

'Not knowing what the Harambee require, I couldn't design any interior pallets,' Anansi said. 'When you do know, come back to me.'

'I couldn't, I already owe you . . .'

'You owe me nothing. It is part of the favour.'

'A coffee-maker for a custom airplane; it seems . . .'

'Reasonably insane.'

Oksana found the touch panel that lowered the tail ramp. It opened on the *waMutugu*, cautiously gathered around the marvel. She followed Anansi into the light.

'No,' he said, holding out a forbidding hand. 'You have to take it up.'

Of course, she thought. I have to make it fly. But she said, 'Here?'

'Is it my engineering, or your piloting you don't trust?'

'Both,' she said. Thinking; you want to see it fly as much as I do. She said, 'Get everyone well back.'

The flight deck greeted her like an absent friend. The familiarities from *Dostoinsuvo* only made the new technology more alien. You are in the middle of a housing project in an untested aircraft hoping to take off under a vee-tol system you've never ever flown before.

Trust. Trust your power. Trust Anansi the spinner. Trust your AI. She blinked it on-line, shivered. A new relationship to forge. It wouldn't be *Dostoinsuvo*. It could never be.

'*Svyatiy*,' she said aloud. 'I shall call you *Svyatiy*: High Holy One.'

Acknowledged, *Svyatiy* said, in Russian.

'Power up. Initiate vertical take-off sequence.'

The surge of energy as the plane came to life, system by system, was overwhelming. The neural interface was thrillingly intimate: a coitus of bodies, woman with plane. She let *Svyatiy* penetrate her, melt through her as she melted through it. There was no Oksana Telyanina. There was no *Svyatiy*. There was womanplane. She had wings for arms, engines in her belly. This was true shamanic flying.

The people on the walkways and pulled back into the arches

looked alarmed as first the left, then the right turbofan fired up. Inside the arena of tenements the noise was shattering.

Where to? Svyatiy asked.

Oksana Mikhailovna laughed.

'Take us to two thousand metres,' she said. 'Then I'll tell you.'

On Kiamutugu football field, the noise had gone beyond something you heard into something you felt. Children screamed; *Svyatiy* screamed louder. The onlookers shielded their eyes against the dust kicked up by the downward-pointing thrusters. Tornadoes of litter chased around the pitch, like an elemental cup tie. And then it went up. In the midst of the storm and scream, it was so gentle most people missed it; the release of pressure on the wheels, the sliver of clear blue air between tyre and penalty area. The High Holy One lifted. It was free now; it went up and up, between the houses, turning like a compass needle, hunting direction. The people of Kiamutugu cheered and clapped and waved. The incautious ran on to the football field to squint up at the dwindling aircraft. As they watched it slid into horizontal flight. The aircraft banked over the satellite dishes and solar parasols of Maryfields and was lost to view.

The people went back to their homes. Team Kiamutugu ran out of the tunnel, kicking their ball before them.

39

Shortly after your first period or wet dream, you learn that what you thought was childhood is memories of stun and haunt.

The play had been at night, in the old amphitheatre. It had been in the good days, when Turangalila could do more than shoot up and argue art. Serena remembered she had been carried to the performance. She had curled up on Gaby's knee sucking her thumb, transfixed by the light and music and magic and dancing. The story – the story she understood – had been about a man who had been given eternal life by the spirits on condition that he did not leave a magic valley. Serena remembered that something had scared her about that deal. She could not recall how the play had ended.

She knew how she would end it.

Gaby had no recollection of the play. Not a thing about that hot, haunted night.

The sun caught the aeroplane as it banked out over the ocean. Flash of wings. Serena shaded her eyes, watched it out of sight.

'You come and see me, any time, just let me know, you're always welcome.'

Easy to say before you got into your white diamond aeroplane and took off in a hurricane of sand and flew right out of my life as easily as you flew into it. You made me trust you. And you really didn't understand when I wouldn't get into your plane and let you fly me up on your big wonderful joyride and look down at all the places I'll never fucking get to see, because you're up there and I'm down here on this beach, trapped in the sand with an eternal life. You were hurt when I said no. You dared to be hurt.

Hussein was running the boat down into the green lap to take Doctor Scullabus into Mombasa for his weekly afternoon delight with a half-Indian woman in a bedroom hung with Arab bird-cages.

'Ren.'

'Doc. Hussein.'

The two men watched the aeroplane vanish into the high haze. 'That is a mighty piece of engineering,' the Doctor said. Hussein shrugged. He did not stand with aircraft. 'Piloting for the Harambee, eh.'

'You want to come into town with us?' the Doctor offered.

'No, thanks.' Yes, more than anything, but there would be the big boats there from down the coast and the islands, and there would be the *pujos* and the new concrete railway, and even airships, and there would be the people going somewhere, doing things, having purpose, and she could not bear them rushing around her to their destinations while she remained mired in hot white sand.

The Doctor and Hussein waved as they skipped into the boat

191

and turned the prow south. They paralleled Serena for a few metres, then drew ahead into deeper water.

Serena watched the little runabout until it vanished behind the point. She took three paces into the tide run. The suck of wet sand under her toes enraged her.

'I hate it!' she shouted. Even the sea was traitor. Gaby was swimming again, in the deep night, with the run of the tide. And the bad days were every day now. The cramps, the fits, the shaking, the tears, the whispered apology of mother to daughter. 'I don't want it!' Serena cursed the sea. 'It's not fair, I shouldn't have to. Why do I have to?'

The sea took her curse, and sucked her bare flesh.

Gaby wished she could open her uterus to the ocean. She knew that if she could get the clean, cold salt inside her, it would douche out the sick and the sin and self-disgust. She might rise from the breaking wave like Venus Umbombarded. But she never could, she was too clenched, her lips too firm. She rolled in the blood-warm dark water, relished the slip of it along her flanks and hips.

She half hoped for an attack. Out here it would be swift and savage as a cruising shark. Gone. All ended. All stopped, thank God.

So what is it to be, Gaby McAslan? Death or resurrection?

To be resurrected, you must first die. Jesus, do they ever think of you, Dad and Reb and Hannah and the girls? That husband, what was he called? Marky. Probably fucked off with the mandatory twenty-three-year-old. Jesus, I used to go out with him. He'd be old and fat and slow now. Fat Marky. They'd all be old. And me, floating ageless in blood-heat water. What do you think I am? I bet you can't guess. The worst kind of junkie to be is the junkie in paradise.

She rolled on to her back, arched her back into a float. The moon was dead; the BDO eclipsed. Rivers of light flowed across the great dark; the Milky Way, mica soft; the arching comet-bow out of the mouth of Éa, aimed at the heart of Venus.

Jesus, what a fucking astonishing universe I live in.

I don't want to die.

I just don't want to go on living like this.

Then she heard the music low on the water. The notes were soluble, most she lost in the water, enough remained to draw a thread of melody. That did not matter. What played them did.

Flute music.

Gaby cried out. The music struck her in the belly like a harpoon, reeling her in. He was back. And all that he brought with him. She had always known that he would not stay away for ever.

Gaby turned on to her belly, stroked strongly for the shore.

40

She woke, not knowing what had woken her. A heard thing. Not the storm, though it still bickered under the deep eaves and rattled the roof scales.

'Room lights. Low.'

She stepped from the bed through pools of low green bioluminescence. Pause. Did she hear? The falls were running high on storm water, lifted out of background mutter to fill the wooden house.

'Close shutters.'

Window covers irised shut. She cocked her head.

The dogs were barking in the yard.

Clothes.

It was three-fifteen.

She waited for the doorchimes, waited one minute, two on the clockwork alarm clock. Out in the rain, the dogs yowed again and then went silent. The wind billowed among the dormers and orioles.

Someone out there.

She got the gun. It was a big repro Israeli automatic, throwing fragmentation rounds. They opened up in flight into a broadside of disc-shaped sub-munitions. Three would shred a human body into a jigging red puppet of meat and bone. Standard issue for front-line Harambee operatives.

'Lights down,' she whispered. She loaded and armed as she crossed the darkened living room. The KLA assassin bugs homed in on thermal profile but needed a visual image to initially identify the target. You could only squeeze so much smart into an aircraft the size of a moth. If the controller was still out there, she might buy enough time to hunt and kill him. Her. Teenage girls had the coldest nerves. If it was already in the house, she was dead.

Stop raining. Stop fucking raining. Let me hear.

She turned in the centre of the room, gun down, gripped two-fisted, diving down into her shamanka senses.

Where are you? Let me feel you. Let me touch you. Let me kill you.

Touch.

At the window.

She spun, fired. The pane flew into a hail of shattered plastic. Oksana was through it and out into the rain.

The dogs were barking.

That was why she did not empty the magazine into the sprawling pale figure, belly-scrabbling away from her across the wooden verandah.

The dogs were not dead.

Two steps took her over the night comer. The nose of the gun sniffed at the base of the figure's spine. Female. Baggy gear, plastered to her skin with rain. A full backsack was tangled in the fingers of one hand. An assassin, with luggage.

'Who the fuck are you?' Oksana Mikhailovna said.

The woman turned, combed long rain-straggled hair away from her face.

Serena.

41

I think it's going to work. I believe her when she says it's not safe – like someone says, come and see me any time, and when you take them up on it, they try and blow your head off – but she knows I can't go back. Won't go back. Not while he's there. So, if I can't stay here, then I'll just have to find somewhere myself. That'll do it. She's that age that sees me wrapped up in a blanket in a doorway, or sleeping under a bus in the *pujo* station or giving blowjobs to fat men in taxis. If she wants to think I can't look after myself, that's okay.

I'm not going to think about her. She doesn't need me. She made that clear. She took him back, didn't she? I said, me or him, and she made her choice and now she can live with it.

I think I want this room. I love this house, I love the sound of the falls, because it's like the sea, and I think I would miss that a lot. I love this place, I love the crazy politics, like the seven tribes that run it don't trust each other so every six months they move round, so the ones who run the courts now run the economy, and they move over to run the administration. The nearest thing we ever had to politics at home – I mean, in Turangalila – was like if Jose-Maria wanted people for a new opera and rehearsals clashed with football practice. It gets kind of boring when everyone just does what they want.

Kirinya is never boring. There's always something happening all the time. I never knew there were so many people in the world, and that's just Kitasha. For the first few days I kept looking at all the faces, then I realized that I'd probably never see any of them ever again, and that's kind of a scary thought. I can be invisible here. Disappear into all these people, but that makes it somehow easier for me to be me. I'm not quite sure I'm saying what I mean here. I'm probably still just high on travel, and being here, and not there. I got let off the beach. I remember now what the man in that play chose. He said that one day among new faces would be better than a thousand years looking at the same old ones.

She's got to let me stay.

I really think she will.

I've got to have this room.

November 30

They have this weird thing here. It's called school. Actually, it's called the Harambee Conservatoire, so you can tell what sort of place it is. I don't have to go – you don't have to do anything in Kirinya, but it's where it's at, and everyone who goes there is a diplomatic brat of some kind, so at least I'm not the only non-African face. What I am, is stupid. Uneducated. You try to say, like just because I've never been to a fucking *school* doesn't mean I don't know anything, but their idea of knowing things is knowing facts and the way Gab taught me is to know how to find a thing rather than know what a thing is. But they don't see that thinking for yourself is proper learning. So I'm the dumb white girl beach bum know-nothing. I fucking hate that. Mathematics. Differentiation. I'm not going to be a rocket scientist, what do I need to know about differentiation for? What do you need any math for? Give me time, I can get hold of anything they need you to know, and more, I can show them how it all fits together, this to that to the other, but they won't respect that.

But I'm on the football team – left winger, Gab would be proud – so that gets me some respect, mostly from the boys. I suspect a lot of this is that they want to get off with a white girl. Does everything have to be getting off with someone? I just want to know these guys as people, as friends, but they can't seem to understand that. And the other girls seem to find this threatening, like I'm moving in on their boys – fuck, I'm not even *this* interested in any of them.

ATR doesn't find me threatening. She's different. That's why we get on, I think. That's my name for her, ATR. Her real name is in Luhya, but she doesn't like it. In English it means After the Rains. ATR. Which she does like. She's a year and a bit older but at the Conservatoire that doesn't matter, we're in the same class. Her sister is an Envoy from her people down in Zanzibar and her parents sent her up to stay with her because they thought she'd get a better education in Kirinya. This was before the current KLA shit – how many schools do all the students carry guns? – but she's not going back now. This is the place, she says.

I know what she means.

I've been reading some of the stuff I've written since I came here. That bit where I say about the anonymity of the big city? Don't believe it. The world is a very small place. Seems that ATR and me are sisters. Sort of. Her father was Gab's cameraman back before; she helped him and her ma – and ATR and her big sisters – get out of old Nairobi when the UN declared open city. Her folks have this idea that Gab's like Batman crossed with the Virgin Mary. So why do I not want to tell ATR what I know about Gab? Okya's more a proper mother, and she's out of town half the time flying Faraway someplace or other. No, now I think about it, that's wrong. Maybe I am like ATR, in that we both live with older sisters.

If Okya minds me drinking her beer when she's gone, she's never said.

December 23

Politics is a real weird business to spend your life on. It's the winter solstice, and so Kitasha is full of pick-ups and moped carts and hand drays and Frog Society people going down the street and Antelope Society people going up the street and getting totally mixed up in the middle. Paper everywhere. And at the top of the street, the Stork Society people are moving into the Frog folk's offices, and it's lunchtime and everyone's trying to get something to eat and there are food vendors coming out of the walls. The thing no one but me seems to have noticed is that for the whole week it takes all the societies to pack, move and settle into their new departments, there is no government in Kitasha. I think the reason no one seems to notice is because no one can tell the difference. Anarchy. I love it.

Government, who needs it? That's the thing about being in a Harambee college; it's like those point paintings Mwanza used to do. The closer you get to them, the more they break up. Because I'm round at her place all the time, I see a lot of ATR's big sister Sarah at work. Seems to me being an Envoy is mostly sitting around in coffee houses talking to other Envoys and maybe once a week or so getting enough people agreed on one thing to influence one of the Elders in Great Boma. But it's talking, that's all. The Ras Nungwi village councils talk to their chiefs, the chiefs talk to Sarah, Sarah talks to the Elders, and somehow something gets done. Everything's talking, and if you listen to what they're talking about, they haven't a clue. The big secret of politics that they don't want anyone to know is that they're just making it up as they go along, like everyone else.

Maybe it's because she's so close that ATR doesn't believe in any of it. 'All they do is talk,' she says. Okay, I'll agree with that. 'They never do anything. They can't do anything.' She argues this with the political science tutor. He says, the point isn't how inefficient the Harambee may be, it's the best democratic solution for a society like ours. ATR says, but what good're political ideals if they can't keep their people safe? I think that's a good point, but he never listens to her and she can't make him understand that there's another way of looking at it. I told her about the Merina sending the gunships to protect Aldabra. ATR says that's what the Harambee should be doing, protecting its members, fighting the KLA and all the other Northern-backed armies of national liberation, instead of trying to negotiate with the UNHCR, because in the end, the UN is a Northern thing, the American and the Europeans, and they won't let the Harambee and the Ogun split it down the middle. Doing, not talking.

There's a lot of sense in this. It feels right, I mean, my gun is right there on the table beside me, all I have to do is reach out. And the mites are quiet now, but if they sense anything, they'll come out buzzing. Jesus, I'm sixteen next month, what kind of society is it sixteen-year-olds are followed around by little swarms of interceptor drones?

The gun scares me. I hate it. It feels oily in my hand, and no matter how much I wash, it never goes away.

There's a place ATR wants me to go with her. This is stupid, I feel guilty writing this, why should I? It's not like it's wrong or anything. That's the thing, isn't it, everyone can do what they want? So I'm not going to feel bad about saying that I'm going along with her, tonight.

Oh God. I've just read this and I make it sound like it's sex, or something perverted. It's not. It's just more politics. She says I'd

198

like it – I'd get respect there, like it's for people who think from the neck up rather than the waist down. University students go, but ATR says they're all right, they don't look down on you or anything. They just want to hear your ideas.

If I had any ideas.

ATR's been going regularly; she says they've had all kinds of people to talk, from old school Free Marketeers to New Age Marxists and about five different kind of Anarchists. They've even had the iMerina ambassador to Kirinya. Tonight it's going to be someone from the Black Simbas talking about affirmative action, whatever that is. It'll be fun, honest. So ATR tells me. Okay, I'm going, right?

So, if I don't feel bad, and it's all right and everyone has the right to do and think anything they want, why have I spun Okya this story about going with ATR to the open air cinema?

February 27

Oh God. I think I just want to die. One would be bad enough, but *two*.

Why do they have to? I didn't ask them to. I don't want them to. I didn't say they could, I didn't give them permission to look at me and think, I fancy her.

Men. They have a nerve.

There's Moh, and there's Blue. Moh – Mohammed really, but he's going through an anti-religious phase because his parents are Envoys from Sulema Nation of God. (Can you see them letting their son go out with a white bitch infidel, even if this white bitch infidel wanted to go out with him?) He's my goal-keeper. He has big hands. I'm not sure I like the idea of running around in shorts with him behind me, leering. Blue is eighteen and he's in the Tuesday night group. He's something on the edge of the Black Simbas. He's kind of cute. Problem is, he knows it. I think ATR's a bit miffed about him fancying me, because I think she has an eye for him herself. Actually, he doesn't fancy either of us half as much as he fancies himself.

And they stand around not quite looking but not quite not looking, and talking to anyone but you, and if they catch you looking at them, they look away, like *that*. And if you try to talk to them, they just go stupid, and either melt, or try to look cool in front of their boy friends. But the thing I really can't make either of them understand is that I am not in the least, tiniest, nano-est bit interested. I just don't do the guy thing.

Trouble is (and there's a two-minute gap between finishing that paragraph and starting this one, while I tried to will up courage – hell, it's my book, no one's ever going to read it but me) I don't know what thing I do do. I mean, the people I feel closest to are all women: ATR, Okya. ATR's sister Sarah. Men, I just don't know what they're about. Actually, you're wrong here, Ren. Men you have no problem with. But that's because they don't want to put their fingers inside your pants right off. It's boys. It's not that I just don't like them, I don't even want to like them. Oh Jesus, maybe I'm lesbian. Why did I write 'Oh Jesus'? Would that be a terrible thing? I don't know. I don't know what I am, if anything. I mean, with Okya dragging everyone and anything up her stairs on Saturday night, it's kind of hard to get the background in clear focus.

Shit. I'm me. Serena. Ren. I can be whatever I want to be.

If one of them says anything, tries to ask me anything, I'll either die of embarrassment on the spot, or explode laughing.

May 16

Well, that didn't last. I knew it wouldn't. Isn't there some proverb about getting what you want, and then not wanting it? Maybe I'm mixing something out of other ones. I told ATR if she wanted Blue she could have him, and after six weeks doing everything short of putting her panties in a chapatti and serving them to him with chutney, he asks her out, and next morning, it's all off.

Sex and politics do not mix, I think.

So we're talking a lot again, and going places, and swearing things like we'll never let a *man*, sorry, a *boy* come between us, because we're sisters, right, which is like total bullshit because if I know anything about sex, it's fuck that and fuck everything else. But maybe we can sort of agree on that. Trust the lust.

Maybe that's why I gave her the link. Like a friendship ring, but more intimate. Like saying, wherever you go, I will be part of you. I think I scared her; ATR's okay with me being an isopath – hell, every other person you meet is Adapted in some way or another, and at least I still look *cute* – but when it got to be something of me, inside her, then she got a bit spooked. But she knew what I was saying, and she didn't want to hurt my feelings – it was when I told her I had a link into Okya, but I'd only ever used it once, that she said okay, and really meant it.

Actually, it's not totally true about Okya, I mean, it's true I've only consciously linked with her once, but I sometimes catch flashes, when she's feeling something intensely. Like fucking. And flying. But that's because we live together, we're physically and emotionally close. I don't think it would be like that with ATR.

Anyway, I found a good spot – it's important that you do these things right. There's a place down at the falls, a little bay the water's carved, overhung by carpets of purple moss. I go there when I want to shut out the noise and the people; you can't see the other houses that back on to the falls, and you can't hear them when they come down to wash and swim and do laundry because it's right up against the water. It's my place. It's good. We went there and we sat on the rocks and ATR said what do we do? and I made the cut in my palm and she let me do one in her hand. Then we shook hands, very slowly, and she asked, was that it? and I said, yes. That was it, except for this thing that freaked me a bit, which was a dead dog washed up in the bay. Like *long* dead, so long I wasn't really sure it was a dog, all blue and floating and gassy.

I've just thought of another reason why I gave her the link. I think maybe it's not a guy thing at all. It's politics. Since we started going to the group, she's got very deep into the whole direct action thing. She's dropped right out of the political science course at the conservatoire. When we talk about it, she gets this hard look in her eyes. I don't know where she is. I try not to talk about it. She loves to. Maybe that's the reason for the thing that didn't happen with Blue. It wasn't him she wanted. It was his Black Simbas. And maybe I gave her the link, because I'm more afraid of losing her to the struggle than to a guy.

My father must have had weak genes. Not only do I look like my mother, but I now know I think like her as well.

I get my own way.

This is Ol Orok. It's a resort lodge up on the eastern lip of the Rift Valley. I mean, the lip. Throw a stone far enough, and it goes over the green edge, and a long long way down. It's green and high and cool and the view goes on for ever. I'm up here on the verandah of the guest house, writing this, drinking a bottle of beer. Over to the left, on the landing field, is *Svyatiy*. Down there, having afternoon tea on the edge of the Great Rift, are Faraway, Cimarron, the folk from the Ogun, the white people from the UNHCR.

It only took three months of wheedling to get Okya to take me on a mission, and this one only because she reckons it's safe. But this is me, right, here? writing, and those are world events going on down there over the *chai* and *mandazis*.

This is not how I supposed world events were conducted. But then again, having seen how the Harambee works, I shouldn't be surprised. And the UNHCR people don't look like the enemy ATR tells me they are. They just look like any bunch of *wazungu*. Except one strange thing. Some of them look, well, I can't really describe it, but I think it must be what they mean by *old*.

This isn't making any sense. Start at the start, do it right.

We were flying in and Faraway asked about Gab, how she was, what she was doing. I told him Jim was back. That was all. He worked the rest out himself. I think I may have sounded too brusque. I don't want to look like an uncaring cow; so, I haven't talked to her or sent her a letter or anything in almost ten months, but, like, neither has she, and she is my mother.

But I think Faraway does think I'm a hard bitch. That's because he cares about her. Come on, Ren, be honest. This is your journal, right? He loves her, he wants her, he's dying for her. And she won't have him.

All that stuff I wrote about it being different between boys and men? I'm thinking, maybe I don't know a fucking thing about males, any of them.

Anyway, we come down at Ol Orok – scary, coming in for

vertical landing on the edge of the great rift – Okya chucks me and Faraway out, tells me to check us in, then she's up up and away and I'm watching her disappear out in the big air over the valley. An hour later she's back, down goes the tail, and out walk the Enemy, who are three men and four women and look like I always imagined my aunts and uncles do. And this is how history is made, folks.

(later)

Oh God, I can't write this. It's just going all over the place . . . Okay. Okay. Way later, like way way later, like it's after midnight and the moons are up, and like way way too much to drink at the dinner. Where I was a big hit. I think. I flirted outrageously with Faraway. Oh God, that notorious Ren McAslan! But enough enough enough. It's being there. That's what. Like all the stuff I talk about with ATR, and in the class, the whole being in the Harambee thing – this is what it's about. It is just people talking in the end. Because people meeting, people talking, people face to face, gets things done, and done right. Done right; doesn't hurt people. Doesn't get anyone killed. That's important. That's the most important thing. Oh Jesus I'm getting all teary about this. All it was was a diplomatic dinner that the kid got invited to so she could get a glimpse of how the world worked. And drank too much and got everyone thinking she's fucking the Missionary. Missionary position hah ha!

Wouldn't mind it, though. He is cute. I can see what Gab saw in him. Oh God! This is so perverse! Mother and daughter!

Go to bed Ren. You're babbling.

No no no. You have to put this down, or you'll forget. What it's all about, is that something happened that's going to change the world – UNHCR recognition of the Southern Consensi – and you were there, and you saw them do it, and you saw how they did it, without anyone killing anyone.

November 23

It's a year now. It doesn't seem it. It seems like just a moment in a crowd, or a party you come into late when it's got going, and time blurs. Then you come out of the crowd, and the party ends, and you're on your own, and it's later than you think.

I've been feeling scared for people recently. I'm worried about ATR. We're drifting apart – I've hardly seen her since I came back from Ol Orok and we had the big argument. She's ditched almost all her classes at the conservatoire – her tutor tells me she won't matriculate, as if I can do anything about it. She doesn't even go to the Tuesday night group any more – all they do is talk, she says. When I asked her what she would do, she wouldn't say. But she's been hanging out more and more with Blue and his people on the fringes of the Black Simbas. I don't need to use my link to know she's fucking him; I'm not jealous, I'm just worried where she might end up. She's different: changed; she's hard, everything's certain. She's right, you're only right as far as you agree with her.

I don't want her to get hurt. I want her back. I want my friend, I want ATR.

And I'm scared for Okya. She's hardly at home any more, flying all over the place, setting up this deal behind the Ol Orok agreement. It's very complicated, very delicate stuff. If the KLA or any of the National Liberation Armies, Jesus, even the Americans, find out, then the whole thing is fucked. So Okya's picking up the UNHCR diplomats from the secret rendezvous point and ferrying them straight in to Great Boma. This is real politics. It's tricky and it's messy and everything connects to everything else and one ball knocks against the other. Not simple me right, everyone else wrong, like ATR and her Black Simba friends.

So why am I scared for her? She's tough, she can look after herself, but it's like the closer we get to the big deal – January 1, New Year's Day, the UNHCR will recognize the Harambee, the Ogun, the CAC and Great Zimbabwe and stage a hostage release from Soroti camp in northern Uganda (Did I write 'hostage'? I meant 'refugee') – the higher the stakes are, the more likely someone could get hurt, or it could all go wrong, God knows. Things being tough and looking after yourself can't touch. Whole world stuff. I mean, I've been up with her on some of the pick-up flights – a different landing zone every time – so she thinks it's all right, but I've got this feeling in my head. My shaman sense, she would call it. Okya says to trust it, even if it tells you *wrong*. So I've been linking into her, without her knowing. I'm best attuned when she's meditating, but mostly I get her when she's in flight – aerodynamic, not mystical.

Just checking she's all right.

And I've been thinking a lot about Gaby too. All of a sudden, I'm scared for her. I try to put her right out of my head, for a year I succeed, and when she comes back in, I don't feel angry, or resentful, or hating her. I feel scared for her.

If anything had happened, I would have heard. Wouldn't I? Okya would know. She would. Even though last time they spoke on the phone, just before Ol Orok, they had a terrible argument; Gab accusing her of trying to steal her own daughter, being a treacherous, lying bitch only looking out for herself.

But I'd still like to think she's happy, she's thrown that fucker out, tied a stone to him, thrown him off the end of the pier, she's not doing the stuff (a voice says, how? who's going to help her if you're not there?), that she's got in with good people. That she's thinking about me, wondering what I'm doing, trying to imagine my life, missing me.

I'm not going back. Ever. *Ever*. But if Okya could fix it so we could like talk on the phone, maybe she could visit me?

42

To the source of the Nile, and turn right. The Holy One crossed terminum on a wave of Sondheim Greatest Hits.

Course normal, rate of descent normal, Svyatiy said as it rode the low-power beacon in to Soroti. Still nothing on her radar senses, but Oksana blinked up the stealth configurations. She imagined she could feel *Svyatiy* shiver as it morphed into the green hills of northern Uganda. The satellites would be up and watching.

Flying north. True journey is return. You must go back again, but only as something different. Thirty kays east of the strip was her true destination: the camp. That was what made this the necessary reciprocal of that other flight from that other strip by that other camp.

The missiles still came to her in dreams. They smiled steel grins as they hooked in on ribbons of fire.

Svyatiy continued its descent, wary as a meerkat for predators.

In the co-pilot's chair, Serena blinked off the glidepath display and opened the fuselage camera icon with a whim. Oksana's surrender had been gradual: passenger pallet to flight deck to apprentice navigator, but it had taken every weapon in Serena's arsenal of pleading, huffing, emotional blackmail and charm to wheedle her ass on to the Soroti mission.

'I don't know, it could be dangerous,' Oksana had said. 'If anything happened to you, Jesus . . . You don't know what it's like up there.'

That, Serena thought, is why I have to be on it. And now she was watching terminum drop behind her in the rearview cameras like the surf-fringed edge of a continent into the ocean. She brought in the lateral monitors, sent the line of transformation racing out on either side of her, curving around the belly of the world. Terminum. Equator. The place of division. She was suspended between worlds. She sent her vision forwards, into the landscape towards which *Svyatiy* was flying. Green hills green trees yellow dust brown rivers. And beyond them, green hills green trees yellow-dust brown rivers. And beyond that, and beyond that, and beyond that. The sameness was terrifying. Only at the furthest limit of the cameras' resolution did the colour and contour of the land change, a soft bleach into the dry beiges and dirts of the southern Sahel.

This must be what they call geography, Serena thought.

Svyatiy banked, pivoting on one wingtip. Final approach to Soroti.

The Ogun representative was already on the ground. The UNHCR people were pulling light-scatter sheeting over his aerolyte as *Svyatiy* touched down in a plume of red dust.

'Yes, but how do you find it again?' Robyn Elders the UNHCR woman asked Oksana as her aircraft faded into the landscape. She was a wiry, tired American woman with good hair and good legs powdered with the red dust. She joked when she could, but her humour was nervous. In the Landcruiser was

206

Stig, who was a Swede, and didn't joke. In fifteen years on the beach and one among Kirinya's twelve million, Serena had never seen a pair of blue eyes before and she fell in love with Stig's instantly.

'Way too old for you,' Oksana said to Serena as Stig hastily swung the Landcruiser on to the Soroti road before the satellite horizoned and laid them bare.

'You just want to keep him for yourself,' Serena said. Ngueme, the Ogun man, found this laugh-out-loud funny.

'Your IDs.'

Robyn Elders passed out clip badges. Serena scanned her new identity. Same name, same face, new past, new present, new life. New age. She liked being nineteen all of a sudden.

'Don't wear them. No one ever does, but always keep it on you. You'll probably not get stopped but if they do scan you the information on the chip matches our database. The regular army is totally inconsistent, one week they'll nod you through, next they stop and body-search everyone. They're getting it up the ass from the Bugandan Royal Army, they're the real godfathers, but you won't see them in the camps, ever. Fucking monarchists. Only thing they hate worse than commoners are whites.' She clawed round in her seat, scrutinizing the passengers. She lit on Serena.

'Your T-shirt.'

'What about my T-shirt?'

'It's not right. They'll know. Believe me. Put this on.'

It was too small and it carried a much-faded picture of a pretty-boy band Serena had never heard of. Ngueme looked out at gazelles as Serena wiggled it down over her breasts. The American woman was sniffing now.

'Stop the car.'

She made Serena squat down in the middle of the road. She kicked road dust over her. She rubbed red dust into her hair. She beat it out of the girl's hair and clothes. She said, 'Okay. You smell right now.'

In the car she gave them the update. All the NGOs were in. ICRC, Oxfam, MSF. They'd begun a collective campaign for quarantine controls to be lifted and refugees repatriated South.

'They're getting a heap of shit from the media, especially the

Americans and the British, but then John Bull always was Uncle Sam's chief ass-wiper. The truth is the EU's split; Germany, Scandinavia, the Baltics, agree with a humanitarian stance. France is almost as hard-line as England. Mother Russia says nuke the bastards; at least they're consistent. Middle East, Jesus. The Red Crescent've had their premises burned in Riyadh, Tehran, Baghdad. Their chief in Yemen was shot dead on his way to the mosque for supporting the NGO campaign.'

With the ground prepared, the UNHCR statement would look like a response to popular opinion. In New York and Geneva, diplomatic rhizomes had been sent out towards other branches of the United Nations world-tree. The Human Rights Commission was in, of course. UNESCO had sent back positive vibrations. World Health would come in. The General Assembly was no longer of one mind and voice.

'This is taking a mother of a risk,' Ngueme the Ogun man said. He was a small, thin, intense Bosembélé, a nation of woodcarvers and mystics. Dictators perched in his family tree, two generations down. He had flown fifteen hundred kilometres on the work of the Ogun in a radar-invisible nanotech moth. He liked to drink and joke, and he was a hell of a fixer.

'Trust us. We know how it works,' Robyn Elders said as the Landcruiser abruptly braked to avoid hurtling into the legs of a meandering giraffe. Serena banged the bridge of her nose off blue-eyed Stig's headrest. 'Word back is, we could get a summit. No shit. The Baltics and Scandinavians have made the offer – nothing overt, through channels. They'd never get it past the Security Council, not with four veto powers against us.'

Oksana said, 'Hey, we're just the engineers, you know? I don't do politics, I just fly the aeroplane.'

'We,' Serena said to the UNHCR woman. 'You said "we could get a summit".'

Soroti was a middle-sized camp. Middle-sized, middle-aged, almost respectable. Settled. On its way to town-hood. But that would have graced it with permanency and the lie of camps is that they are temporary even when they are permanent and their inhabitants are refugees, not citizens. They had shelter and water and food from Northern lotteries and telethons, and some health and less education and something approaching a government and an economy. But they were illusion, they did not belong to the Soroti people, they were things given, not theirs by right. Refugees have charity. And they are thankful for it.

In the consideration of the Bugandan Royalists, who were turning this Nile head-water country into a mediaeval squirarchy of armed principalities, the Soroti were not even refugees. They had not crossed an international boundary. They were displaced persons, awaiting the day when the true *kabaka* would lead them back to their tribal lands to re-establish the Ganda throne on the hill of Kilembe.

Subjects have even fewer rights than refugees. They get it from the king, and they are doubly thankful.

Middle-sized and middle-aged and even respectable in its amenities, but Soroti was still a camp. It was still smoke and sacks and shit when the rains ran off the green hills and overflowed the latrines. It was still lining at the hand-pump five times with the plastic bowls and jerry cans, it was still fighting when the blue and white UNHCR food trucks came swinging in and opened up their tail-gates to shovel out the gifts from the people of the United States of America. If you were a man it was still squatting with your friends, it was scavenging for sods and sorts and shards of dead machinery to make something out of to trade, it was being seduced into the gangs and the petty armies because they had weapons and respect. Even from the blue berets. If you were a woman, it was still queueing and carrying and cooking and cleaning the vermin things from around your children's eyes, it was taking them to the needle-men and the sugar and salt nurses and sitting with them as they shat and sicked everything you tried to give them, and when there was nothing else, it was wrapping them in the sheet and giving them to a foreign earth.

It was still Soroti; small, manageable, remote; that in five days would open its gates and tells its people they were free.

The soldier on the gates was in checking humour today but he seemed satisfied that the strangers in the blue and white Landcruiser were the journalists the chips declared them to be. His pilot-style shades kept returning to Serena. In her dusty Boy-Wonderz T-shirt, she stared back. The soldier stuck out his tongue, luxuriously touched tip to upper lip.

The scanners said the room was clean, but a radio was set outside the door, volume up, against human eavesdroppers. Serena soon discovered that conspiracy is a very unexciting thing. Much of the first hour was spent co-ordinating the UNHCR's supply dumps with the Harambee's fleet of *pujos* and trucks and the Ogun's ground and air cover. She mooched around the big room that smelled of new chipboard and coffee. She read all the maps and the reports and the memos on the boards, and looked out of the window at the camp on the far side of the dirt road. Electrically thin boys were kicking a football made from knotted rags in the air.

Now they were talking about the feeder stations across terminum, and the protection force against the inevitable BRA reprisal.

Serena noticed Oksana looking at her.

'Oh, go on,' Oksana said. 'Can you spare anyone?' This, to Robyn Elders.

Cute blue-eyed Stig was spare.

'Stay this side of the wire,' Oksana warned.

Serena did, at first. As she was shown the workings of refugee camp administration – fewer and rudimentary – Serena realized that Stig was as intrigued by her as she by him. Alien to alien.

'So at what point do you stop aging? I mean, you have to grow, obviously.'

'Every time a cell divides, you lose a chunk of telomere. When they get down to a certain length, the buckies read it and kick in.'

'And how long do you . . . will you?'

'Live?'

He nodded. Your hair gleams, Serena thought. Sun-gold North god.

'I don't know. No one I know's died yet. Well, not naturally.'

The thing he really really wanted to show her was under the infirmary, a windowless cinder-block primary school that smelled of antiseptic and death.

'What is this?' she giggled as he led her down the dark stairs into the shit-stinking cellar. 'Is this going to gross me out?'

He flicked on the light.

'Oh my God!' Serena shrieked.

Upright and unabashed, a forest of wooden penises stood erect on the floor of the cellar. They were ranked in order of length and girth. Serena could not shake the impression that they had grown from the earth floor like fungi. After sixty, she gave up counting.

'Four thousand,' Stig said. 'This was the central sex education visual aid repository for Uganda. HIV, you know? How to fit a rubber.'

'Some of them are, um, big.'

'Tribal vanities. We're thinking of selling them. We've had offers.'

'I'm sure,' Serena said, awed.

Once again in the sun, she said, 'I can't imagine what it's like to live somewhere with only three hours of daylight.'

'Why do you think I'm here? No, it is bad. The suicide rate goes away up in the winter, because of the dark. But in the summer, there's no night at all.'

'Weird world,' she said, then, as the soldier with the shades opened his gate to let a convoy of seven trucks enter the compound, she asked, 'Do you think it's going to work?'

'The release? Yes. I do. I think it's like an avalanche, one small movement starts another, and it gets bigger, and then it all starts to slide. We're just the ones who'll start it.'

'What's an avalanche?' Serena asked. When he told her, she said, 'Snow can kill people?'

'Snow kills.'

She looked across the wire, where street-boys were staring at her hair and tits as unashamed as wooden penises. 'Could I, um, would you, I mean, I'd like to see what it's like? In there.'

She thought he looked cute, the way the sun caught him when he was in two minds what to do.

'Okay,' he said.

There were twelve cups of coffee on the big table in the big prefab hut that smelled of chipboard, and Northerners and Southerners were mired in caffeine-amplified contention. It was a timing thing. Ogun warriors would only be mobilized if the UNHCR could guarantee them safe passage through Soroti. The UNHCR could only divert the Buganda once they were certain of the protection force's movements.

211

Oksana stretched arms above head. Enjoy the pull on the joints. Jesus and Mary, diplomacy makes you feel all your years. She locked. She heard something, she thought: an insect buzz. A disturbance in the air. While Ngueme and Robyn Elders teased strategy out of compromise, she went to the window. People, shit, smoke, poverty, death. Nothing. Back to the table. Where were Serena and the Swede-boy?

'Once the corridor's secured, we can move as fast as you like,' Oksana told the people at the table. 'Eighty per cent of the transports are already at Gombe, the rest will be there by this time tomorrow. We just need to know that it's safe to move.'

Robyn Elders looked at Ngueme. Ngueme looked at Oksana.

And she heard it again. Everyone heard it. Not an imagined thing, or an angry insect. Helicopter rotors, spinning in towards the camp.

Oksana Telyanina ran to the door.

Within ten metres of the gate, Serena was surrounded by children. At first Serena found the reaching hands animal and frightening because she did not understand their language. 'Your hair,' Stig said. They had never seen anything like it. They wanted to touch it. It made them smile. One touch was enough, with a coy laugh and smile from the toucher.

The children drew the women, and the women drew the men. The women were curious but reserved. The men were aloof, cool. She wondered if they sensed she was an alien. She might be sweating off her musky dust bath. These men might smell her.

'Actually, they probably think you're a vampire,' Stig said. 'Round here they have red hair and green eyes, and they don't shrivel up at a touch of sun.'

Perhaps I am, Serena thought. A feeder off hunger and disease. I was the one wanted to see what it's like in a camp.

What it was like, was Kirinya.

The plastic and card shanties felt as new-sprung from the soil as any Kitasha neighbourhood. The rows of tents gave a familiar sense of impermanence. The crowds, the smell of shit, the pools of water, the red mud and the people, doing things together: cooking, feeding, gathering food and fuel, washing clothes and bodies, reminded her of the crowds she watched on the water steps below the falls. The alleys, the clusters of shanties, the rows of tents were all shifting, changing form and substance as their citizens scavenged new roofs, new rooms, whole annexes, little workshops or stalls or drinking holes. The camp was an organic, growing thing. Serena felt right at home in Soroti.

Then the helicopters came. Their flight was low and fast and hard, in over the green hilltops north of the Soroti camp, sweeping down into the valley, ahunt. At first Serena did not know what the noise was. She had only ever seen images of helicopters, never heard their sound. Their blades seemed to strike the air so hard it must bleed. She stood amazed as the five strike helicopters thundered over the alleys, scattering the smoke plumes. They were purple and crimson Chaga-flage; they carried lion's head symbols on their lean flanks. Serena waved to the helmeted, mirror-visored pilots. She turned, hand shading eyes, to watch as they wheeled high in the air over the cinderblock supply huts and spun on their rotors to dive in across the camp.

It was then she noticed the pod clusters under their stub wings.

The people were running before the first missile smoked away from the launcher. They hit Serena like a wave of bricks: she screamed, almost went down, knowing that to go down would be death. She reached for the sun. She seized something, pulled herself up, saw Stig swirled away in an eddy of bodies pouring down a narrow lane between refuse-shack shanties.

She understood avalanche now. A wave of bricks. Or bodies.

Then she heard the screams over the all-devouring hammer of the helicopter engines.

The wave of bodies stopped. Serena was looking up when she saw the lead helicopter launch two more missiles from under its wings. They curved down towards the east end of the camp where they burst in a spray of glitter.

Out of the glitter came screams like she had never heard before.

Serena found gaps in the crowd's confusion to push herself towards where she thought she remembered the gate to be. She pushed past mothers, slipped between men, shoved children out of her way, kicked and punched as the fear of the mob found voice in a rising gibber.

213

The helicopters were stationary, hovering in a goose-skein vee. They were firing continuously now, pouring missiles into the east end of the camp.

The crowd broke. It was raw survival now.

Serena ran. She did not know where she ran, but she must run. Not to run was to go down. She saw an old man go down, saw his hands raised as hard muddy feet came down on his bones. She saw a young woman with her face all blood flailing with her arms, trying to clear passage. She heard a young man's voice, almost singing with fear: *they're dead they're all dead. There's no one left back there*. She heard the hammer of the helicopter engines change pitch and knew without daring to look that they were changing station, acquiring new targets.

The dynamic of the crowd swept Serena to its edge, then cast her off into an empty laneway that veered between huts. Serena ran where it led. Her foot caught something low and treacherous. She rolled, winded, stunned. She stared at the thing that had tripped her. It was a translucent spike, rammed into the ground, edged like a barbed arrow. She tried to pull it free. She cried out. It had drawn a long line of blood across her fingers and palm.

A diamond blade, ten centimetres long. In its millions, it shredded wood, concrete, soft human flesh like rotted sacking.

The engine noise was as sudden and shocking as an explosion. Serena jumped up. The helicopter bore down on her. Its crimson belly passed over her, so low as to ruffle her long red hair, almost affectionately.

You can live, it said.

On the verandah of the camp office, Oksana Telyanina saw the helicopters turn in the air above her and slide in over Soroti. As the missiles leaped from the weapons pods she was running towards the wire gates and the guards looking at the guns in their hands and each other and the helicopters in the sky and unable to connect any of the three. When she heard the first missile explode, it was like it had detonated in her cold and vacant womb. She gasped, gutted, hysterectomized. Target acquisition radars washed over her e-m senses like tongues of fire.

She hit the wire at full speed, clung to it with claw fingers.

'Serena! Serena!'

'Oh Christ oh Jesus oh God oh fuck,' Robyn Elders was saying over and over and over. To the guards: 'Open the gates, open the fucking gates, get them out of there!'

'Serena!'

No way could she be heard.

'Get the fuck out of here!' The American woman was strong, she tore Oksana away from the wire. 'The Bugandans know! They'll fucking murder everyone!'

'Serena's in there!'

'She's dead, man. Don't you understand? She's dead.'

'No!'

She pushed the woman away from her, harder than she needed, hard as she felt. She went sprawling in the red dust. Oksana ran along the fence, screaming Serena's name at the stampeding bodies. Futile as a spark in a blizzard.

Other voices. Go within. That night, the Diamond Jim night, she watched through you, and you knew. You felt it. Deep down, does the river run both ways? Can you make her feel you? No words in that river. It speaks seeing and being.

Breath hammering in her lungs, Oksana forced herself to stop, turn towards the camp. The helicopters were moving over it like slow, annihilating angels. Missiles flew and burst like fireworks. The cascade of glitter did not fool Oksana Mikhailovna. The fuckers were using anti-personnel flèchettes on civilians. No. Don't look. Don't see. Go within. She visualized herself, standing pressed to the wire. She drew in buildings, vehicles, background: *touch me, feel me, see me, be me.*

A shift in engine pitch. The helicopters were moving to secondary objectives. Targeting cameras locked on to the UN truck pool. Drivers leaped from their vehicles. The missiles blew them all away in a spray of flesh and shivered metal.

And *touch.*

Serena stared at the hand. It was all that remained intact of the human. The hand was white, heavy, a man's hand, tanned brown. Blond hairs on the back.

Stig's hand.

She turned. She ran. She did not know where. She did not

know how the flying blades did not find her and flay her to nothing. She ran as if charmed, invulnerable, slipping between bodies, hurdling obstacles that would bring her down. But wherever she ran, there seemed to be a helicopter waiting, and the bright burst of a missile ahead, and a huge cry followed by a more awful silence before the crowd could re-form in a new direction.

She was lost. She would never get out.

As she thought that, she was somewhere else, someone else; a woman, tearing at the wire. Oksana.

A body banged into her, sent her spinning into a tent that collapsed under her. Serena reached within and opened the link into Oksana Telyanina. She superimposed two visions, her own, Oksana's. She knew where to go now, how to get there. If the helicopters would let her.

The soldiers were chasing the people out, *come on come on come on*, eyes on the sky. They scattered into the open country, running, dragging children, carrying the maimed and the dying. Two helicopters held back to work over the remains of Soroti. The other three peeled off to hunt down the fleeing. One locked its nose on to a Red Cross Landcruiser and blew it to nothing. Oksana saw Robyn Elders start to run for the UNHCR 4x4. She made it no further than the bottom step. The air-burst sent her, the whole side of the prefab raving up in a spray of fragments. Dirt and debris and diamond knives rained down on Oksana as she fought to hot-wire the Toyota.

'Start you bitch whore fucker!'

Flash: Serena, the gates within reach.

'Start, fuck you, start!' She cursed the car in all her tongues, and it started for her.

The west end of the camp was burning: fuel from the destroyed truck point. Oksana swung the Landcruiser through tributaries of fire; it clung greedily to her wheels before earth snuffed it out. There.

'Ren!'

For a second Serena did not know what she was seeing. Outer and inner visions coalesced. There was a car. There was a woman calling her name.

Oksana hauled her in by a fistful of BoyWonderz T-shirt. She floored the pedal. The Landcruiser spun away from the torrent of people flooding out from the gates. In the rearview, Oksana saw a helicopter move slowly over the splintered wreckage of the camp to seal off that escape route. She swore under her breath.

Serena watched the blood drip from her fist into the footwell. She said, 'Stig's dead. I saw him. I saw his hand. I touched his hand.'

'They're all dead. They want to kill everyone. They don't care. They want everyone dead.'

Oksana wrestled the big white Toyota over the ruts on to the road west. She pushed it up to ninety.

'Come on come on come on you bitch.'

'Where's Ngueme?'

'I don't know. I don't care.'

'And that American woman. Where is she?'

'She's fucking dead. They're all fucking dead. Don't you understand?' Glance again in the rearview. The helicopters were moving over Soroti like monstrous mosquitoes, greedy for blood they dare not touch. Food too rich for machines. Every few seconds one would casually, almost indolently, let off a missile.

Glance at Serena. God, the kid is out of it. Eyes of lead. The shakes are going to start soon. You're surprised? She was in there. Jesus and Mary, this road was never this long coming in.

'If we can get to the plane we'll be all right.'

'All right?'

'If we can get airborne, we can outrun them. We'll be all right.'

'Airborne?'

Glance in the mirror again. The helicopters were widening their circle. Don't see me. Kill someone else. Kill some poor fucker refugee family, kill them all, blow them into rags, but don't kill me.

'Jesus and Mary God! How did they find out? We were tight, I know it. Who told them?'

'Told them?'

'The Buganda Royal Army, girl. The fucking kings and princes. In their mother-fucking American Kiowa attack helicopters.'

217

'Americans?'

'Oh Christ.'

The words were too banal to pierce Serena's shock. It was the flat tone of inevitability that made her look up from the slow drip of her blood on to the rubber mats. Hunted things run down by the pack, had they voices, would speak like that at the end. She looked behind Oksana's eyes, saw what she saw in the mirror: the helicopter dip away from the others and swoop after them.

'Can we beat it?'

'We can.' But as she said it, Oksana knew that they could not. It was too fast, too certain. Already it had covered half the distance between camp and car. *Svyatiy* was too far. She glanced at Serena: *do you see behind my eyes, do you listen behind my ears, do you hear the lie in my head?*

Yes.

The helicopter was closing fast, nose down, tail high.

Then you know what I am going to do.

Oksana had noticed the dry river cut on the drive in, the hollow rumble of the wheels over the concrete culvert. She slammed the Landcruiser to a halt.

'Out.'

'What?'

Jesus and Mary, they were fast. No time to argue. Oksana leaned across Serena and opened the door.

'Go. Get out. Listen, Ren, the code is "Oh Holy One, preserve us now, and in the hour of our death". The plane will fly itself. Go.'

'Okya . . .'

Serena found herself sprawling on dirt. She scrambled to her feet but the Landcruiser was gone, plunging across country in a high, proud plume of dust. Follow me, fuckers. Here I go.

'Okya!' Serena screamed, a big bare target in the middle of the plain dirt road. The helicopter. It was on top of her. She tumbled down into the dry river bed, crawled into the culvert. Culverted things fled from her. She pressed herself to the earth. The helicopter passed over in a thunder of wings. The ground shook. Serena scrabbled out the far side of the ditch, ran up on to the road.

'Okya!' she cried a third time.

Swearing and blessing by all her holy ones, Oksana Mikhailovna Telyanina drove the Landcruiser like a crazy shamanka, out of her head among the twenty-seven heavens.

'Come and get me you fucking fucks!' she shouted at the purple blood-bloated thing hovering in her mirrors. She threw the 'cruiser left, right: the helicopter dodged and weaved behind her, never sure enough to kill, never quite lost.

'Enough, all right? Enough!' she yelled. A touch of the brake pedal. Oksana Telyanina baled out. The ground hit her harder than she had ever been hit in her life. She rolled, she bounced, things cracked, pieces of her broke and bled. She screamed, she yelled as the Landcruiser plunged onwards. Moments. She only had moments. She fought herself to her feet. Hurt bad. Hurt very bad. Very broken, but she could manage a run.

There was a big shade tree in front of her. It stood apart from a small wood. It was not a baobab, it was not the tree where man was born, but she knew if she could reach it, she would be all right. Forests were her element. It would take her under its branches. It was the tree that was greater than the tree where man was born. It was the world-tree, the universe herself. She ran towards that tree. The tree was all she could see. The tree was all that mattered. Not the swelling howl of Pratt and Whitney turboshafts. Not the prickle of presence in the back of her head that she knew was Serena, unable to leave her.

'Get out of my head!'

No time for goodbyes. The tree was all.

Dust swirled up from the earth around her. Oksana dragged herself towards the healing tree. The engine sound rose to a crescendo, and held.

Oksana Mikhailovna stopped. She turned to face the hovering helicopter.

'Do it!' she yelled.

Serena crouched at the lip of the dry river. Every fibre in her needed to run, linked to Oksana's hopeless flight. She did not. She dared not. But she could not break the link. She could not look away. She saw the hovering helicopter. She saw the short line of fire leap out from under the wing of the Kiowa. She saw the bright flash, and the woman's body leap and jerk into a

219

puppet of red flesh, and the puppet explode into a crimson spray as the leaves and branches of the lone tree whirled up in a sudden storm.

She saw the white light, and the bottomless dark beyond.

The helicopter reared up, banked hard and flew away into the north.

AK47 Hour

43

There were five things in the porcelain jar: a small leather sack of herbs, a spirit catcher from a bedroom window, a pebble of black volcanic glass, the seeds of five trees, a toy plastic aeroplane. They were not the remains of Oksana Telyanina. Nothing remained of Oksana Telyanina.

Being African, and familiar with death, the drinking friends put the jar in the hole and quickly threw in the earth. It was a short job. Kipsang the barman patted the ground flat with the back of the shovel. No one spoke on the run-off where the Gichichi road turned down into the valley of Murang'a. No one laid flowers or read poems or pieces of scripture. No one eulogized. There was nothing to eulogize.

A bus passed, slowly grinding down the dog-legs to the valley below. The passengers stared at the brief vision materializing out of the fog, the black and white figures at the side of the road. Then they were gone. The bus braked to make way for a fast car that suddenly loomed in front of it, headlights blazing. Car and bus grazed past each other. The car drove up the line of official Harambee vehicles and the taxi that had brought the people from the bar. It stopped just above the off-run. Two women and a man got out. One woman was dressed in a long rubber raincape, the other in a black leather trench-coat. The man wore a white *jellaba* and flip-up shades. He was barefoot. The women remained by the car; the man, without speaking, walked to the fresh turned earth, knelt down and touched his hand to the bare soil. Then he stood up, bowed slightly to the people gathered there and went back to the car. It turned a little up the road and came back down. Its headlights swept across the funeral party.

The party was breaking up. The bar folk were shaking hands with the airfield people and going back to their cars and taxis. Faraway shivered.

'Come on, Gaby. We should go.'

'In a minute. I have to talk to Serena.'

Have to. Don't want to. Afraid to. They had held to their sides of the circle while the people from Kipsang's Bar dug the hole, Gaby from fear, Serena from anger.

'Serena . . .'

Serena seized Gaby's hands, turned them over, wrists up.

'So, where is it then? Here?' She stabbed three fingers into Gaby's breast bone. 'Here?' The fingers lunged for the hollow of the throat. Gaby caught the hand, held it, let it go.

You are too much my daughter, she thought. I pity any man you ever have, because you are your most beautiful in anger. You are absolutely stunning. And then she thought, *men*, and, *since when did you become a woman?* Gaby said, 'It's just me. Nothing helping me. No chemicals. No patches. I don't do them any more.'

'You said that before.'

'It's true. Really.'

'You said that before too.'

Serena shook her head, turned to go to the Harambee car where Sarah waited. Tembo's daughter, Gaby thought. What is it that ties us together, that pulls us together however far we travel, and kills us?

'He's gone, Serena. I threw him out.'

She paused, but did not turn. You are going to make me say it, Gaby thought. You are going to make me humiliate myself at my friend's funeral. All right. If that's what you need.

222

'He was cheating, he was sleeping around. But that wasn't why I threw him out, Serena. I always knew he had other women, right from the start.'

'Other women,' Serena said. 'Like me.'

Gaby grimaced.

'He was sleeping with Sudha. But it was more than that. Ren, he was hurting her. Do you understand me? He was hurting her, like he hurt me. And you. Do you understand why he had to go? They had the hurting.'

Serena whirled and Gaby realized that what she had seen before had not been anger.

'She's dead!'

'Yes. Serena, you are not the only one hurts here, you know? You are not the only one who has lost someone you loved. I loved her. She was my . . . my soul.'

'She was my mother!'

'Serena, no.'

'You should have died; it was your place, your time and she took it. It should have been you. She should have had a million tomorrows, and now she has none, because of you.'

'Serena . . .'

She was running for the car.

'Yes!' Gaby shouted at her back. 'She should have! I should have! I wish I had!'

Serena got into the white car. Sarah shrugged, shook her head. Doors slammed. They were gone.

'Jesus, I should have. Can't she hear that? I should have.'

'Give her time. She doesn't understand it. You didn't see her when the plane brought her back to Nyerere. She felt her die, through the link. It was like her dying herself. And she has nothing to mourn, not even bones or ashes. Nothing. She is very young, Gab.'

'I thought, maybe . . .'

'Come on. There is nothing for you up here, and it is cold and miserable.'

In the car, Faraway offered her a silver flask. Gaby sniffed at the open neck. Arak perfume stung the back of her nose. She took a deep swallow. It burned deep, but it was not the water of life.

'Faraway, about, you know, earlier. I'm sorry.'

She had been glad they had sent an airship. It had given her time to try and put all the broken things in order. But when she saw it settle on the same headland as that other Harambee ship, the panic had struck: what if it's him? What if he's come in person to tell me he's sorry? Too soon to face him, after everything. She had almost chickened. Then she had thought, what is it worth, finally banishing the man and memory of Diamond Jim, if you are going to sit like a frightened chicken, unable to face the world? That had given her the courage to carry her bag up the loading ramp and meet whoever was at the top of it. Who had been a politely sombre political kid who, she could smell, had no notion of death.

The young never think they can die.

She had stood by the window and watched the many-coloured lands of the Harambee scroll under her and seen another landscape: the tree-scattered savannah, the dust of moving animals, the cloud peeling back from Kibo, the snows of Kilimanjaro revealed. It had been Oksana's plane that had flown her back from Tsavo West, that first time, when Shepard had taken her up and shown her another world. Another world that was now this world. She saw another dusty plain, marked with white lines, goalposts at either end; Oksana Mikhailovna in her borrowed Team SkyNet shirt and boots and denim cut-offs over green cycle shorts, arguing herself into a yellow card. She saw the Antonovs lined up on Wilson airfield, and the Sibirsk pilots conga-ing between them, singing 'Consider Yourself' from *Oliver*. She saw the bar in the PanAfric hotel, and this-year's-model Out of Africa look clinking Tuskers with Siberian shamanka lesbian chic. Both of them bluffing. Both of them virgins. She thought of Oksana's need for nation, for lives to keep her warm and tell her she existed. She thought of her bottomless capacity for sensation. She thought of the woman's ferocious lust, unfulfilled.

'Big cocks and vodka,' she had said, and closed her eyes and expected tears. They disappointed her.

That was why, when she saw him waiting for her on the field, she ran to him and beat him on the chest, shoulders, arms, belly with her fists. Pounded him. Hammered him, with the same strength she had summoned to drive Diamond Jim out of the Sea House, along the lanes of Turangalila, on to the main road north, south, anywhere but here.

'You killed her!' she shouted into Faraway's face. 'You knew the Bugandans knew, you sent her to her death.'

He let her hurt him until her strength ebbed enough for him to grasp her wrists and stop her.

It was over and the discreet security men were moving out of the cover of the fog to their cars. Faraway said, 'Driver, take us home.'

Gaby looked out at the grey cloud, now eddying, thinning as the car dropped down the Gichichi road. Through rents she glimpsed the villages of the valley, the Chaga dark and lugubrious under the unseasonable overcast. Other world. My world.

'Faraway, that question.'

'What question?'

'The one Okya answered for me. It won't go away.'

The car was lean and powerful, it took the sharp bends as smoothly and sleekly as a speedskater.

'Gaby, I do not think this is the right time to be making a decision like that.'

'It is. I'd be making it even if . . . if she hadn't died. I think I'd already made it. This just . . . just sealed it. Put the sign on it. Does your offer still stand?'

'It does, if you want it.'

'I want it. I want it because I want my daughter never to look at me again like she looked at me over that grave. Do I have to tell you more?'

'You did not even have to tell me that.'

They came out of the clouds into the rain-dirty valley. A steady downpour was dropping out of the heavy cloud. The people abroad on the road huddled under umbrellas and plastic sheets as they kicked through the streams of dirt-red runoff.

'Faraway, I'm going to need your help with something.'

'What is it?'

'Did you hear what I said to Serena, about the, uh . . .'

'That you don't use the patches any more.'

'Yes. But.'

'But you're not over them.'

Gaby looked at the rain.

'No. You've seen . . .'

'I know. I know people who can help.'

'Whatever it takes, Faraway.'

'It will be bad.'

'I'm supposed to say that.'

'Gaby, you've said enough for one day.'

In the front seat, Faraway's aide sat upright, as if stung. He touched fingers to temple.

'Boss. BBC World Service.'

Uninvited, Gaby scanned the frequencies. The Oxford-African Swahili was oddly comforting, delivering its measured and weighted vowels from London into her brain. The world is a trustworthy place while the British play *Lilibulero* at the top of the hour.

The UNHCR had come out.

Faraway was on his mobile. Gaby changed stations, hunting for the FM satellite link. For the first time since the birth of Éa she listened to the voice of SkyNet World News.

' . . . UNHCR and United Nations Human Rights Commission have issued a joint statement calling for the demilitarization of the I-Zone, the scaling down of the UN protection force, and the repatriation of displaced persons into the Chaga states,' the unfamiliar presenter said. It sounded like Distinguished Silver Male speaking. Younger Professional Babe would follow through: 'The United States and Russia have already condemned the statement and have requested an emergency plenary session of the UN Security Council to repair the sudden enormous rift in international security. However, several members have indicated that they will either abstain or vote against any resolution condemning the UNHCR. For the reactions from the Interdiction Zone to today's announcement, we go over live to Lisa Kropotkin in Juba, Southern Sudan.' Who would be windswept and squinting and trying to keep the local kids from waving and grinning into the camera while her Tembo fought with glare and white balance and her Faraway rehearsed the officers in the blue helmets to speak English rather than Military.

The sudden spike of emotion surprised Gaby. It thrust up

through the Lisa Kropotkin in Juba's voice, shattering it. Jealousy. And it felt very warm and fine.

44

The rain had surprised everyone. It was not the season for it, but the weather-prophets all agreed that it would be here for a week at least. Faraway was glad of it. It meant that coffee would have to be taken indoors and not in the garden, as was Tikaram the healer's custom. The tree that grew there would not normally have offended him; it was different when you knew what was hanging in that one, enormous pod.

Tikaram the healer was young, gifted, fecund, third-generation Indian. His annular house, which encircled the healing tree, was filled with children and gods. One of his daughters served coffee on a hand-hammered Benares table from a copper pot.

'She's stabilized,' he said. 'I've replaced her blood with the usual diagnostic bucky matrix; her system should be clean in about five, six hours. It's the psychological dependence I can't do much about. I can keep the pain and the other physiological symptoms under control; otherwise, she has to go through it herself.'

'She's conscious in there?'

Tikaram the healer rolled his eyes up the gilt cornice. A look elsewhere. The fullerene mix he had sluiced into Gaby's bloodstream was feeding medical data to his auxbrain. He listened to voice of her blood.

'Some of the time. She's sleeping right now. She had a seizure an hour and a half ago. Her liver and kidneys are in pretty poor shape.'

Faraway found this patient/doctor relationship altogether too intimate to be professional. Too vampiric. The intimacy of the fluids. In the car coming down the mountain, when Gaby had said 'whatever it takes', his first thought had been Tikaram the healer. Nuya's boy had been within a kiss of death. The allergy to the buckies switching on through his body had been total. Tikaram had saved him. Then he had remembered how the healer had done it, and his second thought had been *she is desperate, but not that desperate.*

'Faraway,' Gaby had said, clenching and unclenching her hands spastically, 'there is a year of my life most of which I don't remember, and what I do, I wish I didn't. You understand?'

'Gaby . . .'

'I whored for those things, Faraway. I whored and he watched.'

At the house in Ena, the healer's colourful children had come splashing out to greet the new client. By then the shakes had started. Gaby left a ribbon of sour thin vomit on the liveskin upholstery of the Harambee limousine.

Faraway set his empty coffee cup down.

'How much longer?'

'That's up to her.'

'Can I see her?'

'Certainly.'

The youngest Tikaram daughter offered him an oiled paper umbrella. He declined and went into the circular garden and let the rain run down him. It streamed down the slick black skin of the healing pod. Strange fruit. He shivered, not from the chill rain. The shell was as shiny and hard as the carapace of a beetle, but it had taken on the contours of the woman within: curve of hips, waist, thighs, breasts, skull. The skull shadows suggested a long scream.

Gaby, what have I done to you?

The tree was a crook-backed gantry of pipes and fans and pulsing organs; the pod hung from its hooked fingers like a mummified puppet. Too many similes, too heavy metaphors in this. Deaths, rebirths, metamorphoses. Think: there is a woman in there. A woman you care for. Faraway's black hand touched the black skin of the pod. No warmth, no movement, no sign of life, or love.

Why do you do it for this woman? he thought. She destroys

228

with a touch, she hurts without thinking, she does not love you. She never loved you.

But you love her.

He left a trail of wet soily footprints across the hand-woven carpets on his way to the official car and the official world. The children descended with mops and cloths to clean them up

Naomi was awake when he came back from the bathroom. He sensed that she had been since the call came, while he got up, while he called the car, dressed quietly, made ready: watching, waiting for him to say what she knew.

No, he thought. I won't play that game. But that was just another game. Games was all it had been for a long time now. Games and spaces. He could not remember when he started looking forward to the court circuit taking her upcountry. She had never said that she savoured the increasing hours his work kept him away from the house. She never would say. No one said anything. The purest game of all is the one in which no one makes a first move.

He caught sight of himself in the mirror: Mr Missionary of the Harambee in his tailored white suit. He looked at the very beautiful woman wrapped up in the pure white throw on the low wooden bed. He thought, how can you be a warrior for your tribe when you are a ball-less boy at home?

'I'm going to her.'

'Of course. She needs you.'

Fuck you, Faraway thought in English. But he did not say it. To say it would demand a passion he no longer felt. He said, 'She's very weak, she's going to need a place to recuperate.'

He knew she would not argue. She no longer had the passion to fight. But he knew she was grateful for the excuses he was handing her. She said, 'If you bring her back, I won't be here.'

'All right,' Faraway said and went out to the waiting car.

It was after midnight, but the house of Tikaram was roused. A different child umbrellaed Faraway in from the car. Another prepared coffee and sweet eats. Gaby huddled in a blanket by a big fire of wastepaper bricks. A third kid was towel-drying her hair. Gaby smelled of washed-off sickness. A flick of Faraway's eyes dismissed the girl.

'Oh, hi,' Gaby said. Her smile and voice and face were wasted thin. Three days in hell had left her skin translucent, her eyes sunken and black. Her hands were hooks, veiny and fibrous. The years the buckies suppressed had caught up with her. She saw how Faraway looked at her. 'Tik says I'll look better once the bucky count goes up again. You should see what that bastard did to my bloodstream.'

'How are you?'

'Wretched. I haven't felt this shit since, you remember that time in Unit 12? That bad. No. I was all alone in that thing. . . . There was stuff I found in there, things I met . . . You don't want to know. I don't want to tell you. Jesus, it's cold.'

She struggled to her feet. She slapped away Faraway's offering hand.

'I'm okay, right? I am okay.'

She shuffled closer to the fire.

'I can't get heat into me. Apparently I can catch cold really easily. And my auxbrain/mebrain linkages are kind of shaky. He had to rewire most of my hippocampus.'

The heavy blanket fell open. Gaby was naked beneath. Naked, starved. Bones, tendons; bruises. New lacerations, old scars. Suddenly moved, Faraway slipped in beside her, under the blanket.

'Hey,' she said, surprised, then pressed her cold, shivering flesh against his heat.

Later Tikaram himself, satisfied with the readings from his portable diagnosticator, laid Gaby out in front of the fire and massaged strength back into her muscles. Faraway watched with twenty-four per cent envy as the healer stripped down to his dhoti and worked his way up and down Gaby's spine. He clenched inside when she said, weakly joking, 'Remember, I used to do this for you?'

He wondered what the other woman was doing back in their dark wooden house.

'So, what have you got for me to do?'

'Gaby, you have to get better.'

'Work is the best therapy. Hell, I've got a lot of catching up to do.'

Faraway sighed. Tikaram the healer smiled as he dug his fingers into Gaby's thin ass.

'All right then. You always were an impossible woman. What you have to do is win the hearts and minds of a continent.'

Tikaram's fingers said, *on your back, clean woman.*

'There has been widespread reaction in the North. The EU, with the exception of Britain and France, is leading the call for an international conference between us and the so-called front-line states.'

'Three days' cold turkey is a long time in politics,' Gaby said.

'The US leads the opposition in the UN. It can only do so as long as its involvement in the Soroti massacre is kept a secret from its own people.'

'That's the cover-up you want me to bust.'

'Our strategic models indicate that a ground-swell of public opinion coupled with international condemnation will swing Washington into an abstentionist position.'

'And we get our peace conference.'

'And the Low War is over.'

' "For want of a nail the shoe was lost, for want of a shoe the horse was lost . . ." ' Gaby said. 'You don't ask much of your ex-junkies, do you?'

Tikaram ran the side of his hand down her breast bone. Gaby winced.

'I thought you said work was therapy.'

'Yes. I did. When do I start?' She tried to get up, wobbled. Tikaram caught her an instant before Faraway. 'Maybe in a wee while . . .'

Not before Tikaram had completed the massage, and another set of checks, and injected her with blood production stimulants, and an hour of hydrotherapy in his plunge pool, and a full body scrub with scrapers and nibbed gloves. And the parcel of herbal remedies, food complements, relaxation tapes, yoga implants and antibiotic bananas and immunoexcitory yams from his greenhouse.

'I still feel like road-kill,' Gaby said as the children – she was not sure how many – ran about transporting her luggage and remedies to the Harambee car. There was east-light beyond the trees of Ena. Another day. Amazing. In the porch her strength ran out. The legs went.

'Jesus, it's an awful long way to that car,' she said.

'No, it's not,' Faraway said and swept her up in her blanket and took her in his arms to the waiting limousine.

There was a woman waiting in Faraway's house when the car turned in in the early pearl grey and Faraway carried Gaby down into the sunken living room. Not Naomi: Naomi had let this woman in as she was leaving. This was Sarah, representative of the Ras Nungwi nation. Sarah, Serena's surrogate mother.

Serena was gone.

45

The storm had taken out the electrics for the whole nation and Fat Tuesday's biolumes were all long dead from starvation. They clung in the corners of the smelly, cheap room, mummified claws locked into the flaking plaster. Wall-running lizards scavenged the desiccated, acidic flesh. Spiders festooned them with cobwebs.

Lightning flicker outshone the candles Serena had arranged in front of the dressing table mirror. Thunder hunted over Nembu. The streets were streaming, the leaking gutter rattled and splashed down the window louvres. Serena sat down on the peeling stool. She studied her image in the dark mirror, the shifting personalities the candle light lent it. She took the big pair of scissors, lifted a long strand of hair and began to cut.

She knew the rooms would be bad when Fat Tuesday said that really, his main business was the little nanofactory in his back yard. She also knew, from the way he sized up this lone young white female who wanted a room, never mind the condition, that he cut his sharpest deals in white slavery. Which was why, when she shook on the price with her right hand, her left hand pressed the muzzle of Oksana's handpiece to the bridge of his nose.

'One round, fragmentation, anti-personnel,' she said. 'Have you any idea what it will do to your head at this range? And by the way, I think you can give me a better price than that.'

It was still too much for the dirty, dark room that smelled of mouse piss and mould. The outspread fingers of the nanofactory solar tree nervously scraped the window, storm-tossed. It would do. She would not be here long. Just enough to transform. Enough to disappear.

The gun lay on the dressing table. Serena lifted a hank of hair straight up. The scissors sheared it off at its base. Every piece that fell to the dirty wood floor redefined her. Every cut set her free. Her hair tied her to pain and anger. The ends of her long tresses coiled around lives, loves, hates, anchoring her.

She cut savagely at the mahogany hair. Strands fell into the candle flames, flared with a blue hiss and the stench of burned keratin. Gusts tugged at the little lights; sneaked through the ill-fitting louvres, the gappy door.

With every cut she studied her reflection. A new face was emerging, one she did not recognize, that was therefore exciting and threatening. Like a sculptor, she created by cutting away. A new face, a new person, sculpted from hair. Welcome, stranger, to my cheap shitty room.

The storm reached its height and passed south down the mountain. The sound of rain filled the world, cascading down the tines of the solar generator. Squatting on the low stool, surrounded by coils of red hair, Serena greeted the stranger in the mirror. She was thin, this female with the skull-cap of badly hacked red hair. She looked very young, a kid. A boy. She looked like a boy. She felt a glow in her crotch at that revelation. I re-invent myself, absolutely. She leaned forward to study her features. The skin seemed paler, the freckles more livid, leopard-spotted, alien. The eyes were huge. She ran fingers over her new-found ears. There were cheekbones she had never noticed before. She turned from side to side, catching the shadows of the few remaining candles on them, trying their effect. She liked them. She liked this human. She liked this Ren. That would be her name. That was what she would be. One name, one syllable, not a girl's name, not a boy's name: her name. Ren.

She set the scissors down, took up the gun. She stepped back to pose with it for the mirror. In her shorts and cropped T-shirt she reckoned she looked long and lean and mean.

In a sudden flurry of elation, she shoved her few things back into her black stuffbag and swung it over her shoulder. She did not bother to close the door.

She left the scissors, and the candles burning down.

Hypnotized by the kick-boxing on the battery TV, Fat Tuesday needed a moment to recognize the person banging the key down on his desk.

'Hey, I'm still charging you a night,' he shouted after the figure darting across the dark lobby towards the street.

The rain had slackened, but it was still enough to keep the people from the streets and paste Ren's thin clothing to her body in an instant. Her boots splattered her with red mud as she ran to the shelter of the shebeen door.

The biolume signs said *Drink* and *Girls* and *Hy-Life*. 'Ey,' said the old man at the tin table taking the admission, seeing wet T-shirt. Then he saw the big silver gun and had no more comment to make.

In the shebeen doorway, Ren closed her eyes, and went to another place. In that place wind-chimes rang from a low eave. Rain beat on roofs, thunder was loud and flat and close. She could smell weather and growing, and bodies. She sensed she was outdoors, but somehow protected, roofed. She lay on a soft surface, wrapped in a soft quilt. Beneath it, she felt she was naked, and that another lay with her. She heard a man's voice mumble, heard her own purr a wordless reply. A mouth kissed hers. Fingers stroked her breasts, gently pulled at her nipples.

Ren whimpered, frightened. Her own nipples hardened. Old Tin Table stirred.

In that other place, a tongue caressed her earlobes. The sound of breathing filled her hearing. She felt her own hands respond, discover smooth, hard man-ass; smooth hard man-dick.

Ren gave a small cry.

'Ey, lady, you all right?' said Tin Table.

In that other, lightning lit the sky. She saw a face she knew.

234

Blue's face. She saw a garden dripping with rain beyond the colonnades of a deep verandah. Beyond, she saw a chaotic skyline of spires and impossibly tall, slender mushrooms. Just for an instant, then the thunder exploded. An instant was enough. The Kirinya district directory would do the rest.

Ren gasped.

She had been entered. She felt Blue's cock press hard into her, gather for the thrust.

She severed the link with ATR. The hunter must remain pure, virgin. Otherwise the hunted would turn and destroy her. It was a sacred affair, the relationship between hunted and hunter. And hunter was the person she had seen in the mirror.

Her auxbrain laid townscapes over the lightning flash of illumination. She clenched a fist: *yes*. It was not close, but she could make it on her own. The rain was a spatter of heavy drops now. She launched herself into it. Oksana Telyanina's gun held loosely in her left hand, Ren loped through the cascading streets of Kirinya.

46

He called himself The Man, but Ren was expecting someone taller. He came for breakfast, and had very bad teeth which he showed a lot as he helped himself to the fruit. He did not think much of Ren.

'So, you the *m'zungu* wants to fight.'

Ren had doubted that one so small, so bad-mouthed, so objectionable could be a Black Simbas commander, but ATR had assured her that The Man was the man.

'There's a reason they call us Black Simbas, y'know?' He smiled, gappily, bent down as if to fix a shoe lace or pick up a dropped piece of ugali. A lunge: Ren gasped as he caught the crotch of her shorts in an iron fist, tugged savagely. 'So, what you got down there, child? Hell, I can't tell. You boy or girl?

Fuck, you white maggots all look the same to me.' Ren kicked free, growled, found the serrated point of the pawpaw knife nudging hungrily at the base of her sternum. 'Vtt. Dead, child. You took your eyes off the ball.' The Man flicked the knife away, buried it in the wooden table top. He twanged it. 'This is war, child, we don't nursemaid no *m'zungu* bitches looking for big thrills.'

'I don't need nursemaiding.' Ren had found her voice. 'I had Harambee protection. I carried a gun every day. And you're just trying to hard-talk bullshit me into being scared.'

'Whoa,' said The Man. 'Well maybe I am and maybe I am not, but what I have successfully done, girl, is get you angry enough right now to cut my jones off with that knife. But you're not mean enough and that is good for you, else I would have to take it off you ungently, child. And if you ain't that mean, you not a Simba, you a fucking liability.'

Ren scowled at him, beaten down. The Man sat back and observed her with spiritless black eyes. Ren squirmed, imagining Man fingers exploring under her shorts and camouflage T-shirt, probing, testing, enjoying.

'She was at Soroti,' ATR said in the silence.

'You do not need to remind me of that, corporal,' said The Man. 'I'll have some more of that coffee, I think.' Blue went into the kitchen to bang the pot against the water pump. Fish, dogs and guests stink after three days. He was getting pissed off with Ren sleeping on his verandah bench-bed. It was the same bench-bed on which he had fucked ATR with Ren riding her frontal lobes. Sometimes Ren suspected he knew, that was why he was could not speak civilly to her. It was not. It was a personal space thing. The home was a bedroom and a wash-room and a kitchen-living room on the ground floor of a heaving project, but it was his place, the first he had ever had, and it was all right for him to invite women into it, but not so right for those women to invite other women. Girls. White girls who wanted to be Black Simbas.

'She saw her friend die,' ATR would hiss at Blue in the shower, hoping that the rush of water would cover her words. It didn't. 'She felt her die.'

Felt, was still feeling. In the cold night, on the wooden bed, under the warm quilt and the big stars the neighbours would sing or fight and the street dogs bark and the early early traffic hurtle past on its way to God knows where, she would wake with a jerk and a cry from dreams of dying. The white light. She had ridden into the light, and learned the truth. God, faith, obedience, the mystic; Oksana's belief of enduring return through the tree of life, all were delusions. Ren had been taken to the edge of the white light further than any who ever returned. She had seen the endless dark that lay on the far side. Beyond this life was no other.

The Man studied her with his black little eyes and drank a full cup of the new coffee before speaking.

'You know, I am doing you a favour. Really. Kids like you, you come to me, say, Man, make me a Black Simba, give me an AK47, send me out to fight for the nation. Yeah. They all as ballsy as you, child. They don't last ten seconds in combat. I seen younger'n you, no faces, no heads. Only reason I ain't sending you back home with a red ass is Rains here says you's a talent. Eye-so-path. Now, tell me, child, why a rare talent like that wants to go running out waving a gun getting her titties blown outa her back? 'S a damn fool don't even know her own value. Damn fool.'

'What are you saying?' Ren had spent too much of her life on water not to know when a prey was hooked.

'What I am saying, child: happen if it were up to me, I'd say no to you child in any shape or form or colour or talent, but the sole reason I am bothered on such a fine morning to come to a shithole like this, drink this fucking coffee – no harm, friend, but this is the most shit coffee I have tasted in weeks – and even pretend to take you seriously, white, is because happen my superior officer, that mighty fine woman Rose, remembers your mother from way back – way back – and owes her a long-outstandin' favour.'

'Gab?'

'You have such disrespect for your lovin' mother you call her by her Christian name?'

'I don't want anything from her. Nothing from her. Nothing to do with her.'

'Well that is a sad shame, child, because it just so happens there is a, hm, special project, yes, I suppose that's what you'd call it, that requires the unique talents of eye-so-paths, and I was just goin' to tell you you were in.'

He has you, Ren thought. The bastard has hooked and played and landed you and you are lying on your side, gasping up at the big blue sky, waiting for the gaff.

'What project?'

The Man whipped the fruit knife out of the table and offered it to Ren.

'I am sorry it's not as hygienic as I would wish, but sure kids your age have turbocharged immune systems.'

'You need a link?'

'Child, would I want to be linked with you? Some of your blood, in this here receptacle, will suffice.'

It felt a strange violation, the faces watching over the fruit rinds and bowls of ugali as she made the slash across the palm, squeezed the blood like juice into the cell base container. The Man capped the jar as Ren winced and willed the wound shut. He slipped the carrier into his pocket and stood up. He looked at the sky.

'Congratulations. You a Black Simba now. Special Forces. Don't that sound mighty fine, white? Don't get all blown up with piss and pride. What you is, is a doggie-soldier. Everyone's better'n you. This child here, my good friend corporal Rains, she is your shadow. She be looking after you. More'n that, she is now your superior officer. Needless to say, but what the hell, I enjoy saying it: if you ever, ever fuck her, or me, or any of the good people you will meet, up the ass, I will find you, and I will cut your cunt out.'

He took the bloody knife and carved a heart-shaped plug out of the half paw-paw on the table. He dropped the soft meat in Ren's lap.

'Good day to you now.'

47

Gaby's videodiary: Busowa Resettlement Camp

Day three. They're still coming. Women mostly, they hover nervously at the door, unsure if they are allowed to come in, and I wave them in and they sit on the ground in front of me and they talk death and loss and pain and the most Christ-awful stuff you can imagine, and it just goes down into my camera like a shopping list. Three thousand one hundred and seven people died at Soroti, and all I can think is, my daughter is missing.

This is the sort of confession you only make to video cameras. I try and make myself feel it, I tell myself Groomsport, the place I grew up, fifteen hundred people. Imagine two Groomsports dying all at once. Everyone dead in their homes and gardens, in the street, in the shops, the bars, on the boats in the harbours, throwing sticks for their dogs on the beach, on the swings at the sea front, eating fucking ice creams, walking on the Point. Now knife them through the heart twice.

Won't work. Serena is out there in twelve million people, alone, and I can't do a thing to help.

The women all speak very softly, almost ashamed to have lived. Later, when the auxbrains start to form – I don't think they have any idea what the Ogun relief staff are talking about, all they know is that they survived – I'll want pictures downloaded. Soft, persuasive, incredibly damaged voices are not enough. As the details of the massacre unfold, the magnitude of the lie the North is telling itself grows. If you have to lie, lie big. The story that it was a pitched battle between rival tribal factions holds. There is no contrary evidence. No one can get on to the site to corroborate stories. No one knows about the anti-personnel missiles, or the American attack helicopters. Or that the only white survivor is my fifteen-year-old daughter. They come and they tell me about their men and their sons and their daughters who died up there and I tell myself, for God's sake, what is the difference? They've lost, you've lost, why the fuck don't you feel? Why don't you cry? What is the difference? The difference is, they know their daughters are dead. I don't know anything, except she's gone.

Yeah, of course Faraway knows the city better than me, he's got the contacts, and Sarah's doing what she can, and I was as much use as tits on a boar back there, but I am this far from hitching a ride on the first *pujo* or truck to Kirinya. If it wasn't for the fact that he'd miss the really important call, he'd have shut his mobile off. You don't have kids, Faraway. You don't know what it's like.

Four days bust-up diplomat hunts for cleaned-up junkie's runaway massacre survivor daughter. I'd love to know what my horoscope said for this week.

Then another voice says maybe the reason you feel nothing is because you're hard. Maybe that's why you gave it up, you saw too much and you grew a shell around you and in the end you found that you were trapped in it, like a hermit crab grown too big and too fat and too complacent. Like a hermit crab, the only thing you could do was crawl right out of it and scuttle naked along the beach. Into a new shell. Jesus, is this all I add up to? Trading shells? There's something old and maybe a bit too comfortable about this work. I slip into it mighty easily; it's a good feeling, having something to do, having a camera to talk to, having a life; but have I just popped back under the old hard Gaby McAslan SkyNet News shell? Around and around and around she goes, where she ends up nobody knows. One big shell game. Find the lady.

Find the fucking lady. Jesus, Serena, where are you?

I'm going to blow these goddam candles out. I've confessed enough to a camera for one night.

The sound was too soft for a cough, too deliberate to be animal or accident.

Gaby hesitated over the video camera switch. 'Hello?'

The woman's eyes caught the candlelight.

'Excuse me, madam, they said you want people to talk to you. Would this be all right?' She spoke Great Lakes French: a Tutsi, Gaby reckoned from her features. A people familiar with genocides.

'Yeah, sure,' Gaby said in her implant French. She sat on the dusty land-coral floor of the round-house, arranged her dresses around her. 'Don't worry about the camera, just talk to me. Tell me whatever you want.'

'May I ask, why do you want to know this, madam?' the Tutsi woman asked.

'So I can prove to the people in the North who did this. Who really did it.'

'Ah,' the woman said gently, rocking forward. 'Then you will need this.' She reached into her fabric folds, drew a glittering thing. For an instant Gaby reached for her gun, thinking she had been drawn on. She had. The woman held out ten centimetres of bright diamond blade.

'Please.'

Gaby took the barbed thing gingerly. It still wickedly nicked her.

'Jesus,' she whispered, turning it slowly to catch the light. 'Where did you get this?'

'From my son's face,' the woman said.

The pool of smooth mud quivered. Ripples ran across its surface. With the slow magnificence of a geological process, Mombi emerged. Rather, Gaby thought among the cycads and hothouse blooms, congealed, like a golem.

The mud-woman took a long time between blinks. Fat drips of slurry ran down the continental shelf of her breasts.

'You are looking good, Gaby,' said the girl in the shiny blue shorts and bra top. Ignore her, Anansi the smooth criminal had said. Talk directly to Mombi.

'I'm not sure I can return the compliment, Mombi.'

'I have put on a bit since I last saw you.' Slab jowls quivered, the woman in the pool was chuckling. Her face was so fat it skewed familiar expression into alien. A smile, or sudden pain? 'Did your friend tell you that I killed Haran with my own hand?'

'No, she forgot that.'

'When you remember everything, you forget that others do not,' Mombi said.

Piling memories like calories on to your body, Gaby thought. Bingeing on data. The word of God that animates the clay golem. She took the package from inside her silk jacket, knelt, unfolded the scarf. She held the blade up in a corner of chiffon.

'Do you know what this is?'

'Dangerous,' said the voice-girl in blue.

'Yes. Very. It killed three thousand people in Soroti last week. Including my friend the forgetful Oksana Telyanina. Do you know what it's made from?'

Mombi screwed up her tiny, beautiful eyes.

'I would guess nanoweave diamond.'

'You would guess correct. Now, can you tell me how the Bugandan Royal Army happen to get their hands on nanoweave diamond?'

'Gaby, you are an old friend and I owe you a long-standing debt, but it would be unwise to presume too much on the strength of it.'

'Three thousand one hundred and seven dead.'

'It is obviously your personal loss confusing you into thinking that we have something to do with this. High quality designer produce, that is our business.'

'Oh, I believe it. Yes. But others may not be as, ah, fastidious as you.'

'This was not manufactured in the South.'

'You're very sure of that.'

'The thing about an empire is that it must be well run, and have good information. Something you Harambee should be mindful of.'

Gaby sat down cross-legged. She stabbed the blade into the short turf.

'I agree with you. I don't think this was made here, or anywhere in Africa, or even Australasia or South America. But the buckies that built it were. Like you said about running an empire: the Emperor has to know what's going on, or his head's on a spear. Mombi, who's running designer fullerenes into the North?'

The thing in the pool heaved, sent honey-brown ripples lapping at Gaby's toes.

'You may have heard that I am still engaged in hostilities with the Black Simbas.'

'Twenty shootings in as many days is hardly what you'd call discreet. I thought it was a territorial thing. They're running fullerenes?'

'Your information is not as complete as you assume.'

'Weapons systems fullerenes? To the North? To the NLAs, UNPROFOR, the Americans? Mombi, come on, give me something I can believe.'

'Mistake, Gaby. There are no such things as weapons systems fullerenes. There are just molecules, moving other molecules around. They have no will, no sense of purpose. No conscience. Just molecules moving molecules. Once they are out there, they can make them do whatever they want.'

'But the Simbas, Mombi . . .'

'Everything changes, Gaby. Are you thinking of going after them?'

'I'm just asking questions.'

'It's who you are asking them for. Gaby, I would strongly advise you against this.'

'I need to know, I need to get every step in place, one after the other, like stones in a river. Otherwise we don't get to the other side.'

Mombi quivered. Gaby read it as a shrug. It cast up a small mud storm.

'Very well. If you are insistent upon this foolish course, at least allow me to extend you protection.'

'I don't need your protection.'

'You most of all, Gaby.' Mombi moved into the deep centre of the pool, slowly submerging. The interview was over. Gaby pulled her weapon out of the fake soil.

'Leave it.'

The voice-girl – Gaby remembered Anansi had called her Rewa – stood over her. She knelt down, picked up the blade in the light scarf. Their eyes met. A sudden shiver chilled Gaby. The eyes were as dull and blank as mud. The red-linered lips said, 'Gaby, I gave the Siberian woman another message to give to you. I wonder if she forgot it too.'

'What was that?'

'Ask Gaby: how long will she keep her spear hooded?'

'She told me that.'

'What was your answer?'

'My answer was, I have no spear.'

243

Neither Mombi nor Rewa gave a reply. Bubbles rose and burst in the honey-mud lake.

The Russian wars had made Gaby wise to BVMs. The glint of a hub-cap, the tilt of a wing mirror, the lane-shift three cars behind you, a cigarette butt under your window, the echo on the telephone, the moment's hesitation in the PDU link. Black Van Moments.

They're coming for you.

Mandé the Shit was that invaluable but infuriating journalist's source, not an informant but a corroborator. You leaned on him, and he told you what else you could trust with your weight. All truths came in with the deliveries to his bespoke Afro-Asian foodery among the trunks of the great banyan tree, and you could eat them and they would not give you the shits. But he had his Italian suits updated weekly from Milan and he was addicted to needless cosmetic dentistry and he was irredeemably The Shit. Gaby was always careful to call him Mandy. The right and wrong doctor.

'The thing about Mombi is, she does not lie,' he said. 'If she says a thing, it is so. For good or ill.'

'From you, I believe the Black Simbas are smuggling nanotechnology to the North.' Gaby rolled the cardamom-studded banana up in the chapatti. The waiter uncapped her beer bottle with his teeth. Someone deserving of instant canonisation had at last worked out how to replicate decent Tusker. In her memory, Doctor Scullabus's Prescription tasted like engine oil. 'Believe, but don't understand.'

'Did Mombi say where?'

'Do you know where?'

'I've heard rumours.'

'That's what I pay you for.'

'I've heard the supply line ends in India. Bangalore.'

Cyber-navel of the planet. All webs node in Mother India.

'What do they want in India?'

Mandy the Shit spread his hands in that gesture Gaby hated so much she wanted to hit him.

'This I do know, if Mombi says go carefully with the Simbas, this also you can trust.'

'I'll be careful,' Gaby said. 'I've got too big a tab here not to.'

Then, as the mopedcab lurched out in front of an overloaded *matatu*, she glimpsed in one of the many wing mirrors the too-timely pull-out of the too-smart car parked at the end of the street. BVM.

'Go left here.' Gaby tapped the driver on the shoulder, pointed down a roofed-in alley thronged with pedestrians.

'This is not the way I would go to get to the New Thorn Tree,' said the girl rider.

'But it's the way I would,' Gaby said. Follow me down this, faked-from-Japan. The mopedcab honked its way through a busy cloth market of brightly swathed stalls, bulbous, aromatic vats that spun the fibres into fabrics and solar powered looms. First there had been the boys playing football a little too seriously outside Faraway's house. Second, the echo on her handshake at Henry's. Third, the over-conscientious pet-buyer in the Embu bird market. And now the well-timed car.

You could call it paranoia. She liked to think of it as pattern recognition.

No twitch in the journalist's senses as the white-gloved *maître d'* tip-hatted her in to the bar where all the newspeople went. The contact who would be squaring the travel arrangements with the UN had not arrived yet, so she had Aaron set one up and went for a shit. Pants down panties down, contemplation on the cold ceramic. Jesus, a cigarette would be good. Helps keep the weight off. Needs something. The classic post-addiction weight-gain pattern. Give me three weeks I'll be there with Mombi wallowing in mud glorious mud. Why don't they do something useful and invent buckies that eat fat and piss alcohol?

That would be too easy. Like it would be too easy for one damn thing to lead to another damn thing to lead to another and the whole thing would string together like ducks in a row. Or martyrs going over the falls. And she could wrap it up and sneak it North and the whole planet would love her. And all the Lisa Kropotkins would just go and die of awe. Too easy for you, Gaby McAslan. You fucked up. Now it's karmic payback night.

Night? Year. Lifetime.

She realized she hadn't thought about Serena for a whole morning.

BVM. The washroom door had opened, but the restaurant beyond was unusually quiet. The footsteps had crossed to the cubicles, but no other door opened. The footsteps had been slow and measured. Looking. Gaby bent over, peered under the cubicle door. Shadow of legs on the tiles.

She had the Harambee-issue firing piece out of her jacket, armed and aimed in one silent, silken motion.

Still out there.

Moving like a glaciation, she got up, slid back the bolt. She stood upright, naked from waist to boots. Slow, slowly, slower. And *go*. She whipped the cubicle door open. Found herself muzzle-to-point with a fabulously thin young black woman in killer leather, biker gloves and absolutely no hair aiming a spear as tall as herself at Gaby's forehead.

'Fuck!' Gaby McAslan yelled, panties around ankles. She and the spear-woman stared at each other long enough for Gaby's gun-arm to begin whimpering. Then the woman snatched away her spear, snapped it butt down on the floor tiles. In the middle of the women's toilet in the New Thorn Tree Bar, she bowed to Gaby McAslan.

'What the fuck are you?' Gaby McAslan said, clutching at her clothes while keeping the gun trained on the woman. In answer, the woman thrust her spear-arm forward. The head hovered in front of Gaby's face. She recognized it: her blade, the diamond blade, pulled from a dead boy's face in Soroti. It had been melded seamlessly into the shaft of the weapon. High alchemy had been worked on it: the spear was one monstrous, flawless white and black diamond.

'Mombi says, now you have a spear. I am to bear it for you.'

Sixty-four channels of shit on the bedroom terminal, she didn't feel the equal of Lisa Kropotkin on SkyNet – yet – and even amortal life was too short to sift the endless trivial chaff of the world web. Four fingers of that good fake whiskey Faraway brought back from New Harare was all the entertainment Gaby required. Lately she'd seen more of the bottle than of him, and that was going down by the handful. Careful, Gab. Yeah. But the house was big and strange and not hers. You can't comfortably slouch around dressed in fuck-all when you still catch the perfume of the woman who was there before you in the closets or find her pubes in the shower. Or when there is a mad leather fetish woman with a diamond spear out in the garden who does not understand the meaning of the words *I do not need a bodyguard.*

She wondered what it must be like not to have to sleep.

She no longer thought of her predecessor as a sexual enemy. Naomi. Her name is Naomi. She is a Gikuyu lawyer, and a good one. And you can talk about her in the present tense. Right now, she is much closer to you than the man you share. Gaby almost felt sorry for the bitch. It's hard when they leave you. Unbidden, an image of Diamond Jim, smiling, boyish, cute, sun-bleached, bubbled out of her whiskey glass. She found she could look at it, and turn away. So, Naomi, unseen sister. There is men's leaving and women's leaving. They were always leaving us, but we left them. She tilted the glass to the ghost. Because she did that, she knew with a sinking certainty that was also a resigned elation, that the thing was starting with Faraway.

Would that be so bad? she thought. A Faraway thing. He is kind, he is patient, he is handsome, he has a good body, he is funny, he commits like a sin, he worships you, he will do unthinkable things for you. He has done unthinkable things for you. Why not Faraway? Gaby recalled this same soliloquy, almost image for image, behind the wheel of an open-top SkyNet runabout, smirking with sexual satisfaction down the palm-lined beach road south of Mombasa. You were fucking him then, and he is ten times that man now.

But I am one tenth the woman.

He loves that tenth.

Why not Faraway? Wherever he leaves for, he will come back. He isn't going to fly off to explore a Big Dumb Object and make excuses about scientific camaraderie to cover his little expeditions into other vaginas and finally fade into some kind of metaphysical singularity that only whales can understand, and never come back.

So: why not Faraway?

It's different when you're under his roof, when he's still

carrying you across his threshold, when you can't choose yourself where to go and how to get there.

In a time, maybe. Now; he's down in Pretoria and you have to follow a trail of fullerenes all the way to Bangalore without ending up wearing your intestines round your neck, so turn the lights way down and take your whiskey to bed because it's the only warm glow you'll get there tonight.

'Lights down,' she ordered the room. Her voice almost covered the scriff of foot from the living room. Almost.

'Cletho, get out of my house,' Gaby shouted wearily.

The first time she had woken to find the figure standing at the end of the bed, she had almost blown it through the painted fabric partition. The woman had been in classic warrior-pose, one leg bent, right foot pressed against left knee, holding herself up with her spear. The thing about the Masai pose, Gaby remembered, is that they can hold it for hours without tiring. As she clearly had.

Gaby liked everything about her bar her ubiquity. Like all Mombi's girls, she was a talent. Her lack of need to sleep was merely a useful adjunct: her primary endowment was sensory enhancement. Her vision went up into the ultra-violet and down into the infra-red. She had something akin to cranial radar. She had the sense of smell of a tracker hound, the hearing of a bat and, like a shark, her skin could pick up the electrical fields of living beings. She was a mother of an early warning system. She was as black and beautiful and adamant as ebony.

Gaby had learned another thing about Mombi's girls. Their mothers were all old Nairobi whores. They had been warped in the womb by Chaga fullerenes tunnelling in through the molecular underworld of the HIV4 virus. Daughters of the infected. After that she found herself softening to her pretty, savage protector, but not enough to let her into the house.

'Come on, Cletho.'

The kid sneaked joints from the diplomatic stash when she thought Gaby wasn't around. Old senses doesn't mean no senses, warrior.

No answer. She pulled on a T-shirt and soft cream leggings and went down into the darkened living room, glass in hand. Nothing no one nowhere. But she had heard another scuff of foot on floor. She moved cautiously into the room. Where is your gun, Gaby? The one Faraway said never to be without? On your bedside table. You are going to take out an assassin with a glass of Great Zimbabwe whiskey?

'Cletho?'

'No. It's me.'

The thick glass hit the floor and bounced, sending a lap of brown whiskey tonguing through the air.

'Lights.' The word almost choked Gaby. The biolumes slowly filled the room with yellow glow. Gaby clapped hands to mouth as the night-comer moved from the window to the carved scissor-stool. The figure in the skin-hugging flage suit was as lean and wary as a night-hunting cat. A stroke of the wrist control reset the fabric pattern to a garish purple, orange and yellow leaf dapple.

Oh Jesus, it is you, inside that suit, beneath those muscles, under that hair, behind those cheekbones and eyes that were never that colour before and that hurt, hungry face. Gaby sank into the woven grass sofa.

'Serena.'

'Listen. I'm not staying. I'm only here to tell you this. You're messing with dangerous stuff.'

'Cletho, how did you get past her, what have you done with her?'

Serena pursed her lips in exasperation, shook her head. Gaby had lived with that tic for almost seventeen years. The girl unhooked a black, vaguely sea-foody device from the tack-patch on her left thigh, all shell and antenna. From Harambee briefings Gaby recognized the prawn-thing as an un-gun. Phased e-m pulses generated resonances in the auxbrain that cascaded into the mebrain. Grand mal, petit mal, amnesia, blindness, unconsciousness, paralysis, hallucinations, docility all lay in the weapon's aerials. Death, at the right setting. Cletho with her spear never stood a chance. The thing ripped through her enhanced senses like a leopard gutting a lap dog.

Who gave you such a pretty toy to play with, child?

'She's okay. She's going to have a sore head for the next couple of days, but she's not damaged.'

'Who are you with, Serena?'

'People who call me Ren.'

Ren. Re-in-vention. I recognize this person barely. I know her not at all. And neither do you, I think, boy-girl soft-hard tough-vulnerable daughter-enemy of mine. But whoever she is, it suits you.

'I'm not going to try to talk you out of it.'

'You couldn't. That's what I'm here to do to you. They'll kill you, Gab. They've the contract ready. All they have to do is call it in. It's bigger than you can imagine.'

'What's bigger?'

'I can't tell you.'

'Do you know?'

Ren closed her eyes, grimaced. You know, Gaby said.

'Jesus, what've you got into?'

'The Black Simbas!' Ren shouted. 'You know that!'

'Because of Oksana?'

Ren could not look at her. She shook her short, soft red hair. Gaby flinched, so strong was the sudden desire to tousle it, run her fingers through it, feel out the shapely skull beneath, tell her daughter she was magnificent, beautiful, precious, loved.

'It's war, right?' Her eyes flashed their old colour. 'And you either sit back and do nothing, or you fight, and I've seen what sitting back and doing nothing does, it gets people killed. So I'm saying, hey this is me, I'm going to fight. My way. My war. I'm doing something that matters. I'm making a difference, I'm not just sitting back on some, some, fucking beach, getting out of my head while the whole thing goes to fuck. Jesus, I don't know why I bothered. You don't understand.'

I do, Gaby thought.

'I'm a warrior, understand?'

She heard the pain and the pride and uncertainty, and she said, slowly, still not looking at the fierce, ardent child across the room from her, 'Then you know why I have to do this.'

'I don't have to know, I don't have to do anything. I don't have to be here. I don't have to give you this warning.'

'But you have.' Now she could look at Ren.

'You're messing me around, you're trying to get me to say, to say . . .'

'Say what?'

Ren flung the words across the room with a sudden inarticulate slash of her arm.

'Fuck you! Fuck you! I'm going.' She surged up. She moved like a thing trained, liquid, disciplined. Her suit colours ran like oil on water. 'Don't mess with the Black Simbas. They will kill you.'

Gaby let her get to the window before saying, softly, 'Ren, I have to.'

Her hand rested on the catch.

'Ren, you think you're the only one feels anything? You think you're the only one hurts? The only one misses her? No. No no no. You see, I didn't just lose Okya. I lost my daughter. I lost you. And I deserved it. I deserved to lose you, because you're right, in one year she was more a mother to you than I ever was. And I don't care if this sounds whining and apologetic and that I'll say anything to stop you walking out, because I will, but it also happens to be what I feel. Because you know a hell of a lot for your age, Ren, but you know fuck about guilt, and you know fuck about what it will make you do and say.'

Ren shook her head.

'Gab, it's not the Simbas.'

'What do you mean?'

'The ones running the fullerenes. I mean, yes, we are, but not the ones you're looking for.'

'Who is?'

Ren took a deep breath.

'It's a Hutu group over on the west side of Lake Victoria. The Tororo Empire. The Haut Zaire Reunification Army have a mercenary deal with them, nanotech for training and arming them for an expansion into CAC territory.'

'How can I find them?'

'Gab, don't.'

'Ren, like I told you, you have your cause, I have mine. It generally goes without saying that you're prepared to die for it.'

'The H-Zras have links with the KLA in Samburu camp.'

'Thanks. So what are the Simbas running?'

Ren swallowed.

'Amortality. We're selling complete bloodstream bucky systems to fat Indian capitalists who will pay anything you ask to get off the reincarnation carousel. Telomerazers, free-radical scrubs, anti-viral suites, cancer-busters, cell-repair systems, aux-brains. The lot.'

'Why?' Gaby asked.

'No,' Ren said. 'That I can't tell you. Jesus, I've told you too much already. I have to go. She doesn't know I'm doing this, she'll miss me if I'm not back by dawn.'

'Ren . . .'

'I got to go.'

'Ren!'

Breeze straying though the open window stirred the insect nets. Ren had slipped away, pulled up the hood of her camouflage suit and become one with the night.

48

After the Rains ran her hard. Five kays in the morning, ten in the evening. The people of Mururi's steep terraces and techno-shanties grew familiar with the lean figure in the tight green bodysuit, ascetic and muscular as a Bach prelude, weaving a course of grace and concentration between the overhanging Great-houses, and the pretty black woman on the moped, pacing her grimly through the clayey footpaths, down the precipitous staircases.

The first time, Ren had thought she would die. Now it was her life. For an hour and a half each day, her uncertainties and contradictions were consumed in the purity of running. Nothing existed outside of the exigencies of her body. She was absolute, physical, mindless.

After the run, she submitted to the warm fingers of water in the hygiene unit while her own fingers explored her flat breasts, her smooth flanks, the taut belly muscle. Then she lay under the fingers of the masseuse, exploiting all their weaknesses and aches. Then ATR's fingers, working the aromatic oils into her spotted hide. Last, the obscene, swollen finger of the leech nuzzling between her shoulder blades, the brief needling pain as its tongue pierced and sucked her. She had glimpsed it once – she had turned her head a moment too early – a translucent chaplastic maggot, swollen and dark on her blood. ATR sealed it into the sterile carrying case, and the bike boy had taken it away.

'A warrior must be strong,' ATR told her. Ren had balked at the vast amounts of food her officer/trainer prepared: she found she could eat it all and still be hungry. Once the linkages commenced, she came out of them ravenous. There was always food for her. She knew she was as trained and groomed and single-purposed as a beautiful racing dog. It was right. She was a Black Simba psy-warrior.

The linkages were what she was shaped for. Two hours a day zazen in the contemplation room in this safe house, dimly lit by what daylight eked through the woven grass walls; ATR sitting by, watching, listening, ready, in case; the street sounds of Mururi exactly five thousand two hundred and twenty kays away as she sat behind the eyes of Mrs Meenakshi Khandewal, wife of Mr Jogendra Khandewal of JTT Industries of Bangalore, age forty-three, theoretically immortal. When she went to the shops and looked at clothes and shoes, Ren was there. When she took coffee with her friends, or went to the races, and joked with them about adulteries and lesser infidelities they were all too terrified ever to commit, Ren was there. When she picked up her two daughters from the school and gave the house girl instructions that they were not to watch satellite television, when she hired the caterers for the big dinner for the other directors on the table they used twice a year, when she made the vegetable cook's life hell because she had forgotten to salt the *bhindi*, Ren was there. She saw the trivialities with which a rich, useless woman sought to fill an eternal life. She saw the cracks and the shadows. She saw the cold of the bed every night when they rolled away from each other and slept. She saw the way she looked at the boy from the courier company who delivered the packages addressed to her husband, and felt the lust. She saw her take the people-mover through the thronged streets of Bangalore to the special doctor, and the guilt bit like cancer in her belly as the needle slipped into her and shot her full of illegal fullerenes from out of Africa, spiced with Ren McAslan. Meenakshi Khandewal had a fine life for spectating.

In the time Ren had with herself – a few hypnagogic moments before tumbling into exhausted sleep, the morning run awaiting her – she would trace the physical links between herself and Mrs Meenakshi Khandewal: blood to blood. Needle to slug, slug to bike boy, bike boy to the secret mission headquarters where they distilled out essence of Ren McAslan and injected her into sealed phials of medical fullerenes. Lab to coast by private taxi; then into the low, fast radar-transparent boats that ran them to the Sri Lankan pirate ships waiting beyond the continental shelf. Off the Malabar Coast they transi-shipped to coastal dhows, then to the ports of Kerala and Mysore and so into India's arterial system of planes, trains, trunk roads until a bike boy brought them to a doctor's surgery in an elegant suburb of Bangalore. There he filled the syringe, stabbed the needle into the slightly flabby arm of Mrs Meenakshi Khandewal, and put Ren into her bloodstream.

Every night, except the one she left her bed and slipped on ATR's flageskin suit and ran further and faster than she had ever pushed her body before with a warning for her mother.

It was a simple plan. Simple, unstoppable and bloody. And after six weeks and six hundred and thirty kays through the byways of Mururi, it was ready to go into operation. All the warning Ren had was five minutes to stuff her things into her black bag.

'This is it, isn't it?' she asked ATR as the mopedcab took them away from Mururi and its Great-houses, zigzagging slowly southwards down the foothills of Kirinyaga. It drove a long way out, beyond where Kirinya disintegrated into a jostle of villages and tribal nations, beyond even those into scattered settlements that hugged the coral road, as if afraid of the high, dark Chaga at their backs. The driver left them on a featureless verge, turned and drove away. The sound of his engine was a long time dying. No other vehicles passed. In every direction smooth red-boled trees rose sheer for a thousand metres before unfolding in a vaulted roof of huge red hexagonal leaves. Things not birds chimed in the sunlight above. Water dripped from the edges of the leaves, glittering in the shafts of light that fell through the canopy.

'What happens now?'

'We walk,' ATR said. 'That way.'

They ran, that way. It could have been any way. Direction was meaningless to Ren. There was no Ren. She was pure action. She ran through the deep crimson gloom beneath the Chaga canopy, hurdling roots, splashing through streams. It was the apotheosis of everything she was, everything she had made herself, and been made into. She could run for ever through this alien wilderness, beneath this roof of leaves.

She stung with anger when ATR, winded, called for her to stop. The fire burned out of her. She was herself again, a person, a face. She shivered, cold in the highland gloom. Low.

'Save yourself,' ATR panted. 'You've got a battle to fight, tonight.'

The camp was an hour's trek further. It was not country you could run in. ATR and Ren picked over piles of crumbled masonry, detoured around tilted slabs of decaying concrete. Reinforcing rods jutted like compound fractures dripping stalactites of lime and rust. Skeletons of fighting vehicles crouched under shrouds of sulphur yellow florets and copper mould. Ren paused before the twin golden arches of a lost McDonald's, shattered and slumping into a gobble of pseudo-fungi. A city had died here. Strange flowers bloomed from the corpse of Nairobi.

The base grew like a fruiting body out of the green decay of a drive-in cinema. The screen had slumped into rubble. At the centre of a *cheval de frise* of concrete listening posts was a construction like a dozen ribbed eggs, ends half buried in the earth, clutched together. A black man in Chaga-purple combat gear sat on a stool by the oval door. A repro AK lay across his knees. He was Bamileke, unit commander.

The interior of the building was cool and vaulted, lit submarine-green by biolume globes. The other isopaths were being prepped by their trainers. There were four of them; three men, one woman: Ismail, Farad, Johnson and Beauty. They knelt on the packed clay floor. Beauty nodded to Ren as she took her place and ATR started to work on her neck muscles. The men were already out riding their hosts. ATR stretched Ren's legs out and loosened up the calf muscles.

No fear, she thought. No feeling of any kind. This is the time, and you will do the job. Feeling will make you weak. You are a warrior, and a warrior is strong. Strong and brave. A warrior allows nothing that will threaten her strength and her courage.

She saw the tree by Soroti Road with its leaves and branches torn away. She saw the white hurricane that stripped them bare. She saw the tiny red scream in the eye of the hurricane. She felt herself shredded into nothing. She felt herself die. She saw the white light and the deep dark and the helicopter turning in the air and flying into the north.

A touch on her shoulder, not ATR's. Bamileke knelt beside her. The silver flask in his hand smelled of spirits.

'Drink this. It will make you strong. Relax you.'

'I don't need any,' Ren said.

They ate, vast platefuls of food. The long link would burn megajoules of energy. The last thing Bamileke did was order everyone to the toilet. Squatting in the curved ceramic shell, Ren pulled the flageskin suit out of her black bag. She struggled into it. She loved the way it made her look and feel. She was ready for battle now.

The isopaths took their positions on the earth floor. Their corporals knelt beside them with pots of water and thermal blankets. The warriors would lose two degrees of body heat during the attack. They completed their preparations. The run began.

Out beyond Lamu, where the green of the coastal waters turned to the indigo of the deeps, the captain of the Sri Lankan pirate cutter took delivery of a sealed casket. The flimsy little reef-runner that had couriered it fled for shore. A swell was getting up. The pirate captain started his big engines and headed for deep water. Three minutes out, an explosion tore his ship in half. Wood, metal, flesh, carbon fibre fountained into the air while fore and aft sections settled into the deep. Squabbling gulls dived upon the smoking flotsam.

As one link was cut, another was made. Ren opened her eyes in Mrs Meenakshi Khandewal's cream Western-style living room. Mrs Meenakshi Khandewal was facing a severe dilemma.

The Scottish whisky, or the cigarettes? Both were Jogendra's, and really not proper for a lady; she would probably not like either of them, but she wanted to take something of his so that he would know how annoyed she was that he had allowed her to tell everyone that they were going to the evening racing when all along he was booked for the Institute of Directors.

The whisky. He knew the ayah pilfered the cigarettes.

Reclining in the folds of Mrs Meenakshi Khandewal's auxbrain, Ren saw an opportunity. Find a wedge, ATR had told her. Use hesitation, indecision, exploit any mood, habit, addiction, guilt. Any crack of concentration can be forced wide enough for you to step through. Use the hand as if it is your own hand. Use the body as if it is your own body.

Not the Scottish whisky. I want a cigarette.

Mrs Meenakshi Khandewal opened the ivory box, took out a cigarette and lit it.

Ren almost recoiled into her own body in shock.

Mrs Meenakshi Khandewal saw what she was about to slide between her lips and made to stub the thing out in consternation. The moment's lapse was all Ren needed. Mrs Meenakshi Khandewal tried to shriek but Ren had hold of her vocal chords. I am the stranger within, Ren thought. I am in your blood. She tried to phone for help: Ren made her sit down and finish her cigarette. The Indian woman had no idea who or what was possessing her, only that her body obeyed another will. A battle was being fought over a contemplative cigarette on a cream upholstered sofa. Mrs Meenakshi Khandewal's tenacious struggle for self-control was eroding Ren's will power. She had to deliver the coup now or she would be forced out. A beat of her mind activated bloodstream buckies. Neural fullerenes wove molecules, synthesized cascades of hallucinogens. Mrs Meenakshi Khandewal tripped out of her own head. Lost in neurospace. Buckies built neural bridges between auxbrain and mebrain. In the space of half a cigarette, Ren had extended her control over motor, perceptory and autonomic systems. She was Mrs Meenakshi Khandewal.

The phone rang. It was Farad with the directions to the gun shop. Ren went to the kitchen to get the knife. The cigarette-thieving ayah stared but fear of the madam kept her silent.

Ren took the Merc. She put the top down and the radio up. Mrs Meenakshi Khandewal did not know the street, but once in the district the on-board took her straight to the door. She paid for the short barrel pumper and two boxes of ammunition by Amex. The gun shop man had an expression of numbed stupefaction, as if he would not be surprised if every respectable industrial wife in Bangalore came and bought heavy ordnance from him.

Ren hid the gun under the back seat shawl and drove the remembered way to JTT. She laughed as she pulled the big powerful car out past buses and trucks and teenagers on motorbikes. Up up up. But not police-arousing fast. E-messages appeared on her windscreen display: Ismail and Farad were on site. Johnson was entering the compound. Beauty had been held up by a religious demonstration; she would be there in five minutes.

Ren turned in at the gate. The very dashing Sikh security man came out of his box to greet her personally. He saluted as he swung up the barrier. Ren parked in the reserved space at the administration block. She breezed past the front desk with a cheery 'good evening'.

'Mrs Meenakshi Khandewal.' The desk-boy's querulous voice stopped her ten paces down the corridor. 'Excuse me, maybe you've forgotten, but Mr Jogendra Khandewal is at the Institute of Directors tonight.' Querulous could too easily become suspicious. Ren turned, smiled apologetically. She pulled the pumper out from under the shawl and fired both barrels.

In the echoing fake granite corridor the reports were shattering.

Blood. There was blood on the mottled stone behind the desk. Splinters. Something had taken two savage bites out of the reception desk. Ren saw the splintered tree, and the dancing blood in the spray of blades. She had shot on sight. She had killed without thinking. It was as if the gun had possessed her as she possessed Mrs Meenakshi Khandewal.

Move, a voice said. You are a soldier, you are a psy-warrior, it is your purpose to fight and to kill your enemies. They will kill you on sight, without thinking.

She could not run in this body and shoes. She could trot

aggressively. Doors that opened, faces that appeared in corridors, figures suddenly revealed behind elevator doors, she threatened with shot-gun and kitchen knife.

'Get the fuck out of my way!' Mrs Meenakshi Khandewal shouted. 'Fucking fucks!'

They did not look like enemies. They looked like shift workers and cleaners and receptionists scuttling away from this bourgeois monstrosity.

Weakness. Be strong. A warrior must be strong.

Only that the man in the designer sportsgear was carrying a shotgun saved him. Ren rounded the corner and there he was, in the middle of the corridor. She swung her weapon up. He lifted his. That was the moment where Mrs Meenakshi Khandewal's memory recognized him, Arun Agarwal, Gajraj the CE's wastrel brother. They had met fleetingly at the Mishra's pre-wedding reception. He had been a friend of the groom.

'Farad?'

'Ren?'

A man in a security hat poked his head out of a door behind Farad. He whirled, loosed off a warning barrel.

'You okay, Ren?'

'I had to shoot the guy on reception.'

'Yeah. Well. Johnson's only just now taken out the IT centre.'

'You've seen him?'

'He did it.'

'The others?'

'I saw Beauty make it in. We're almost back on schedule. Johnson bought us enough time. Good luck.'

He was almost around the turn before Ren called him back.

'The boardroom's right.'

Farad shrugged.

'They could have found me a body had an idea where he was going.' Then he turned, let off a shot down the corridor, reloaded and advanced, firing steadily. Ren kicked off her shoes. Barefoot gave her a little more speed. The lights suddenly flickered. Elevator doors opened and closed spastically. A low, fast object darted out of a flap in the wall, veered across the floor towards Ren. The second blast spun it down the corridor in a tangle of metal and circuitry: a cleaning drone. Johnson had reached the plant's cybernetic nervous system. As if in confirmation sudden cold whirled through the corridor. But Johnson was beyond confirming anything.

Ren's route to the Processor Hall Three took her past the IT centre. A filigree of black fibres, delicate and complex as spiderwebs, crept from under the door, feeding, growing on the hydrocarbons in the nylon carpet. Ren pushed the door open. The takeover was well established. Soft fingers of pseudo-coral reached for the ceiling, which dripped in swathes of tar black tendrils. Piled folds of yellow-flecked fungus had already shattered the windows and spilled down the outside. Dark yellow crystals, some several metres long, crowded most of the room. As Ren watched, the top of the plastic skull of a monitor embedded in a mess of crystal spikes blistered and broke out in thousands of diamond quills. Ren could just glimpse the body collapsed on the desk. Tiny crimson blooms were visibly advancing over its outspread fingers, up its arms, across its shoulders.

Not Johnson, she made herself think. Johnson is two left of you on the mud floor of a Black Simbas base somewhere in the former northern suburbs of the Nairobi. That is the wife of Mr Chatterji who plays golf with Jogendra every Friday afternoon, whose name you could never remember.

Mrs Meenakshi Khandewal had visited the processor halls precisely once before, and that had been in a Bertoli dress with fine wines and the best people in Mysore. The nanodiamond car had been unveiled and received the appropriate adulation from the best people while the Bangalore press wallahs surged in for close-ups. Then everyone had put on their complimentary diamond tie-pins or brooches and gone on the tour of the processor halls. Mrs Meenakshi Khandewal had thought the jewellery vulgar. The boast was that this new technology made diamonds as cheap as dirt. That did not say much about Bangalore society. She had noticed some of the yellow press had obviously come to the same conclusion as her, for they had steadfastly refused to adorn their ties or lapels with diamonds worth less even than paste. In the cavernous processor halls, she had been intimidated by the monolithic nanofactories. She would have thought it ironic that processing the smallest of elements required the use of massive blocks of engineering, had Mrs Meenakshi Khandewal possessed a functioning sense of irony. Intimidating, frightening. She had hated that her husband spent his time with these huge, metal mistresses. Crude, unsubtle, unfeminine. She hated that she lived in the house they built, ate the food they wove, spent the money they milled. She had vowed never to set foot on the factory floor again.

Ren kept Mrs Meenakshi Khandewal's promise. She was not setting foot on the factory floor. She came in on the tenth level service gantry. She peered over the edge. Thirty metres down the canyon wall of the number one processor to the ground. You would faint sheer away, Mrs Meenakshi Khandewal, Ren thought. You should thank me, that I'm teaching you things, taking you places you never would dare tread. But you're still tripped out in there. You'll never know. You'll never know a thing.

Beauty was on top of the processor four, Hall One. She wore the body of Mrs Tapan's handsome son Kishor. Mrs Meenakshi Khandewal had an eye for him. Partly he was a fancy of an amusement for herself, more a prospect five, six years down the line, for her Savita. He would be well-established then. The talk of the circle. Lawyers at least kept their hands clean.

Beauty said, 'I saw Ismail down by the airconditioning and he didn't do it right, not right at all. I mean, he did it, and they're all over the place by now, but it was too quick. He didn't get to see what was happening. So I'm not going to follow orders. I'm going to do it this way.'

The knife was in the inside pocket of the soft black silk blouson. It was a folding American-style hunting knife, hooked tip, serrated blade. Beauty unclasped it, admired the fine, clean blade. Then she touched the tip to her left wrist. With one sure, straight jerk, she opened the left arm almost to the elbow. Ren almost cried aloud at the spurt of sudden, scarlet blood. Kishor's handsome face contorted, he dropped the knife. Only Beauty's will kept him from clamping a hand to the massive wound.

'I reckon, I've got seven, eight minutes. '

He waved his red, gushing arm over the top of the nanofactory like a blessing. Where the blood was sprinkled, the ceramoplastic blistered and bloomed into hundreds of pin-head-sized orange flowers.

More than immortality. More than the Trojan horse buckies extracted from the bloodstream fullerenes of isopaths. The shipments that ran in from the Malabar coast to the black medical markets of Mysore and Tamil Nadu were laced with fullerenes that turned their carriers into walking, talking, aspiring biological packages of Chaga.

The flower patches fused, sent out fern-coils of delicate crystal. Beauty was now waist-high in yellow, glittering fronds. Kishor's body wavered. His face was white, his breathing shallow. He slumped, caught himself, tried to focus on the beautiful destruction leaking out of his body. He could not focus. He fell on his side. The crystal fronds rang like breaking glass as they shattered. Ren could hear faint sirens. The apotheosis of Mrs Meenakshi Khandewal pressed urgently.

Barefoot, she ran the narrow catwalks, climbed the steel ladders, crossed the mesh bridges slung over terrifying chasms. Processor Hall Five. Centre stack. She stood in the middle of the big rectangular roof. She tried to imagine the nanomachines, churning away beneath her feet, weaving dirt into diamonds. Ren wondered, what if the roof gave way and dropped you into the molecular fury beneath? Like a pool of piranhas, it would strip her to the bones within seconds. Beyond piranhas, it would reduce even bones to soup. She shuddered, then the incongruity hit home. You should worry, Ren McAslan, balancing at the top of the spinal column of this sack of sabotage fullerenes? The sack, that soon will be torn open, and die? She would not go lingeringly, like Beauty, entranced by her host's death. She owed Mrs Meenakshi Khandewal a swift dispatch.

She pressed the point of the kitchen knife to the corner of her jaw bone. She relished the sensuality of blade against flesh. She was in the land of the suicides now, the torments and dark joys to be found in committing crimes against your own body. She pushed, a prickle of pain, a slow well of blood. The warm run of it down the side of her neck shocked her. Ren's grasp on the blade faltered.

The tree stood before her again, its leaves, branches, bark stripped bare. She saw the explosion, and its red eye. She saw the explosion of the shotgun in her hands – once, twice – and the spray of wood, and the red running down the wall. She saw

Kishor's forearm spraying infected blood and the look of betrayed realization glazing his eyes. Beyond the light, is only dark.

Ren took the knife away from Mrs Meenakshi Khandewal's neck. You are a warrior, she shouted at herself. You must destroy your enemies.

She looked for those enemies. She found vain, trivial, kindly Mrs Meenakshi Khandewal. She found Savita and Little Meena, and Jogendra, and her friends and the places they went and the things they did. She saw her parents behind her, and her grandparents standing behind them, and the hopes they held for her and the plans they made for her and the life they planned for her. She found the hopes and plans and lives she held for her own daughters, and the joy she took in their triumphs and the pain she felt at their disappointments. She found a well-dressed snobbish middle-class Indian woman who had nothing she could call her own but her two daughters. She saw a human being.

She brought the knife up to her throat. She could not make the slash.

With a cry, Ren threw the kitchen knife away from her. It fell glittering down between the stacks. Mrs Meenakshi Khandewal could not run, but Ren ran her. She ran her back across the high bridge, along the gantry work, down the metal staircase. Mrs Meenakshi Khandewal's body protested. Ren pushed it on. Across the factory floor. Sorry Mrs K. Is it worth a promise to save your life? Ren pushed up the bar on the emergency exit, ran across the dark loading area towards the distant flashing blue lights of the emergency services.

'Help me!' she shouted. 'Help me!'

Paramedics in fluorescent green jackets hurried to her aid. Safety was assured. Ren shut down the isopathic link, jumped out of Mrs Meenakshi Khandewal across a sub-continent and an ocean into her own body. In her final moments in Mrs Meenakshi Khandewal's body she had tried to envision the isopath chamber, the kneeling figures with their attendants. Imagination might lessen the disorientation of opening her eyes in her own body again. She still came out of the jump as if from a vivid dream, dazed and tired and not knowing what to believe. She

263

fought with her body. You cannot afford this. You need every instant. But she was cold, and deadly tired. She tried to focus on the other figures in the ring. Johnson was curled on his side in foetal position. Ismail was rocking back and forth in his foil blanket, breathing loudly. Neither could see her. Beauty and Farad were still out there. They could find out. They might already know. ATR draped the thermal blanket around her shoulders. Ren shook it off.

'Bag,' she croaked.

ATR slid her the black canvas bag. Ren's fingers fumbled among the smelly clothes and the hygiene stuff and the cheap body ornaments until they closed on the handle of Oksana's gun.

It was one smooth, swift motion. Bag to brain. The side of the barrel knocked ATR a metre and a half. 'Sorry sorry sorry,' Ren gibbered but she did not stop to see if her friend moved. Beauty's and Farad's aides were getting to their feet. Ren turned the gun on them. 'Down!' she screamed. 'Down the lot of you! Nobody make a fucking move!'

She ran out of the chamber straight into Bamileke. Ren jabbed the gun at him and screamed wordlessly. He reeled back. Ren dashed past, out, into the light. She heard movement behind her, glanced: Bamileke had fetched the AK47. She narrowly avoiding hurtling into a drive-in pillar. Ren swung the gun in the direction of the threat and fired three shots. The recoil almost sent her headlong. She stumbled, recovered. The gnawed concrete pillar to her left exploded. Ren screamed, peppered with shattered concrete. She dived for cover as the Kalashnikov opened up on semi-automatic. Ren rolled, jabbing at the flage-suit's wrist control. She saw herself turn, uncertain. She hugged herself, not daring to shriek, as Bamileke raked the lost drive-in with shells. She pulled up her hood, pressed her bag to her belly and crawled for the cover of the rotting city and the tall trees.

'You're dead, you know!' Bamileke's voice echoed from the curve of the old cinema screen. 'We'll find you. You can't hide, we will track you down, we will find you and kill you. You are dead, you fucking white bitch! You hear me? Dead!'

The loudspeaker pillars leaped and shattered under the assault of bullets until not one was left standing but Ren was gone, out among the root buttresses, running.

49

In the High Atlas the snows were melting and the springs and freshets of Marrakech burgeoned. Red rock aquifers filled; nano-pumps siphoned the deep earth-water into wells and reservoirs. Irrigation canals swelled, aqueducts gushed and chuckled. In the souks and medinas of the royal red city robot water sprinklers laid the winter dust; palace pleasure grounds, royal parks, courtyard gardens, rooftop allotments, wallpots and window boxes burst forth. A thousand swimming pools heliographed. In the great square the water sellers clinked their brass cups and saucers. In the coffee houses the men talked politics over small sparkling bottles named after saints and Sidis. The kids gathered around parked mopeds showered their faces with bottled Atlas melt. Discarded plastic litre bottles blew and bounced through the tortuous covered streets. The children still danced under the public hydrants; the drunks, the hash-heads still cavorted in the fountains. The ancient buildings drank spring water through their roots, like rising sap it surged dizzyingly to their crowns; rooftops sprouted green, bougainvillea and bitter orange grew dark and glossy. A cool humidity exuded from the walls into the streets; whole districts seemed to fill and stretch. The city grew taller and prouder, drunk on water.

The little palace had been an after-ripple in the cascade of architecture that marked the advent of the Alaouite dynasty. It had been built to house the less favoured women and eunuchs of Moulay Ismail. He had filled it with light and space and water. The harem had flustered and intrigued through its airy colonnades and chambers for three weeks before being moved with the rest of the court to the new capital of Meknes. Now UNESCO ran it as a guest house for visiting dignitaries. That definition included the current clandestine delegation from the renegade hemisphere. The whole building had been reserved for the Southerners, its bugs and monitors fed a careful synthesis of faked conversation.

Gaby was entranced by the house. Every morning she swam in the Pool of the Women. Three hundred and fifty years ago four and twenty concubines had amused themselves in these waters; now one woman slid naked over the geometric mosaics. She would dive down through the cool green ripples, hair floating around her like a banner, to trace the lapis lazuli outlines, the patterns of embedded pearls. Afterwards she would take her breakfast coffee in the courtyard garden and read her newspaper to the muted plash of the fountain and the swooping whistles of the caged birds.

Marrakech, city of waters.

She scanned the day's briefing. The contact would be delayed again. Another day in the markets and street cafés with Faraway. Another night in the restaurants and free-jazz cafés, talking and talking and talking, and knowing, and wanting to, and going back to their exquisite, sensual, separate bedrooms. Because you're scared to start it.

No, she thought; not scared to start it. It started the moment the plane took off from Nyerere. Its first movement was in the hasty, sneaked transfer at Tibesti, the false idents, the credit cards, the dash through the dust storm to the Sibirsk cargo shuttle.

A self-smile, an affectionate memory. Not Faraway, but Cletho, in the departure zone at Nyerere. The only airport on the planet you can bring a spear into the concourse.

'Wherever you go, Cletho goes.'

'This is a covert diplomatic mission. You aren't exactly inconspicuous toting two metres of razor-edged nano-diamond.' But the girl's loyalty had touched her. She had been standing under the lip of the canopy as the diplomatic shuttle pulled away, spear in hand.

Then the adagio of desert flight, so high you could see the curve of the planet and the Sahara seemed softened under the sun to the colour and texture of caramel. The whole five hours she had leaned against the window, hypnotized by this raw, natural world that seemed more alien than anything that had fallen from the stars. Third movement: rondo, allegro: the wonder-filled exploration of this ancient, beautiful house, the memory of sensuality impressed on its walls like faience, and the red, water-sprinkled city beyond. No, it's already started. You're scared to complete it. Bring it to its natural cadence.

Faraway was a bear in the mornings.

'Mm.' Coffee and croissants. Three, and two coffees before he could manage a polysyllable.

'He's been held up again,' she said. 'It'll be tomorrow before he gets in.'

She did not want to say that it could even be a different city. Marrakech had been a last-minute switch when Ogun intelligence unearthed a mole in the Lagos network.

'Shit.'

So it was another day in the souks and the squares and the coffee houses, and another night in the restaurants and walking among the jugglers and snake charmers and fortune tellers and Islamic preachers blazing with *baraka* in the Jemaa el Fna and in a free-jazz club they talked and talked and danced close to a tune that Gaby did not tell Faraway had been written by Diamond Jim and had somehow preceded her North across terminum, and afterwards they went back to their exquisite, sensual, separate beds. In the morning again she swam naked in the Pool of the Women and ate her fresh croissants and read her newspaper and the daily briefing came through on the house PDU and said, *he's here*.

The driver of the big blue taxi made sure his passengers knew that his vehicle was the last word in modernity. If he could, he would have stopped and made them get out to look at the coils of ceramoplastic and organic circuitry under the hood. 'Shit and water,' he said. '*Vraiment*. Plastic, paper, household scraps, dead vermin, any old shit, you throw it in the tank and the car goes. Those niggers down South don't know what they're sitting on.'

'Savages,' Faraway said.

Gaby realized a thing about terminum. When she had been an exile she had seen it as an iron curtain, an armed *ne plus ultra*. Looking from the other side, she saw that it was a membrane, a placenta. It was impermeable to big things, like people and ideas

267

and economies, but permitted the osmotic creep of small things; molecules, notions, jazz songs.

The rendezvous was in a clattering coffee house overlooking a bus station. Ceiling fans wobbled nervously, waiters in tassled *tarbooshes* brought and took on silver trays. Gaby was the only woman. The coffee house chatterers stared twice, first at the red-haired white woman, then at the black man with her.

He sat at a table by the window. Street noise and bus traffic made conversation discreet. What had been plump sixteen years ago was now fat. His hair had retreated to a final redoubt at the base of his skull. He still grew it long. He still affected the white-man-in-Africa linen suits, though he now looked hot and stuffed in them. His face was rounder, but underneath thin, weary, overburdened with too much seen. Not so much a boiled owl, Gaby thought. Now a smoked owl. A pickled, preserved owl.

Gaby could walk right up to him without him recognizing her. She knew he had been looking for someone older. Someone who looked less like the memory of a dream.

'T.P.'

He looked up, suddenly terrified. Then, recognition. T.P. Costello surged to his feet, amazed. Hands met; suddenly flustered, he had to sit down.

'Jesus, it's true. You don't . . .' The North Dublin accent was impregnable even to time.

Gaby sat across the mosaicked table from her old boss.

'We do, just slower. A lot slower. God, it's good to see you, you look . . .'

'Shit. I look like shit – it's the job. Jaysus, you've no idea what it's like to be back in the field again. What've you got?'

'No idea,' Gaby and Faraway said simultaneously in the old litany.

After the elderly waiter had served the coffee and the brilliant, horrifyingly calorific sweet things, Gaby set the cell memory in the middle of the table.

'The whole thing, step by step by step.'

'You can prove it all?' T.P. asked. 'This is absolutely solid?'

'T.P.,' Gaby said. 'This is me.'

He smiled. 'I've heard that before. Usually I just had to call in some favour to get your ass out of the fire. Seriously, Gab, they will jump on any weakness, any flaw or uncorroborated fact. And this isn't just the Press Complaints Commission, or a libel suit if you're unlucky. This is governments. This is the fucking CIA.'

'The Tororo Empire is using Haut Zaire mercenaries to take out local non-aligned nations. I've talked to prisoners. It's all in there. The H-Zra funds its campaigns on both sides of terminum by illicitly trading Tororo cha-tech. Straight swap: buckies for arms. It never gets outside the MI complex, but I've got the names of the brokers. They're in there. Half a dozen big name Northern industrials are using Tororo diamond weavers – blue chip companies, major players – and paying off the NLAs with experimental weaponry. This time, it was the Bugandans' turn to play with the big boys' toys. The Soroti attack was a field test. It just so happened it had a geopolitical kickback, but primarily it was to ascertain the effectiveness of a new anti-personnel missile system. US Army pilots were flying American Kiowa attack helicopters; I can give you the serial numbers. The bastards were so sure of themselves they didn't even file off the maker's marks. It's all down in there. The missiles are manufactured by Nanoweb-Raytheon in Kansas, the flèchettes were designed by JTT in Mysore. Seventy per cent of stolen nanoware leads end in India. I've traced all the steps, from a fucking ten-inch diamond blade a mother pulled out of her son's face to J.S. Chandrasekahr's desk of the fifty-fifth floor at JTT. It's in there, I can prove it. The whole I-Zee, Low War operation is a testing ground for new weapons and military strategies. I show that. But it's more. The political strategy is to keep the South isolated and divided until the Northern corporates can develop bucky technology to the level where they can survive contact with us. Because right now, we would be fatal to them. It's the classic alien first contact scenario: in almost any permutation, contact with an advanced interstellar alien civilization, human society comes apart. Human society? Fuck. Western corporate capitalist society comes apart. They have a strategy for it, I've seen it, I had it wormed out of the Pentagon: quarantine, control, access restricted to government and military channels. The Chaga fucked that up; there were no aliens – no aliens they could recognize. No spaceships, nothing landing on the White

269

House steps, no grey pixies with slitty eyes and twitchy fingers giving people enemas. The Chaga was an alien alien. But now they have aliens they can recognize. Us.'

'It's a hell of a risk.' T.P. Costello said.

'Come on, you're sixteen years in the same company in a business where they cut your throat because they think the colour of your tie clashes with red. You wouldn't be here if this was going to be terminal to the career of Thomas Pronsias Costello.'

'You know, I've just remembered what it was about working with you that so pissed me off. Faraway, what did you ever see in this woman?'

Gaby scooped up the cell memory.

'It can go right back South with me again.'

'Gaby, just give it to me.'

But she hesitated.

'This is more than T.P. Costello getting a story he can retire on and sticking it up the asses of his enemies.'

'And maybe I'm here because I don't give a fuck about any of that. Maybe I'm here because this message comes on to my desk and I meet the contact and I find this woman I haven't seen for seventeen years, that could have been dead for all I knew, wants to meet me. Maybe that was enough, to find out where she's been, what she's been doing, see her again.'

Gaby pressed the little plastic container into T.P.'s hand.

'You still talk the biggest load of ould shite, T.P.'

T.P. barked with laughter. They went on to an achingly kitsch *tajine* restaurant, and then to a bar, then down to the Square of the Souls to see if the *sidi* were preaching there again to fill them with spiritual dread, then to a club where Gaby did not know any of the tunes.

'A kid. Jesus, I can't imagine you with a kid,' T.P. said while Faraway was trying to summon a club girl to buy a bottle of wine.

'Kid? She's seventeen years old,' Gaby said. 'All oestrogen and angst.' And camouflage gear and big guns. And you have been running around doing deals, breaking stories, plotting and scheming and falling in love in a foreign city and you do not know if your Serena is alive, dead, hungry, pregnant, poor, fighting off five bastard men, in love, in a body bag, in bed, in hell. This is the first time in five days you've given her a thought.

'What's she like?' T.P. asked.

Gaby raised one eyebrow. T.P sucked breath in through pursed lips.

'The men must be queued from here to Capetown.'

She had three dances with him after that, one fast, two slow. He asked Gaby, 'Did you ever get that bundle of files from Shaw Wayt?'

Gaby had to reach into her auxbrain to recall the name. 'Shepard's records,' she said. 'I did. That rumour you told me.'

'What one was that?'

'The one about Shepard making it into the fifth chamber. Do you know, what happened, has he . . .'

'Did he?'

'Yes,' she said, thinking, you can only say that because you are a little drunk and the band is playing music that is the echo of old aches.

'You have to understand, the BDO is the one thing that's even more taboo than you people. And they don't have forty thousand kilometres of border to defend, just a lot of space and a lot of big guns. The place is the fifty-first state of the Union. What is it?'

'Fortress America. So you've heard nothing.'

'I've heard, but nothing I can prove.'

'About Shepard?'

T.P. had caught the expressive Gallic shrug from SkyNet's Paris European headquarters.

'All you get from the military is freeze-dried ice-cream. You have to go to the amateur networks; the astronomical groups have been noticing a lot of thruster burns out there recently. The talk is they're moving against the Space Monkeys.'

'T.P., we don't call them that where I come from.'

'Sorry, probably some of your best friends . . . But the army's on the move. The big university telescopes can resolve surface detail down to a hundred metres. They've got tugs quartering the surface. Also, the satellite watchers have noticed perturbations in the orbit of Gaia.'

'I thought that had burned out long ago.'

'Just the cameras. What it is now, is a handy-dandy guided missile.'

'Jesus. Why now?'

'SETInet's been monitoring radio traffic – there's not a hell of a lot else for them to do with their PCs and satellite dishes now we've actually made first contact. Over the past six months the Monkeys – Big Sky Nation, sorry – have found someone to talk to down here.'

'Someone in the South.'

'Good guess. Yes. An outfit based in Madagascar.'

'Jesus. The Merina. Do the SETI people know what they're talking about?'

'They've cracked the coding – they're the kind of people do this sort of thing for a hobby – but what it sounds like is – they tell me – whale song.'

The little band had begun another tune. Gaby looked over to her table. Faraway nodded, got up to order wine.

'There's another thing,' T.P. said. 'This only recently got declassified under new EU freedom of information rules. The BDO isn't the be-all and end-all of space exploration. In fact, since the US annexed it, it's freed up the rest of the universe for us bit players. There's an Indian satellite – AUGIE, Azimuthal something or other – it's carrying a Danish experiment making a gravity wave map of the sky. About the time when Shepard and the others went into the fifth chamber, it registered a gravitational anomaly.'

'Like?'

'Like I'm not a scientist. What it recorded was a disturbance, a gravity ripple, right across the solar system. Just for an instant, a few thousandths of a second. The woman I talked to described it being like the wake of a fast boat, only it appeared everywhere at once.'

'It can't do that.'

'It did.'

'You're going to tell me it originated from the BDO.'

'I'm going to tell you that it led straight to Éa.'

'Jesus, T.P.'

'There's more. They're only getting the data in now because of the distance and all that, but it made a turn at Éa, like the thing was a lens, and headed out of the solar system. Straight as an arrow.'

'Rho Ophiuchi?'

'No,' T.P. said. 'That's what they'd been expecting. That's what's weird. It's aimed in a totally different direction, into this big empty sector of the sky. No clusters, no nebulae, just a lot of red dwarfs and out about seven thousand light years, what could be the accretion disc of a medium-sized black hole. The thing is, Gaby, the evidence they're getting now seems to indicate that the ripple is still simultaneous. Wherever it's going to, it got there the instant it left.'

The set ended. The dancers broke and applauded. Before Faraway returned with the new wine, Gaby asked the one question she needed an answer to. 'T.P., did Shepard ever come back?'

'No,' T.P. Costello said as they all sat down and Faraway poured.

That night the spirits of the old house were awake. A new wind blew through the arches and courtyards, the hot wind from the south, out of the heart of Africa. No one would sleep tonight. Faraway followed Gaby through the sensuous, elegant rooms to the Pool of the Women. He watched, quivering with want and uncertainty, as she scattered her clothes and descended the marble steps into the dark, rippled water. She let the cool water caress her vulva, then launched herself out into the deep. Mica flecks twinkled far below her, capturing the moons held in the skylight. She was swimming among stars. She dived down, but tonight she could not touch them. They seemed to have receded beyond her reach. She broke surface, flicked her hair behind her, trod water. Faraway hesitated on the top step.

'Come and swim with me.' Gaby turned on to her back.

'I can't swim,' Faraway said.

'I'll teach you.'

Still he stood. He looked in torment. He shook his head. Gaby slid towards him. She stood on the bottom step, extended Faraway her hand. He walked down, into the water, all the way. He stood chest deep, stiff, afraid, as Gaby swirled around him like a sea-succubus, removing his clothes.

'Gaby.'

'Faraway.'

'I'm scared of water.'

She touched her finger to his lips. She stood beside him in the shallows. One hand on his chest, one under his thighs, said *lie back*.

'Gaby . . .'

'It'll hold you. Trust it.'

His face said he did not, could not. But he trusted her hands. He tensed, almost panicked as she moved the hand on his chest under his back. Her face said, *still. Relax.*

'Arms out,' she said. Her arms easily supported the weight of the big man. 'Just float.' In the moonslight she saw him not as a naked man, or as a soon-to-be lover, but as a sheer, magnificent skin. She said, 'I'm going to take my arms away now. You'll float. Don't worry.' But he did. She saw the sudden realization that no one was holding him cross his face. He tensed, panicked, went down. Gaby dived after him, wrapped her arms around him, hauled him into the air.

'You let go,' he said.

'Sorry,' she said. The wind in the gardens, the women in the walls said, *kiss him*. She kissed him. He came up hard against her belly at once. In the near free-fall of water, she wrapped her arms around his neck, her legs around his waist. He drew her out of the deep water, up the steps. On the third step he settled back, Gaby on top of him. Ripples lapped around his chest. Gaby's hand squeezed his balls. His tongue jammed against hers. He entered her. She pulled out of his mouth, arched her back, laughed sharp and loud. The walls echoed. Her forefinger found his asshole. He stiffened as she burrowed in, one, two. His fucking took a deeper urgency. Got you now, negro. Fingers right on the thrust button. I can run you like an old tape machine. Fast forward. Rewind. Pause. Play.

The two finger exercises racked him out to twenty-five minutes before he came. Gaby spent the last ten minutes in a blur of multiple orgasms. She curled up against him in the now-chill pool, humming tunes from *The Sound of Music* as she watched the ropes of semen sink through the dark water.

They gave her a new, better idea.

The braided velvet curtain ties made soft fetters to hog-tie Faraway over the carved wooden coffee table in the drawing room. He stared upside down at the carved Moorish door, laughing filthily. A noose of the under-gardener's twine went round his ball sack. His laughter turned to wide-eyed dread as she threaded the long ends back through the loop, pulled hard and yanked his balls into two bulging, velvet-skinned black plums. Gaby bestrode him. No arms, no legs, no head. The classical male torso. She settled on to his chest. A stool, upholstered in exquisite black leather.

She warned him: 'Most males can only take ten minutes of this.' She waited until she felt him struggle against his bonds before adding, 'You're getting an hour.'

She set to work on his cock. She worked it hard, she worked it soft. She worked it fast, she worked it slow. She seized its full length in both hands, she devoted minute attention to the lining of the meatus. She gave him mouth, she gave her nipples, she gave him tongue and teeth. She gave him fingertips, fingernails, hair. She slid carefully selected objects up it. She paused to tighten the noose around his balls until they throbbed. She pushed him to the edge of orgasm, she pulled him back, a dozen times. She kept him hovering unendurably on the brink. He went from laughter to high-pitched animal keening through inane chatter, blasphemies in five languages, warnings of consequences if she did not stop right now, pleading, vowing any and every kind of service for ever amen, shouting, silence. Gaby wondered how the word-spam computer was conveying this to the listeners. After forty-five minutes Faraway had passed into an altered state of consciousness. After an hour she jerked him furiously until he came with a cry like a hurt child. Then she untied his balls and his body.

She saw his face when he came back from washing off the sweat in the pool. She thought, with a deep, abandoned thrill, Oh My God, he is going to make me pay for this.

She was still paying for it when T.P. Costello came barging in followed by the flapping, protesting *gardien* with the news that JTT Nanotechnology Bangalore had been destroyed in the night by the Black Simbas.

'Put your fucking clothes on and get us out of this,' T.P. demanded.

'I'm in my fucking clothes,' Gaby said, swaddled in soft ecru bed linen.

'Hi,' Faraway said, smiling at the man in the white suit at the foot of his bed. 'How are you?' Seven hours of sex had quite cured him of being a bear in the morning.

Two terrible words penetrated Gaby's post-coital aura.

'Black Simbas?'

They mapped the extent of the damage in the courtyard garden. The satellite channels followed up the early-breaking on-line news sites with live pictures. To the three old news people, it was the first days of the Chaga again: the cordon of soldiers, the confused, frightened evacuees, the shaky suggestions of alien life-forms rising through the geometries of twenty-first century Indian industrial park. The contagion zone had stabilized at a kilometre across. Forensic teams had gone in. Meridian, AOL News and Microsoft Direct carried details: the infected blood, the possessed wealthy. StarEast satellite had the survivor, a kind-faced, plump, hysterical woman covered in blood wrapped in a foil blanket. Paramedics led her to an ambulance.

Gaby drank her breakfast coffee and watched the carnage and told herself, do your work. Be your work. Think about how you are going to save this. Don't think about your daughter. Don't think about what she has done.

'Our calculations are wrecked,' Faraway said. 'But they haven't mentioned Soroti. That is one thing we still have.'

'If we make the connection, it could look as if we're condoning terrorism,' Gaby said. 'We're certainly explaining it.'

'It could go either way.' T.P. poured fresh coffee. 'Up North no one understands what's going on down South. They can't tell the difference between the Harambee or El Sur and the Black Simbas or the Chaganistas. You're all anarchists, terrorists and probably communists to boot. On the other hand, Washington isn't exactly in love with Delhi. After the great capitalist Chinese Empire rumour failed to scare everyone, India's the new Faceless Asian threat. So there'll be condemnation from the White House but not a hell of a lot else. Strategically, it could work in our favour: conference now, or it's NanoWeb-Raytheon next and everyone wakes up and finds they're not in Kansas any more.'

Faraway paced up and down the gravel paths. Gaby thought of his clothes still lying at the bottom of the Pool of the Women, and the silk drape tassles still tied to the table legs. It's not right, she thought. After sex you will remember for the next thousand years, you should not have to make a decision like this, the biggest decision of your career, utterly on your own. Dr Dan's mathematicians in Great Boma have all the permutations mapped on to their big model, they could tell you the consequences of your every action, but you're blind and deaf, you are in Marrakech, *incommunicado*.

'Our hand has been forced, we play our card now,' he said. 'This is not the best time, but it is the only time. If we wait, our enemies grow stronger. Can you do this, T.P.?'

'Yes.'

'Then go with it.'

Faraway wanted to buy the Moorish coffee table but the *gardien* could not sell United Nations property and the wood would not have survived contact with the Chaga. In the UNESCO car, at the airport, in the R.A.M. Boeing as it climbed over the snows of the High Atlas, Gaby was quiet, distant. Chilled.

'Are you all right?' Faraway asked, thinking it was somehow him.

'Yeah,' she said, leaning against the window, looking at the gentle golden desert, thinking about Serena.

50

In the dream, the Hound of God had brought her down. She lay between its steel-clawed paws, looking up into its six black eyes. She could not run. In dreams, you can never run. The hound unfolded its mandibles. She screamed as the long tongue slid out and locked. It held her entranced, like a charming chromium snake. One thrust. She tried to cry out but the poison needle had impaled her voice box. She took a long, wracking time to flail and die.

She woke with a cry. Something had touched her. She scrambled out of the nest of papers and rags, away from it, away. The door-frame brought her up hard. But she had the gun now. Two-fisted, she pushed it in the direction of the touch.

'Hey, whoa, sorry!' The young man in the saffron Buddhist robe held his hands up. 'It's okay, it's okay, I was just checking you were all right.'

She slid up the door-frame to her feet, backed away, never taking the gun off the man's face.

'I'm not going to hurt you, I just thought you might need some help.'

She turned. She ran, again. She had let herself sleep. One moment's weakness, and she had lapsed. The timer patch on her wrist said, fifteen minutes. You cannot afford even fifteen minutes. Her body said, Ren, you must sleep. But you cannot sleep. The Hound of God never sleeps. Never sleeps, never stops. Keeps coming and coming and coming. Once it has your pheromone pattern, it will not give up until you are dead.

Three rounds left. The thing was armoured, it could take all three frags to put it down. To be sure of a kill, she would have to wait until the very last moment to fire. When the thing was coming down from its death-leap. But she was so tired. She did not know she could fire straight. Sleep, food, fatigue: her body's needs betrayed her. Trotting on its six ceramoplastic legs, the Hound of God knew no such imperfections.

She had instinctively run for the city. Two thousand square kilometres, twelve million souls. Big city, your city, she had chanted like a mantra as she fled through the deep Chaga towards the road. She had hit the Kirinya highway and re-set the flage-suit to neutral, waving a desperate thumb at the buses and *pujos* growling past. No one was prepared to give a ride to a white girl in a tight suit, whatever its markings. She was far beyond her reserves when she came on the small wayside mosque. The concessionaire selling hot food to hungry Muslim drivers had stared at Ren, stumbling over her slew feet, crazy with fatigue, but did not say a word as she hauled herself up the rear ladder of the little country bus swathed in improving *suras* in elegant Arabic and snuggled into its black thermal fibre mane, among the bundle and bales. It was only because the sound of the engine starting woke her that she realized she had been asleep. She peeped out between the bundles. Her senses had told her true, the road was rising. The bus was taking her in the right direction. She could rest a time. First she must open one more isopathic link. She wrapped hands and feet in the luggage ropes, closed her eyes.

She opened them on a fist, a sudden white blast of pain. The link almost ruptured. As her borrowed body rolled, she glimpsed a purple-clad figure tall over her, the swing of a boot, a crushing impact. On the roof of God's bus, Ren cried out. In the shell-shaped room, ATR cowered against the wall, hands over face, arms over breasts and womb.

'Don't hit me, don't hit me, please!'

Bamileke drew back his fist and casually back-handed her. Ren flinched. ATR's shriek subsided into muffled sobbing.

'She was yours, understand? Your responsibility.'

Another blow. ATR held one hand out, pleading to stop.

'The white bitch shot at me.' Bamileke kicked her twice.

'I'm sorry. I'm sorry.'

'She tried to fuck me up the ass. No one fucks me up the ass. Do you understand?' He dragged ATR to her feet. She held her hands up in front of her face. She saw that he would hit her again, and that he would not stop until she told him what he wanted to hear.

'Someone has to die here. Do you understand?'

He let her drop. ATR crawled across the floor, spitting and retching.

'Do you understand?' Bamileke roared.

'Yes!' she screamed at the man. 'Yes. I understand! Give me the hound, and I will bring you her head!'

The link broke. Ren's power was gone. Woven like a fly in a web of Islamic ladies' luggage ties, she had lapsed into unconsciousness. She awoke with a shock, sticky with drool, arms and legs aching, hands and feet numb. Her head ached. She needed desperately to piss, but had never been so thirsty. Dark: night? The watch patch said she had slept three hours. Ren untangled herself from her web and pushed through the heavy baggage.

279

Night: lights. City lights? Then she was under a big curving roof of ivory ribs, and into light again, and noise, a big open space. People, engines, swinging vehicle lights. Kianyaga *pujo* station. She was home. Her city would protect her. As the bus jolted over the pot-holed coral Ren clambered down the ladder. She dropped to the ground, melted into the crowd. She found an unvandalized *choo*, treated herself to a luxurious piss and gulped down mouthfuls of water from the spigot that warned in three languages that this was not drinking water. She scrubbed dried yellow grit out of her eyes, caked drool from her face. She emptied her bag and pulled denim cut-offs and fake fur top over the flageskin. She checked the gun. She had wasted half a magazine on that bastard Bamileke.

The mirror was broken into radiating shards. Ren studied her shattered image. She moved her head until the epicentre of the shards lay over her right eye. She challenged herself: Do you know what you are any more? If you smash your fist into the hole over your eye and all the pieces fall out on to the piss-swimming floor, what will you put them back into?

You were sure, so absolutely sure, the night of the storm over Fat Tuesday's.

She looked beyond the face in the mirror. Fullerene called to fullerene. She opened After the Rain's eyes. Walls she knew, a bed that bore her impress, a clock that kept her time, a magazine that wasted it. She was back in her room in Mururi.

So fast: how? Too fast. The Islamic bus, an old sow dawdling to market.

Something else in her room. Something sniffling, clicking. A movement, between the bed and the wall. As ATR left the bedroom she glimpsed a glossy, dog-sized object, nuzzling at her body-mark on the bed. Into the kitchen. Clicky tippy-tapping behind her: Ren clenched her fists at the frustration of not being able to turn ATR's head to look. Unwashed bowls, piles of left-overs. She waved flies away from a spoon stuck in a mound of *irio*. She knelt and offered the spoon to the thing clicking behind her.

The hound trotted on tiny needle toes. It was a thing all pins and blades: six sprung insect legs, a gleaming, thorn-studded carapace of iridescent purple, a hatchet of a head that unfolded nested sets of mandibles to lick up the taste of Ren. Feather-frond antennae brushed the bowl of the spoon, learning her scent. ATR set the plate of rotting scraps before the hound. It crouched on its spindly legs, scrabbled in the decaying, flyblown mess with its busy busy mouth. Fuelled, it drew itself up, turned, and went hunting Ren.

It hunted slowly, steadily, at an easy trot. It hunted with insect inevitability, tasting the night with its antennae for Ren-musk, drawn to her with the blind magnetism of a luna moth. Through ATR she watched it pick its precise way down the steps of the Great House and disappear into the dark alleys of Mururi.

And she had found herself facing her broken image in a bus station toilet. And she was running with the unresting, unhasting, silent as light Hound of God on her heels. Running where? She could make Okya's place easily. She could ambush the thing, kill it, tear its beaked skull off. But there was no help there any more. She would face the hound alone, in the dark, cold, shut-up house.

Gaby. She has friends, resources, she has the power of the Harambee behind her. She'll know what to do. She is your mother. But if she doesn't? The hound will take down anything that comes between it and its prey. Mombi's spearwoman. Faraway. Your mother.

Nowhere to run, psy-warrior, but run is all you can do. And your strength is failing, and your will is sapping, and the black sleep seems like bliss. They say that the purest love is the love between the hunted and the blade.

She caught herself, asleep on her feet. You can't go on like this. Maybe I could get a lift, get right away, far and fast. She thumbed, she waved, she yelled and swore, but the traffic on Uhuru Highway howled past. High then. Maybe those tiny needle feet can't climb, and I will live the rest of my life on roofs and tree tops.

Where am I? An open space under stars, crossed by foot-trodden paths, muddy after rain. Behind her the growl of the big orbital highway. Before her a deeper darkness; a wall of vegetation, no lights, no features. To her left, biolume huddles underlit the ribbed canopies of domestic processors. Some petty nation or other. To her right, street glow highlit the tall cylinders and silos of a manufacturing tribe. As good a place as any to play out the end-game. Four fast, deep breaths of cold mountain air; Ren jogged towards the factory lights. And was on her face, down, too stunned even to curse. Squirrel hole, discarded litter: too dark to see. But in the silence where her next footfall should have been, she heard a tiny, delicate clicking. Needle legs, knitting unhasting haste.

She was on her feet, cursing them on towards the lights of the big processor stacks. A glance back. She saw what she expected to see. Darkness. You won't see it until the end, when it comes down out of its kill-leap and the needle takes you in the throat.

Perspective had tricked her. The lights were closer, the stacks smaller than she had thought. What she had thought was a full-scale molecular engineering facility was a neighbourhood nano-factory. The processor pillars stood three times her height. Good cover in the linking web of veins and cords. You have to use it now. Run another kilometre, and you will be too weak to shoot straight.

She chose a strong defensive position between four big supply pipes. There was an escape at her back. She pulled out Oksana's big gun and checked the mechanism. She pressed it to her cheek and listened to the sounds of the liquids burping through the feed pipes and the traffic on the orbital highway and the radios and television from the nanoworkers' homes and her own breathing.

Click.

She had dozed off, for an instant. Nothing to see out there on the floodlit clay. Then where was it?

Click click.

Ren looked up. Ceramoplast mandibles unfolded in her face. She dived forwards as the poison tongue stabbed space. She rolled, fired until the empty chamber clicked as spastically and terminally as the limbs of the hound.

She stood, panting, pointing the gun at leaking tubes and punctured veins.

A glitter of movement caught the factory floods. The Hound of God dropped to the foot-smooth clay, a tight ball of legs and chitin. Click. It sprang open like a trap, poised on sprung toes.

Ren ran. High. You've nothing left but to get high and hope

you can flick this fucking thing to the ground and drop something heavy on it. It's slow, you can beat it. She hit the tube webbing , scrabbled for fingerholds.

Something hit her hard across the kidneys. She dropped like a spider.

'That for fucking sea-food gun,' a woman's voice said. Ren rolled on to her back. She must be dead, for standing over her was a bald-headed woman dressed in slick leather carrying a diamond spear in her two hands. Angel of the assegai. Behind her, advancing at its inexorable lope across the wet clay, the Hound of God. Not dead then. Not yet.

'Cletho had mother of headaches for three days,' the woman said, planting the butt of the spear on Ren's sternum.

The Hound, Ren knew she should say. *The Hound is coming to kill you.*

The spear woman saw the slant of Ren's gaze.

'Oh, that.'

The movement was so fast that Ren could only see that it was a woman when she crouched, hands spread for combat, in front of the Hound of God. She was dressed in rubber pants and a rubber jacket covered in soft rubber spines. The Hound hunkered back on its rear legs, extended its tongue, pumped power to its jump engines. It leaped. The woman was dead. Except the woman danced out from under its leap and while it was still in mid-air, twisted its hind leg and flipped it on to its back. Before the Hound could right itself, the rubber woman had dived in with blinding speed and wrenched its back left leg to a twitching spastic stalk. Shivering, the Hound bounced, righted itself, bounced again, needle aimed for the centre of the woman's forehead. She was not there. She rolled out from under the needle, knocked the hunter three metres with a *savatte* kick. It landed on coiled plas-flesh muscles, sprang instantly. Its speed took the rubber woman by surprise. She rolled out from under its kill leap by the merest shim of rubber.

'L'Oriente, she fast,' the spearwoman said.

L'Oriente, she very fast. The Hound came for her, she jumped high, brought her boot down in the middle of its gleaming carapace. The Hound gave a little shrill, skittered away leaking yellow ichor. Nanorepair systems slipped into heal as it rounded fast – very fast – on L'Oriente. A bladed toe lashed out, opened a gash across the back of her jacket. The woman slid out from under its jaws as it buried the tip of its poison fang in her shadow. She put distance between her and the thing in a blur of motion. She shrugged off the jacket, looked distastefully at the shoulder to hip slash.

'You've got me angry now.'

The Hound rounded and charged. Not slow, not steady, not tireless. It came like a missile, like a hunting helicopter, locked on. It had kill-crazy in it now.

L'Oriente stood, unmoving.

'Cletho.'

With one liquid motion, the leather woman flung her spear at L'Oriente. Head to heart. Her aim was true. It would run the woman through like a gutted tilapia.

'No!' Ren yelled.

It was too fast and beautiful to be possible. In a flicker, L'Oriente was where the spear was not. Her arm moved in a blur of light. She caught the spear in flight, spun, dropped to the clay. But the hound had leaped. The hound was coming down, poison tongue dripping. And the diamond spear head was there to meet it.

L'Oriente knelt in the classic Masai moran attitude; the lion-killer's stance. Impaled by its own hunger, the Hound of God thrashed and kicked on nanodiamond. It did not die clean. It clawed with its needle toes at the shaft, trying to haul itself, lubricated by its own ichor, for a final thrust at its assassin.

L'Oriente up-ended the spear, thrust the head deep in the clay. The insect head stabbed and pecked as she snapped its hunting antennae, pulled out its plug eyes. Her fingers were too fast. She wrenched off its legs. The thing clung ferociously to its artificial, raging life. L'Oriente twisted off the jagged head. Now exhaustion broke over Ren. Between waves of blackness, she saw L'Oriente pull the spear from the carcase, then a hallucinatory glimpse of a beautifully polished limousine on the shiny wet clay. The stretch limo of God, she thought. Fetish angels, come to carry me home.

'Mombi?' she asked, curled on upholstery as smooth and warm as living skin, city lights blurring past the windows.

'Ah, you with us again,' said the spear-woman – Cletho, Gaby's bodyguard Ren remembered – absently stroking her matted fake fur.

'Lexus,' Ren said, then, 'Gaby's?'

'Listen to the child, will you?' Cletho said. 'These white brats have no respect, calling their mothers by their Christian names. I and I mother would have tanned I's ass for such familiarity, *m'zungu*.'

'Your mother sucked pig dick for Arab pornographers,' L'Oriente said behind the wheel. Ren stared at the air-conditioning panels in the ceiling. The car was very big and quiet and she could hear noises beyond it she recognized. Big fans: aircraft engines.

'Nyerere.'

'She all names, this one,' Cletho said. 'Yes, sister. You taking a little unscheduled trip for which you don't need no papers, don't pay no fee.'

Ren forced herself upright. A great roar and glare of white rushed over the Lexus. She ducked, fearful of the things in the sky: a heavy transport with Great Zimbabwe markings thudded down beyond the perimeter.

'Where, what?'

'So, Mombi has no love for your former employers,' Cletho said, 'but not so little that she risk her best operatives unless there gain in it for Mombi. You and your kind have become tradeable lately.'

'Isopaths?'

'Smart girl. Cletho knew she hadn't knocked you hard enough.'

L'Oriente sniggered.

'Negress, shut your mouth,' Cletho said. 'But for I's generosity, you be on end of that hound-fucker's needle.'

'Who else wants isopaths?'

'So happen you about to find out.'

The Lexus swung in at an empty stand. Cletho extricated her spear from the footwell and assumed guard position, foot propped on the inside of her knee. Ren shivered, shoved her hands in her armpits, jiggled up and down. High and cold on the slopes of Kirinyaga.

285

'Coming in now,' L'Oriente said.

A cluster of lights detached itself from the city glow of Kirinya. A tilt rotor swooped in low and fast, swivelled its fans into vertical mode. Downblast streamlined Ren's fake fur. She squinted through hot air and grit. Cletho held her stance, adamant.

The engine howl ebbed. The tilt-rotor settled on cantilevered legs. Hull lights came on. Nose and fuselage bore the green hand sigil of iMerina.

51

Seven tokes of Moroccan *kif* baited the trap. Seven micrograms of Judas psychotropics sprang it. Gaby stepped over the purring Cletho, on her back on the rug in front of the fire, wiggling her fingers at the ceiling.

'That'll teach you to raid the diplomatic stash.'

The designer had guaranteed five hours of guilt-free vacationing through inner space. Plenty of time. Gaby slipped the Harambee issue PPP into the gripskin holster inside her street coat. The taxi hooted again. The house secured itself.

Mandy the Shit had been as close to concern as his neurochemistry would permit.

'Gaby, this is foolhardiness of a very high order.'

'I need to know.'

'You are still at war.'

'It's my daughter.'

'I know nothing of this parent thing,' Mandy the Shit said as he pushed the slip of paper with the address scrawled on it across the bar.

The taxi took her as close as the driver dared to the end on that slip of paper. His sentiments echoed Mandé.

'It's personal,' Gaby said. She asked him to wait. He asked her to pay in advance.

Of course guerilla armies have their headquarters upstairs from a pool club. The men in the street yipped and yelped at the lone white woman. *Hey darlin', you c'mon over this way, what you doin' out all alone on a night like this?* The mere motion of the hand towards the fastdraw holster was warning enough. *Okay, okay, no offence, ma'am.*

The yard at the back was dark and stank of dog piss. Her eyes night-shifted: wooden pens, dull-eyed bitches, heavily pregnant, suckling litters. A staircase.

The soft-eared bitch nuzzled her offered hand. 'Hello there, girl.' I am of dog people, Gaby thought. A long time ago, in another country.

'Hello there, girl.'

The muzzle in the side of the neck belonged to a heavy calibre handpiece. The voice belonged to a short, toothy teen with the moiré patterns of nightshades swarming over his eyes. The smile widened as he frisked out the PPP. He knew a Harambee weapon.

'You would use these on me?' he asked as he shook out the fragmentation rounds. 'You would blow me up like a bomb?' He screwed the muzzle into the soft nerve bundle under Gaby's ear. She could see in his teeth and smell on his breath that he really, really wanted to watch the shells tear out her skull on his night vision glasses.

'Rose!' Gaby yelled.

'You be quiet now.'

'Rose! Gaby McAslan! Unit 12. You owe me.'

She felt the hammer go back.

'Leave her.' A woman's voice, a darker-on-dark figure at the top of the stairs. The gun dropped away. 'Lucky for you, Gaby McAslan, I pay my debts.'

Dogs attended Madam General Rose. They lolled beneath her desk and around her chair, they laid their sleek heads in her lap, they bickered and fretted for the unthinking attention of her fingers. They were not the Chaga dogs she had once bred, that guided raiding parties past the United Nations and the Kenyan Army to pick the fruit of the forbidden zones. Rose and such a dog had guided Gaby and Jake Aarons on the hallucinatory trip

287

into the Kilimanjaro Chaga that had ended in Unit 12. The soldiers had shot that dog. The memory of the South African officer came clear and sharp across twenty years; gun, skull, detonation. These dogs would not go so. These were battle dogs, quasi-organic combat systems seeded through them like cancers. Reconnaissance rigs turned them into relentless hunters. Rings of one-shot lasers studded the brow ridges, nestling under short copper fur. *Plastique* organs in their bellies made them waiting time bombs.

'She deserted under fire. It is a capital offence.' The dog moved its head. Rose fondled its soft jowls. Glossy scars marked the ancient amputation of the little finger of each hand by Mombi's enforcers. The amputations were supposed to have taught Rose obedience. But you got out, Gaby thought. You deserted to the Black Simbas.

'JTT was destroyed, it doesn't matter that Ren didn't go through with it.'

'The action is already taken.'

Grip in the heart, ice in the spine, the eyes of the dogs were all lead.

'What does that mean?'

'The Hound is loose.' Rose saw Gaby look to the war dogs. 'No. Not these. Worse. Gaby, I owe you but I cannot help you. She was a soldier, under orders. She betrayed her people.'

'She's my daughter!'

Rose had left the room. Her dogs padded after.

Room to yard to cab was sick featureless numb. The city and the night gave her nothing but her own reflection in the window; an intimate study of the most hideous of anguishes: the mother who has failed to protect her child. Half a lifetime ago you took her up to a high place and offered her to Africa if it would give back what it had taken from you. Africa, continent of time and cruelty, heard and now she is fallen, broken, swept out on the tide. You wanted it, you never wanted her. Are you answered?

Somewhere on another planet, the driver swore and banged the horn, entangled in a knot of traffic. The taxi suddenly bounced, as if a heavy object had dropped on its hood. One had: standing legs apart on the custom-painted cha-plastic, spear-point aimed through the windshield at the paralysed driver: Cletho.

'You want to know something, you not go running to them Simbas. Bastards shoot you soon as look at you,' she shouted. 'You want to know what's with your daughter, come to Cletho, right?' She jumped down and got in beside Gaby. The driver did not want a diamond-edged spear so close to his anatomy, so it stuck out the window like a lance, where it posed a major threat to the street people.

'You always underestimate I,' Cletho said. 'You think Mombi send out her best bodyguard without number-one blood-scrubbers? Woman, I was off that floor soon as you shut the front door.'

'Cletho, right now, you are *this* important to me.'

'See? This is where you have no respect. Now, if Cletho were to say, don't worry, be cool, she know where your daughter is, then you have respect.'

It was the numb again, but a different numb: breathless, white, spinning.

'Serena? Jesus, you know where she is? Is she all right?'

'Don't ask questions. All you do, ask questions, why this, what you mean, how, who? Listen to Cletho. Ren is safe. Cletho should know. Cletho and L'Oriente save her ass from Simba Hound.'

'Take me to her.'

'That is difficult.'

'Why? Where is she?'

'Madagascar.'

For an instant it was as fabulous as Xanadu and Shangri-la.

'The Merina? Why?'

'These questions ... Okay. Remember, Cletho is under strict contract, Mombi ever finds out, your bodyguard take early retirement.' Cletho leaned over and licked the driver's ear. He shuddered. 'Okay. He knows I know where he live. These Merina, they wanting talents.'

'Isopaths.'

'Yah, but not just isopaths. Also looking for precogs, and Spacemen.'

'What would the Merina want with Spacemen?'

289

'What else anyone want with Spacemen?'

'Send them into space?'

Cletho's possible response was aborted by a volley of curses from the street. A woman in Islamic dress had been nicked by Cletho's spear. She clutched her arm and called the anger of God upon the godless.

You don't know, Gaby thought. It takes an outsider to teach you. The God of Africa is cruel, certainly capricious, but he knows his people in his big land too well to be angry with them.

52

World turning.

In the 2032 online edition of the Bartholomew atlas, the globe of the world has a northern hemisphere but no southern hemisphere.

In SkyNet's European headquarters, the duty desk logs five thousand calls following its report on the Soroti massacre.

In Madison Wisconsin, Mrs Rosemary Blaney upsets her Sunday lunch guests by asking them if any of them saw that thing on the news channel about Africa?

In London, T.P. Costello defends his station's reporting policy in a live question time show against a hostile interviewer and audience.

In San Bernardino, Kayley Holmes, an engineering student, hits the search key for 'South+Chaga' and turns up fifty newsgroups in the Greater Los Angeles area alone.

In Kansas City, NanoWeb-Raytheon prepare libel writs against SkyNet News.

In Paris, Sorbonne students picket the US embassy with banners declaring *Guerre Bas: Finez!* Riot police break them up.

In a shell-shaped wooden house on the slopes of Kirinyaga, Gaby McAslan discovered lust and lies. The sex was tremendous. The lies were greater. She would make any sound, utter any blasphemy, do any filthy thing Faraway suggested, except tell him that her daughter had fought with the Black Simbas in Bangalore, was training now with the Merina for a higher, harsher battleground.

This will come for me some day, she thought. When it does come, it will have grown into a juggernaut that will roll over me and I will go down under it. I am trading in destructions: my own to come, or my work now. It is not so hard a decision. I've been destroyed before. I know what it's like down there.

She rolled back under Faraway's fingers. The planet rolled on.

Within a week five hundred mirror sites are carrying the complete SkyNet report on the Soroti massacre. NanoWeb-Raytheon's war-chest is bottomless, but with every injunction they take out to close down a mirror site, three new ones spring up. Their share price has dropped forty points. The North American media fight back by highlighting the Bangalore attack. *Village Voice* reports membership enquiries to South support groups up two hundred per cent. In Kansas City, Chicago, Akron, St Louis and Indianapolis there are Saturday demonstrations outside NanoWeb-Raytheon offices and subsidiaries. There are students, high school kids, library assistants, lawyers, car workers, waitresses, actors, short-order cooks, nurses, writers and college professors there. They are videoed, digitized, identified and filed in an intelligence database. Congressional e-mail post-boxes are crammed solid by flaming campaigns. Professional lobbying groups are hired, funded by ten thousand car washes, cake bakes and garage sales.

The giant is waking.

Great Boma, like the body it contained, was a noble ideal enthroned in chaos. Its nested domes struggled against the skyline of Kirinya's oldest, vilest shanty. One hundred and eighty thousand people stewed in Kagumu's four square kilometres of open sewer alleys and collapsing piles of residential cylinders, but the township wore its squalor like a sash of pride. It was the legacy of when it was a camp. When Nairobi destroyed itself in boy-gang warfare and the Black Simbas had evacuated those who had no other way of escape up the northern corridor, Kagumu was the place that had taken them in. It had been invented by a man who called himself M'Zee, the old wise one. He devised and shaped the big, open-mouthed tube-homes that could shelter and give water to a whole family, he had grown the roof gardens and guided the nascent democracy. He had died breaking up a knife fight. He never saw his faith fulfilled. The cylinders piled higher, the streets gained names, the refugees became citizens, camp became city. None now remembered his name. His spirit liked that. Kagumu considered itself the seed of Kirinya. It was one of the few parts of the city that proudly remained outside the Harambee. It regarded the Great Boma in its heart with the mildly proud embarrassment of farming parents whose son wants to be a dancer. But the official cars were safer there than any other part of the city. Pairs of thumbs spiked on Kagumu gate made good community relations.

Even in her capacity as Harambee media agent, Gaby felt like an impostor every time she entered Great Boma's ribbed wooden domes. Those Adapted that could sense truth and falsehood had the true scent of her soul. Liar, hooker, junkie, bad mother. And promoted beyond her talent. She sat at meetings nodding at the proposals and making her suggestions, which were always agreed to, thinking, you know, don't know? But you're not going to tell me. You're waiting for me either to confess, or fall on my ass.

The media monitoring group especially creeped her. She had never been comfortable with orthos. Ones hooked by their umbilicals into the necklace of comsats, and beyond into the North's computer net; these were the suckers of sins. They knew everything right down to the cat noises she found herself making when Faraway woke her in the morning. Most of their work, it seemed to Gaby, consisted of sitting around a table out of their symbiotes drinking coffee, gossiping and waiting to see what their simulations did.

'The American press is still solidly anti-South,' the Harambee man Kibeki said. His orthobody squatted a long loop of umbilical away on the bare wooden floor, looking almost wet under the dome floods. 'However, the tack they're taking against the South Support Networks and the Peace Movement should start to backfire on them in about three days. Most of the online newsnets are wavering.'

'This Hart-Wately Bill is throwing up fractal futures,' said Moab. She was a fat mathematician who smoked a lot of cigars safe in the knowledge that her orthobody would scrub out all tars and carcinogens. 'At the present there's a probability of seventy-two per cent that it won't get passed, but I'm getting basins of attraction around Richard Kinghan and the Mid-Western Republican Senators. It would not take much to swing it to an increase in the defence budget. It looks good with an election eighteen months away. The Military Industrial complex is a safe card to play. '

'But you can never ignore popular pressure in the United States,' Kibeki returned. 'The Moral Majority, the Southern States black democrat swing. This is the biggest mass movement since the Vietnam War. Certainly bigger than the Iraq Offensive.'

'I thought we would have got America by now,' Faraway said. 'Europe will go like dominoes.'

'It does not matter if we do not get America. Gaby?'

She shook her head and opened her hands in the way that says, *it was out of these a long time ago.*

'It's still working,' Bartimaeus said. He wore a goatee, a disreputable pair of yellow football shorts and a straw hat and was the best stochastic analyst in east Africa. 'Given the usual *caveat* that this is a living thing and can either sing hallelujahs or peck your dick off. Coffee? It's that Uplands blend.'

Elsewhere.

In Northampton, Massachusetts, a drama teacher at the junior high school is fired when parents find out that she is a member of the local South Support Group.

In Chicago a linguistics professor is dragged by two police from under the wheels of a delivery truck to NanoWeb-Ray-theon's South Side plant.

In Paris the Foreign Ministry announces that it will be supporting the motion in the United Nations General Assembly by the Nordic and Baltic states for an international peace conference.

In Washington the well-paid lobbyists press Congress to

immediately withdraw American military advisors and end all military and economic aid to the front-line states. *Bring the Boys Back Home* is the slogan.

The Sudanese government calls a hasty conference of all front-line states in Khartoum. Less than forty per cent of the Latin and Central Americans turn up. Coverage in the European and North American media is low-key. The Federation of Islamic States issues a condemnation of the United States for its lukewarm support of Islamist aspirations in Sub-Sahel Africa and South-East Asia. The *Washington Post* delivers an editorial questioning United States foreign policy in Africa. *Are the interests of our nation being served by maintaining an interdiction zone that no longer enjoys United Nations and international support?* Buoyed by what it sees as a sea-change in the nation's opinion-setter, the federation of South Support groups plan a walk on Washington. Buses bring old and young, black and white, men and women, of all religions and political shadings, to the shadow of the Washington Monument. To marching bands and samba *baterias* and *mariachi* ensembles and a float with a Blue Beat outfit, they walk past the White House and up the other side to the front of the Capitol where tiny distant specks of the speakers make pertinent points no one can hear because the sound system is so overloaded.

Fifty thousand people walk that day.

Bartholomew's hemisphere turns in space.

In the dark hemisphere, the people of Africa talk. They talk in the markets and the street cafés. They talk at the bus stops and by the side of the roads as they meet with no other purpose than to swap chatter with their friends. They talk under trees and in barbershops and gathering food from their *shambas*, waiting for their cars to be recharged, playing *mbao* on shop doorsteps, picking the kids up from school, wondering when it is going to stop raining, on sunny porches swapping stories from the papers and the radio. They debate the failure of the American Congress to ratify the Hart-Wately Bill, which would impose trade sanctions on any outside nation dealing with the Chaga states. They argue the ramifications of the lead story on the radio news that, as a result of massive budget overruns on the BDO project, overseas aid, both economic and financial, has been slashed, especially to Meso-America and sub-Sahara Africa. They point to lines in the editorials that come through the village news links: *'Reservations over continued levels of involvement in the front-line states'. 'Budgetary drains.' 'Long term stabilization strategies.'* Will they agree to the 'Frozen Four' summit proposal at the next General Assembly? the woman warriors ask. The mothers and old women say, it is men. They do what they will. Peace? the young men ask. The old men shrug and spit and say it looks as good as it has ever done. In Harambee and Ogun and the Central African Confederacy, in the cantons of Great Zimbabwe and the nations of KwaZulu and the states of the Federation of South Africa, the people listen and discuss with intelligence and passion, because it is their world these people in the North are talking about.

It came just as Gaby was rubbing patchouli oil into Faraway's elegantly curved ass as he lay face down on the big ebony bed. A communicator squeep, the apologetic voice of Faradje, Faraway's aide. The relationship with a good PA is as close as marriage, and as sensitive to adultery. Sorry boss. Yes, I know what time it is. But they've pushed the vote up.

Faraway left a treacherous trail of patchouli behind him as he swept into Great Boma. Elders, Envoys and Missionaries had gathered in the big dome. The gloom sparkled with dozens of micro-televisions. Gaby, Faraway, Faradje and the three forecasters gathered around Faradje's hand-held.

Dr Dan entered. Elders and Missionaries alike made way for the slow-stepping orthobody. He came to join Gaby and the stochastic wizards of the mountain. The symbiont settled on its massive hams. Its belly rested on the wooden floor. Lips of flesh peeled away from Dr Dan's face.

Faraway had warned her, but when she first saw what he had done to himself, Gaby had been horrified. For ten years the auxiliary body had been all that held his collapsing bones and organs together. But he had always been the great political survivor. Not even his body could be allowed to subvert his purposes.

The General Assembly vote was in open session: observers

and activists jostled with world media for floor space in the public galleries. Ambassadors from the countries that no longer existed had made sure of their seats. The representatives from the next-to-front-line states, who had equal amounts to gain and lose from opening terminum, had also turned out in force.

'Europeans and North Pacificans are solid,' Kibeki commented.

'Central Asia and Middle East look patchy,' Moab said. She sniffed. 'Who's wearing patchouli?'

The big five were all in place. It was too close even for the amazing Bartimaeus to call. The speeches ended. The voting began. Gaby found she was holding her breath. She exhaled gently. History, she thought over the soft breathing. I am making history. No. I have done nothing. They have done everything, the people, who have decided they are not going to be ignored any more.

The rump and front-line states were unanimous no. India, the North Pacific Rim, Siberia, Central Asia went yes. North Africa went yes.

'Jesus,' Bartimaeus said. 'I wasn't expecting North Africa. The EU's coming through now.' Finland, Estonia, Sweden and Iceland, the Frozen Four who had proposed the motion, voted yes. State by state, Europe came through in agreement. France hesitated; France said yes.

A cheer rang out under the dome of Great Boma.

'Quiet, you bastards!' Bartimaeus shouted. He bent towards the tiny organic television. 'Britain abstained!'

'That's good?' Gaby asked.

'For the US's barking dog, it's good.'

The voting continued. Central America said yes, to a man. Mexico said yes. Canada said yes.

'It's all down to the US,' Dr Dan said.

The camera caught an aide weaving a path between the desks to whisper animatedly with the US ambassador. The ambassador shook her head repeatedly. The aide left hurriedly. She looked stiff and angry.

No one spoke in Great Boma.

The US ambassador reached forward. The white abstention light came on.

Great Boma erupted. In New York, the public gallery exploded. Through leaping and cheering and slapping backs and high fives, Gaby tried to watch the wildly veering screen. In the Assembly chamber, the Finnish ambassador slumped forward over his desk. His Icelandic counterpart had come over to slap him on the shoulder.

In the Great Boma of the Harambee under the snows of Kirinyaga, Moab handed out the cigars. Gaby smoked one. She had forgotten how good they were.

At the Peace Party that night in a Kagumu bar, Mr Missionary Faraway propositioned Gaby McAslan.

'I'm going to make you an obscene proposal,' he said.

'When do you make any other?' Gaby said, light-headed from cigars and beer.

'This is not like any other,' he shouted over a dance combo that had started up. The orthobody people were performing an amazing lumbering dance: people moved back, fearful of being trampled on the night of national victory. 'Gaby, I need a press agent. I know no better than you. Come with me to Helsinki.'

Someone was now singing the Bob Marley song *War – No More Trouble*, to syncopated handclaps. Black lies flocked around Gaby like filthy insects. They had no place in this bar, on this night. She drove them away.

'Yes,' she said. 'I will. Yes!' She jumped up and locked her legs around Faraway's waist and he held her and danced her to the gentle reggae backbeat.

53

Serena's Journal: May 17 2034

I must be the only person ever got press-ganged into the space program. Actually, there's *this* much chance of me going up: I'm first reserve, understudy in case something happens to the main pilot. I do all the same hard work and get none of the glory stuff.

Whoa. Stop right there Ren. You're doing exactly what they tell you never to do: launch in, make it up as you go along. In space, that gets you dead. You follow the system. One thing after another. The order is life.

My name is Ren McAslan. I am seventeen years old, I am a trainee reserve astronaut with the iMerina Space Directorate at the Flight Training Facility on Nosy Bé. Which sounds like an affliction or a curse but is a tiny coral island off the north-east tip of Madagascar and, to a Turangalila kid, is home sweet home. With rockets.

Dr Scullabus used to tell me his people had a thing they did: after any long journey, they would sit down and wait for their souls to catch up with them. That's what I'm doing here: waiting for my soul to catch up with me through these slow marks on a white page. Too much, too fast. If I put it down, one thing after another after another like they tell me, maybe I can start to believe it.

Anitraséo tried to explain on the plane, but I just wanted to sleep and when we came in over Ambositra, I was just so amazed: a city that's one big building, twenty kilometres across. I mean, Kirinya had three times the population, but it's just something that grew up one night and sort of assed it out into being a capital. Ambositra, lying over its green hills, was designed to be the capital of a great nation, and knows it. Okay, all I saw was the diplomatic transit lounge in Antsirabe airport, but even that was amazing. Nyerere is just a bit of land that no one else could think what to do with, so they made it into an airfield. Antsirabe was purpose-built, an integral part of one enormous organism.

But this is Nosy Bé: sand, palms, reef. If I open the louvres in my room I can hear the waves in the night and I know where I am.

The examplar-trainee relationship is spookily like my relationship with ATR. Anitraséo is my lover mother sister tormentor confessor friend and enemy. She knows everything about me. What I know about her is that she is Merina of iMerina, the ancient Malagasy royal house. She's surrounded by a cloud of taboos: she was not allowed to tell me her name, the pilot had to introduce us at Nyerere. I suspect Anitraséo is not her true name.

Whoever she is, she has six months to turn me from Black Simba psy-assassin into Merina space warrior.

They're going to run the blockade on the BDO. The Merina are major players in a coalition of Indian Ocean Rim nations – interplanetary war's too big even for any one state to do on its own. They've got allies in Sumatra, Java, East Australia, even the Mozambique coast and the FSA. Ozzie rocket engineers and Merina nanoware designers have been growing a fleet of simple two-stage launchers evolved from stolen Russian booster designs. There are launch sites all around the Indian Ocean basin. You'd think the hardware was the difficult bit; rocketry is easy, it seems. Building eighty boosters isn't much when you can grow an entire integrated capital city out of the Ankaratra Hills. It's the meatware that they can't nanoengineer.

Which brings me to my Flight Group. Ofé, Irya, Infana and Ren. Precog, spacer, mission commander and isopath. All women. Yay! Infana engineers, Ofé foresees, Ren flies. Irya's time will come. If we survive. We aren't getting up there without a fight.

I said Ren flies. The ship flies itself – it's linked into my autonomic nervous system, leaving my higher cognitive levels free to get us out of trouble.

Maybe I'm secretly glad that I'm almost certainly not going up there. I get this suspicion that most of what goes up isn't coming down again. Tomorrow we start training proper. Anitraséo took the sample from me about an hour ago. More blood and running. Every morning and evening. Watch me, Merina bitch.

June 5

Well, hot-shot, the Yankees are going to blow you clean out of the sky. I don't think I'm ever going to be able to run this link. Every morning they shove me into a tank and flood it with acceleration gel, and I just panic. Okay, the stuff is an aerobic membrane, but I know I'm drowning. I crash the link. Anitraséo's taught me yoga techniques to help me relax: they're great out on the deck, but the moment I feel that stuff rising over my belly . . .

Then there's the philosophical problem. With birds or animals there are analogs for every part of my body: paws for feet, feathers for fingers. But a cha-plastic tank the size of a house that looks like an over-ripe fruit crossed with a diseased heart: no fingers, no toes, no hands or head. No analogues. I feel like a woman in a fairy story, trapped inside a tree by angry spirits. Anitraséo is patient with me. Open your eyes and see stars. I open my eyes and see nothing.

When I'm not learning to have a spacecraft for a body, I'm practising tactics with Ofé. The theory is she sees it three minutes before it arrives, and I get us all out of harm's way. I link into her extended time sense. Simple. Wrong: Ofé's perceptions freak me almost as much as the tank. I lose it every time and we end up spread all over geostationary orbit.

Running is my special space and time; sea on one side, on the other, climax Chaga with the white shell shapes of the Space Flight Centre rising out of the palms and hand-trees, the beach-front *bandas* and bungalows. The place has been designed so that when the American spysats look down, they think, *beach resort* and fly on. Like they'll look at the launch sites and say, *huh, coral island* and fly on, never imagining there're silos with rockets in them grown right down in the roots of the island. On a clear day, you're supposed to be able to see the site on Nosy Mitsio. I never have. I never will, this beach is as close as I'm going to get to it. This is what I think most in my running time: *I can't do it.* And no one will believe me when I tell them that. They think I'm not trying, or I just have to learn something; they can't see that this is as good as it's ever going to get. Sometimes I think I would've been better taking my chances with the Hound. I cannot do this.

June 22

I can do it. I *can* do it. I can *do* it. And it's simple. It's so simple.

They podded Ofé up and then I went in. The cap sealed and I was in the dark and it was like I had died and been buried. The gel came up and this time I didn't fight it, I wanted it to rise up over me. I wanted it to be water, and drown me so I wouldn't have to have another day of doing this. But it wasn't, and I didn't, and you can yell and scream and the gel takes your words away.

I wanted to be dead.

I opened my eyes. And I saw stars. I saw *stars*. There was no pod, no module, no systems and engines and tanks. I was naked to the sky. I was Ren-ship, I could walk among the stars. I didn't have to visualize an action, will a hand to be a jet cluster, or think 'run' for my legs to start main engine burn. I just did it. And it was so simple, so easy, I couldn't see how it had been so difficult, what it was I couldn't understand.

Anitraséo asked me, 'Are you all right?'

That just broke me.

Maybe you have to be as low as you can go before you can come up again.

She runs the simulation. I take us up in one big beautiful burn from booster separation to transfer orbit. I bring us to I-point, join the Fifth Group, get behind Ofé's eyes, look up through the layers of futures to the one two minutes thirty seconds from now when the US Death Stars acquire lock-on and charge up their lasers. Down in the present, I link into the escorts' AIs, set them on target for this future, and watch them scatter into dozens of sub-munitions. Eat smoking buckies, Death Stars! Up into the future again: the second wave of orbital artillery is charged up and rolling in on combat orbits to cut me apart with million-degree scalpels. Hold it. Hold it Ren. The pain . . . They are taking off my breasts with razor blades. They are sawing me in half from pube to skull . . . And into the present. I move my hands, we roll away from their predicted targeting arcs. Two minutes thirty seconds later, lasers rip apart empty space. I'm not there. I've flown away. I deploy the inflatable mirror: a passing shot reflects off into space. Before the first wave can recharge, my missiles reduce them to blobs of bubbling slag. Group Five hits I-point. The big burn takes us into cis-BDO orbit. The second-wave Death Stars have recharged and are reacquiring targets. No point looking into the future now, we haven't enough fuel to evade them. We can only trust our second-level escorts. Seven gigawatt EMP capacitors discharge at once. Earth Defence Battlegroup, as well as much of the North Eastern quartersphere, crashes and burns.

And *out*.

When I came out, I sat on the gantry for ten minutes, shaking with energy. It was like all the fear and failure and depression was dark heavy fuel in my tanks, and some unknown spark had caught it, and it was burning hot and hard and holy, pushing me into places I'd never been before. Anitraséo brought a thermal sheet; she did not even need to touch me. 'You're burning up, girl.' I couldn't even nod. She had me brought a cup of cold *chai*: she's not allowed to handle food herself, and all I could think was, I can do it. I can *do* it. Ofé was towelling down, and she said, 'What happened?' I just burst into tears.

I never knew I had such tremendous, tempestuous highs inside me. I feel like I want to hug all the people I meet and tell them what happened. I'm in love with everyone. Anitraséo warns me, half-joking: love is not an accessory you need on a space trip.

July 22

Toatéu. Pronounced: Toe. Ah. *Tay*. Oo. Meaning: Transcendental Object At The End of the Universe. And what is that? Anitraséo's not sure. No one's sure. No one can be sure: it's a singularity, so you can't know anything about it. Like a black hole? I ask. Yes, but historical and psychological, rather than physical. Meaning that it's the end and the beginning of the world. An alpha and omega point. Control of Toatéu means control of reality. Whatever that is. Anitraséo thinks it's a kind of evolutionary bootstrapping machine; that somehow, in some far future or incredibly remote past time, we are the Chaga-makers, and have sent the BDO to engineer our own uplift.

Magic, I say. Magic, Anitraséo agrees, given that anything that operates outside the laws of physics is by definition magical.

This is pretty trippy stuff. And it gets trippier. Toatéu's existence was deduced by Aldabran isopaths linked with whales migrating through the Diamond Reef. The Reef was a giant molecular computer, using whale song as a kind of computing language to draw this map of history that all focuses on Toatéu, the beginning and end of the world. This is just like, whoa, but now I know why the Merina and the Harambee were so keen to get their hands on Aldabra. And why the Americans are so keen to keep the BDO to themselves.

And now we're going to steal it from them.

My diplomatic past is a source of amazement to my team sisters. 'Your mother's a what?' Irya asked.

'A Harambee information officer.'

'My mother taught French in a Christian School,' Irya said. 'You should have seen what happened to her faith in Jesus when I came out of her womb.'

Of all the team, I think I'm closest to Irya now. I admit it, I was wary of her at first, I was hesitant of her gesture of friendship. All those hands, those arms. She freaked me, pure and simple. Isn't this a terrible thing to say? I must have hurt her a lot, she was only trying to be friendly, she was as scared and on her own and wanting someone as me. More, probably. I'm only different on the inside.

Funny. It takes one tiny shift of the light to change how you see someone. I was coming back to the unit house after a swim, and I heard a voice singing an old-time Christian song that Gab used to sing for me: she'd learned it from her sister, who'd had this Christian phase. 'I know His Name, I know His Name, His Name is Wonderful, It's everything to Me.' It was Irya singing it, lying in her hammock on the verandah. And for the first time I saw her as a person, with a past, and things she liked, and songs she knew. And now she does the best neck massages ever – you haven't been massaged until you've been worked over by a spacer's lower hands – and she's very into body painting. She envies me my white skin: fresh canvas. I envy her hers: charcoal black, matt, *magnifique*. She wants to do an apocalypse on my back: God and his angels versus the Yankee Death Stars. Turn all my freckles into constellations. I'm willing. But she still won't come with me for a swim, though I tell her water's the nearest thing to freefall until we actually get into space. She says she's not built for it, it's her enemy, it'll drown her.

Actually get into space. The simulations and the combat runs and the training schedule are all so exact, so real, that they mask the fact that we won't be the ones fighting their way past the Death Stars to reveal the secrets of Toatéu and gaze at the naked singularity at the beginning and end of time. We'll be sitting on the verandah barbecuing fish, watching the smoke trails go up from Nosy Mitsio as sonic booms roll across the lagoon. If you think about this too much, it knocks the spirit right out of you. All that energy, that epiphany I had in the tank, flickers like a candle flame in the night. What's the point of it? There's only going to be a point if someone gets hurt, or dies. Or there's some kind of disaster.

It's bad when you start hoping that people have nasty accidents.

Our exemplars think we need a morale boost. So this morning we're going to go and see a rocket. Not any old rocket. Our rocket. The one we'll be flying, if . . .

Reserve Silo 1 is on Iles Glorieuses, which is way too grand a name for a chip of cha-coral halfway between Madagascar and fuck all else. Nothing to see on the surface: a bare patch in a spine forest was the landing pad. The site crew threw a light-scatter net over the tilt-rotor before the fans stopped turning. A spysat was due over the horizon in five minutes. Underground: fast. First thought: maybe flight training is not so bad. These people live like coral, squeezed into tiny tunnels and cells so small they fit like segments of orange into its skin. They crawl everywhere, you have to bend double to get through the doors. They sleep hanging up. I don't think the word 'upright' exists in their language. Grubbing round underground, hardly ever seeing the light of day, or feeling the wind, or the water. I think I'd die of claustrophobia, but Irya feels right at home

But they've got the spaceships. Our guide – an army Major in shorts, beard, luck bangles and BO – squeezes us through this heavy blast door so tight it's like being born, and we're there. On the edge. Wedged on to this rickety gantry on the side of a launch silo. Fifty metres up, fifty metres down.

Never mind the silo. That's just empty space. In front of me is the machine that's going to take me to the stars.

'Touch it if you like,' the cool Major said. I reached out my hand to the white plastic, and jumped back.

'It's warm,' I said. 'I can feel a pulse. It's like it's alive.'

'It is,' the Major said.

I knew all the facts. Liquid fuel, high thrust aerospike engines, two stages: booster and orbiter. We're taking the fast track. At lift-off we'll be pulling eight gees. Thus the acceleration gel. Facts, data, specs: the briefing buckies were hardwired into my blood. But standing skin to skin with the big launcher I was overwhelmed by the sheer *physicality* of the thing. It was like it was there just for me. Waiting for a bit of me to be put into it, so it could wake up, and burn. I knew that the next time I went into the simulator, a big, hungry part of me would be in that aerobody orbiter up there, white as an ocean gull.

'I come and look at it every day,' the Merina Major said. I would too, just to make sure it was still there, that it hadn't flown in the night without me. Well, Major with the BO, you've got a rival now. It worked, Anitraséo. I want more than anything to ride that big fucker.

August 8

The exemplars are in a huddle again.

Bad sign on bad sign. The flight crews are shipping out. Two, three times a day, a tilt-rotor comes in across the lagoon. Half an hour later, it goes out again and there are empty seats in the refec at dinner. The rec is a mausoleum. You can't get a volley-ball team together. It's difficult even finding someone to shoot pool. Nosy Bé feels empty, and strangely scruffy, like it's all going to fall apart if there's no one left to look after it. Except the Amazing Left Behind Sisters, picking up the trash, cleaning the weed off the beach, dusting the rooms and making the beds.

The thing about having a precog on the team is that sudden meetings can be bad news but you aren't going to die of shock. So before we go in we know that the United Nations has ratified a motion for a full emergency summit between North and South at the end of the month. But our exemplars still have to tell us this, otherwise Ofé couldn't have foreseen it.

We've all got questions.

Infana: will iMerina send a delegation?

It's inconceivable that a major nation like iMerina would not be represented in Helsinki. Ambositra is assembling a high-level negotiating team.

Ofé (though she already knows the answer): what happens to the mission?

The mission continues as planned. We go to launch-ready status on September 15th. Launch is still confirmed at twelve hundred GMT October 3rd.

Irya: The Northerners are going to say, we gave them what they wanted and then they stabbed us in the back.

You think Helsinki is going to give the South anything? exemplar Soanierana says.

Me: what about us?

What about you? Anitraséo says. Back sitting on the verandah watching the monsoon clouds pile up on the horizon and the tilt-rotors scurrying beneath them, that's what.

Little grace note. Irya and I are sitting around watching CNN. Now that reporting bans've been lifted, it's like the news nets are making up for seventeen years pretending only the top half of the planet exists by suddenly taking an interest in every tiny detail of life in the South. Hey! Look! We've got this whole new world right on our doorstep, and you should see the cool things they do! What's sickening is how eagerly we go along with them. Smile and answer their stupid questions. Some woman from Great Zimbabwe's just made a fool of herself talking about great aspirations and hopes for a new world order and unifying the whole family of man. Now it's a spokesperson from the Harambee.

Irya tilts her head to one side, then to the other. She frowns, says, 'Ren, that woman has freckles, same as you.'

I say, 'That woman has red hair, same as me.'

Irya says, 'That woman . . .'

'Is my mother.'

54

Look out the left, the captain said, it's right below us. The big
Airbus banked. Gaby looked down on a clutch of summer-
brown islands nestled in an ultramarine sea. Sketched-in fortifications, diagrams of barracks and drill grounds, geometrical
bastions and revetments. Bridges linked the islands; incongru-
ously oriental to Gaby in this high north. A big ship, tall as a
skyscraper, negotiated a strait channel between tree-covered
shores. The island fortress disappeared under the wing.

The captain announced three minutes to landing. The cabin
staff moved to check seats, seat-belts and upright position seat-
back tables. The aircraft slid down over microwave masts and
oil refineries and apartment blocks. Gaby prodded Faraway
awake.

'You missed it.'

'I'll be seeing quite enough of it.'

'You've drooled.'

While he got the seat-thing checker to fetch him a microwaved
towel, Gaby called up Dr Dan on the earphone.

'How was it for you?'

'Unspeakably tedious, my dear.'

'We're going in now.'

'I can feel it.'

'Word is there won't be a press call at the airport. They're
going to transfer us straight to the conference site.'

'Anything that gets me out of this crate sooner is a good
thing.' The cabin staff took their seats for landing. 'It's a bit
different from the last time we flew together, Gaby.'

She laughed.

'What is the old goat saying to you?' Faraway asked.

'Last time we were on a flight together, Dr Dan said he'd
never visit an aeroplane toilet again without thinking of me.'

She watched Faraway think up a dozen Faraway comments.
He didn't make them. Jesus, we've moved a long way, Gaby
thought. But part of the thing was the dirty innuendoes, the
single entendres. The wheels went down and locked. The diplomatic charter hit the runway. On its way to the secure stand

discreetly distant from the paying traffic it taxied past an aircraft with Cyrillic on its belly and tail. Gaby closed her eyes at the black throb inside. Air travel is travel outside time; it all connects, one after the other, like Christmases, and sex. In aeroplane time, it's only moments since you sat in the cockpit of *Dostoin-suvo* on the strip at Wilson while your new friend Oksana Mikhailovna Telyanina showed you her beloved Antonov and you tasted her burn of pride like an old whiskey.

'All those trees,' Faraway said at the top of the steps. 'And they're all the same.'

Gaby shivered. Cool north August. A string of black cars snaked out from under the terminal building and formed a semi-circle facing the aircraft. Behind them, constrained by men in long coats, Planet Press came sprinting out to fire their stills and shoot their cut-aways. Cameras on the roof, cameras on cars: a sea of celebrity. Gaby polarized her eyes dark against the camera flashes and looked over the wall of lenses: yes, there were people lining the glass fascia of the terminal building. Many held cardboard placards. Finnish South Solidarity. Paris Africaine. London Liberty. A pallet shifter moved in to the open hold hatch and locked on to the cargo pod. Welcome to Helsinki, Dr Dan.

A tall, dark young man stepped forward to meet Gaby and Faraway at the foot of the steps.

'Welcome to Helsinki, Ms McAslan, Mr Muge.' He actually bowed slightly. 'My name is Kalevi. I am your liaison for the duration of the conference. Whatever you need, don't hesitate to let me know. First, if you please, there are a few inevitable formalities I have to observe.'

He speaks better English than I do, Gaby thought as he scanned the UN diplomatic clearances. His greeting called up memories of farewell; with Cletho, in the verdant mist-watered garden of Faraway's shell-house.

'You cannot come with me. You would not like it there. You must trust me in this.'

She could still see the way the kid looked after her as the Harambee car drove away.

'That's all in order. If you would come with me?'

The semicircle of black cars re-formed into a snake, each replete with an African delegation: Harambee, Ogun, CAC. In two hours, they and other Kalevis and the placards in the terminal would be back for Great Zimbabwe and FSA and iMerina. Swaddled in leather upholstery, Faraway took Gaby's hand. She gripped him hard.

Motorcycles escorted the Africans through outer Helsinki. The cars drove smooth and fast. The roads were empty. At each junction was a squad cruiser or a motorbike cop, or just a neighbourhood cop, drinking McDonald's coffee from a styrofoam cup. At some, people were standing, staring with puzzled expressions. Me too, Gaby thought. She fought the urge to wind down her window and shout to the outrider next to her that his thighs looked fabulous in those tight breeches. Speedskater thighs.

Aho.

The car took her to a boat. The boat carried her across the narrow water to the island. On the island, a 4x4 took her and Faraway and the rest of the Harambee delegation along dusty gravel roads across bridges to their suites.

'I hope you'll be comfortable,' Kalevi said. 'Even though, for us, it's been an unusually warm summer, I've had the heat turned up.'

The Harambee suite was in an old barracks that smelled of new paint and carpeting. Suomenlinna was an operational military garrison; the squaddies would come back to white walls, bare wood and pale fabrics. And the diplomatic bar. Gaby unearthed a bottle of some black brew that reminded her of Guinness.

'I don't know about you, but I want a drink.' She poured two glasses. 'Prost, or whatever the hell they say here.' They drank. Her eyes bulged. Liquorice, salt and vodka. Consistency of engine oil. 'What the fuck is this?'

Faraway smacked his lips.

'Actually, I am rather warming to it.'

After three glasses he was warmed enough to fuck her like a dog on the elegantly bare wooden floor. Gaby looked at the Kalevala walls hangings. Madness and incest in your bedroom.

'Well, that's that anointed,' she said, towelling her hair dry afterwards. Her PDU binked. Dr Daniel Oloitip had arrived.

Kalevi was waiting on the wharf as the mobile crane unloaded the container. Naval ratings unfastened the catches. The door unsealed with a hiss. The ramp went down. Dr Daniel Oloitip stepped out into the sunlight and late summer dust of Suomenlinna. For a moment un-diplomatic, non-political, animistic dread crossed Kalevi's face. Yes, I would do the same, Gaby thought, I did the same, the first time. But only for a moment. He presented himself to the hulking orthobody. He bowed, slightly.

'Welcome to Suomenlinna, Dr Oloitip. My name is Kalevi, I am your aide.'

The fleshy lips around Dr Dan's face unsealed. The old Masai politician stepped out of the open maw. Kalevi shook the offered hand without hesitation. You're very good, Gaby thought.

The sailor boys glanced distastefully at the coiled umbilical. Kalevi's raised finger brought the low-loader.

'Thank you, but, after twenty-two hours in that crate, I'd like some exercise,' Dr Dan said. 'Which way?'

Kalevi walked with him. Gaby fell in behind, appreciating the incongruity: tall, reserved host, hands clasped behind back side by side with the monster from out of Africa striding slowly on its two huge clawed feet.

There was a reception that night for the African delegates. The room was a former officers' mess, stripped down to Nordic spareness and hung with floor-length tapestries depicting scenes from the history of the island fortress. A vocal group greeted the guests with traditional music. Magnificent in full-length forest-green silk, Gaby's entrance turned every head like compass needles to magnetic north.

The Finnish Foreign Minister, ostensible host of the conference, welcomed his guests. The rest of the Harambee delegation was already established. Dr Dan was engaged in tripartite talks with the Ogun's Tundé Allotey and a tall, thin-faced white woman Gaby remembered from her briefing as the Estonian Secretary of the EU Diplomatic Corps. Dr Dan nodded to Gaby. A long golden burnous, exquisitely brocaded, covered the immodesties of his orthobody.

A nudge at Gaby's elbow.

'Second tapestry down. The drinks waiter has just passed her.'

A.O. Rananatsoa, two metres ten of sheer Merina hauteur in

white shot silk. As if she could feel the temperature of a gaze, she looked up from her conversation to Gaby and Faraway. Faraway bowed gently.

'Time for round two.' Faraway slipped between the moving diplomatic bodies towards her. Gaby chased down a drink. Careful now. You've got a press conference in the morning. And God knows the diplomatic damage you would wreak by getting drunk at an official reception. Though it would be very very good to accidentally spill a glass of that black liquorice/salt stuff down A.O.'s fucking pure and perfect white silk dress.

Despite her admonitions, Gaby found it took at least three champagnes to face political small talk. God, I'd forgotten how good the real stuff tastes, she thought while a red-faced Icelander talked without break or respite about the virtues of turf roofs on houses.

'Excuse me, just a moment.'

She and Faraway exchanged orbits in the centre of the room.

'If she didn't hate me before, Madam A.O. really hates me now,' Faraway said. 'When she gets annoyed, her nipples go hard.'

'Help me, I've just met the most boring man in the world,' Gaby whispered. They waltzed apart, on into the party. The Icelander was looking round for another victim.

'Ms McAslan.' Kalevi, superb in formal frock coat and silver at his collar. 'I am sorry to have to bring this up now, but there are a couple of points I need to clarify for tomorrow's press conference.' They were clarified in moments, but Gaby stayed talking to him under the tapestry of the Surrender of Suomenlinna.

'You see the space in the third bay?' he said. 'A tapestry commemorating this peace conference has already been commissioned. This is history in the making. I am very privileged to be part of it.'

At least you are trained for it, Gaby thought. I fell into history. Sudden applause. In its wake, the room fell silent. The President was about to make his welcoming address.

Shuttles had been laid on to ferry the delegates back to their suites after the reception but it was a clear night and a strange country and Gaby needed to walk off the champagne because the good is always more dangerous than the fake. Kalevi insisted on escorting her and Faraway. He walked fifty metres ahead and never once looked back, but Gaby did not doubt that he was aware of their every move.

'You are all right about this press conference?' Faraway asked.

The night smelled of dust and deep water. Gaby looked up at the northern constellations that she had once known like the features of her face. Blue-white Vega, to Deneb in the tail of Cygnus, down to Altair in Aquilla: the summer triangle. Behind them, on the edge of visibility in the dark beyond the city airglow, the soft dust of the Milky Way. The moon was a sharp crescent, strangely upright. Not at all like the lazy moon of Africa, sprawling on its back like an infant. The BDO was low over the city lights.

'I can handle it.'

Kalevi was waiting with a boat in the morning.

'I'm thinking how this must seem to you,' he said as they cast off and negotiated a course through the channels and rocky islets and big bulk carriers. 'All of you on the island. It's not like you're being quarantined.'

'Of course not,' Gaby said. Official cars drew up on the harbour cobbles. The boat tied up, security went ashore to move the gawkers back. In the car to the hotel she glanced over the questions she would be answering. No problems. Kalevi fretted backstage while Gaby checked her face in the ladies' room. A tech miked her up in the wings. She could read the logos of a dozen news channels on the microphones taped to her lectern. SkyNet was there. The front of the platform was thick with recorders. The buzz was audible, the cigarette smoke tangible.

Kalevi walked on, welcomed the media and introduced himself in Finnish and English. Then, 'Ladies and gentlemen, Ms Gabriel McAslan, Information Officer for the Harambee delegation.'

And on. The conference hall was full: faces lenses lights mikes ranked up in the tiered seats. She set her speech and the question cards down on the lectern, took a few deep breaths. It is no problem. You've done dozens of these things. Yes, but that was a long time ago, and you were on the other side of the lectern.

She scanned the seats for faces to pick on. Ah. Ms Lisa Kropotkin. You'll do very nicely.

'Good morning ladies and gentlemen, thank you for coming. I have a prepared statement from the Harambee. Afterwards I'll take questions.'

Afterwards, she came storming offstage so fast she left even Kalevi in the blocks.

'I made it quite clear that only pre-submitted questions could be put,' he said for the twelfth time as the boat pulled away from the berth.

'Not clear enough for Lisa Kropotkin.'

'I'm sorry. I apologize. It was my fault.'

'No it's not. She's just doing what she's supposed to do.' What I would have done in her place, she did not say.

That night there was another reception, for the Asian delegations which had been arriving that day.

'Would you mind if I gave it a miss?' Gaby said as Faraway pulled on the formal *jellaba*. 'You can only take so much folk singing. And you should wear something under that. No wonder you're cold all the time. And what if you get a hard-on? Major diplomatic incident.'

He put on the waistcoat, kissed her and went out to work.

The blue evening called Gaby outdoors. Swifts darted low over earth and water, hunting dusk bugs. She wandered where the paths led, past the laid-up gunboats and quiet, empty barracks. The blue deepened, a touch of cool came into the air. Gaby pulled her wrap around her as she kicked up stones from the dusty paths. Past vacated houses with herb gardens and kiddies' tricycles left where play ended. Up on to the greened-over fortifications, to a stone bastion where a great iron gun leaned out to sea. She jumped, grabbed the empty muzzle, pulled herself up to gaze in. Cigarette cartons, Coke cans, condoms. Out in the channel a cormorant was fishing. The familiarity hooked a claw in her heart.

I want this dusk, she thought. I want the magic hour, I want a lingering quietus between day and night. I want this cold, that will grow a little every day until this sea locks into ice and if I were here I could skate away from island to shore. If I could skate. But I could learn to skate. I want seasons, I want trees that all look the same, I want real champagne, I want subtle, imperceptible autumns, I want sea-fishing birds and kids that fuck in fortifications and smoke afterwards.

I love Africa but it's not my home.

A brief bright light burned on the eastern horizon. The unceasing nightly punishment of Venus. Gaby wandered the line of the walls under a shell of intense blue. She discovered she had come round to the reception hall. Kitchen staff were kicking a ball on a quadrangle behind the service area, running and hacking and heading and yelling. Piles of chef chic marked the goals. A ball bounced wide, Gaby moved to intercept it. She threw the ball to the goalkeeper, who kicked it up midfield. The players closed on it with shouts. The sky turned indigo. It was too dark to see in the quadrangle but the footballers played on. Gaby left them to their game. She passed through an arch under a clock tower on to the wharf. The lights of small craft were moving on the water.

The trill of the PDU was as sudden and incongruous as a cannonade. Kalevi's ident. She called his face onscreen. In the background, wide angle tapestries and politicians, and politicians' noise.

'Ms McAslan.' He frowned. 'Is there something wrong with your PDU? I'm not getting a clear picture.'

'I'm outside.' She brought the tiny lens closer to her face, turned the gain up as far as it would go, but the low light warning flickered at her.

'Ah. I have a personal call for you.'

'Who is it?'

'Your sister. She would like to see you.'

Kalevi complained, politely, about his schedules, but Gaby reminded him of his pledge at the airport. 'Whatever I need.' He bowed and arranged it.

His security was very good. You could not tell them from regular guests. Gaby took a seat in the bar where she could see the door. There was real Irish whiskey on the optic. Suddenly she wanted one. Suddenly she was more afraid of this meeting than any press call or interview or television-to-camera. She looked round for her security. They were reading their newspapers, chatting over their coffees, watching for threats. She saw

314

a bargirl. She leaned forward, raised a finger. In the same instant, she saw the woman in the doorway.

I'm standing up, Gaby noticed. I should not be. I should be on the floor. I should be hiding under the table.

The tall, thin woman was coming towards her. Her expression changed with every step: confusion to uncertainty to recognition to surprise to bafflement.

'Gaby?'

'Reb?'

They embraced. They broke. They sat across the table learning each other's faces. The bargirl hovered a table away.

'Oh my God. It is true.'

Gaby wanted to cover her betraying face with her hands. I should have your face, she thought. I am the older sister. Your face speaks what I've lived through. Your lines, the deepening of your eyes, the grey in your hair, the experience in your bones. My face says nothing of my experience.

'I'd heard that you don't age like we do; then I saw you on the television, in that press conference, and I thought, well, television, it's supposed to make people look good. But here . . .'

'It has its disadvantages,' Gaby said. 'You're looking, ah . . .'

'Older.'

'I was going to say younger.'

Reb smiled. My point is proved, Gaby thought.

'Would you like a drink?' Gaby said. 'I just sign chits and the UN pays for everything.'

The bargirl came in.

'What's the hotel like?'

'Oh, I'm not staying here. You can't get a room anywhere in Helsinki. I'm out in a motel in Espoo.'

'Are you long here?'

'I got a flight yesterday.'

Morning coffee was served.

'They do these really good rolls in this country.' Gaby offered the plate.

'Actually, I'll pass. I'm vegan.'

'Since when?'

'Since Jimmy, and he was about eight years ago. Same sort of time I started calling myself Bec.'

315

'Bec. And Jimmy?'

'Oh, I'm well past Jimmy now.'

'Is there a current?'

'No, I'm on my own at the moment. I'm back at the Watch-house, though.'

'And Hannah; her's must be some size now.'

'Ciara's expecting her first in January, Sirya's doing an MA in theatre design in Galway.'

'Jesus, I'm an emergent grandmother. And Hannah's husband, what's his name? I used to go out with him, God!'

'Mark.'

'Marky.'

'They divorced eight years back.'

'Shit.'

'She was with me for a while, but she re-married in 2028, and it's going okay. He's a divorcé too, so they know the ground-rules.'

'And Dad, is he still warden of the Point?'

'No, he gave it up a couple of years ago. I'm warden now.'

'I suppose he must be, what, seventy-one, seventy-two? How the hell is he?'

'He has cancer of the liver. He's dying.'

Help me, Gaby called to her security. Protect me. I'm hurt, I've been wounded. They read their papers, drank their coffee, powerless to keep her safe.

'How . . . how long?'

'Maybe a couple of months. It was pretty far gone when they diagnosed it. They've got all these new anti-cancer treatments, but you have to get it early. They wanted to put him in a hospice but he wouldn't have it. He's come back to the Watchhouse. I'm looking after him. He's good.'

'Why didn't you . . .'

'How could I, Gaby?'

She looked up. Her sister was now older than she would ever be.

'Gab, I didn't come here to get you to drop everything and rush off to his bedside. I just came here to tell you, because I wanted you to know, before he dies, so you wouldn't blame yourself; and because . . . well, because I wanted to see you.'

316

'Hell,' Gaby said. Her PDU sang. She set it on the table among the coffee cups, adjusted the lens. 'I'm sorry about this.' Kalevi. She had two minutes to get to the ABC interview. Her car was outside.

'Yeah, okay Kalevi, I'm on my way.'

She folded the machine into her pocket.

'Shit, I'm sorry, Reb.'

'This wasn't really a good time . . .'

'Is it ever?' Gaby got up. The security people decided it was time to stop whatever they were idly doing and get up also. 'I've got an interview. Um, could we meet up for dinner? Here.' She scribbled a number on the back of a receipt. 'My direct access. I got your mobile number when you called – sorry, but we have to log all callers. Security. It's stupid, I know. Good to see you, Reb. Bec.'

She waved from the door. In the car, thirty seconds from the ABC temporary studio, she discovered she had cried all her make-up down her face in big smudged tears. She gave a good interview against tough questioning from Saul Pesci, who tried to hold her personally responsible for the Bangalore attack and the threat to American industry from Southern nanotechnology. He drew an analogy with economic cancer. She imagined him twisting and gutted on the blade of Cletho's spear as she very calmly, very professionally took him back down the chain of connections from Soroti to missile factories in Kansas. After the interview was a short filler with BBC, and a one-to-one working lunch with a woman from *Time*, then on to a live patch-through to the Chinese main evening news in conjunction with V.P. Ambohidratrimo, iMerina's press agent, and Winifred Oboté from Great Zimbabwe. And out to the next engagement, security clearing a wedge through the media while Gaby told Kalevi to reschedule her evening meeting with Dominque Celibidache at News Inter and book her a table in whatever passed for a good restaurant in Espoo and send a car.

Dominque Celibidache was not accustomed to being rescheduled, nor being walked out on before the end of an interview. A call had come through from Faraway. The South American delegations, arriving all that day, were being detained at the airport. The US had launched an objection to the presence of

Adapted at the summit. Such talents gave the Southerners an unfair advantage in negotiations. The US would not enter into discussions until all supernormal abilities were removed.

'Never mind that the CIA probably has bugs up our asses,' Faraway said as he met Gaby off the high-speed naval launch. 'They want them all: isopaths, precogs, sensors, truthseers, lucks, right down to arboreals and aquatics. They also specifically mention orthos.'

'Dr Dan. Fuck.'

'We cannot fight them on this, and they know it,' Dr Dan said in the sonically silenced meeting hall. He paced ponderously across the wooden floor. 'Without America there is no summit.' White spots high in the vaulted roof found glossy highlights in the muscles of his symbiote. 'We should have expected this: they cannot be seen to acquiesce too easily.'

'We need you,' Faraway said.

'No. You do not. There is more than enough talent here to negotiate for Harambee. It is just aggravating that all I will be seeing of this will be on a screen in Great Boma.'

Gaby called the emergency press conference for midnight. By eleven forty-five the room was full and cameramen were squabbling for places on the steps. She drank a lot of water, went to the toilet twice and marched on without waiting for Kalevi to introduce her.

'Ladies and gentlemen, thanks for turning up at such short notice. I have a brief statement; I'll be taking questions later. The United States of America's demand is blatantly racist and aggressively white supremacist. Also, a new human social disease: species-ist. These people with whom the United States cannot negotiate are not disabled or mutated, they are not alien miscegenations, they are not hybrids or mongrels or monsters. They are human beings. Beyond skin colour, or hair colour, or bone, or even blood, they share the deepest common factor: in their genes, they are human. We are one species.'

She challenged the faces she had selected. Her smoky hint of underlying anger was holding them. Good. 'However, in the interests of furthering this peace process, the Harambee has decided . . .'

'Good speech,' Faraway said when she came in, sweaty and

dirty and tired to death. He had bath, glasses, cold champagne ready.

'Improvizing,' Gaby said. She sank into warm deep water, melted as the whirlpool came on. Faraway slipped in behind her. Water slopped on to the floor. His fingers found her out. She squirmed away.

'Faraway, I've had a fucker of a day.'

'Sorry.'

'It's okay. Faraway, my sister turned up.'

'I heard.'

'Jesus, is nothing private?'

'Was the restaurant good?'

'They had arctic char. And this sea view, all islands and trees. Yeah, it was good. Faraway, my father has cancer.' She set the champagne glass in a puddle on the floor. 'Do you mind if I don't drink this? I just don't have the taste for it tonight.'

She leaned back against the solidity of his chest and belly.

'Faraway.'

'Yes.'

'Could you just hold me?'

She lay in his arms until the water grew cool.

The isopaths, the precogs, the ones with Cletho senses and the ones who knew truth from false and the ones who were just plain, incredibly lucky, the arboreals and the amphibious ones and a single Sumatran Spaceman and the orthobodies flew out the next morning. Two hours later the Americans flew in. Media attention flowed to them like rats to sewage. With twenty-two hours until the Summit opened, Faraway was shuttling among the South Americans making deals and trying to stitch together voting blocs. Gaby's head-to-head on CNN with Washington spin doctor Madchen Connors was not until sixteen hundred local time; she spent the morning processing feedback from the world news. With the exception of the British, the Europeans had liked her attack on the American banishment. The Chinese and East Pacificans objected in practice but agreed in principle. The most interesting feedback was from a phone-in on East Coast breakfast news: overall the tone was two to one that the Southerners had no ground for protest, but among the Afro-Americans, Hispanics and Asians, the minority of callers, support for her stance was one hundred per cent. Give me your poor, Gaby thought. Thank you, huddled masses. The computer models showed a drift Southwards in most of the news magazines, broadsheets and specialist news channels, while the mass market tabloids and networks, bucking a bulge in predicted popular support, were hardening by the hour. The worldweb was the usual chaotic stew of opinions from thoroughbred Marxist class war to bomb-the-bastards! neo-imperialism. Microsoft Online was solidly pro-North, as usual. Her species-ism sound-bite did seem to have caught. No doubt everyone else's models were telling them the bulges and spikes of popular opinion were working in their favour.

Faraway called in half an hour before the CNN bout.

'How did it go?'

'We've got about sixty per cent agreement. The far South still has this machismo no-one-tells-us-how-to-vote attitude.' He looked weary to death. His skin was dull, his body heavy on him. There was no light in his eyes.

Gaby looked at her cue cards. Fuck it, she thought. She laid Faraway out on the floor and worked him over the way she had on the beach at night on Aldabra. When he was purring she answered the insistently chirruping PDU. She had pissed Kalevi off, though he was too polite to show it.

'I'm Irish,' she said jumping into the boat. 'We lack clock genes.'

One minute to airtime Washington replaced Madchen Connors with Latoyah Wellesley.

'I know nothing about her,' Kalevi said. He was as close to discomposed as Gaby had ever seen.

'One thing I know for certain,' Gaby said. 'She'll be black.'

She was. Her entire strategy was, subtly, by insinuation and innuendo, to make Gaby out to be a racist. Gaby clung tenaciously to the multi-cultural, multi-ethnic character of the Harambee but conceded ground to Latoyah Wellesley's attack over Islamic fundamentalist communities. She could not get any ripostes home over American violations of UN charters in their support of the front-line states. An openly partisan newsjock did not help.

'Jesus, if that's their standard of negotiation, we're fucked up the ass before we even start.' Gaby wiped down her face with mineral water.

'I thought it was a points decision,' Kalevi said.

She very much wanted Faraway to be there when she got back to the suite, but he had left a note on the house unit that he was meeting Australians in the refectory which was a former brewery. He would be late. Gaby fell asleep on the sofa with the entertainment centre burbling *Tosca* at her.

She woke to invasion. The door crashed in. Blinded by lights. A figure: silhouetted in the white room.

'Faraway? What time is it?'

'Three-thirty. Get up. The Merina. The fucking Merina.'

Faraway swearing. She rolled on to her belly, tried to get up still drowsy and shocky. Lights outside the window; the island was blazing, there was the sound of many engines: boats, aircraft.

'What about the Merina?'

'They've launched missiles.'

55

She dreamed a hand was shaking her, a voice calling her name. In the dream, she told hand and voice to fuck off, couldn't they see she needed to sleep?

'Ren.' The dream unravelled. 'You must get up.' She blinked, still shadowy between worlds. 'We have to go, now, Ren.' The body behind the hand and the voice held up a black backsack. 'I've packed what you'll need already.'

She sat up.

'My things?'

'Ren, there's a car waiting.'

Anitraséo.

'What time is it?'

'Eleven ten. Get dressed Ren.' The hands gave her shorts, T-top, sandals. Her arms and legs couldn't find the appropriate holes. 'You'll need this.' A plastic weather sheet. On the bungalow verandah the sudden shear of wind, sharp with rain, swept her into the waking world.

'Where are we going?'

The car took her to the airstrip. A tilt-rotor stood ready. Ren halted midway between car and plane. The rising wind tugged at her weather sheet, the rain soaked her thin clothing in an instant.

'Where are the others?'

'Only you, Ren,' Anitraséo said.

The tilt-rotor sealed and lifted before she was belted into her seat. It scuttled away under the rim of the lowering monsoon. The aircraft lurched as it slid into horizontal mode, big engines fighting the buffets.

'We're going, aren't we?' Ren's fingers were white on the armrests as the bucking tilt-rotor struggled clear of the storm.

'Yes,' Anitraséo said. 'We're going tonight.'

Twenty twenty-two local time: Merina Launch Facility 3 on the island of Mayotte experiences an accidental outgassing. Twelve tons of toxic booster coolant are vented to the surface. US Planetary Resources Satellite WorldWatch 12 on a five-degree two hundred kilometre orbit registers anomalous activity on Mayotte. 'Planetary Resources' being a euphemism for Military Intelligence. WorldWatch 12 relays the data to WorldWatch control in Greensboro, North Carolina. Twenty-one eleven: Merina time; primary analysis of the satellite data is complete. The neural nets assign an eighty-three per cent probability of an outgassing of rocket coolant. The thing about neural nets is that their total lack of imagination allows them to contemplate the unimaginable.

The niggers have rockets.

Twenty-one eighteen the information and prognosis is passed to the Pentagon. Initial threat assessment is complete by twenty-two twenty-four. The War Room staff ask for a neural net analysis of Merina territories for possible further sites. Recommendations are forwarded to the Joint Chiefs and the White House by twenty-two thirty. The President is disturbed at a lunch for workers in the many charities of which he is patron.

The Presidential advisor speaks slowly, quietly and calmly. The lunch guests watch the Presidential motorcade drive away while the First Lady apologizes. By the time he reaches the Oval Office, the Joint Chiefs have identified eight possible launch facilities in the south-eastern Indian Ocean. The options before the President range from wait and see to limited nuclear strike. At twenty-one fifty he decides. Operation Screaming Eagle goes into effect.

Valley Forge is a single-stage-to-orbit heavy shuttle. It runs a five-day patrol arc in an eighty-kilometre orbit. Its crew is tight, trained, professional, bored, mystical. It carries two orbit-to-ground Black Arrow cruise missiles with FAE warheads. At nineteen hundred GMT, twenty-two hundred local, *Valley Forge* enters the attack window for targets in the western Indian Ocean. Three minutes later it drops both missiles from its open cargo bay. Re-entry sequence commences at twenty-two fifteen. Twin ionisation trails burn across the night skies of eastern Africa, long bright meteors. At fifteen kays wings unfold, scram-jets ignite. The missiles descend to cruise altitude, skimming the wave-crests, fixated on the palms and corals of Mayotte.

At twenty-two thirty the first missile impacts Mayotte, totally destroying Silo Four and its escort rocket. Thirty seconds later the back-up missile takes out Silo One. A cluster of satellites monitors the fireballs. From the size and spectrum of the blast, they conclude that silos, rockets and fuel systems have been destroyed. What they cannot know is that fifteen people have been incinerated in the firestorms shrieking through the narrow coral tunnels. Among them is the isopathic pilot who had been in the crew module monitoring system links.

Operation Screaming Eagle is a success. Empty of weapons, *Valley Forge* rolls on to its belly and commences de-orbit.

'Mayotte is dead?' Ren asked.

'We are switching to back-up. You understand, Ren, we have to go now. The orbital defences will be on guard. They could catch our ships in ascent phase. They may even use nuclear weapons against the rocket sites. If we launch immediately, we may be able to take the Death Stars by surprise.'

Turbulence gripped the plane and shook it like a rat as it descended through squall lines towards Iles Glorieuses. Ren grabbed the seat-back in front of her as the bottom dropped out of the sky. You are about to be fired into space on a rocket, and you're scared by bumpy air? Fall one kay, fall one thousand kays, it's all the same.

'The rest of the Coalition is in agreement with us about this,' Anitraséo said. 'New Perth's models estimate a three-hour window while Washington evaluates the threat and draws up a strategic response.'

The tilt-rotor pilot told his two passengers to prepare for landing.

'The rest of the Mayotte team will be coming in about forty minutes behind us,' Anitraséo said.

'But I don't know them.'

'You don't need to know them.'

The cabin rattled as the tilt-rotor lurched into vertical mode. Ren looked for sure things to hold on to. She saw her face reflected in the window: pale face, bare head, sharp bones, glowing goblin eyes. Animal afraid. Yes. Because when you are in that pod on that rocket there will be no place for fear. But the fear must go somewhere, so it has come back here to meet you flying in, for fear, like other universal constants, is conserved.

She glimpsed a circle of light down there in the rain.

'I'm not ready,' she said.

'No one is.'

The tilt-rotor touched down. The cool Major was waiting with a big paper umbrella. He did not seem so cool tonight. On the steps, Ren turned to her exemplar.

'What about the peace talks?'

'You think there can be peace talks now?'

Raindrops catherine-wheeled from the tips of the slow-turning rotor blades. A gust stole Ren's rain-sheet and turned the Major's umbrella inside out. It was not so bad to be soaked again. She had not properly dried out from the last time.

The Major was not so cool tonight because one of the escort drones was showing anomalous readings on the pre-flight checks.

'Can you get it fixed?' Anitraséo yelled over the wind.

'I've got all the teams I can spare on it,' he yelled back. With emergency launch forced on him, that will not be many, Ren thought. A fresh gust sent them staggering. 'But I'm most worried about this weather.'

Down below, out of the storm, Ren was given warm towels to dry in and hot water to drink.

'Can't risk anything stronger under those gees,' said the doctor as she laid Ren on the table. 'Okay, you know the procedure by now.' The needles sought out her soul. 'We're going to have to crash-breed these to get a workable colony. They'll be here in fifteen minutes.' She heard the doctor leave. She lay on the soft couch and thought, make the most of these minutes alone, they are the last you will have for a long time. She stared at the raw coral wall and tried to push her vision through it. Beyond that wall is a tunnel with people hurrying in it. Beyond that tunnel is a chamber with equipment in it. Beyond that chamber is a huge tank full of liquid hydrogen. Beyond that tank is a great tall silo. In the centre of that silo stands a rocket. My rocket.

On the wall were three counters. One showed local time. The second showed GMT. The third counted hours, minutes and seconds to launch. Two hours eight minutes twenty-three seconds. Fuelling would be complete, the boosters settling out gas bubbles and quantum eddies, the empty feed tanks filling with inert nitrogen. The flight computers would be flicking through preliminary diagnostics, a thousand checks a minute. In a breeder tank, buckies were boiling out of a drop of blood, voraciously multiplying. On the surface, football-field-sized patches of Chaga were melting, running off in the driving rain in rainbow-coloured tears, revealing deep geometric gouges in the bare bones of Iles Glorieuses. In Silo Four, sheltered by two metres of coral cap, engineers were prying into the close-packed guts of Escort 1 with molecule-sized tools. Out to the west, flying into the storm, a Merina tilt-rotor would be on final approach.

Ren McAslan watched the figures click down. Soon, it will all be, but in this moment I am warm, I am dry, I am alone with myself.

At t minus one fifty-two, the team from Mayotte came in. Ren's meeting with them was perfunctory: William Bi, a first-generation precog in his thirties. Ren recognised a Kalenjin name. Space Cowboy the Spaceperson, young, sexually indeterminate, friendly as a dog. Tsirinana: flight engineer. High-caste

Merina name. Visibly pregnant. When they had gone, William and Tsirinana to medical for link shots, Space Cowboy to scrub-down, Ren said to Anitraséo, 'That woman, she's several months gone.'

'Yes,' Anitraséo said. 'It will be explained to you. There is not time now.'

Have you secrets from me, exemplar? Ren thought as they squeezed through the narrow tunnels to final scrub and seal. As the razor scraped her clean, as the jets of water pummelled her, Ren tested the link. She willed herself into another body, one taller, stronger, whiter, waiting bathed in hard white light. Selves superimposed; she was a shaven rocket, she was a teenage girl naked in the spotlights. Hot air dried her off; in her other body she felt her many complex systems, checked their state and condition. She was well. She was fit. She was ready to fly. Anitraséo wrapped her in a thermal quilt and took her into the white room. It was one hour fifteen minutes to launch. The others were already in the quiet white room, with their white quilts. They nodded, no one spoke. Space Cowboy was in an inverted yoga asana made all the more complicated by two sets of arms. Male, Ren observed. Tsirinana sat with her legs pulled up and her arms wrapped around her, as if by enfolding herself she were also enfolding the child within. William sat with his head back against the wall. Ren did not need to look into his head to know that he was living three minutes in the to-come. Ren sipped distilled water and sat cross-legged on the floor. She looked at the faces of the people she would go into space with. She saw there were different kinds of fear. There was the fear of dying badly, and there was some of that in every face. There was the fear of getting it wrong, of failing others. There was the fear of being seen to be afraid. There was the fear of the unknown, and the fear that is like that but is not it, that is the fear that whatever your anticipations, whatever your prepara-tions, whatever your resources or skill at improvizing, there is something out there that is beyond all of those and will shatter them. She wondered which they saw when they looked at her. Perhaps they saw a fear all her own, the fear that your achieve-ments and abilities are mere luck, or guile, and that in the hour

326

of crisis, you will be exposed as a fraud and a liar. That you can't do it. That you never could.

Space Cowboy had unfolded into the standing triangle asana. Ren shrugged off her quilt and copied his posture, enjoying the sensuous pull of sinews and joints. He smiled to her. Everyone did what they did with fear. That was what the white room was for.

There was no clock in the white room. There were two opposite doors. The further door opened. The exemplars came in.

'It's time now,' one said.

One hour to lift. They took the crew up a steep narrow companionway on to a gantry. This was higher than the one from which Ren had viewed the spaceship, and abutted the curved back of the orbiter. Four open orifices waited. William's was that on the furthest right. He shook hands with his exemplar and climbed in. Space Cowboy hugged his exemplar with all his arms and, with some difficulty, squeezed into the slit on the far left. Tsirinana bowed to her exemplar, and slipped in next to the Cowboy. Anitraséo and Ren kissed. Ren wriggled between the cha-plastic lips into the remaining pod. She squirmed to find a comfortable position in the yielding flesh. Get cosy, you're going to be in it for some time. She closed her eyes, not wanting to see the lips seal out the light. Out there the orbiter would be reforming its ceramoplastic integument. Beneath, the pods redistributed themselves around the central core. Each was a self-contained re-entry body: in theory, should the orbiter sustain catastrophic damage, they would blast clear and return to Earth. In theory.

She blinked up the auxbrain displays from the exterior cameras. The tunnel was empty. The gantry dissolved into the wall. Main engines good, first stage good, separation collar good, orbiter good. Looking beautiful. Feeling so scared it passed into an emotion more than fear, something crystalline and solid in her belly, like obsidian cancer. Surface cameras: a weather balloon whipped away like a fugitive spirit.

Link to William. Shattering layered futures like a supersonic bullet shattering sound-waves. Three minutes from now Anitraséo would tell her Escort 1 was dead.

Link to Tsirinana. System checks a strangely intimate mantra; sharing your body with another woman. Nominal, nominal, within acceptable parameters.

'Ren.' Anitraséo: another inner vision showed her in the cramped control room. 'You're looking good. We're going to pressurize now.'

Always, that clutch of panic when the acceleration gel came oozing in from every side, nowhere to turn, nowhere to escape it. Rising up, invading you through every slit and hole. She choked, it went down into her lungs, kept pouring into her. She stopped breathing. Internal and external pressures rose and equalized. The gel matrix stiffened. Ren was embedded in amber. There was now no boundary between her and the ship, physical or mental. She bore herself in her own cha-plastic womb.

She curled into the foetal position that was the strongest and safest against high gees.

Count t-20. Tsirinana switched the ship to internal power. Anitraséo came on to tell Ren that Escort 1 was beyond repair. Pre-flight checks were completed satisfactorily. The course computer was updated. Inertial stabilizers were reprogrammed. Meteorological reports predicted a slight lull in surface wind speeds. The mission was outside abort parameters. Barely.

T-10. At three widely spaced locations on the wind-swept coral spine of Iles Glorieuses, thirty metre discs of bed-rock dissipated into spores and were swept away on the storm wind. Rain swirled around the aerodynamic contours of the orbiters cowering in their silos. Ancillary services were disconnected. The launch was at Level Two Abort: if there were an accident now, the second stage engines would fire, throwing the orbiter clear of the ascent booster to splash down in the ocean. Main engine compressors were brought up to speed.

All these Ren felt as potencies in her body, awakenings, empowerings, penetrations, conceptions. Moment by moment, she was reinvented. It was birth to adulthood in minutes. Tsirinana switched her on, system by system. She was electrically alive.

T-5. The digits counted down in her visual cortex. T-4. *Wait*!

she wanted to shout. Hyper-oxygenated acceleration gel swallowed her words. T-3.

'We're committed,' Anitraséo said. 'Launch in one hundred and seventy seconds.'

Seconds. It was down to seconds now. It was a joke. They couldn't do it. This sort of thing didn't happen. There were no such things as rockets, there was no such place as space, the sky was a hollow shell of plaster and paint.

Sixty seconds. Fifty-nine.

'Commence primary ignition.'

Oh God. They were going to do it. It was real after all.

'Twenty-nine, twenty-eight, twenty-seven, 'Anitraséo counted.

Listen to me! Ren tried to shout. I'm not ready, there's stuff I've forgotten.

Count zero zero five. The main engines lit. Count zero zero zero.

No, please . . .

The scream froze in Ren's throat as eight gees of thrust turned her into a living fossil.

56

From the shores and islands of the Indian Ocean, the Coalition fleet launches. Three full four-ship squadrons from New Perth's Eighty Mile Beach sites. Two battle groups from the Dreamtime Nations in Arnhem Land. Eight ships from the Sunda Federation's Barat Daya bases. A Level One abort keeps one of High Sumatra's two orbiters in its silo in the Barisan Mountains, but the escorts kindle the dawn sky. Twelve pillars of fire burn from the mountains behind Port Elizabeth: from the valleys of Transkei, KwaZulu throws its two battle groups starwards. In Xai Xai the single orbiter and escorts of the Royal Mozambique Navy send the birds flapping and screeching across the salt marshes. On its many islands, the Merina launches. Four ships from

Réunion, eight from Mahé and Coetivy. From Comoros, four ships. On the storm-swept verandah of the beach bungalow at Nosy Bé, a precog, a Spacewoman and a pregnant engineer watch four fingers of fire reach up from Nosy Mitsio into the low, hurtling clouds. And from Iles Glorieuses; three ships climb towards orbit.

Multiple gravities crush Ren McAslan. Her bones creak, her inner organs are spheres of granite, her blood is liquid lead in her veins. Her brain is a numb throb of weight and blindness. Buried deep in red blood, a voice nags: *you could do it in training in the centrifuge, with the simulator. These people need you to do it now. Do it now or you will all die.* The gel matrix enfolds and upholds her. Suites of bloodstream buckies link to form architectures of nanocarbon around her tubes and sacs.

Ren tries to move her muscles against the cocoon of gel and gravity. Tearing agony. But she feels the matrix yield, just a millimetre. That's enough. Her body will obey her. She has control.

T+40. Iles Glorieuses Control detects oscillations in Escort 2's flight. The rocket is unstable. At t+60 the destruct command is given. Escort 2 consumes itself in a blast visible over several hundred square kilometres of eastern Indian Ocean. Orbiter and Escort 3 continue ascent.

Seventy-seven space craft climb over the dark half of the planet.

Low orbit missile shuttles *Bull Run* and *Shenandoah*, WorldWatch satellites 6 through 9, MIsats *MacArthur* and *Schwartzkopf* and space station *Unity*'s planetary observation platform simultaneously report multiple violations of their operational envelopes. Booster plumes from twenty sites in the Indian Ocean. The high-speed link at Greensboro glows with orbital data. Majors and generals analyse and assess the initial threat.

The Pentagon is advised of a Class One nuclear alert. Early warning radars track the ascent. Any of these bogies could sow multiple warheads over the western United States within thirty minutes. The acceleration is terrifying. The war room transmits the primary level authorisation codes for Operation Defender. The defence satellite weapons charge up their weapons and acquire targets.

The President sets down the emergency PDU as the attaché arrives in his office with the nuclear briefcase. Outside, a military helicopter sets down on the well-watered lawns.

Pictures form out of the pain. Images in red, fragmentary glimpses of stars through an envelope of glowing air, at her feet three pillars of fire, beneath her, a map of Madagascar and South-East Africa. This is your body, Ren yells at herself through the gravities. Live in it. Be it. Burning. Her body is on fire.

The vision stabilizes. The dome of her skull is lifted away: three-dimensional space rushes in. She sees in further senses than sight. Those actinic dots rising far across the curve of the planet are her sister ships. The pain is forgotten: she is a burning woman, flying free. She opens the link to Tsirinana. Her aux-brain tumbles with engineering displays and command buttons. First stage separation is imminent.

Somewhere, Anitraséo is shouting at her.

I hear you, she subvocalizes. *I hear you. Ascent is . . . normal.*

T+240. Automatic stage separation blows the dead booster clear. It tumbles towards the dark ocean, glowing with re-entry fire. The orbiter's three aerospike engines take over. The acceleration eases back, three gees, two gees, one gee. The acceleration matrix relaxes but still keeps a secure hold of its foetal crew. Too sudden a pressure drop would kill them with the bends.

Ahead, rendezvous at I-point.

The President with his generals and majors is climbing to thirty-five thousand feet above the Washington/Baltimore conurbation. In Air Force One's war room they sit in swivel leather chairs before a wall screen. The nuclear briefcase, which is more like a chromium egg, rests in the President's lap. It is chained to his wrist. There are three views onscreen. The first is a map of Earth, the ecliptic sining across it. Dots, arrows and lines display the array of forces. The second is a plan view of the planet surrounded by concentric discs of the near-to-high defences. Coloured lights are slung around it like decorations on a Christmas tree. The colours change as each sector is brought up to combat readiness. The third view is a vertical cross-section of a chord of earth. A narrow vee radiates out from the equator: the forces available ahead of the hostile fleet, their status and response times. The defence strategy and its weapon systems are only named after Star Wars. They are not fast, lean little fighters, that seemingly need no fuel to perform their high-velocity astrobatics and fire their incredibly destructive ray guns. This is Space War, fought out with limited resources and opportunities on a battlefield of fractional orbits, firing arcs, recovery times and gravity wells. This is where the computers fight.

A major says: 'NORAD confirms that the hostiles are not on ballistic trajectories.'

A general interprets for the President: 'It's not a nuclear strike.'

The President closes over an open cover on the chromium egg. The generals and majors pretend not to have noticed.

Another major says, 'We have projections from Greensboro.'

A new schematic presents itself to the President: the Earth-BDO system. Hostile red lines loop away from the equator across space to tangle the BDO in a web of parking orbits.

A major says, 'The fucking niggers are going for the Star Gate.'

It is not necessary for a general to translate that for the President. The President looks at the screen. He looks out of the window at the summer-dry woods and geometric farms of Maryland.

'Stop them,' he says.

The slaughter begins.

Ren knows the timing of main engine shutdown to the millisecond, but it still takes her by surprise. Free-fall is the one experience Anitraséo could not simulate. The closest Ren can compare it to is the flight into Iles Glorieuses through the monsoon. But those drops bottomed out. This never will. Falling and falling and falling. Her stomach knots, she wants to be sick, but all there is is distilled water and a hard plug of gee-gel. She feels lost, vertiginous: her three-dimensional vision betrays her; is Earth up or down? Are the stars around her head or under her feet?

Doesn't matter, she realizes. That's two-dimensional, ground-ape thinking. You are the centre of a sphere of senses that moves through time, not space. She thinks, this must be how precogs perceive their world.

Thinking: precog, she perceives radar images on the edge of her sensory globe. Death Stars, moving on attack vectors. The battle is already joined; the East Indian and Australian ships have deployed their defence mirrors. Three minutes from now Ren feels the second wave of Death Stars gain lock-on and target their weapons. Her auxbrain feeds the information to the navigation computers. Manoeuvring thrusters fire, outflanking the Death Stars.

But up ahead, in the new future, an orbiter out of the Dreamtime explodes in a silent blossom of white energy.

Something is wrong with the plan.

Air Force One is coming down to earth again, now that Washington is not going to end the day as a crater of radioactive obsidian. The big plane banks. On the screen, red dots scatter and squirm away from the stabbing white rays of the Death Stars.

'It's like the fuckers know what we're going to do,' a general says.

'They do,' a major ventures. 'I'm betting they have precogs on those ships.'

'Precogs?' the President asks.

'They have a limited foreknowledge of the immediate future.'

'Sperm of Satan,' another general whispers.

Greensboro reaches the same conclusion when the first wave of orbital lasers fire on empty space. They watch, trapped by their own recycle times, as half the primary targets unfurl dozens of secondary munitions. One hundred metres from target, the missiles explode in a spray of fullerenes. Solar panels erupt in sulphur-yellow flowers; spears of pseudo-fungus erupt through the plastic skin. Nuclear generators run critical. The first wave of Death Stars die in radioactive and molecular meltdown.

White stars nova and fade in Greensboro and Washington. Orders come from under the Pentagon. They can see three minutes into the future. Use that against them. Draw them close, then cut them apart when they can't manoeuvre out of the firing arcs.

The second wave of Death Stars drop lock on. Beyond them, Space Defence Sectors Three and Four come online and position themselves to cover the BDO orbital windows.

The Coalition fleet flies on. Orbital mechanics are implacable. There are two points from which it is possible to reach the BDO, and two only. Combat Group One, four Arnhem Land and four Sunda Federation ships, fly into the sights of twenty-five fully charged orbital lasers. The precogs look ahead. They see twenty-five fully charged orbital lasers, doing nothing. They look again. The Death Stars hang, silent. A third time they look. They see themselves dying in fire. The isopathic pilots burn thruster fuel. The precogs look again and again, and again. Wherever they look, they die. There is no way out. The Australian and Javanese crews spend their last two and half minutes living their deaths. The Death Stars fire. Bevawatt lasers sweep away the inflatable mylar mirrors, carve refractive scales like a scalpel dead flesh. Exploding liquid hydrogen tears ships and crews apart. Combat Group Three throws its escort missiles at the gunline; burned-out Death Stars use their last drops of fuel to intercept them as the main group takes Combat Group Two apart.

Ren sees orbiters exploding silently, beautifully, spilling hydrogen fire across the orbital marches. Escape pods tumble Earthwards, Death Star reinforcements swoop in on fast return orbits: two shots, and out. Dead defence satellites close with Coalition missiles and detonate their nuclear power piles. Fission bursts pin-prick high orbit. A dazzling light, a scream on her ship-senses: an EMP drone has detonated, blinding an entire squadron of satellites. While Death Star computers activate self-repair systems and reload AI targeting software, a single High Sumatran orbiter pulls away from the rout.

For it is a rout. The South's ships are well designed, their crews skilled and courageous, but they are untried. And they are not equal to the task. The United States has had fifteen years to prepare for this.

Now the Federations of South Africa, the KwaZulu and the Royal Mozambique Navy run the killing zone. The Americans are good at this now. The Death Stars that have discharged their capacitors on the second wave turn to deal with the escorts at close range while the reinforcements dive through on assassination orbits, gutting African ships like market fish. It is simple slaughter. A battle group of twenty ships goes in. Nothing comes out. Ren's extreme range senses register thruster burns around Unity: tugs despatched to comb out survivors. *There are no survivors!* she wants to shout to them. *Once you start the machines killing, they will never stop.* Coiled in her inner ear, Anitraséo is whispering, *disengage. Get out. We will contact Washington.*

We will be orbiting dust by then, Ren thinks. You have to talk to Ambositra, Ambositra has to talk to the White House, the White House has to talk to the Pentagon, the Pentagon has to talk to the war machines and all the time the machines are obeying their orders to hunt and kill. And I have a plastic mirror and an EMP drone to fight them with. Her forward vision is a constellation of falling Death Stars. She looks three minutes into the future. She sees million-degree blades swing across space towards her white body. Back in the present, *Mahé*, one hundred and fifty kilometres above, commences erratic manoeuvres. A brace of Death Stars bracket it as they fall past: lasers flash. *Mahé* dies noiselessly, cut in half, spilling its crew into ten thousand kilometres of vacuum. As they pass through the Merina fleet, they squeeze off a fan of close-range, low power shots at the interceptors closing in on them.

And now the next two defsats are on their approach, swinging their lenses to bear on the Nosy Mitsio squadron.

Tsirinana orders the mirror deployed. Silver foil explodes from the nose of the orbiter. *No!* Ren subvocalizes. She vents the inflation gas. The mirror collapses into a tangle of crumpled streamers and folds draped over *Iles Glorieuses* like a thermal blanket around a refugee.

No! Ren insists again. *They all did that, and they're dead.*

A trinity of Death Stars punches searing holes through *Nosy Mitsio*'s mirror. The ablative shielding on the front of the orbiter glows white hot, vaporizes, peels away. The front half of *Nosy Mitsio* vanishes in a ball of plasma. The rear of the orbiter tumbles earthwards.

Tsirinana: *Recommendations?*

Ren: *I don't know. I just know if we do what they did, we will die like they did.*

She feels targeting radars from four Death Stars wash over her. They taste like the breath of the Hound of God. They feel like the hot down-wash of Soroti helicopters. They look like sick blood seeping under a Bangalore office door. They have lock-on. In sixty-three seconds they will be in arc. She can see them in all of William's futures. She dies, trapped in burning amber, screaming.

Space Cowboy: *What's the situation of our reaction mass?*

Ren: *I know what you're thinking. Go for orbital insertion early.*

Tsirinana: *We do not have enough to get back.*

William: *There is no coming back from this.*

Tsirinana: *We are not in the optimum window.*

William: *We will be dead by then.*

The computers give Ren course options. The Death Stars are closing.

Tsirinana: *Go. Now.*

William looks into the future, picks the best option. Ren feeds it to *Iles Glorieuses*. The aerospikes kick in at five gees. The Death Stars are fast: they spin immediately on their gyros, but Ren has a final surprise for them. Her last chance card. Escort 4 detonates in the middle of them in a seven gigawatt electromagnetic pulse. Ren cries silently as feedback arcs from *Iles Glorieuses's* raped circuitry through her auxbrain. The Death Stars spin out of control. Smart and fast, *Coetivy* follows *Iles Glorieuses* on a high-gee burn. The figures are relentless. Burn-time, fuel reserves, nano-repair systems, the recovery rates of US laser defence satellites, all meet at one point, and one point only, that says *you live*. *Comoros* and *Réunion* miss the point by a second. They die the death meant for Ren.

The fourth and fifth waves of Death Stars arrive at the insertion window to find it empty. They furiously try to bring their weapons to bear on the fleeing ships, but they cannot get an arc.

Ren shuts the engines off. *High Sumatra*, *Coetivy* and *Iles Glorieuses* free-fall away from the orbital marches.

In an oval office in a white house, the President of the United States of America sees the last red dots kindle and fade on his wall screen.

'How many?' he asks.

A major says: 'Thirty defsats destroyed outright, beyond self-repair or temporarily incapacitated.'

The President watches the white lines whipping close around the world, and the three red looping away from it.

'How many?' he asks again.

The same major says, 'One ship from Sumatra, two from installations off Madagascar. We have alerted BDO base, Operation Close Star Gate is in effect.'

'How many?' the president asks a third time.

A general answers. 'From debris analysis we conclude that each orbiter has a crew of four. Our count is sixteen ships destroyed outright, two managed to eject escape pods; three suffered re-entry failure and have burned up.'

'Sixty-five people,' the President says. He closes his eyes a moment. The general who called the Southerners sperm of Satan imagines he is praying. He is, but not in any way a fundamentalist general would recognize. 'All right. I think we can downscale Operation Defender. Thank you gentlemen, good evening.'

57

Suomenlinna was an island of light. The windows of the diplomatic suites in the big barrack blocks gleamed with lamps. Yellow sodium lanterns illuminated the bridges and roadways. Fans of white arc-light lit up the bastions and magazines. Mast-mounted floods along the wharf edge cast silver on the lapping water. In the strait known as Gustav's Sword, channel markers blinked red and green. Vehicle headlights dashed and darted along the dusty yellow-lit roads. Aircraft and ship navigation beacons moved out on the dark water, shuttling to and from the greater lights of the city. Lights shone from the windows of the brewery which was the delegates' bar. Within, LEDs burned on PDUs and microprinters and coffee machines. Television screens glowed end-of-the-world blue. Matches flared. Cigarettes smouldered.

Faraway paced. He could not pace very far, or very hard. The brewery was crowded. All the diplomats still talking had gravitated there. The noise was incredible for five in the morning.

Faraway was angry. Gaby had not seen Faraway angry before. Deep under all the other, more urgent fears, she registered it as a thing to be wary of, some day.

'Fuck them and their mothers and their mothers' green seeping cunts! A.O. Rananatsoa; she is mother of syphilitic maggots, she fist-fucks herself, her mouth is full of pig come.'

Across the crowded bar PDUs chirped and warbled, a predawn chorus. Faraway ripped the latest statement from the Coalition out of the printer. At oh two six GMT all ships had successfully completed staging, orbiters and defence escorts were on course to transfer orbits. At oh two eight Coalition ground stations at Nosy Chesterfield and Sindangbarang reported US orbital weapons redeploying to combat-ready positions.

My daughter could be there, Gaby thought. Lasers could be seeking her out. She almost screamed the fear to Faraway. Kalevi's arrival stopped her.

'Excuse me, but the others are all ready. We're only waiting for you.'

Faraway looked at Gaby.

'I'm ready,' she said.

The Ogun, CAC and Great Zimbabwe people had already boarded the boat. It was a big navy hydrofoil; as soon as Kalevi shepherded his charges aboard the ratings cast off and the burbling engines sent white water frothing over the stone wharf.

Gaby went up on deck. The most important press conference of her career lay ahead among the city lights. She needed elements around her: fast movement over black water, the wind streaming her hair back like a war banner, the edge of east-dawn lightening the tremendous curve of sky arching over her. Doubts in the under-dawn: what if I make my statement and answer their questions and they still do not believe that we have nothing to do with it? This is not another story. This is not the upward spiral of Gaby McAslan's career, which could, and did, glide effortlessly from one thermal of world events to another. This is history you are fucking up. This is the future.

Serena, she thought, where are you?

'Ms McAslan.' The wind of the fast boat's passage tugged at the flaps of Kalevi's jacket. 'I'm sorry to disturb you.'

'It's all right, I just needed time to myself.'

'Yes, it is very difficult to find time to be alone. Our society does not seem to much value solitude.'

'It's the same in Kirinya. Africans like to be together, they don't really understand that you might want not to be with someone else, once in a while.'

Kalevi joined her at the rail, apart, respecting the distances. The hydrofoil swung into the harbour.

'It's a very beautiful morning,' Kalevi said.

'There's something, isn't there?'

'There's been another communication from Ms Rananatsoa on behalf of the Coalition. The Americans have opened fire on the fleet.'

Gaby closed her eyes as the fast boat sank down on its foils into the water.

'Are you all right, Ms McAslan?'

'Have there been casualties?'

The little ship glided in to the jetty. Engines reversed; sailors threw ropes to shore crew.

'Yes, there have. Heavy casualties.'

The black cars were drawing up on the harbour, among the market traders erecting their stalls and unloading their vans. The men in suits waited on the quayside.

How can you expect me to make statements, answer questions, have anything to do with any of the things you represent in your suits and cars, when I do not know where my daughter is?

'Ms McAslan?'

'I'm coming.'

They drove through the empty, cavernous neo-classical streets. Faraway cursed constantly.

'Shut up!' Gaby rounded on him. 'Just for once shut the fuck up.'

He stared. She looked out at the early tramcars, with the brave little flags above their cabs quivering in the breeze that came

339

with the dawn. He did not speak to her until they were in the hotel and the delegates were in their seats behind the conference table.

'Good luck,' he whispered.

'Thank you,' she said. He ran a finger down her thigh as she stood up to address the wall of faces.

'Good morning, I'm authorized to make a joint statement for the organizations present here: Harambee, the Central African Confederacy, the Ogun and Great Zimbabwe. This statement is in response to the recent news of a mass launch of space vehicles following the attack by US cruise missiles on the Merina installation on Mayotte.'

She checked her selected faces. Disbelieving. Expecting. Waiting. Hunting. Too much hunger in Lisa Kropotkin's expression. Be careful of this one.

'We make it known that we had no foreknowledge of this action by iMerina and its allies in western Australia, Sunda and High Sumatra, and Southern Africa. We have had no part in its instigation or implementation, we have been taken as much by surprise by this as you, ladies and gentlemen.

'This should not be taken as tacit condemnation of the Coalition. We support the right of any Southern political entity to enter into association with any other, or form any kind of alliance or coalition they see fit. We also support their right to the peaceful exploration of space, and we condemn in the strongest possible manner the United States' attack against unarmed civilian space vehicles. Likewise, we condemn the United States' assault on Mayotte with two space-launched cruise missiles. We join the international community in protesting the US's *de facto* annexation of the artefact known as the Big Dumb Object. We maintain that the Big Dumb Object is a unique, irreplaceable and powerful resource that should be held in common for all humanity, not merely those groups that possess the technology to reach and exploit it.

'We reserve our deepest concern for the consequences for the peace process. We feel that this action may be used by certain parties as an excuse to quit the process. We would regret that. The parties represented here remain firmly committed to the

340

Helsinki process, and I reconfirm that we will be in attendance at today's opening session.

'I call upon the United States to immediately cease attacks on the Coalition ships and the territory of Coalition members. I call on the Coalition to return all space vehicles to Earth as soon as practicable, and for both parties to proceed by the Helsinki process. This statement was agreed by delegates of the Harambee, Central African Confederacy, Ogun and Great Zimbabwe as of oh five thirty local time today. Thank you. Questions. Gentleman from CNN.'

Lisa Kropotkin had been on her feet first. Way too eager. You wait.

'I don't know if you know, but we've just heard that the second and third groups of Coalition ships have been destroyed. Can I have your reaction?'

My reaction. No. You won't get my reaction. My reaction is to go over this table and up those steps and grab you by the throat and shout in your face *what have you heard, what do you know? Tell me what you know.*

'I hadn't heard. I mean, what more can I do than deplore this pointless waste of life, and reiterate our call for an immediate cease-fire?'

Lisa Kropotkin was sitting forward again. Wait your turn, pushy woman.

'Okay, MSN.'

'Your joint statement: how completely in agreement are you? I'd like someone else to answer, please.'

Afo Bayu from the Ogun leaned to the microphone.

'I'm not prepared to discuss the policy of my own government in open forum, but I can't think of any circumstances that would compromise our solidarity.'

The others at the table nodded and murmured assent. Gaby watched the faces in the steeply tiered seats. Her news-sense itched, something going down here. Setting up a one-two.

'Ms McAslan.'

All right, Lisa, I'm ready for you.

'SkyNet, Ms Kropotkin, isn't it?'

'It is, yes. Ms McAslan, do you recognize this photograph?' Lisa Kropotkin held up an A3 of four shaven-headed women in white T-shirts and pants. One had four arms. One was white, so young. Green eyes.

'Where did you get this?'

'That doesn't matter. Ms McAslan, could you confirm that this is your daughter Serena?'

'It is. Yes. Serena.'

Not a whisper in the conference room. Not a hand raised to interject a question. They know, Gaby thought, They want to see her tear me apart in front of a planetful of cameras. I know what is coming next.

'Ms McAslan, can you confirm that your daughter was a member of the Black Simbas team that attacked and destroyed JTT Nanotechnology in Bangalore, and killed five people?'

Eyes met, green and blue.

'Ms McAslan?'

You bitch.

'Never mind. Ms McAslan, can you confirm that your daughter Serena is a member of the Merina astronaut training program?'

Faraway, help me. No touch, no look. She was alone. She was naked.

'Do you confirm that, or deny it? Ms McAslan? No comment? Okay, one last question. I have evidence that your daughter is crewing a Merina space vehicle launched from Iles Glorieuses. Any comment, Ms McAslan? No? I think we should know whether the daughter of the Harambee spokeswoman has been, and is now, actively engaged in terrorist activities against the North.'

Alone, naked, in the dark water, drawn towards the reef. You tell me everything I have feared, but not if Serena is alive or dead? Gaby wanted to shout at her destroyer. You take everything and will not even throw me this one thing? But Lisa Kropotkin was finished. She took her seat, the media rose as one. The wave of voices broke over Gaby. She went down beneath it.

58

Drowned in soft nectar, Ren floated between worlds. The three survivors of the Coalition fleet straggled across five thousand kilometres. Course corrections were completed. Eight hours until rendezvous with the Big Sky people. Living on the outside of the BDO. She could not imagine it. The widths of continents lay between the tiny cha-plastic darts, yet to Ren, curled in her protecting womb, they seemed as close and familiar as triplets. *Iles Glorieuses* was embedded in black as she was embedded in fullerene carbon honey.

'Ren.'

A soft, man-woman voice in her inner ear. Space Cowboy was walking the hull, his blue-black radiation-tight hide sealed in translucent pressure-plastic.

'I'm clear. I'm coming round.'

Ren felt Cowboy's hand-feet on the skin of the ship as if it were her own. It was at once intimate and alarming. Groping his way over her body.

'Oh. Gods.'

She popped open her skin eyes at the sound of Cowboy's quiet awe. She saw a wonder. Cowboy stood erect on the humpback of the hull. His lower hands gripped ship-skin. His upper were lifted in a gesture of involuntary worship. He stood silhouetted against the rising Earth, an eye of ocean, Africa ascendant, the monsoon a river of cloud streaming across the deep blue towards India. It defeated every simile and likeness, it was Earth, the mother of all metaphor. Anything to which it could be compared was lesser, out of its self and substance, and degraded the source.

You could lose yourself in it, Ren thought. You could fall in and in and never stop falling. To her it was not a sphere. It seemed inverted, a hollow bowl, full of water. Its fragility terrified her. The slightest knock might spill those waters into space. The blur of atmosphere at world's edge was a breath on a mirror. The soft line of night at the far edge of the continent looked like a sickness. That terminator bisected another line of division. When she had looked through the camera-eyes of

Svyatiy, Serena had been amazed by the absolute boundary terminum drew across the landscape. Through *Iles Glorieuses'* eyes, looking down from vastly greater height, terminum was a wound, the skilful cut of a fruit seller's knife, that split a guava so that it fell in two halves in your hand. Two hemispheres, two worlds, separated by a hair-fine film of air, that happened to share the same gravity and atmosphere and sun and length of day. They were Siamese twins, separated at birth, now eager to emphasize the distance between them. The land-heavy North dressed modestly in duns and dusts, wore its jewellery of cloud sparingly. The beautiful South dazzled Ren with colours and patterns, swirled cloud around it like stoles and wraps. Like many of the people of the South, its face was marked; the tattoos, scarifications, disease pockmarks of Chaga-fall. The ring structure of early growth patterns underlay the contemporary landscape: Ren traced linked loops and spirals across the land. She tried to find cities and towns, places she knew: the white line of the reef at Turangalila, the harbours and island of Mombasa, the high white peaks of Kirinyaga and Kilimanjaro. She saw a sweep of cloud-jewelled coast, she saw a high, many-coloured tableland broken by the Rift Valley. She saw no cities or nations or anything made by humans. She saw Earth. She imagined she could smell its perfume.

'Cowboy.'

Tsirinana broke the magic.

'Sorry, boss.' Cowboy moved to the nose of the ship where the mirror lay in a tangle of deflated struts and sheeting. 'I'm starting cutting now.'

Ren watched how his body took the best orientation, how it balanced him against reacting forces, how one lower hand would never let go its grip until the other was firmly anchored. Instinct, a million years of divergent evolution bred in one generation. Cowboy worked slowly and steadily, blades cutting through the writhing plastic. It was beautiful to Ren in the way that men move with unconscious beauty when they think no one is watching them.

Anitraséo's presence resonated in Ren's auxbrain an instant before she heard her voice on the comlink.

'Orbiter Three, acknowledge please.'

Tsirinana responded.

'We've heard from Helsinki that the Americans have pulled out of the conference.'

Ren sensed a glow of satisfaction from Tsirinana; less so from William.

'It seems likely that the front line states are going to withdraw as well. It looks like the conference is finished before it even began.'

Ren saw Cowboy give a little victory dance on the hull. I am not so sure, she thought. Maybe we will reach Toatéu, maybe we will see a naked singularity with our own eyes, maybe we will pass through it and become something we can't begin to imagine, but what does that mean for the people down there? The Low War will go on. There will be more armies of national liberation, more children carrying guns to school. There will be more Sorotis. There will be more Death Stars, and ships fighting. Maybe we will have control of the balance point of history, but can we stop more people dying?

She looked again at Cowboy diligently cutting free the mirror. But that is not what you are here for, she thought. She switched senses. Bright contacts were moving into defensive cover around the BDO at the extreme limit of her forward radar vision. Intra-orbit tugs, unarmed, but capable of carrying armed and armoured Marines. The battle of the BDO would be fought at grappling range. That's why you are here, Space Cowboy. You are one, they are many, but you will be fighting on familiar ground. On Nosy Bé Irya had not spoken about her simulator sessions that had left her exhausted, shaking, withdrawn. Ren had learned from Infana. Edged weapons. Man to man, hand to hand to hand. The theory was that space people's innate three-dimensional orientation gave them a crucial advantage over lumbering Earth-apes.

I know His Name, I know His Name, His Name is wonderful, it's everything to me. I would sing that song too, Irya, if every day I gutted people.

Cowboy had freed the mirror. He stuck the cutter to the tackpatch on his lower arm, anchored himself with two hands, swung the glittering knot of mylar. It weighed nothing, but its mass was not insignificant. Ren saw muscles bulge under translucent pressure skin; behind the face mask, Cowboy grimaced. And let go. He almost overbalanced. All four hands grabbed hull as the crumpled mirror tumbled away from *Iles Glorieuses*, changing shape as radiation pressure moulded and unfolded it. It caught the wind from the sun. A ragged disc of silver set sail for the stars.

59

She did not see it in the hotel, or in the car. She did not see it in the boat back to the island. She saw it in the big, bare, wood-floored rooms of their suite, the thing she had warned herself against, Faraway's true anger.

'You knew.'

'About the Black Simbas, yes.'

'So, in Marrakech, that night, when you were fucking me, the time in the water, the time with the stool, in the bed, all that time, you knew.'

The thing about the true anger was that it showed itself in absence. Faraway did not pace, did not shout or swear violently and imaginatively. He stood in the lattice of light from the window and did not move, as if anger were a spear run through him, pinning him to the bare wood floor.

'Yes. I knew.'

'I loved you.'

Don't do this, Gaby thought. Don't play it with your heart. I can't stand against that.

'I know,' she said.

'How long had you known?'

Your skin, she thought, it changes when you're angry. It goes dull and waxy, like the skin of a diseased guava. It loses its light and life.

'The time you went to Kama-Kivu, when I didn't go with you. She came to me. In the house. She warned me not to provoke the Simbas. She told me about the Tororo connection. She gave me that lead.'

'You lived in my house, under my roof, you ate my food, you slept in my bed, drank my water, and you brought an enemy into it.' He was shaking. He closed his eyes, dipped his head to one side, as if shying from an expected blow. 'And she goes to the Merina and they say, you come to us, we will make you an astronaut, fire you into space, and how long have you known, and kept it secret? How long have you been laughing at me, at the stupid negro?'

'Faraway . . .'

'Faraway, I remember him well, all he thinks about is women and dick. You can lie to him. You can tell him whatever you like, because he will believe you, because his brain is in his dick. Women and dick. Stupid negro.'

'They'd have fucking killed her! They had a contract on her. The Merina saved her life.'

Don't stand there and take my arrows, Gaby shouted silently at Faraway. Don't be a martyr, I don't want to put my finger in your wounds, I don't want to taste your blood. I don't want you to kill me by maiming yourself.

'They saved her life. They had a contract. I don't know what you are talking about. I know nothing. Stupid. Ignorant. A fool. So, the Merina tell you they have saved your daughter's life, and you keep this secret from me. '

'Not the Merina. Cletho told me.'

'Ah, Cletho. So Mombi is in this too, and still people treat me like a dumb dog. Yap yap yap, see? He can do tricks. He can stand up on his back legs and pretend to be a diplomat. He is quite good, for a stupid fucking dog.'

'Faraway.'

'Do you not think this might be important, that my press agent's daughter is going to be shot into space?'

'I didn't know anything about that.'

'I do not believe you.'

'I swear to God, I didn't know.'

It's happening again, Gaby thought. It is all coming apart around me, right down into the atoms so that nothing remains. I could have spoken. I should have spoken. But I was afraid that this one trust I have been given would be taken from me, when it is my silence that has taken it from me more surely than any words I might have spoken. I am losing another man. I have pushed him away from me by secrets and fears.

'We have lost, you know? They cannot trust us now. I cannot even trust us. The peace conference . . .'

'Fuck your peace conference!' Gaby spat in Faraway's face. He was a head taller than her, but he recoiled from the sudden heat of her anger. 'Fuck your peace conference. My daughter is up here and I can't do a thing to help her and I am scared, I am so scared that she is dead, you understand? My daughter is dead, and you think your stupid fucking peace conference matters a damn?'

She saw two things she had never seen before. She saw what hate looked like on Faraway's face. She saw what his hand looked like wanting to hit her with all his strength. He saw these things too. They terrified him. He dropped his fist, covered his face with his hands.

'Gaby . . .'

He took a step towards her, arms open; forgive, make it all as it was. Gaby danced back across the big bare room.

'Get away from me.'

'I'm sorry.'

He advanced towards her. Gaby backed towards the door.

'Get away from me. Don't you come near me, you bastard . . .'

'Gaby, I'm sorry . . .'

The doorway was empty.

She saw him coming from a long way off, along the grassy parapet. He was dressed Northern style, jeans, a thick sweater, though the sun was high and the day hot for the Northland. An inverted perspective appeared to apply to him; with every step towards her, he seemed to grow smaller. By the time he reached where she was sitting cross-legged on the grass, he was so small, inside Gaby could pick him up between thumb and forefinger. He said, 'I'm sorry.'

'I'm sorry.'

'Can I?'

He gestured at the ground beside her.

'Of course.'

He sat. He was not comfortable cross-legged. Bones too big. Gaby could not look at him. Her gaze went past him, to the water, the islands, the mainland.

'I'm sorry,' he said again. 'No man should ever . . .'

'No man ever will.'

'Yes.'

'Faraway, I'm leaving.'

'I promise, I will never . . .'

'It's not because of you.' That is only partly true, Gaby said to herself. I couldn't trust you again, not as I would, if I loved you. But I never did. I lusted you, I passioned you, but I never loved you, and you know it. 'You know why I have to go.' She looked at him, into his eyes, the way that African men find threatening. Now we will see how adult you are. 'You understand?'

'I hoped you could stay.'

'I can't. I'm a liability to the mission.'

'The mission is dead.'

'But I still betrayed it. You know why I had to, but I betrayed it, and you.'

'I would say come back with me, but . . .'

'I would cost you your career. You'd be always defending me, the white bitch, the traitor. I'm finished in Africa.'

'Where will you go?'

'Home. Can you fix the UN travel permit?'

'I'll make it permanent. What will you do?'

'I've got a couple of pension funds that have been slowly accruing while I've been out of the country. I can cash those, they'll tide me over until I find something. Maybe T.P. will give me my old job.'

'When will you come back?'

'Not for a long time. Maybe . . .'

He touched two fingers to her lips.

'Don't say it.'

'Are you crying?'

'Yes, I am. When are you going?'

'Today.' She saw the pain on his face. 'I have to, it's best.'

'It is,' Faraway said. 'Best. Yes.'

'Faraway, would you mind not coming with me to the airport?

Would you mind just staying here, and not coming after me?
Just let me go. If you came after me, I don't think I could go,
and I have to, you understand?'

'I understand,' he said.

She hugged him hard; muscle hard, bone hard.

'Thank you,' she said. 'I can't give you anything like you
deserve.'

He kissed her and she knew from it that he did still and
always had loved her, and she felt like shit. She bit his ear-lobe.
He yelped. Gaby broke free in the moment's distraction. She
walked away down the long green battlement. She never looked
back.

60

The airport was full of eyes that glanced and whispering lips.
The girl on the enquiries, over-imperturbable as she handed over
the UN diplomatic visa. Yes, I'm her, the one who died on
prime-time, the quisling shot by a firing-squad of cameras. The
boy on the check-in desk, tagging her bag through to Ireland.
Face on the visa, face in front of you, same face you saw in the
paper this morning over your breakfast rolls. The people in the
shops and newspaper stalls, glancing from front pages to her
face: isn't that her, isn't she the one, here, look?

One face did not say traitor. It was waiting for her at the
bottom of the ramp to passport control.

'Ms McAslan.'

'Kalevi.'

He bowed shallowly.

'How the hell did you know I was here?' Gaby asked.

'It's my job,' he said. Gaby could not suppress the smile. 'I
wanted to see you before you left. I have very much enjoyed
working with you.'

'Even if I fucked up everyone's last best hope for peace.'

'I think the Americans and front-line states were looking for an excuse. I'm sorry it has happened like this.'

You know nothing about sorrow, Gaby thought. She took his offered hand.

'I would like to say I look forward to meeting you again, but I think that's highly unlikely,' he said.

'I'd say so, but thank you anyway. Thank you for everything. You were the perfect diplomat, even if I wasn't.'

He blushed and walked away quickly to cover his emotions. A woman passed him, walking towards Gaby. She was tall, black, dressed in impeccable silk. She was Madame A.O. Rananatsoa.

'Gaby, I'm so glad I caught you, the car was delayed by traffic.'

'What the hell do you think you have to say to me?' Gaby said.

'Something you should know before you leave. If you please?'

Merina security was low-profile to the point of invisibility: the inter-faith chapel had been discreetly emptied of faithful and fearful. The two women sat in the many-coloured rose of light from a small stained glass window.

'You set me up,' Gaby said.

'Yes. I regret that it involved your public humiliation.'

'Anyone other than Lisa Kropotkin.'

'She bore a personal grudge against you ever since your exposé of the Soroti massacre. She is a woman capable of much personal malice.'

'And you're not.'

'Please believe me, this was not personal. This was a precise political tactic.'

'To destroy the Harambee's credibility.'

'To isolate the Harambee from any present political alignments.'

'And into one with iMerina.'

'Eventually, yes.'

'Why?'

'I cannot tell you that. It will become apparent.'

'You had this planned all along. You were always going to do it, whether or not you launched. That was just the *coup de grâce*.'

351

'In a way, it is fortunate for you that we did. We were prepared to totally destroy you to make the conference fail.'

'Like you destroyed my daughter.'

The chapel shook to the subsonic rumble of aircraft take-off. The Malagasy woman said, 'I have not yet told you what you should know.'

'Then tell me now and go.'

'Our Earth station on Nosy Chesterfield reports that at fifteen twenty-three GMT the orbiter *Iles Glorieuses* made a successful landing on the BDO and contacted our agents there.'

'Serena . . .'

'It could hardly have made a landing without its pilot.'

Suddenly, Gaby found tears on the back of her hands. Suddenly she found her body shaking. Suddenly her heart seemed frozen between beats, time suspended. The light from the rose window poured into her and filled her up. As if from a great distance, she heard A.O. Rananatsoa say, 'It seems that her very inexperience and indiscipline bought her survival when those crews that followed the plan of engagement were lost.'

'Serena . . .'

'Is a remarkable young woman. And fortunate. I envy you your joy, Gaby. My eldest son died this morning. He was a trainee technician on Mayotte, he begged me to let him be part of the mission. I could not refuse him. He was incinerated in the tunnels around Silo One when the fuel air explosive struck. So I am glad that there is one child who was thought dead who is alive. Take joy in your daughter; I wish I could share in it. It is always the mothers who suffer.' She stood up, absently stroked the creases out of her dress. 'I could not let you go without being certain, Gaby.'

'Thank you. You know I can't forgive you.'

'I neither need nor wish you to. By the way, you have seven minutes to make your flight.'

The departure hall was ringing with Gaby's name. She was last on to the Boeing. It pushed back as she was fastening her seat-belt. As it turned into its take-off run Gaby remembered she had wanted to get a bottle of that black salt-liquorice stuff to take home. Then she was up and the trees that all looked the same and the long, many-islanded lakes fell away beneath her as the plane took her into the exile that was a kind of homecoming.

61

Cowboy called her name. Ren woke in darkness. She cried out. She kicked, pushed at it with her fists. The soft enfolding substance yielded, but the darkness did not lift. She was trapped in the pod, embedded in fullerene gel like a fly in sap. The ship had died around her, the pod would follow, last of all she would die, far beyond any reach or help, lungs bursting, bleeding, screaming to draw oxygen from the stagnant, choking gel that filled them.

'Ren.'

The voice was in her ears, not her head. There was air in her lungs, not acceleration gel. Ren wriggled her arms over her head. Her fingers found purchase. Day blinded her. She blinked away after-images as she forced the slit of white into a circle. Eclipse: Cowboy's grinning face filled the frame of light.

'Ren! How are you, did you sleep good?'

'I thought I was on the ship.' She took a deep, slow breath. The air was rich with stinks human and alien: breathed through many bodies, dense with Chaga pheromones familiar and exotic. She filled her lungs, coughed, spat out droplets of golden polymer. She hauled herself forwards. The door valved to its maximum aperture: light flooded in on Ren.

She stared at her hands, her wrists. The pod gel had dried on to her in a close-fitting skin of translucent amber. Three narrow fluorescent stripes ran from knuckle to elbow on each arm. She glanced down her body. Three stripes on the side of each calf, from ankle to knee. Three stripes from navel to crotch. She twisted round. She glimpsed white fluorescent stripes in the valley of her ass. She became aware of a constriction around her face: her fingers caught the edge of a hood. She pushed it back from her head. Three white stripes.

Being dressed in her sleep seemed more a violation than being undressed.

'You need a hand?' Cowboy asked. The one he offered her bore the symbol of three spirals. She took it and pulled herself into the light.

She lay, chin resting on folded elbows, in the mouth of a pocket on a cliff of Chaga-coral. A similar cliff faced her a kilometre away across a steep, narrow canyon. Hundreds of pockets covered the valley sides. Cascades of vegetation tumbled down the cliffs; figures moved over and through them, harvesting. Lines were slung between the canyon walls, a web hung with biolume clusters and spongy water traps. As she watched, a four-armed figure moved with dazzling speed up the net, leaping from node to node with thrilling confidence.

Ren looked up. The canyon walls met overhead. The point of the sky-arch was densely forested; tendrils, roots, strings of bladders, waving fans of porous moss hung many metres into the canyon, entangling with the rope web. The climber disappeared into the roof jungle of knotted tubes and orange flowers.

Ren looked down. A hundred metres below, the cliffs were cut off by a plane of light. The floor of the canyon was a concave hemisphere of translucent fabric, guyed to the mountain sides by thousands of adhesive threads. Looking up and down the canyon, Ren could see where the edges of the world-floor rose to meet the valley roof, on the world's close horizon. A roof on the world, a carpet of light, that was the only safe way to see this place. To see it as it truly was to invite vertigo: a bubble clinging with spider-silk to the outside of the Big Dumb Object, a dome of air pressurized by centripetal force.

Mandelatown, its seventy-three citizens called this tender balloon of gases. After the hard-shelled terror of *Iles Glorieuses*, it was home and safety to Ren.

Cowboy clung head-down to the wall above Ren's nest.

'How long was I out?' she asked him.

'A couple of hours.'

'I'm sorry. I just couldn't stay awake.'

'Don't be. You needed it. Tsirinana's called a meeting.' Cowboy scuttled around the spiracle mouth until he was underneath Ren. '*Coetivy*'s come in.'

'It's all right?'

'It's fine.'

Ren shivered in her nest. The flight was still written in the ache of her muscles and bones. The long loop around the dark side of the BDO, American radars like the fingers of unwelcome men on her skin, Marine tugs pulling away from the hub on intercept burns, fuel reserves dwindling by the second. Always running. Always the hunted. *High Sumatra* had been the first to go in. A terse crackle of communication, the stutter of attitude jets, then the heart-stopping dive to within fifty metres of the surface, the American tugs swooping down behind. Somewhere in the warren of canyons between the sprawling kilometre-high mesas of the Dirac Massif, there had been a fight: bloody, hand-to-hand at three kilometres per second. Against one Marine squad, Chaga-born adaptations might have prevailed. Not against two. *High Sumatra* was grappled, gutted with cutting lasers, snatched away like a broken songbird. Then it had been Ren's turn. She took *Iles Glorieuses* out over the pole, spun her on her tail, and went in. Claws of ice reached for her; she danced clear of them, threw her ship between ten-kilometre icicles and bergs the size of cities. She twisted *Iles Glorieuses* through great CO_2 Ginnungagaps, William scanning seconds ahead, the briefest thruster squirt between her and destruction. She plunged through sudden outgassings, rolled to narrowly avoid massive iceteroids melted loose by the heat of the sun and flung outwards by the BDO's spin. Then she was over the rim, belly scraping the uppermost fronds of the vacuum-Chaga canopy. The strategy had been to confuse the defence by taking widely divergent approaches to the landing site. For once the strategy worked. Tugs looped wide from the north cap on surface grazing orbits. Too far, too slow. Ren had gone radar-dark among the fissures and the towering heat-exchange fans of South Fermi. With the last fuel in her tank and strength in her muscles, she had brought *Iles Glorieuses* in to the wide valley where four-armed figures in abseil harnesses moored it fast against the centripetal spin and shrouded it with thermal profile netting.

Gravity, Ren had thought, naming the new force pressing her

spine into the soft placenta of the life pod. No. Gravity draws you in. This repels you, throws you away. Traitor gravity. Anti-gravity. Sleep, her body told her. You are thinking about gravity? You have fought a battle and survived, warrior. You have brought your ship and your people safely to the destination. You have lived where others have died. Sleep. Eat. Get strong again. She shivered in the blood-warm amniotic fluid. Darkness flooded in. At some point she felt shifts in this anti-gravity. The Big Sky people are ejecting my pod, she thought. Again, a sensation of gentle acceleration. They will be taking me to their nation, she thought.

Sleep is a great punctuation, Ren thought as she pulled herself up to sit in the mouth of her mountain nest. It makes a new day of everything. A spider-line was attached by a gobbet of adhesive to the cliff face just above her head. Cowboy watched as she reached for it and failed.

'You are in no state to climb,' he said. 'Get on my back, I will take you.'

She glanced down at the strong curve of pressure-skin. Its strength was egg-shell thin: a body, a heavy tool, almost any object falling from half a kilometre would punch through into vacuum beyond. Mandelatown would pop like a bubble. Ren wrapped arms and legs tight around Cowboy. She closed her eyes and pressed her face against his back as he swung them out over the white drop.

'Don't you trust me, Three Stripes?'

'What?'

He stroked her wrist.

'It's how people are named here. I think this will be my name for you.'

As Ren contemplated it, and found she rather liked it, night fell. There was no twilight on the Big Dumb Object, darkness was sudden and absolute. Ren battled primeval fear with briefings. *There are two nights on the outside of Big Dumb Object, Little Night, which happens when it spins away from the sun, and lasts six minutes, and Phase Night, which is when the BDO passes into occultation behind earth, and is gradual over a period of seven days.* As her eyes accustomed to the short dark she saw Mandelatown become a constellation of lights: biolanterns swaying in the air currents that stirred the web, bioluminescent fungi on the canyon walls, green glowings from the cave-mouths, the stripes on her wrists and ankles, Cowboy's spirals. A sudden gust shook the web. Ren felt Cowboy's lower shoulders tighten as he secured his grip on the bouncing rope.

'You okay?'

'I'm okay,' she whispered in his ear. A sound; a rising stuttering shriek high above. Machine noise, engines. Ren looked up. Red and green navigation lights were moving up in the low-pressure zone close to the surface of the BDO. Warning beacons pulsed white, yellow, tiny jewel-points burned blue for an instant. Attitude thrusters: one of the Big Sky People's two pirated tugs was returning. The ground crew had lifted the upper edge of the air canopy, spilling atmosphere into space, allowing the ship to slip through to dock. Ren saw suit patterns dancing around the tug, cocooning it in faintly glowing silk, like spiders that had ganged together to hunt a swallow.

Cowboy held the line until the pressure stabilized. In that time, night ended, a new little day began. The floor of the world was a curve of white.

This world is missing a second dimension, Ren thought. Everything is either one- or three-dimensional, the line or the volume. There are no planes, no flat surfaces in Mandelatown.

The meeting place clung to a crevice in the northern wall. Ren was reminded of worm casts in the soft lagoon mud at Turangalila, tangles of spit-glued sand, a soft, feather-gilled monstrosity lurking within. The trumpet mouths of these tubes were the height of two people. A warm gust of human-stink stroked Ren's skull-stubble as Cowboy swung down the clamber-netting.

The meeting took place in a chamber shaped like a human ear. Ren and Cowboy descended a curving ramp between high ridges of crimson coral to a central whorl where William and Tsirinana waited with the leadership of the Big Sky People. Tsirinana's pressure-skin, signed with a white triangle, seemed to emphasize her pregnancy. 'It will be explained to you,' Anitraséo had said as they met the crew from Mayotte off the tilt-rotor. It seemed seasons ago. It was only hours. She felt like she had known Tsirinana all her life. She was hardly less a stranger than these three Big Sky People. They perched on stools fitted to their complex anatomy. One, an African man with a skin so blue-black it seemed oiled, who wore two linked circles on his pressure skin, was staring at her. He jumped off his stool, bounced on his lower hands over to Ren, caught her shoulder and examined her scalp. Ren shied away.

'I thought so,' he said.

'Thought what?'

'It is red. I did know your mother.'

'My mother?'

'I was in Unit 12. I had another name then; I was called Juma.'

'Gab got you out?'

'You are not the only one,' William said suddenly. The one who had been called Juma spun on his lower hands. He stared at William's face. He frowned. Recognition dawned.

'The precog. Yes!'

'What's going on here?' Ren asked. 'I don't understand.'

'I also was held in Unit 12,' William said. 'Your mother got me out. She also got me in there in the first place.'

The Big Sky man said to William, 'Red Three.'

'Ah. I am sorry.'

'Don't be. I have a wife, many children now. And we are free. And you, the red woman's daughter.'

'Small world,' Ren said lamely. Juma Two Circles laughed.

'Yes, and I have been from one end of it to the other. Space is curved, you will always come back again.'

'Two Circles,' said the Elder who had South American features and carried the sign of two commas. 'The kid's tired. She's come far and fought hard.'

'And we do not have time to waste,' said the third Elder, a woman with the fine, heart-shaped face of the Nilo-Hamitic race. She wore two blue rings around her wrists, ankles, neck and waist.

'We will talk later,' Juma Two Circles said to Ren. 'I owe your mother.'

'The tactical situation is evolving by the minute,' Blue Two said. She was Big Sky Nation's military leader. She came from Galla people, a warrior race. She had been part of the tug hijack that had sparked the Space Monkey rebellion; she had crawled across ten metres of hull, naked to vacuum, to blow the canopy latches and consign the white meat to space. 'There has been a change of plan.'

Stools flowed out of the chamber floor. Cowboy showed Ren how to be almost comfortable on one.

'As mission commander, I should have been consulted before any changes were made to operations,' Tsirinana said.

'No time,' Blue Two said. 'Our forward observation posts report increased traffic through the main lock. General Mc-Kittrick is about to move on us.'

'In the past she's been put off by fear of heavy losses,' Commas said in heavily accented Swahili. He shifted his weight on the stool. 'Her last major engagement, we took another one of her tugs; she lost three soldiers. Fear of a hull breach has prevented her from throwing the *Gaia* probe at Mandelatown.'

'Your arrival tipped the balance in favour of action,' Blue Two said.

'How soon?' Tsirinana asked.

'Imminently. She will want to strike before you enter the fourth chamber.'

'For us, it is imperative that we relocate Mandelatown,' Two Circles said.

'You're going to move all of this?' Ren heard herself ask. Two Circles smiled at her ingenuousness.

'We have done it before. We have a suitable site already picked out in the Oppenheimer Escarpment. The pressure sheet is all that is essential.'

'But the farms, the plants,' Ren said.

'We carry the seed with us wherever we go.' Ren saw a secret smile on Tsirinana's face; she brushed her long, elegant fingers against the swell of her suit. Two Circles continued: 'It will be hard for a while, but we are Big Sky People, we can live anywhere. We adapt. But we will need all our people for the move. All our people, all our resources.'

'We can take you to the second entry point,' Blue Two said. 'But once you are inside, you are on your own. We cannot guide you.'

Tsirinana was halfway out of her seat.

'This is not what was agreed with the Coalition!'

William's fingers restrained her. Ren thought she sensed something protective, proprietorial in the touch. Is that your child, swimming in there? But who would sanely send a pregnant woman into a war zone, through a space battle, on a rocket? Questions: no answers.

'The safety of my people is not negotiable,' Two Circles said. 'In keeping with standard US military practice, Alice McKittrick will only engage if she is certain of absolute victory. She will annihilate the tribe to the last child.'

'These Americans are not barbarians,' Tsirinana's eyes challenged him.

Two Circles held her look. 'She sent us a message.' A circle of floor in the centre of the ring of stools flowed into screen. 'Our rim watch relayed these images to us twenty minutes ago.'

The observation post was concealed in a clutch of low egg-shaped hills a few kilometres from The Hub. It commanded a panorama of the south cap and all the traffic that moved between the main lock, a two-kilometre wide blister rising above the dense surface growth, and High Steel, the one-time front step to the BDO. Over the years it had expanded into the transfer point and re-fuelling depot for Unity tugs. It hung fifteen kilometres above the out-lock, a sprawl of modules, solar panels and booms on which tank farms clustered like a heavy harvest. Ren could just make out intra-orbit tugs nose-in to the fuelling points. Alice McKittrick's space fleet jostled like piglets at the teat. The sleek white delta of a Merina orbiter was as inappropriate among them as a bride in a boneyard.

The camera zoomed in on the imprisoned ship, pod ports open, mirror nacelle empty, then refocused in a sudden swirl of ships and stars on The Hub. The lock was opening, petals sliding over each other. The interior had been rigged with floods; it blazed with light. Out of the light, into the dark, came four sudden bright specks. The camera tracked and zoomed. At its highest resolution, Ren could see that they looked like tiny five-pointed stars.

She closed her eyes. She heard William's intake of breath, Cowboy swearing softly in his own language, nothing from Commander Tsirinana. When she looked again the screen had returned to the floor and Two Circles was staring at her as if her reaction were the one that truly mattered.

'In space no one can hear you say "Geneva Convention",' Blue Two said.

'We will take you and the team from *Coetivy* to the entry point immediately,' Two Circles said. Tsirinana nodded. 'We cannot afford to have one of our ships out of service any longer than necessary. Blue Two will brief you more fully on the tug, but I can assure you that you will not find yourself without, ah, allies inside the fourth chamber. You will also find yourself with enemies: the military have kept a base there since the Big Sky rebellion. Blue Two will take you to the ship now, this meeting has already eaten up too much of too little time. Good luck, you will need it. '

He called Ren back from the curving ramp. 'Hey, red woman's daughter!' He pressed a thin, flat object into her hand. 'You will need this, I think.'

It looked like an innocuous few centimetres of strip plastic, but Ren knew from experience that a twist would lock its molecules into a wicked little blade. She nodded her thanks, pressed it to her thigh tackpatch and went to where Cowboy was waiting to carry her on his back to the ship at the top of the world. The roof-crews were already unfastening the mooring cables as the crew of *Iles Glorieuses* strapped in.

'You all right, Three Stripes?' Cowboy asked, noticing that Ren in the next seat had closed her eyes.

'Just trying to let my soul catch up with me,' she said. She felt the warmth of his hand on her hip. It felt almost like a soul. A sudden lurch jolted her eyes open as the tug dropped from its cradle under centrifugal gravity. She clutched for Cowboy; then the engines took control. The Big Sky pilot steered his ship beneath a canopy of inverted jungle. Ren glimpsed dangling tendrils and flowers through the tiny ports. The sky forest was lashed by a sudden hurricane. Vines whipped, fungus caps swayed, flowers shed hand-sized petals. The Big Sky People had lifted the hem of the pressure curtain. The tug was blown free in a gust of wind, ice crystals and flash-frozen petals.

A flowery way, Ren thought. Maybe it is a good thing that I have moved too far and too fast for my soul to catch up with me. Maybe the real name of that soul is fear. She looked for clues of soul in the faces in the pod. Cowboy; yes: his touchings begged as much intimacy as they gave. His *Coetivy* counterpart, a fine-featured Malagasy boy, also sat with their isopath, an aristocratic Merina man. Ren judged him in his late twenties. They both had the fear-soul on their faces. They could not touch to take it away. William sat with his co-precog, a Mozambique mulatto woman with a beautiful pale skin and liquid brown eyes. She saw Ren looking at her. Fear there too. Is that because of the future you can see, or the future you cannot? At the front of the pod, Blue Two was in intense conference with Tsirinana and the engineer/commander of *Coetivy*. Also a woman, Ren noted. Also, Ren concluded from her unconscious self-touchings and the heavy, liquid-filled way she could not get comfortable in her seat, deeply pregnant.

The sudden brief night came again.

62

The clear-up teams moved through the reception hall. They were quiet and efficient. They unpinned the frontals and folded the cloths, they collapsed the spindle-legged tables. They dismantled the dais where the singers had performed and unhooked the white backcloth with the blue logo on it. Faraway watched men on ladders take down the tapestries of Suomenlinna's proud legacy, shake out the dust and carefully roll them up. They could cancel the commission for the new tapestry, now that history was not going to be made on this island. Men with big black refuse sacks moved around Faraway, emptying ash trays, dropping in half-eaten morsels of food, picking up detritus from the floor with litter sticks. They worked with the single-minded purposefulness of drone insects, as heedless of Faraway as if he were a piece of furniture. Less so: furniture was to be stacked on trolleys and taken out to the waiting service vans. He was functionless, redundant.

He looked around at the hall that was swiftly being stripped of its diplomatic finery. He turned at the sound of Kalevi's voice, suddenly raised outside.

'I would strongly advise you against trying to speak to Mr Muge.'

A tall woman silhouette in the bright archway.

'You should heed Kalevi's advice, Mme Rananatsoa,' Faraway said.

'I have things I must say to you.' She came down into the hall. Kalevi hovered in the doorway, flustered at the breach of protocol, even at the end, when it could no longer matter.

'What could you possibly say to me?' Faraway said. 'Your words have already destroyed this mission, finished me as a diplomat, and cost me the woman I loved, and there is still more?'

Now the workers were aware that there was more than work in the hall. A self-consciousness crept into their actions, as if they were the ones being overheard or overseen in their private moments.

'The essence of a diplomat is that he takes nothing personally,' A.O. Rananatsoa said.

Faraway looked around him again. Only Kalevi knew him well enough to read the conflict of emotions in his face.

'Very well. I will hear you out.'

'Not here.'

'Agreed. Kalevi, I will see you at the boat. I will not be very long.'

They crossed the parade ground, followed the path that curved around the hill on which the campanile stood, to a hump-backed wooden bridge. A.O. Rananatsoa paused and looked over the hand rail into the water.

'Despite what I said, I am aware that I have caused you a great deal of personal pain. I apologize for that.'

'You have something to tell me.'

'My most recent update on the progress of the Coalition fleet was that the crews of both orbiters successfully passed through an exterior circulatory vent and entered the fourth chamber. If you have any way to contact Gaby, I think she would like to know this. She should know where her daughter is.'

'I will make sure she does. Is that it? I have a boat waiting.'

'Beyond the fourth chamber is the fifth chamber. We have evidence that this chamber contains a singularity.'

'I know. It was Aldabra's entry ticket to the Merina empire. Toatéu. The Transcendental Object at the End of the Universe.'

Sea ducks swam under the bridge, a bright-plumaged male with a drab female, heading out into the channel.

'This singularity; the Americans believe it is some kind of interstellar transportation device, a kind of star gate to other sectors of the galaxy.'

'You do not.'

'Our theory is that it is a cognitive and social nexus. An evolutionary crisis point: the end of the socially constructed world and the beginning of a new one. I suspect neither we nor the Americans are wholly correct, the nature of a singularity is that it exceeds any system that would contain it, be that space, time, or language.'

'I can see that this would be a prize worth having.'

'More than any other, if what we suspect about its capabilities is correct. But what use is control of a singularity without access?'

'Eight astronauts are going to hijack the Big Dumb Object from under the noses of the Americans and fly it back to Madagascar?'

'Not Madagascar, Mr Muge. Africa. Kirinya.'

'This is insanity. You are speaking insanity, woman.'

'In its current form, of course. We will have to make some structural alterations. Our evidence from the Big Sky People is that the singularity in the fifth chamber is effectively the control system of the entire object: if we can reprogram that, we can re-engineer the whole artefact. That is currently in progress; the whole purpose of breaking the blockade was to bring a number of specifically designed fullerene packages into the Big Dumb Object. You could call them seeds, or eggs. However, my contribution is no less important, though, right now, it has never seemed less attainable. Without the co-operation of the Harambee, the plan is lost.'

'Why should I listen to you? You have manipulated me shamelessly.'

'Only because it was imperative that the Harambee be politically isolated so that this offer would seem more acceptable.'

'It is a strange gesture of friendship, to humiliate the Consensus before the world community, and then ask favours of it.'

'Even if that favour brought the Harambee far greater standing than any agreement you might have wrung from the North?'

A fast catamaran bound for Tallinn was negotiating the narrow channel to the gulf. Wake water sent the purposeful ducks bobbing. Waves lapped at the piers of the wooden bridge.

'What do you have now, Faraway?' A.O. Rananatsoa said.

'Do not ever, ever call me that name,' Faraway said. 'Only she is allowed to call me that. And you destroyed her. You sent her into exile; her child, Serena, you sent to a war. What has Gaby done that you hate her so much?'

'It was nothing personal.'

'Of course not. It never is. But she suffers. We make our schemes and our plans, and our political decisions, and someone suffers. Someone dies.'

'I know.'

There was a colour in the Merina woman's voice, a tone to those two words, that Faraway knew she did know, personally, intimately. Painfully.

'I have no authority to make policy decisions for the Harambee,' he said.

'Of course not. But you can recommend a submission to the Consensus.'

'Not without some idea of iMerina's proposition.'

'Certainly,' A.O. Rananatsoa said, and told him. All of it.

Faraway was late for his boat. He was so late that all the other diplomatic launches had left and the first of the reinstated ferries from the city was tying up.

'Madame Rananatsoa will be taking this launch?' Kalevi asked, stiffly. Faraway took satisfaction that, in the end, he had managed to piss Kalevi off.

'Madame Rananatsoa will be travelling with me,' he said.

The day-trippers swarmed ashore, curious and eager to tread boards, walk roads, cross bridges, pass through doors and under roofs, sit on chairs at tables that had felt the imprint of dangerous aliens.

63

Deep blue, edging into indigo. Muted surf on island rim. Cloud over all, purple hemmed with red. A dim sun, a crimson sky, the sea was a world-arch, the ocean snake swallowing its own tail. The water was clear far down deep. You could see all the way. Beneath the ripple-run, a shape, a shimmering; almost as liquid and evanescent as the medium through which it rises. Shape flowed, became certain for a moment of recognition: a bubble, rising rapidly, shedding uncertainty, gathering form and substance. Curled inside, a yolk, a golden foetus.

The bubble broke the surface, bobbed on the wine-dark ring-sea. Waves tumbled it towards the break line. The golden creature within struggled, kicked, punched at the shell. The birth-bubble rocked, the wind caught and luffed it. The golden woman went head over heels. Sharp glittered in her hand. A point penetrated the shell, drew into a slit. The bubble burst. The woman struggled clear from the clutching, drowning rags of skin.

Venus Rising from the Ocean.

Ren rolled on to her back, breathed ten, twenty lungfuls of clean air, took her bearings. Beyond the rags of crimson cloud the island-studded world-ocean arched over her. The islands were all perfectly circular, all exactly the same size. One of them is a traitor. One of them is a melanoma among freckles: an army observation post. The sun was a blood-red disc in the centre of a dark wall that seemed to rise sheer from the sea, like the castle of an enchanter in childhood Celtic faery tales. Lifting her head above the lap, Ren could just make out the ring of white water around world's end. Empire of the Rising Sun. But the sun never rose or set here. The Empire on which the Sun Never Sets. South.

The sun is south, they told her. *North is where you are going, castaway.* Ren could feel surf-break as a tremor through her body. She was within swimming distance of an island. *There is no guarantee where you will arrive,* Blue Two had said. *But wherever it is, you will arrive together.* It could be that they would all swim ashore right into the arms of the US Marines.

Ren trod water, studied the low meniscus of dark purple vegetation. She reckoned it was ten minutes to the beach at the paddle that was all she could manage after the transit of the gas exchange system. She pushed for shore. A beach-bum childhood had taught her ocean-sense. A vibration in the water, pressure shifts: something beneath her, rising fast.

The briefing had said nothing about big predators.

Her senses said, *trust your instincts*. She plunged away as the bubble burst the surface. The wind caught the bubble. Ren dived as it rolled over her. She glimpsed struggling arms within. Too many arms. Cowboy. She surfaced to windward; the breeze was carrying the bubble away from the island into open water. Cowboy beat at the transparent shell as Ren tried to find a purchase on the sly, slippery thing. Waves broke over her, she spat strangely spiced water.

'Get back!' she tried to shout as she stabbed with the twist-knife. The blade went in and held. Cowboy shifted his weight to roll the cut upwards; Ren's weight dragged a long slash through the tough membrane. The bubble burst silently. Cowboy tumbled out and went down in a flail of arms. Ren dived after him. He fought her. He was an octopus. Ren had hunted octopus. She knew how to take the clever old man of the sea. She punched Cowboy hard between the eyes. He went straight out. Ren grabbed him by his pressure skin hood and hauled him skywards. She turned on to her back, cupped her hands beneath his chin and kicked for shore. They staggered out of the surf line on to the beach of soft red cilia. Cowboy flopped like a drowned spider, water sucking at his lower fingers. Ren pumped him dry. He coughed much phlegmy water.

'Can't,' he whispered.

'Can't what?'

'Swim.'

The communicator patch on Ren's wrist said nothing but static to her auxbrain. She jumped up and down, ran a little way up the beach to jog some body heat into the batteries, but they were sea-chilled, moribund.

'I can't contact the others.' She scanned the curving seascape for breachings. Tsirinana was pregnant. She might need help in the water. She might equally have washed up on the other side of the island. 'I'm going to look round.'

Cowboy was sitting up now.

'Three Stripes.' For a moment she did not recognize his name for her. 'There's something watching us.'

Thing. Not one. Ren unwrapped the plastic strip from around her wrist. A twist turned it into a weapon.

The thing-not-one was some tens of metres distant in the deep shadow where the island canopy overhung the beach. It was not until it moved that Ren was certain it was not part of the vegetation. It was a thing that could only be comprehended by likenesses to things she knew; part lizard, part caterpillar, part elk. Its glossy body ran on ten short caterpillar legs. Like Cowboy, it carried four arms on its upright trunk, two powerful lower, two delicate upper bearing a clatter of long-jointed fingers. There was no head. The trunk flared into an array of curving antlers and bony fronds, like many cupped hands. She could see no facial features. It was too peculiar to be frightening, or threatening, but Ren kept grip of her knife. The thing tilted its left antler array towards her. Vents opened in the smooth beige skin between them.

'Please, put down your weapon,' it said in perfectly accented Swahili. 'I am meek and harmless. You are welcome to me.'

It moved fast for its size, a ripple of millipede legs. It paused a few metres from the castaways, inclined its head first to Cowboy, then Ren.

'You are in as good health as can be expected,' it said. The skull vents fluttered. Ren caught a waft of cinnamon, oil and Chanel from the thing. Her nose prickled. She fought a sneeze, lost.

'Gesündheit,' it said in American English.

'Are you, are you . . . are you a Chaga-maker?' Ren asked in English.

The vents rippled.

'Heavens no,' the creature said in her own African English. 'I am, at best, a manifestation of this place. An emanation. Since individual identity is a trait of your species, you may call me Locutor. I am that part of this entity with which you can may

368

most readily interact. Now, if you are recovered from your ordeal, I will take you to your colleagues.'

My name is Ren, and this is my diary. I've kept diaries on paper and on video, this one is different. It's not written on paper, or cell memories. It's written in my memory, in the cells of my auxbrain. This diary is mental. I write it in whatever moments I have to myself, whether I am walking, or working, or waking from sleep. It's a deliberate act of will, *now, I am going to commit this to my mental diary.* That way I won't forget it. There is much to remember here.

Locutor is good at talking, but not at language. It took William to explain to me what it had been trying to tell me on the beach, all that stuff about emanations and manifestations. Locutor is not this funny lizard-insect-elk thing: Locutor is the whole island. The entire ecosystem is one individual alien. The race is these archipelagos scattered across the circular sea. What's that saying about no man is an island? With these people, every man is an island, literally and metaphorically. And the islands are alive. One living thing.

One thing, and one of everything. At first I had the same problem as some of the early Chaga explorers, everything was so new and alien that I couldn't recognize anything. I couldn't see where one thing ended and another began. Now I'm beginning to know the shapes and the patterns – they're very, very different from anything at home – and part of my problem was that no two are the same. There is one, and only one, of everything. Thousands, maybe millions of different forms, but only one member. Only one of this thing like a half-buried cup that I'm sitting under, making this diary. Only one of that flying thing that sings like Diamond Jim's flute. Only one of that ball-shaped yellow flower at my feet. Only one caterpillar-elk Locutor. It's like an orchestra with only one of each instrument, but every instrument you can imagine. I was going to say that this is a world with no me, only us. But at the same time, it's no us, only me, unique, alone.

Locutor's species has been transformed by the Chaga. It came to their world two hundred thousand years ago. His was the last sentient race to symbiose with the Chaga. The last are always

369

the exemplars to the next. What his people were before, he does not say. What we might become, he will not answer.

At first I was disappointed that Locutor was not a Chaga-maker. Now I think I'm glad that he isn't. I think I would have thought, is that all there is, a caterpillar with antlers, a living island? I'm glad there's a mystery beyond this mystery: perhaps even the fifth chamber is only a door to another level of mystery. Locutor's species – they find names uncomfortable, they have big problems with the essential human experience of *self* and *not self* – see themselves as gatekeepers, ones who point the way. A species of John the Baptists. Maybe all we can know of the creators is the creatures they shaped.

Ocean-sense woke her. It was not night – there was no night on Locutor's homeworld, a satellite of a brown dwarf orbiting a cool distant red giant, and none in this red-lit simulacrum – but a sub-aural rumble had broken Ren's sleep. The others dozed on, even usually sensitive Cowboy, his arms wrapped around him. A bruise blackened the blue-black skin on his forehead where Ren had straight-armed him. She crouched, listening. Nothing. But a definite *feeling*. A dewdrop ran down the crease of a lolling red leaf-tongue, shivered from the tip for a few moments before the vibration knocked it loose.

'You are not unconscious?'

Locutor could be as stealthy as vermin in the shadowy mono-forest that was his own body. Where there was no night, there was no sleep. He found it as incomprehensible as death.

'We're moving,' Ren said.

The antler-antennae scanned her with subtle senses.

'Yes. You're most perceptive. We're underway to the north coast. You require transportation and I'm providing it.'

Having analysed the tones of all the humans on it, Locutor now talked to each in his or her own voice. Ren found listening to herself most unsettling.

'You can move, like a ship?'

'No. I'm walking.' The coronet of horns read confusion on Ren's face. 'I'm not making it very clear, am I? I support myself, both literally and metaphorically, on many thousands of root legs – they filter minerals and plankton from the sea water. We

370

can use them to get around. We all need to move about, how else would we ever get it together?'

Ren struggled against visions of islands humping each other. Images of sex and reproduction fertilized Locutor's comment on transporting his guests.

'Have you ever carried any other humans?'

'A Marine whose microlyte engine failed her.'

'Not soldiers. Scientists, from outside.'

'Not I, but I remember them. It was a very long time ago, I was a mere polyp at the time. They came through at the foot of the south wall.'

'The soldiers have closed that way off. We used the gas exchange ducts.'

'That must have been testing.'

Squeezed like a hard birth through gas capillaries, the bubbles tight, claustrophobic; always the fear that you're never going to get out of this. Then bowled through cavernous aeolea like a pin-ball in Dr Scullabus's pachinko machine. Tumbling, bounding, rebounding, rolling, dizzy beyond nausea.

'You could say that. These scientists; do you remember where they went?'

'I forget nothing. That is our purpose, to witness and record. And assist when requested. They were taken, as I am taking you, to the north coast. We observed them climb to the portal and successfully enter the fifth chamber. We have records of a series of events that indicate they encountered the singularity. Shortly after, the Marines arrived. Things got very complicated then. I had an unusually eventful childhood. You people lead interesting lives.'

'The one who went in, did any come back out?'

'Oh yes. The majority. All bar three.'

'And did they go back across the sea? Did you take any of them?'

'No, they remain on the north shore. They have a community there.'

'Locutor, you understand reproduction, children?'

'Darlin', sex is sex in any species. You have just taken a deep breath. Are you anticipating respiratory distress?'

No, I'm trying to say something that I have kept pressed down

371

in my mind so long, but has burst up like a brilliant bubble. A bubble with a life in it.

'Locutor, one of those scientists was my father.'

Day two. Being what follows after sleep one. Locutor's sea-bed crawl is so slow it's hardly perceptible, but this morning when Cowboy and I went to the beach the northern shore was noticeably closer than yesterday.

Sailing towards my father.

Walking actually, but it doesn't sound as good in a mental diary. Locutor says it will be another day before we reach the shore, but quite frankly, I wish it was for ever. Because then all the things I've imagined about him will be made real. I'll see him as he really is. I'll see a fifty-six-year-old man from Nebraska who once loved my mother and did the biggest walk away of any man ever. I don't know if I want to see the man I'll find under all the clothes and jewels I've put on him. I'm scared he won't be strong enough to carry it all. And what the hell am I going to say for a opening line? Hi Dad, I'm your little red-haired girl? What's strangest of all is that the one I can tell this to is an alien island-insect-elk entity, and not Cowboy, who's the closest thing to close I have on this planet. Maybe that's why. Too close. I feel good when he's around. I think about him a lot. He's kind, and he's cute, for someone with four arms. And he doesn't talk about himself all the time, unlike most males I've known. When he calls me 'Three Stripes' I go all warm, down there, under those middle three stripes. Jesus, I'm in the middle of a fucking interplanetary guerilla war, and I'm worrying about parents and boyfriend.

What did I just say there? So, I saved his life, but it's a long way from that to the B-word. I know what's doing it. Locutor is moving through an area where there are many islands; sometimes so close that the channel between hardly seems wide enough to allow him passage. There are things moving in the water, like long, silver torpedoes. They move so fast I can't make out details, just a sensation of speed and silver. They zip under the outer edge of the beach, then loop out again, turn, zip back, buzzing us like chrome barracuda. I'm sure there aren't as many as there look, it's just they move so fast.

They're sperm, Locutor tells us. It's the mating season. Each of those torpedoes contains the genetic information for a whole island ecology. But Locutor is having none of the soliciting of the other islands. 'I am on a mission,' he says. 'Dirty boys.' I thought there was something more in the air than the usual mix of buckies and scents. Mating pheromones. On humans, this is like six beers straight only you can still walk and talk, and with turbo-charged steel jizzum down in the water, it's no wonder Three Stripes is getting a little sweaty under the skin-suit.

Locutor says he will be glad to be clear of this unwanted attention. He's not the only one. Apart from that time when I was washed up and didn't know where anyone was, we've kept radio silence. Security. Somewhere out there on that big sea is an all-seeing eye. We don't even know for sure if the *Coetivy* group made it in. William says he thinks he's noticed a shift in position of one of a group of islands twelve o'clock high from us. We lie on our backs and squint up through the wispy clouds at the dots on the big blue. A definite northward trend, he says. They never look the same twice to me whether they're moving or not. The scary thing is, if William can see an island not where it should be, the Eye in the Sea can see it too. And us.

Tsirinana risks a frequency scan. A lot of weird noise on long wave – Locutor apologizes, his species gossips a lot in the lower electromagnetics on abstruse topological theorems and improvized song cycles – then a big silence until, up in the short wave, we hit chatter. A lot of chatter, on several wavebands. Coded, of course. They're relaying important stuff back to The Hub. No conceit to imagine it concerns us. We're just trusting that it's going to take them a long time to get enough GI Joes through the hole in the hull to stop us.

Meanwhile, sail on, slow, stately ship.

'Three Stripes.'

'Yeah.'

'What do you think it is?'

They lay on the carpet of fine red hairs that fringed the island, looking north, to the white line of surf and the improbable parabola of land curving out of it towards the dark ovals surrounding The Hub that were the portals to the fifth chamber.

Ren rested her head on Cowboy's belly. His lower fingers unconsciously felt out the nap of her orange stubble. It made her want to purr.

'What do I think what is?'

'Toatéu.'

'A singularity.'

'But what is a singularity? I mean, what does it mean?'

'The Americans have this idea it's some kind of gateway to the stars.'

'Is that what you think?'

'I don't know.'

'If it is, then Locutor, his island-people, they could have come through it from wherever their homeworld is.'

'There are a lot of them, and they are kind of big. Hard to transport.'

'Yes. So maybe it only seems to transport things across the universe.'

'How do you mean?' You can keep doing this for as long as you want, Space Cowboy, she thought, moving her scalp under his thick, strong fingers.

'That maybe all it sends is information. They just send the blueprints for Locutor's species through the singularity, and build it from what's around at the far end. The original stays behind. Or maybe the original is destroyed. You couldn't really have two Locutors, even if they're never likely to meet.'

'What's the problem?'

'Well, which is real, and which is the duplicate?'

'Does it matter? I used to have a friend who knew these professional forgers; they'd fake perfume, whiskey, watches, clothes. Their philosophy was, if it's exact right down to the atoms, what's fake about it?'

'Used to have a friend?'

'She died.'

'I'm sorry.'

'So am I.' And now all there is is a scar that is a little sore when I press it, and a few flakes of wood ash on the wind. She felt Cowboy move beneath her.

'For a long time I didn't understand what my exemplar meant when she said that Toatéu was a social and historical singularity.

374

But if it's like what I think, if it's a place of pure information, then a human could walk into it, and be reduced to information. And that information wouldn't have to go anywhere. It could just be changed, edited. Improved. Then it could be printed out in its new form. You would become whatever you wanted to be. Thousands of ways of being human. Or more than human. Or other than human.'

'My friend, the one who died, she believed in the power of language over reality.' Ren felt emotions tight in Cowboy's muscles. She turned to look at his face. She saw old anger and waiting hurt. 'Hey, are you all right?'

'Do I look all right?'

'What's wrong with you?' Ren said.

'What's wrong with me? Look at me. This is all right?'

'You look good to me. No, more than good.' Speak the truth, Ren. You owe him nothing less. 'You look beautiful to me.'

He had left off massaging her skull some time before. He held up his big, broad, work-worn lower hands.

'And these?'

'Those especially.'

'Tell that to my mother, who gave me away when I was two days old. She could not look at me. I was the punishment from the spirits. They told me in the home that she wanted to crush me under a rock.'

'Jesus, Cowboy. I'm sorry.'

'When I get there, I am going to make myself into something that is not this. That is not a punishment. That my mother would press to her breast.'

'What more could you be, that you aren't already?'

'Like you,' he said.

'You don't want to be anything like me,' Ren said. She kissed the calloused palm of Cowboy's lower hand.

At last. Something I can do. Something I'm good at. Something useful. Something no one else can do. No one handles a canoe like Ren.

It's funny how you have all the big things covered, and it's the unexpected details that trip you up. Tsirinana had it planned, all the way up to The Hub, and we were stopped in our tracks by two kilometres of reef, surf and shallow lagoon. Locutor could not take us any closer in.

'I can't swim that,' Cowboy said. No one could, the reef would tear you apart in seconds. We stood on the shore and looked at the other shore, the tiers of Chaga sweeping up and back to the centre of the world, and then it's Ren has the idea.

'Is there anything we could use for a boat?'

We went scavenging. William found this long pod with a hollow down one side. No idea what part it played in the island ecology, but to me it was a canoe tree. Locutor was none too happy about giving up a unique part of his biomass: he grumbled about wasting energy in re-routing ecosystems. His language facility has recently come to grips with griping. Time to get off before he learns sarcasm. But he dropped the pod and William and Cowboy dragged it to shore while Tsirinana and I whittled down rudimentary paddles from driftwood. Then we put Cowboy in the nose, and ran the thing out in the water. It was as stable as Gab after a night at the Mermaid, and you had to paddle like shit to keep the thing moving fast enough not to roll over, but it was a boat. My boat. I sat in the back with the steering paddle, and it was Turangalila again. That sounds crazy, you're thinking, you're halfway between the earth and the moon in an artificial space habitat and the sea curves up and over your head and it's full of living islands that walk. But you take all that away, and you have me, a boat, my hands steering it, the sea around me, the sound of surf on the reef. You never get that sound out of you. Part of you hears it always.

I took us along the line of reef, out beyond the surf, looking for the change of colour where the channel opens. I'd told everyone what to look for, but William kept glancing at the sky, south, into the sun, and frowning.

'Problem?' I asked him.

'In two and a half minutes, there will be,' he said. At the same instant, Tsirinana shouted: 'There!' We all saw the channel of deep indigo water. I stabbed down the steering oar, we just managed to come about without capsizing.

'Paddle like fuck!' I shouted.

They did. A roller lifted us and surfed us through the pass in the reef with the waves crashing on either side, and we were through into the clear green shallows of the lagoon. Then William gripped the sides and turned around in the canoe. We all looked where he was looking, shading our eyes against the glare of the sun. There was a dark spot in its centre, like an iris in an eye. As we watched, the dot expanded to a circle. I saw a thing like a gleaming fleck of gold fly out of the eye of the sun. A ship. The Americans had arrived.

Ren sealed up the suit and sniffed around where she had buried the shit. Clean. No one was taking any chances since the armoured tug came through the portal from Chamber Three. The canopy in this shore forest was impenetrable, but Ren imagined she could feel the weight of it, pressing on her bowed neck.

Something.

She snapped upright, listening, looking for pattern and movement in the dense understorey of rustling crimson cane. To her right. She turned slowly. Don't let them know that you know they are there. She uncoiled the knife from around her wrist. In that head of reeds. She turned one hundred and eighty degrees past it. Someone in there. No one who meant her well. Anyone who would, would have identified himself. All the way round, and back. In the concealment of her body, she twisted the knife. And now.

The drop to fighting crouch, the leap, the battle scream were one seamless action. She went through the reed bed like a bullet through a heart. Something went sprawling out under her. She landed on top of it, knife high to plunge it through the throat. Hands and eyes begged for life. White hands. Blue eyes.

She spared the knife.

'Jesus,' Ren said.

Helpless before her, squeezed between her thighs, was a surf nazi: fair skin, blond hair, blue eyes. Naked but for a patterned sarong, body pierces and paint. He was not a day over thirteen.

64

His name's Marco. I did him an injustice; he's fourteen. That's very important to him. I think he sort of fancies me. Well, I am the first female of his age group he's seen he hasn't been vaguely related to. That's what you think, Marco.

We're at Omega Point. 'Point' because it stands on a spur that lifts it high enough above the forest roof to see all the way to the ocean. 'Omega' because, well, of what's waiting up there, high above, behind the portals. It's pretty cool, for a place built and named by scientists. What it's like is a flock of weaver birds nesting all over the root buttresses and lower trunks of the canopy trees. Imagine hundreds of rush baskets woven into and on top of and through each other. Rooms spill all over the place, the dark doors and windows make them look like spirit faces. Empty eyes and mouths.

Thirty people live here, the ones who came down from Toatéu and their descendants. They looked into the face of the singularity, now they weave their basket homes and forage in the hanging forests and raise children. There isn't a hell of a lot else to do. You're either over forty or under twenty at Omega Point. These faces, these people, they knew my father. They're real. And because they're real, it somehow makes him real. They take all the things I've imagined about him, the things I've heard Gab say, the stories she's told, the glimpses I've seen inside that wooden box of hers, that she thinks I never looked at, and they make him solid, Trisha Aldred and David Pao and Hector Moraes. No, that's not right. It's more like they make a hollow mould of him, a space like my father.

Because he is a space, an absence. He never came back from the fifth chamber. And I think I'm kind of glad of that, really. I won't have to ask or answer any hard questions. I won't have to make room for him in my emotions – in the middle of space battle, I have to come to terms with finding my long-lost father. But I can't help wondering about him. I think I need a little gold to fill the hollow mould. I think I want to let people know who I am.

*

'Jesus. Shepard's kid.' The woman threw a knot of deadfall wood on to the fire. Sparks swarmed up to the chimney hole; the collapsing coals flared briefly. 'I should be amazed by this, but when you live this close to a singularity you get kind of used to synchronicity. Come closer to the fire. Let me get a look at you.'

Ren shifted closer to the heat, settled into a half-kneel, leaning into the fire glow. The woman studied her face intently.

'I don't know. Hard to say. Cheekbones, maybe. You got his jaw. It's a long time since I saw him. Since any of us saw him. Faces fade.' The woman poked the small blaze with a cord of wood. Firelight gleamed from the walls of the basket house.

'Trisha.'

'What?'

'What was it like?'

'The fifth chamber?'

'Yes.'

'I never saw it. I didn't get in. You won't get in either, unless it wants you. It's stayed closed for sixteen years. It opened once, and only once. It was his idea. After the Curators – your friend Locutor's people – told him what it was they were curating, he had to get into the fifth chamber. It wasn't enough for him that we had an entire sentient alien species set down in our laps – first contact, not counting the Chaga, and no one's still certain what kind of alien that is – when he heard there was a singularity, nothing else mattered. Nothing else was real.'

'The island-people – the Curators – they were just artefacts too, things made by the Chaga. The singularity, it wasn't. It was the thing itself.'

'Jesus, you are like him. Always looking for the big truth.' Trisha Aldred shifted on her stool. 'We went up there; it's no joy-ride, kid. When you get above the vegetation line, and you've no food, and the fog comes in, and then the snow . . . At least we'll be sending Hanuman with you. We had nothing. Hell, I wouldn't even think of it now, even if that fucking portal opened and Jesus and Mary and the whole fucking circus of heaven came flying out. But, we got there. And we sat down and we waited for the thing to open, like all the other ones. And we sat and we sat, and we scratched our asses and played pinochle, and we waited. I can't remember how long, it was long and cold and miserable. But the idea that on the far side was this place where everything begins and ends, where all the rules break down ... We talked a lot about what we thought it was in there; all kinds of wild, wacky, theories. Real blue skying. All the physical theorems you could prove, all the metaphysical stuff; like space-time worm-holes, and hyperspace, and where the Chaga-makers came from. Then Hector said, hey, is it my imagination, or is getting warmer? I don't know why I did this, but I felt the surface of the portal, and it was warm. In fact, it was glowing, a very dim red, even dimmer than that shit-pile of a thing calls itself a sun over there. And getting brighter. But not hotter, that's one of the weird things. Within a few seconds, it was glowing white hot, like a sheet of white fire, but all there was was this slight warmth off it. And then Shepard walked in. He got up and he went right through it; just walked clean into the white fire. Then Adeline went, and Elia. Then David tried, and he bounced. It was like he'd walked into a plate glass window. No visible difference in the portal, but he couldn't get through. We all tried. Not a thing. It wouldn't let us in.'

Ren stared into the fire. The woman fed it fresh fuel, though the wicker room was still smoky from the previous stoke of wood.

'He's gone, kid. He just walked away, and I can't tell you where he went.'

Ren shivered; a wind was rising in these foothills of the south cap, gusting through the tall trunks of the great forest, through the unchinked gaps of the reed house, through her soul.

'Trisha, there's me, and I know he had two other children, two boys. One of them died a long time ago, before I was born, but do you know, are there?'

'Any others?'

The woman smiled. I know what you would say, Ren thought. You're thinking, not for want of trying. But you think I'm still a kid, and that it would embarrass me, so you'll just smile.

Trisha Aldred pulled her wrap tighter around her and prodded the fire. 'Do you think it's cold in here? I just can't get heat into me.'

*

She had never pegged Cowboy for a mouth breather. Curled on his side, eyes shut, mouth wide open. Snail-tracks of silver saliva on his face. He had kicked the blanket off and hugged it to him like a child or a toy, wrapped in all his arms. It seemed a thing crueller than war and atrocity to wake him.

'Cowboy.'

She barely touched him but he was awake on the instant. He sheepishly wiped drool from his cheek. Hey, it's okay, Ren wanted to say. I could do that. I would like to do that. What she said was, 'You got to get up. We're moving out.'

'What?'

'William says they're coming.'

His things were bundled together in moments. He pulled on the patterned serape that was one of many gifts of the people of Omega Point to the warriors.

The guide Hanuman, a dark-haired white boy with bad skin and shy eyes, was waiting with Tsirinana on the open place at the head of the settlement. William was looking out to sea.

'Any moment now,' he said. 'Yes. Look.'

At his word, Ren saw flowers unfold across the sky. Five, ten, twenty tiny white blossoms, far up the curve of the world, curling in towards her, driven by Coriolis force. Every second, more were opening; white, ruched petals. Thirty, thirty-five. The slow, soft falling beauty was a lie. Pretty army parafoils. Alice McKittrick was air-dropping her warriors on the north slope of Chamber Four.

'They're opening about a kilometre up,' William said, awed. I understand that, Ren thought. The other seventy-four kilometres, they must have done in free-fall. She shielded her eyes with her hands, squinted for the tug. It was a tiny golden beetle almost directly above her. How badly they must want us, that they take on the unimaginably hostile environment of the third chamber, then jump into seventy-five kilometres of thin air over an alien ocean.

By the time the first wave hit the drop zones along the coastal strip, the hunted were two kilometres above Omega Point, climbing fast up through the trunks of the soaring crimson trees. They climbed for many hours under the dense canopy. The slope grew gradually steeper. Ren noticed that Cowboy was finding it difficult. When he thought no one else was looking he would take the weight off one hand, clench and unclench his fingers. Hanuman taught them the foraging tricks of the coastal forest. He was a taciturn, aloof youth but a good hunter. This bulb held sweet meat, that fruit had seeds you could chew when your energy was low. This gourd gave a sip of water, that flower a drop of nectar.

When they stopped to eat and rest, Ren sat down close beside Cowboy. She opened his lower hands, which he had clenched into painful fists. She ran her thumbs over the big knuckles and tight tendons, massaging out the cramps.

'My mother taught me to do this,' she said. He was glad of it, though he would not say so. Ren noticed Hanuman watching them from the root buttress where he sat apart, sucking flesh from his foraged fruit.

An hour beyond, the canopy forest ended as abruptly as a line on a map. Before the travellers rose an open land of shoulder-high hemispherical hummocks of green and purple mottled moss. Easy climbing – wide corridors meandered between the mounds, but Ren kept glancing at the sky.

'I'll let you know,' William said.

It's one thing knowing, Ren thought, it's another doing something about it.

He let them know fifteen minutes later at a halt in a small boggy hollow where four tussocks met.

'Look at the sun,' William said. As they watched, a black dot appeared in its heart. Within seconds it had opened into a circle. Through sun-glare, Ren glimpsed the tug vanishing into it. The portal closed.

'Where have they gone?' Cowboy asked.

'To get more.'

Up the trail, Hanuman was waiting for them to follow. There was little to eat in the moss-mound country, though water was plentiful, running and trickling down the winding channels. An hour's walk and four kilometres higher the landscape began to change. Some of the moss domes grew cracked crowns of quills. A few minutes higher and the crowns pushed out jagged stalks tipped with spears of folded florets. Higher still and the stamens rose, three, four metres before blossoming into bell-shaped white blooms. Hanuman hacked a flower head down with his knife. A symbiotic creature like a winged seed could be found inside the blossoms. It was considered a delicacy in Omega Point.

There were other changes, non-botanical. Now when the group paused, Ren became aware of an increasing lightness in her step and a chill in the air. She leaned her hands on her aching thighs. The gravity was gentler, but the slope was crueller. And getting nothing but steeper. Ren looked up the way she must go, through the cloud-shrouded sky reefs, and the snow country, and up beyond the snow country, the high bare places towards the hub. It would be sheer scramble at the end, to the shelf at the base of the portal.

And even then there was no guarantee it would let them in. Tsirinana remained convinced that the gates would open wide and bid them enter.

'Way to go yet,' Cowboy said, seeing where she was looking. 'Don't worry, every step takes me towards country I like. I will help you, Three Stripes.'

Hanuman pressed them on. He did not want to camp in the moss country. It was a bad place to be caught if the clouds came in. They broke for sleep under a fan of filigree clamshells a few hundred metres into the coral country. Ren sat with Cowboy and worked on his hands, which she knew pained him much more than he would say. She noticed that all the time, one or other of his upper hands kept in gentle contact with her. She liked that. He pulled his serape close, hugged his blankets and was noisily mouth-breathing within seconds.

Twenty-five kays up, Ren filed in her mental diary. Top of the world. If my legs and shoulders didn't hurt so much, if I wasn't so cold, if I didn't want something hot and filling to eat so much, I think I'd be having just about the most fun I've ever had. If it wasn't a war, if there weren't soldiers down there hunting us, if space ships hadn't fought and people hadn't died.

There was more she knew she wanted to say but the thoughts would not focus. Tired. Sore. Sleep. She rolled up in her blanket and curled up against the warmth of Cowboy's belly. She remembered feeling arms move around her.

While they slept the fog came down. Ren woke shivering, sniffling, soaked under heavy wet blankets. They toiled all the first march through dripping coral gardens under grey cloud so thick Ren at the back could not see Hanuman in the lead. Her stubble itched. Her legs ached worse then the day before. Her saturated pack weighed a ton and chafed her wet skin. And the way grew steeper and the air thinner. She found herself labouring for breath on the tougher ascents.

'Look on the bright side,' William said. 'At least we can't be seen.'

An hour into the afternoon march, the solid mass of fog began to ripple and rip, and in the space of a few metres blew away. The sky was clear and the sun was bright and they found themselves on a high knuckle of rock where the support ridges of the north cap, splayed like fingers, joined together. Ren spread her silver-dewed serape on the bare rock to dry. She sat down and tried to get some sun into herself while Hanuman divided up the fruit of his foraging.

'It's back,' William said peeling a bulb of meat. Three minutes later, the tug came out of the portal. With the perspective of altitude, Ren could now make out details of the ship. It was a brutal barrel, built for heavy pressure, white and blind as a cave fish. It was ponderous even in zero gee. Ren glimpsed letters and the colourful patch of the stars and stripes on its belly as it manoeuvred.

I see you. Do you see me, this little speck of sun-warmed gold on the side of the highest mountain in the solar system?

Within the hour, the parafoils were falling like spring blossom.

'They're going for *Coetivy*,' Tsirinana said.

You want to call them, Ren thought. I would too if I were you. I would want to know. But what could it do, except tell that big slug up there, here we are! Come and get us. At the next pause, where the coral gardens gave way to wave upon wave of mushroom-trees that grew horizontally from the ground before turning upwards and unfolding spotted red caps, Tsirinana scanned the wavelengths. Down there, the soldiers were talking a lot. Talking fast, in a strange jabber that confounded all of Tsirinana's language implants.

'Klingon,' Hanuman said. 'It's from an old television sci-fi show. They were some kind of aliens; someone made up a whole language for them.'

'I've never seen this show,' Tsirinana said.

'Neither have I,' said Hanuman. But he knew some phrases in it. 'Let me hear.' Tsirinana plugged an ear jack into the wrist communicator. Hanuman pressed the bud to his ear. 'Abrams is moving into position. Georgiades has the defile covered. He's asking mobile for thermal images. He's relaying them to the squads. Abrams wants heavy weapon support. He's taking up position in the moss forest. He has them on thermal imaging. He says he thinks they know he's there. They got one of those fucking freak precogs. There's no word in Klingon for precogs. Or fucking either. He said those in English.'

'Go on,' Tsirinana said.

'Andersen has contact. Abrams is going in. They've got them. It's over.'

No one spoke much the rest of the day's climb. They could not fail to notice the busy traffic of dragonfly microlytes between ground and heavy tug. Camp was thirty-five kilometres high in the fungus forest under the breath of the snows. Ren entered in her soul-diary: We're on our own now. And I don't want there to be the least suspicion of bold and defiant and fuck-you gung-ho in that statement, because it makes me take a long, cold look at what we are. And that is a seventeen-year-old white kid with a knife, a shy man who can see into the future, a guy with four arms and sore hands, and a pregnant Malagasy woman. And behind us, down there, getting a little bit closer all the time, like age and death, is the most efficient killing mechanism the world has ever seen.

She saw Tsirinana sitting apart, hunched under her serape. William went to her. He sat beside her. Ren saw them talk intimately. William touched her belly. Tsirinana laid her hand on his. She saw that Tsirinana was shaking. She is crying, Ren realized. She is scared. She does not know what to do. She needs another person to touch her and tell her she is doing the right thing. For the first time, Ren thought of Tsirinana as having an age. She had been Tsirinana: lofty Merina bitch, engineer, commander. Pregnant with a piece of nano-engineering so audacious it bordered on fantasy. Now Ren saw a woman in her mid twenties. A handful of years separates us, she thought. Little years, vast responsibility.

She rolled over in her blanket and stroked Cowboy for warmth and comfort and maybe, she thought, a little bit more, just a little. But he was deeply asleep, drooling out his dreams of a childhood of rejection as absolute as infanticide.

Snow dazzled Ren. She knew what it is, and how it worked, she had even seen it, from a distance: that white stuff on the top of Kirinyaga that glinted in the sun. She did not know that it made a sound when you walked on it, and that it had a taste, and that you could throw it at other people, that under the dwindling gravity it piled high and steep and turned the magic mushroom forest into wonder. And that after half an hour it was colder than she had ever known cold in her life, and that her eyes hurt and her head pounded from squinting through the dazzling, universal white. Then it started to fall.

Ren discovered white-out.

'Here. To me.' Somewhere out there was Hanuman. 'To my voice. Walk straight ahead of you. Here.'

Mushrooms were monsters, snow devils, looming at her, luring her to burial under coat upon coat upon coat of interlocked ice flakes. Hands seized her, pulled her ungently into dark and shelter and warmth.

'There's always a nest hole close by up here,' Hanuman said. 'You just have to know the signs.' The pouch in the living skin of the mountainside confined the iMerina Expeditionary Force like multiple births in a womb. Outside, white screamed past the open cave mouth. 'The thing about the weather up here is, whatever happens, it never happens for very long.'

After an hour William said he could make out the shapes of fungi. Within five minutes the air had cleared completely. The blizzard passed down the mountain; in its wake the world glittered, new made.

'I think we can go now,' William said. 'It's beautiful out there.'

'You would not think it so beautiful if you had to walk on your hands,' Cowboy said. 'My fingers are blue.'

'Your fingers are blue anyway,' Ren said, but breathed on them for him. Then, on a gleeful, thrilling whim, she pressed them against the three white stripes of her groin. 'Warmer now?'

'I would walk through ten thousand kilometres of snow, just to get them cold enough for you to do that again,' Cowboy said.

Tsirinana said, 'Before we go, there's something I should tell you. I reckon we're about a day, maybe a day and a half at most, from the portal. I'm activating the biochemical triggers. I'm going to give birth in forty hours.'

They climbed for two hours through the ice forest. The gradient was now so steep it was hard scrabble for every hand and foot hold. Ren stopped abruptly at the foot of a pitch.

'I can't see,' she said, terrified. 'My eyes hurt so much, it's all just glare.'

Cowboy tore a strip of cloth from his serape and wrapped it around her eyes.

'Take my hand,' he said. He led her up the ascents, telling her where to step, where to grip, where to trust and where to lean on him. Time stopped. Space ended, movement ceased. All that existed was gradient and gravity and cold the point at which they intersected, Ren's shrieking muscles and numb hands. She became aware that Cowboy had stopped abruptly.

'What is it?' she whispered.

William answered. 'Cover.' They scuttled under a stand of fungus caps, shovelled snow around themselves, huddled and shivered and feared. A few seconds later Ren heard a low insect drone. It grew louder; she thought she could make out a pattern in its sound: loud, then fading, then growing again. She slipped her blindfold, flinched at the pain of the light.

'What is it?' she asked again.

'Microlyte,' Cowboy said. 'Just pray it doesn't pick up our trail.'

The sound faded to the right and disappeared into the susurrus of the wind over the snow fields. The ascent continued. In the shelter of the burrow where they camped that day Cowboy unbandaged Ren's eyes. She blinked in the gloom. Black snowflakes eddied, solidified.

'I can see!' she said. 'Oh God, I was so scared.'

By the cave mouth, Tsirinana listened to the advance of her enemy.

'They're in the coral gardens,' Hanuman translated. 'They're talking to squad about eighty kays clock. They're already up above the snow line. Everyone's being pulled in.' He paused, pressed the bud deeper into his ear. 'They're saying about microlyte thermographs. They know where we are.'

Snow dazzled, Ren slogged a first march behind Cowboy. She never wanted to know or see or hear or touch or have anything ever to do with snow again. Evil white powder. But she noticed that the going did not seem to be getting any harder, though she knew that the wall must be very steep at this altitude. The centrifugal gravity was dropping off.

The lies eyes tell you.

And she was feeling warmer. Impossible. The ground seemed warm under her feet. Her next handhold, she let her grip remain on it for extra moments. Blood heat under her suit glove.

'Ren.' Cowboy unbound her eyes. She blinked, winced, shut her eyes, opened them again, squeezed away the blobs of dark light.

'Oh, my God.'

She was above snow and clouds, above everything. The world lay at her feet like an empty offering bowl, arched above her like the dome of the temple. Looking up, she saw the wall of world's end flare out into the vault of heaven. Only the black circles of the portals were higher than she was, ringed around the hub like seated saints. And not so high, from this altiplano of sparse, ground-hugging scrub wind-sheared into weird, agonized topiaries, the closest seemed no more than a morning's stroll. If you could do a trick with gravity, and turn it ninety degrees so you were not climbing an almost sheer wall but walking down a gentle grassy slope, you could do it in one big, joyous run.

Only gods could do such tricks. It would be a day and more, and Tsirinana was already pressing her fingers to her belly, frowning. Ren had already heard her retching shallowly among the aromatic bushes. The climb continued. Ren sighted was little better than Ren blindfold. All she could see was ground, fingers hunting for a handhold, Cowboy's lower hand reaching down to help her up. In the afternoon pitch the microlyte returned. There was nowhere to hide from it on the naked north slope. Ren turned to face it. It passed so close she could see the fur trims of the pilot's parkas.

They ended the day with the portal a tantalizing kilometre above them. That kilometre was at an incline of almost sixty degrees. Final camp was in cavities scooped out of the living flesh of the mountain. Cowboy and Ren shared a cave. They huddled in the back from the bitter wind that had battled them for the last few hundred metres of the ascent. Within minutes the temperature had risen enough to make serapes and blankets uncomfortable. A few minutes more and Ren had broken sweat.

'There must be some kind of heat exchange system just under the surface,' Cowboy said, exploring the chamber's leathery skin.

'My shoulders ache,' Ren complained.

'Lie down on the floor,' Cowboy said. She lay face down on the floor. 'Take that off,' he said. She unsealed the top of the skin suit, wriggled out of it. 'You smell,' Cowboy said.

'You're not exactly a rose garden yourself,.'

She felt Cowboy's fingers work the cramp out of her shoulder and upper arms.

'Cowboy,' she said, 'my front hurts as well.' She turned over. She touched her small, big-nippled breasts. 'Here and here.'

He kissed them. In a moment she was out of the suit and on top of him.

'There's no reason why we shouldn't,' she said.

'None at all,' he agreed.

She fumbled for his seals.

'I mean, I think I know you well enough.'

'Certainly well enough.'

Fingers. He was all fingers, everywhere, all at once.

'This is just something we've both wanted to do for a long time.'

'A very long time.'

She straddled him. Her back pushed into the receptive roof of the nest. Skin above and skin below. He could do it all at once. Left tit, right tit, clitty.

'Oh! Jesus!'

One up her ass. Was this what people did? What do I do? She found what she was looking for, squeezed his balls with one hand, grabbed his dick with the other. It was like a rocket. I know all about flying rockets, she thought. She manoeuvred over it. It kicked in her hand. Hot sticky wet clung to her thigh. There was a smell of wheat and musk.

'Sorry,' Cowboy said. 'I'm sorry. I'm sorry.'

'It's okay,' Ren said but it was already going down between her fingers and the heat of the moment had passed. He was asleep, sprawled on his back, snoring, within a minute. Ren slept draped over him, cheek against chest, rocked by his breathing. Her sleep was filled with dreams of vertigo.

The next day's climb was sheer and arduous and punctuated by frequent rests. During one, William glanced skywards at the tug, holding position in the axis over the ocean. His concern became apparent at the next halt. Slowly, very slowly, the tug was moving.

'It's coming down our throats,' Cowboy said.

'It's going to try to dock in The Hub,' William said. Tsirinana stood staring, mouth open, her face half wonder, half fear. She touched her fingers to her belly.

'I've just had a contraction.'

The last eight hundred metres to the lower lip of the portal were worse than Ren had imagined bad could be. So she would not have to think about the pain and the fear and the tiredness and the hunger, she divided her attention between the steadily approaching ship and Tsirinana pausing to grimace and spasm. We aren't going to make it, she thought. She is going to have it out here on the side of the mountain. By the time they hauled themselves over the lip on to the wide flat apron of the portal, Tsirinana's contractions were five minutes apart. Still she insisted on walking up to the face of the gate. She peeled back her glove and pressed her hand to the adamant black.

'It's warm,' she said. A fresh contraction seized her. She doubled over. William set her down, tried to make her comfortable with blankets and folded serapes. The door remained closed. 'Help me.' Tsirinana fumbled at the gusset seal of her suit. 'Get this off me, please, now. Now. Now!' William made it just before her waters broke. Ren could not contain her grimace of revulsion at the spreading gush. Body fluids, womb-juice. She stood back, repelled, redundant. She felt as unfeminine as a boy next to this defining moment of womanhood.

'Oh guys,' Cowboy said from the brink of the ledge where he was keeping watch. 'The Marines are here.'

Fifteen kilometres above Ren's head, the tug nuzzled at the puckered rosette of cha-flesh at the centre of the spin axis. It spun up to match the BDO's rotation, docked and locked. The image was immediate, inescapable and intimately sexual.

'Fifteen kays,' Cowboy said. 'They could be here in a few hours.'

Tsirinana let out a cry. William knelt beside her.

'Give me a hand!'

'I don't know what to do!' Ren cried.

'Help me get her clothes off.'

Tsirinana was droning now, legs pulled up on the nest of blankets, long, keening animal moans broken by panting. Her grip left bruises on Ren's arm.

'Oh Jesus, what's wrong, why does it hurt so much?'

'You're not dilated enough,' William said. 'Try and hold back.'

'I don't want to, get it out, get it out of me,' Tsirinana wailed.

'I'm going to try something,' William said. Ren saw him do something with his fingers around Tsirinana's vagina. Tsirinana heaved and screamed. 'There's something over the head of the vagina,' William said. 'I tried to push it back.'

'Don't you fuck with me you fucker!' Tsirinana swore, then lapsed into agonized burbling in Malagasy as another spasm tore at her. 'Get it out of me!'

Ren mopped her sweat with the hem of her serape. It was the most useful thing she could think to do. Cowboy came loping over on all fours.

'This is probably not the time, but they've started landing soldiers.'

Tsirinana screamed again. She pushed, gasped, pushed. There was nothing left of her but pain and effort.

'Oh God!' she shrieked. 'Help me.'

She fought the thing inside her for an hour. William and Ren and Cowboy yelled encouragement, wiped her sweat, held her shaking limbs. Hanuman glanced over from his position. Every look was more apprehensive than the last. Tsirinana pushed and fought and the thing refused to be born. William took Ren aside. Cowboy sang to the trembling Tsirinana and stroked her limbs.

'Her energy is spent,' William said. 'She is weakening. She does not have the strength to do it.'

'What are we going to do?' Ren asked.

'I am trusting that the Americans will look after her,' William said. 'Give me your knife.'

Hanuman was called over to hold her wrists while Cowboy and Ren took a leg each. Tsirinana bit down on the twisted corner of blanket and clenched her fists and closed her eyes tight. Ren looked away but she knew when the knife went in. She had not thought the human voice capable of a sound like that. She wanted it to be over but it went on a very long time. Then William handed her her bloody knife and a gnarled black oval of slime and blood the size of two fists. Ren shied back from the thing William had taken from Tsirinana's womb.

'But the portal's closed.'

'Take it,' William ordered. 'Dig a hole. Bury it. It will go active in contact with organic circuitry.' He saw Ren fascinated by the terrifying wash of blood from the open belly. 'Do it!'

Ren scuttled away. She hacked two-handed at the spongy, porous substance of the portal apron. Every cut and slash was a joy and release. She levered out chunks of Chaga-stuff. She dug down until she laid bare the fibrous nervous system of molecular circuitry. Ren pushed the womb-thing into the hole, covered it up with loose debris, pounded the surface flat, ran back to Tsirinana. She was unconscious. Her lips were blue. William's face was grey. Blue, grey, red. So much red. William held fistfuls of belly, trying to seal up the wound with his own flesh but the blood ran from between his fingers.

'I can't stop her bleeding,' he said. 'I can't stop the blood.'

Two hours later the first Marine platoon completed its traverse around the portal and arrived on the lower lip. There were four men and one woman. They wore hooded real fur parkas and carried light automatic weapons. They found a white boy and a black man sitting with their legs dangling over the brink. Further back they found a red-haired white girl and a four-armed humanoid. The humanoid had his arms around the white girl. The girl had cried herself into exhausted, heaving sobs. By the obsidian disc of the portal they found a half-naked woman lying on her back in a glossy pool of drying blood. The Marine meditech checked her out. She had been dead for at least an hour. The medic crossed himself and closed her eyes.

65

They called the shuttle run through Chamber Three the Pizza Express. One mistake and you were thin and crispy with an undergenerous portion of sauce.

Ren was learning Marine humour. It was unsubtle and often gory and ran to complex in-jokes and multiple layers of allusion. Binding her hands and ankles with cable grip was not one of their jokes. That was security. 'We already lost two ships to you Space Monkeys,' said the woman soldier who had been assigned to watch over her. The dangerous survivors from *Iles Glorieuses* had each been assigned a cramped, windowless cell in the cargo hold, and a trooper to guard them. As a guard Ren's was tough, as a Marine full of soldier-shit, as a woman, she could be made to talk.

'What the fuck was that all about back there, anyway?' she asked.

You'll learn, Ren thought. For she had seen, quite distinctly even as she was bundled into the tug, the ring-shaped wave starting across the world-ocean of Chamber Four from south to north. Then the hatches sealed and the little metal holding cell trembled as the engines powered up. Ren found herself drifting towards the back wall under gentle acceleration. The woman soldier grabbed her.

'You could untie me,' Ren said. 'You don't have to do this.' That was what had prompted the comment about the Space Monkeys. Yeah, and we're doing it again, right under your noses. If you're going to steal, steal big. Acceleration within acceleration. When will you notice? When will you work it out?

She still saw Tsirinana as they left her on the high, bare plateau. A whole world for a life. I don't buy that deal. If she could, Ren would have clawed the dripping black seed out of the ground and forced it back into Tsirinana's belly.

The cabin creaked. Joints groaned. Rivets strained. Ren read fear on the woman soldier's face. Coming under pressure. Pizza time. The tug was a cacophony of strains and agonies as the pressure built to gas giant levels. The woman soldier fingered a rosary and closed her eyes. Acceleration again playfully pushed Ren. She tumbled head over heels.

'Please, let me go.'

She caught Ren, pulled a blade and cut the ties. They floated facing each other, each with their arms wrapped around their legs, while the tug made the transit of the third chamber, listening for whatever tell-tales death whispered in the atmosphere of a gas giant.

'There's things out there,' the soldier said. 'Living things. I never seen them, no one ever has, it's dark as hell, but they're out there, flying in that. They see them on the radar. Huge great fuckers.'

They looked at the creaking curve of hull, sharing unspoken imaginings of dark wings brushing the painted metal.

It did not last as long as Ren had feared. Certainly not as long as it took to climb to a portal, or for a woman to bleed to death from an improvized Caesarean. The groaning and clicking dwindled and ended. The tug moved on. The woman Marine jacked in her earplug radio and did not speak until a trooper at The Hub undogged the door and released prisoner and guard. Then she said, 'Hey. That was impressive, what you did.'

Bright light blinded Ren's snow-burned eyes as soldiers ghosted her through the pods and tubes of The Hub. One windowless room to another. But through the painful light-fog she noticed that a lot of people were moving around in a high state of agitation. They have noticed. They have worked it out. She kept her smile inside her skull. To have worn it on her face would have peeled the skin from her cheekbones.

Alone in a small room. Not alone. Tsirinana was with her. Mrs Meenakshi Khandewal was with her. Oksana Mikhailovna Telyanina was with her. They made the room very small. They were not people she wanted in so small a room with her. She tried to distract herself by making herself as still and motionless as she could in the middle of the cell and imagining she could feel the minute pressure of the BDO under acceleration. She tried to imagine the great ice-fields beyond the fifth chamber thawing, deliquescing as the mass-momentum drive consumed them for micro-gees. She tried to imagine what was happening in each of the worlds she had passed through. The Curator-people gripping bedrock hard with their ten thousand toes as the tsunamis raced towards them. The big ring-waves breaking, sweeping away the one-and-only ones. The unseen things in the third chamber; how would they react as the pressure waves raced the length of their dark world and back again? The flying things in the second chamber, the primeval Africas far below her, would they stare as the fixed stars began to slide across their windows?

Bigger changes to come. Nothing is lost, Locutor had said. Everything is held in Toatéu. She was glad. She had had enough of death, without becoming the destroyer of worlds.

She tried to imagine herself on the outside, walking along the crack in the earth that had suddenly appeared between the third and fourth chambers. She could jump over it, but already it was widening into a fault line, a rift, a gulf. In the end it would sever the Big Dumb Object into two smaller, smarter objects. She hoped the Big Sky People had made it to the safe side. When she had run through all her imaginings and was back in the small room with the bloodstained women, she was taken before General Alice McKittrick.

'Ren.'

The woman was a corpse. Years of microgee had gnawed her bones to twigs, her muscles to knotted string. She hung inside her too-big uniform like a jigging puppet on wires. Over sixteen years of zero gee General Alice McKittrick had learned the trick of being intimidating in free-fall without the props of desks, surfaces, partitions, levels. She kept the light from her small office's window at her back. Silhouettes and halos. A bright blur of authority. She floated in comfortable Lotus. Ren struggled to hold herself upright. Gravity will kill you, bone woman, she thought. You can never go home again, and I am taking this one away from you. She asked, 'I want to know about the others, what's happened to them?'

'Of course you do. They're being held in solitary, but they're fine.'

'Fine.'

'You understand that, right now, you are not exactly our top priority. Atmospheric pressure in the Chamber One is down ten per cent in the past hour. We've reports of mass extinctions.

Whole species are lying down and dying out there. The hominids, they're dying.'

'Nothing is lost in Toatéu.'

'Well, you keep telling yourself that.' General Alice McKittrick reached out for a drifting water bottle. She took a sip. 'I just know intelligent creatures are dying. I should congratulate you, girl. You lost every battle, and you still managed to win the war. Our entire strategy was contingent on your going for the Star Gate – Toatéu as you insist on calling it. We'd never imagined anything like this space elevator plan.'

'It's just moving atoms around. That's what we're good at.'

'Yes. So this is what's going to happen to you now.'

'Out the main lock, like those people on High Sumatra?'

'Where do you get your ideas from, girl?'

'We saw what you did. Don't lie to me.'

General Alice's face said, I can lie to you, I can do what I want, child. This is all still mine.

'You saw bodies go through the lock. I'll admit, it was a scare tactic. I'm telling you they were dead even before we opened up the ship. Some little trick with that secondary brain you carry. Now, you can believe me, or you can call me a damn liar to my face, but it really doesn't matter. It's not going to bring them back.'

'You mean, they all killed themselves?'

'I mean, they flushed that egg thing they were carrying and then gave themselves heart attacks so we couldn't talk to them and find out what they were really after. Because had we known, I would have nerve-gassed the entire fourth chamber to stop you. By the time we found out from the crew of the *Coetivy* ship, you were already at the portal.'

'The *Coetivy* people . . .'

'They're alive.'

Ren felt the air tremble around her. Ripples ran across the surface of the globe of water in the transparent blue bottle floating beside Alice McKittrick's head. Altitude trims as the BDO approached geostationary orbit. Over the next few days the fourth and fifth chambers would split off and withdraw to a slow eighty thousand kilometre orbit while the rest of the object began to spin itself into a bridge between Earth and Heaven. Just moving atoms around.

'What's going to happen to you,' General Alice McKittrick said, 'you'll be taken to High Steel and transi-shipped to Unity. From there you'll go down to Kennedy. We've got a media operation already underway. You'll be tried in a US court on war crimes charges. After all, we don't yet recognize Merina, or any of the Coalition states – in fact any of the Southern states at all. So you are legally international terrorists. And you did pull off the biggest heist in history. Of course, we all know that you're hostages. Except that the United States does not take hostages, so you'll just be treated as ordinary criminal prisoners. Almost certainly, there'll be a trade-off some day. I can't say when. It could be a very long time, given the current climate towards the south in Congress. So. Congratulations. You won the war, but always remember, you didn't fucking beat me. All right. Take her. I got stuff to do.'

Two guards swam through the hatch. Ren did not resist as each took an arm. General Alice McKittrick turned to her evacuation plans. The water bottle spun slowly in the dusty light from the window, a miniature Big Dumb Object.

The engines shut off. The tug fell clear of the BDO. Behind it, the main lock irised shut. Hanuman pressed himself to the tiny triangular port.

'What is that kid staring at out there?' the woman guard said. It was the same woman who had guarded Ren on the Pizza Express.

'Stars,' William answered. 'He's never seen them before.' The woman soldier thought about that.

The drop to Unity would take eighteen hours. The guard had velcro-backed cards to pass the time. 'Any poker players?' she asked, managing by great dexterity to riffle the deck. 'What about you?' she said to William. He looked at her. 'Okay, I hadn't thought about that. Anyone else?' Ren shook her head. Cowboy held up his free upper hand. The other was handcuffed to the chair. He alone of all the prisoners was secured. The Marines mistrusted Space People. Soldiers are a superstitious race. The guard balked when he picked the cards up with one lower hand and fanned them with the other.

'Two,' he decided.

Hanuman glanced over his shoulder. It was long enough for Ren to read more than stars in his face. She joined him at the window.

'Look at this,' he whispered. They clung head to head and peered down on the stars. 'There, see? Those red and green stars; they're moving together.'

They watched them move across the star field. The distances between them seemed to be increasing, though they stayed in the same relationship to each other. And they were occluding other stars. Ren thought she glimpsed brief, bright bursts of blue light around the edges of the constellation.

'Those aren't stars,' Ren said. The same instant, the tug pod was electrified by proximity alarms.

One-eyed jacks and black queens tumbled end over end in space. Sudden acceleration sent them raining down on Ren and Hanuman.

'In your seats. Get in your fucking seats!' the guard shouted.

'It's a ship,' Ren whispered to Hanuman. The woman had pulled a stinger. The fierce little hand-piece fired neurotoxin darts. Human-lethal, hull-friendly. She waved the weapon at Ren.

'Get in your fucking seat!'

She slowly fastened the straps, held her hands up. The klaxons ended. The flashing lights went out. The guard swam over to the intercom. Gravity shifted again as the engines burned, swung the Marine against the bulkhead.

'What's going on!'

The whole cabin heard the reply from the crew module.

'The fucking Space Monkeys are trying to board us!'

The soldier cut the speaker. The cabin jolted again and again as the tug crew tried to outmanoeuvre the Big Sky raiders. Ren glanced out the window. A darker darkness moved across the stars. Warning lights flashed in her face: the glare of small thrusters lit up the cabin.

'To me!' the guard shouted. 'No one looks anywhere but at me, right?'

Nothing happened. The guard held her stinger to her chest. She was breathing heavily. There was a clunk, heavy enough to shake the ship. She looked up. Another clank, a slithering sound

398

across the hull. She looked down. A series of loud bangs, a screeching hiss. The soldier toggled the intercom switch. Static. She whirled, backed away from the hatch.

The outer lock unsealed. The inner dogs turned. The cabin hatch opened.

'Don't come a step closer.'

The Big Sky warrior threw up all four of his hands as the muzzle of the stinger stabbed at him. But the woman could see all the others behind him, and beyond them, a ship she could not fly, clamped like a hunted sparrow in the grappling arms of the stronger, faster Big Sky tug. Her grip wavered.

'Don't,' Ren whispered. The American soldier looked at her. Her face said, you can read my mind? Yes, Ren thought. You are thinking, it can go two ways. Either you can push the gun into the side of my head and make me a hostage, or you can press it into the roof of your mouth and pull the trigger. I do not much want either. I want you to take the third way.

The woman soldier closed her eyes. She let her hands fall. She reversed her grip on the stinger, handed it butt-first to the Big Sky commander.

'I surrender,' she said. He would not take her gun.

66

All ready on Iles Glorieuses, Ren said.

All ready on the Dark Side of the Moon, the Big Sky captain said. Grapples released. Manoeuvring jets pulsed. *Iles Glorieuses* dropped from the skeletal embrace of the tug. Ren flew free. At ten kays she burned the engines one last time. She was committed now. She was going home.

Iles Glorieuses on de-orbit, she said to the Big Sky tug. *And thank you. What are you going to do now?*

Go home, what do you think? the captain said. *It's our home, we live there. Anyway, a space elevator is going to need lift boys.*

In her augmented vision, the tug faded in her hindsight to a faint radar contact. Its engines fired twice. Going home. Earth now filled half her vision. It dominated all her senses, drew all things to its hypnotic blue. She fell towards it, spiralling down its gravity well like an insane wall-of-death rider.

Yee-hah! Cowboy hollered sub-vocally.

In a niche of her mind, Ren felt William smile.

Iles Glorieuses, *respond please.* Nosy Bé was coming through. Ren felt an almost painful rush of recognition at Anitraséo's voice. Iles Glorieuses, *can you hear me? Respond please.*

Iles Glorieuses *responding. I can hear you, Anitraséo.*

We have you on long range scanners. Did she hear a catch in the voice? *You're clear for the landing window for Réunion. Please make the following course adjustments.* Vectors, moments, fractional orbits, trim burns flowed across the isopathic interface between her auxbrain and the computers that flew the ship. The systems responded. *Automated landing systems have engaged. Lie back and enjoy the ride. You've deserved it.*

Curled in the womb of amber acceleration fluid, Ren thought, yes, I have deserved it. And I shall enjoy it. I shall observe and savour and remember every moment. It's not one many humans have ever made. I shall never come this way again. Few will ever need to, when the Freedom Tree is grown.

She was in the ship from Mandelatown, in the moments before the landing at the vent into the fourth chamber. *We're going in,* the pilot had said and the fear and the tension had blown away like summer storms and she had felt a vast and electrifying serenity. *I call it the Freedom Tree,* Tsirinana had said, touching the swell in her belly that had betrayed her. *That's not the proper name, but it's my name. In Sierra Leone, in the town of Freetown, there was a tree at the top of King Jimmy's steps. When the slave ships were captured, the slaves were brought to the tree and had their chains struck off beneath its branches. It was they who called it the Freedom Tree.*

Yes, that is what history will call it, Ren thought. The Freedom Tree. Rooted in the earth of Africa, watered by the snows of Kirinyaga, rising out of the mountain through storm and cloud and ozone, through stratosphere and ionosphere, climbing out of the atmosphere. Higher than this tough little shuttle, climbing into space, beyond Unity and the orbits of the Death Stars and the spysats and the comsats, to geosynchronous orbit. And beyond.

The forces must always be in equilibrium, Tsirinana had said. Her face had lost its high Merina composure when she spoke about the Coalition's staggering concept. *It must grow in both directions at the same time, inwards and outwards.* Cowboy explained Tsirinana's radiant enthusiasm. She had been a member of the engineering design team. She was pregnant with her own dreams. *And at the far end, we have to hang a counterweight.*

Beyond, to the singularity. Toatéu. Star Gate. Names for the mystery. At the far end of her space elevator, Tsirinana hung the universe.

Ren remembered another tree that grew to heaven; the world-tree of Oksana's shamanic legends, its roots among the unborn souls, the nations flowing up its trunk, along its branches that reached out to other worlds.

For the Earth terminal, we need something that will anchor it firmly, something with its roots in the mantle, something with enough altitude to lift the ground station above the worst of the low level weather.

Something like a five thousand metre mountain, less than one per cent of a degree south of the equator. And if that mountain happens to be someone else's, get them to share it with you. By any means.

They will have to talk to us then, Tsirinana had said. *They will come to us, and then we shall tell them what we want. And they will give it to us. We will have their respect.* And their people, and their commerce, and their wealth, and their ideas, in a buzzing cross-fertilization of cultures and races. Kirinya's future was greater than the mere capital of a dynamic new nation. Its destiny lay as capital of the human species. The navel of the world. And the great umbilical, connecting us to those other ways of being, out there. Birth, and death. Death on a high plateau at the end of the world, under a leafless acacia on a sun-burned plain. The Freedom Tree, the Tree Where Man was Born, the Tree of Souls, half-living, half-bleeding. Like all of us.

I may never come this way again, but this is a sight I hope I will see many times in my years to come: Africa beneath my feet like a carpet of spices, a whole world in a continent, the mother of man, as the Freedom Tree lifts me to adventures and experiences I can't begin to imagine. And when they are done and I am changed by them, I will see Africa as I see her now, rising out of the dome of ocean and the arc of night like a legendary child being born, that is old and wise, and at the same time for ever young and curious; as I come home.

She felt the little ship buck and kick; skipping like a stone on the upper edges of the atmosphere. Soon surface heating would close down her skin-eyes; she would fall blind and burning across the winter constellations. Through tongues of plasma fire licking over the hull, she glimpsed the white mountains of East Africa. Kirinyaga was the eye of a tremendous spiral weather system. She imagined a line of light rising out of that eye like a ray, higher than she could see, shooting into the eye of heaven. She saw terminum striding across the curved land and now she saw it not as a line of division but a place of joining. She did not see two hemispheres, separate and hostile. She saw one world, and though it swamped all her senses, it seemed as small and fragile as a newborn. She saw a blue earth on a black sky. She saw a white girl in a dark forest. She saw red blood on a pale plain. She saw her cheek on Cowboy's chest. She saw the Freedom Tree climbing out of the heart of the line of division. Then the hull sensors shut down and she saw no more as the little ship shook and shuddered and shrieked and fought the air, drawing a line of fire across the dawn breaking over Africa, coming home.

Freedom Tree

67

The dying was done in the house by the sea. It was all healed over, sealed, committed to fire and earth, but it lingered in the things that remained, the bookcases, the wardrobes, the larder, the magazines on the tables, the astronomical equipment in the Weather Room that looked out over the shipping channels to the changing blue of Galloway across the water. The late summer evening made it strong. It had been his season, the hot, tired days when the effort of coming autumn seemed too much for the world. The lazy days. Gaby could not stay in the house with them. She whistled up the shy black cross-breed bitch. They went out on to the Point.

The paths were baked hard by ten rainless days. Beyond the barbed wire fence, the barley bowed seed-heavy heads. The sky above the grain field was an intense, infinite blue. No rain, no change in sight.

Strangely undignified, to be committed to fire on a day like this. Weather should mark it, unexpected rain, a strong wind flapping the jackets and dresses at the crematorium, high fast cumulus. Not shimmering, changeless blue. It was like a chord of eternity.

Time had not overgrown the secret, remembered sea-path through the dry gorse. Time was no part of this place. Here the seasons turned and things were born and bred and died but nothing changed. All things moved but went nowhere, like the bobbing painted ponies of a carousel. Jude the silly bitch frolicked back and forth, ducking into tunnels among the twisted trunks, plunging out again a few dozen metres ahead or behind, looking to see if Gaby was still there. Still here, hound. She had the palest yellow eyes Gaby had ever seen in a dog.

Black dogs; the house on the headland; the Point, its sea and seasons; Galloway across the sea, the hills of Antrim on the far side of the lough; a McAslan to care for it all. The constants of life in this place. And I, as unchanged as any of it.

Word is faster than flight. The Heathrow transfer had been swift and anonymous, but the press had been waiting for her as she came down the escalator into arrivals at Belfast.

'Ms McAslan, have you any comment ... Ms McAslan, are you responsible ... Ms McAslan, how long have you known that your daughter.... Ms McAslan, what future for the talks process ...'

'My father is very sick, I've come home to be with him.'

They mobbed the big black Landrover, thrust cameras and recorders through the open window as Bec paid the car park attendant. Jude the dog barked excitedly at the hands banging on the glass. Their cars were parked for half a mile along the back road from Bangor: the Landrover turned on to the rough dirt track down to the Watchhouse to find them ranked on the low concrete bridge over the stream like vigilantes. Bec slowed, but did not stop. Later she went out to the ones who had come up to the house and were ringing the bell.

'My father is terminally ill. Please, respect his privacy and allow him some dignity.'

In the end the police were called. They moved them on.

Her father spent most of his days in the Weather Room. He had a chair by the window where he could feel the sea on the glass and watch the weather moving across the sky. On a small side table were the fingerpad for the computer and the little hip flask of morphine. He was listening his way through his favourite recordings, many of which were sixty-year-old vintage waxings from the punk era of his teens. The floorboards would shake to 'White Man in the Hammersmith Palais'.

Pushing open the door of the Weather Room, Gaby was again an eight-year-old, apprehensive of the grown-up mysteries of her father's sanctum. He sat by the window. He looked thin and old and tired of being tired. He looked like what he was: a dying man.

He set down his copy of Henry James.

'This man is an anal retentive,' he declared. 'Why am I wasting my precious reading time on this overblown twaddle?'

'One of those writers you always said you'd get around to reading some day but never did?'

They embraced. Gaby found herself tearful.

'It's good to have you back,' her father said, and she heard the break in his voice. He pushed her back from him so he could look long at her. His eyes read her face. She had been dreading confronting her father's imminent mortality with her a-mortality. Now they sat face to face overlooking the sea and she found that it was a compact between them, not a source of separation. They were both far beyond the common, he in his embodiment of death, she in her denial of it. They met in extremity. They talked trivia; the flight, the reporters, the house and how she might find it changed and how not. Gaby wanted to say a thousand things to her father, about her life, her fears, her hopes and betrayals and where she had come from, where she might go to. Instead she talked about airports and how she hadn't looked at any of the papers to see what they were writing about her and how little and how much the house had changed and those things remained unsaid. This was not her time.

'So, a daughter,' her father said. Gaby looked away.

'It's complicated.'

'You're telling me. That's one good thing about this. It makes everything simple. It pushes you into the present. Things like doing the crossword in the paper become major aesthetic experiences. It's there, it's absolutely immediate. Completely present. More important than bloody Henry James. Excuse me.'

He broke off for a sip from the flask.

'Does it hurt?' Gaby asked.

'Of course it bloody hurts. You know, it's a wonderfully selfish

405

thing, dying. You can get away with anything. The revenges I've planned, the murders I've committed, knowing I would absolutely never be brought to book for it. I even got you back.'

'That wasn't you. That was my own decision.'

'Are you absolutely sure about that? You know, when I heard you were coming, I didn't want to see you. You terrified me. You would be standing there, with all those things in your bloodstream, that this thing, living inside me, couldn't begin to touch. You wouldn't even have to think about it, to be invulnerable would be as natural as breathing for you. Totally taken for granted. I hated you quite a lot for that. Now, I think actually Dylan Thomas said it best. At the end, wise men know dark is right.

'"And you, my father, alone on that sad height,
"Bless, curse me now with your fierce tears, I pray."'

'I'm not exactly raging against the dying of the light, am I? There's a lot to be said for going gently. Or at least going as you wish to go. Without bloody Henry James.'

He flung the broken-spined paperback across the floor.

And now the dog was chasing across the mud flats sending wading birds peeling up to hover a moment in a flick of wings and then settle again, long toes spraddled wide. Back and forth she dashed and the birds fled from her. Gaby wondered which was taunting which. The moon was high, the crescent moon of the western islands, upright, looking into the future. Its bright companion was just below the horizon. Some said they could already see a change in its shape, a spindle to the old moon's crescent. But they were the kind of people who are always first to any new thing, to cling to its leg like a masturbating puppy.

After three days a breaking boy-sex scandal involving a holy local politician drove the journalists from the door of the Watchhouse. The others remained, the ones you were not supposed to see watching you, that anyone less practised than Gaby in the arts of political surveillance would have missed. Keeping an eye on the dangerous subversive in case she tried to rape and eat school-boys, or squirted her infected blood over mortgage-payers. Gaby walked up the dirt road past the roofing contractor's van and the dog-walking couple into the village. She bought chocolate and a satirical magazine in the shop and a whiskey in the bar from a barkeep barely old enough to have pubes. He served her and went down the far end of the bar and pretended to talk about lottery cards with a friend for rather too long. In the shop, the owner had at least waited until she had left before gossiping over the microwaved sausage rolls and broccoli and mozzarella lattices. Unclean alien witch. Perverser and more grotesque by far than any Free Presbyterian boy-fucker. Don't you worry, bar-boy. What makes you think this fortysomething in a twentysomething body has any interest in you? She kept her visits to the village to a minimum after that, and drank at home, with people she knew.

A parcel came for her. It took her quite by surprise. It was a big padded envelope, trans-shipped through Helsinki, carrying many UN priority dockets. It had been opened, poked into, prodded at, sniffed and sampled and sucked so many times it was more tape and official seal than envelope. She opened it and tipped out the horoscope tapestry Bec had sewn for her so many years before. Pinned to it was a note. It was from Faraway. It said: *You will need these to find your way back to me.* There was another message on a slip of paper in the bottom of the envelope. It showed signs of having been much read before Gaby. It read: *All is not lost: our enemies are our allies, it seems. Something very strange and wonderful will be happening, and everyone will see it. Come back to me.* She sat a long time alone in the kitchen, twisting the tapestry of stars between the fingers of one hand, beating the others softly on the raw pine table. She hung it on the wall of the big, bare room with the view out across the Point that she had slept in all her childhood. Yes, Faraway, she thought. I will need these stars to find my way, but not back to you. I can't come back to you. I don't love you. There's another. There always was.

She spent much of her days with her father, making up time both of them knew could never be made up. They solved crosswords together. They solved the world's woes together. They talked about issues and politics that could not possibly have any significance now, except for the moment, the pleasure of the spark of one idea off another, the present in which her father lived. They talked about new world orders that were, and that could be. Every time they spoke, she heard more death in his voice, saw more of its dark shading over him. She did not find it terrible or morbid. There was a fitness and dignity in its dark colours and sombre tones. It was as essential to what he was as his birth. It became him.

The night he asked her to take the boat out the moons were full and the tide was high and the evening was full of the still, shimmering heat that it carries in it at the end of summer. He was sick and weak and very tired, but Gaby could not refuse him. He sat in the bow of the little wooden shell as Gaby steered it away from the jetty, looking back at the lights of the Watch-house and the sunset glow still hanging over the Point. She took him past Seagull Island, out of the harbour and around the little headland. She navigated by the lighted windows of the Watch-house into the tide-water channels between the sand-drift islets. She noticed how her father sat in the bow of the boat and looked around him at the Point in the twilight and she knew he was making his farewell to his place. Venus burned low over the eastern sea. As Gaby steered the little boat through a narrow rocky cut out towards the open water again it brightened to a comet impact.

'Three hundred and eight left to go,' her father said. 'There's still a lot of speculation on the astronomy newsgroups about what they're going to do with what's left of Venus. They've got the rotation period up to twenty-two days.'

'Crash terraforming,' Gaby said.

'No doubt, but whose terra?' He laughed darkly. 'Matter of damn. Always be a mystery to me. I quite like that. I don't think we should get all the answers in one lifetime.'

Around the high headland seals had come ashore on the tidal reefs. They rolled on to their sides, lifted heavy heads to scan the visitors with their black eyes. Gaby circled the islet until the seals merged with the dark and the water was streaked with the yellow lights of the big town across the bay.

'Time to go?' she asked.

'Time to go.'

Two noons later he died.

You knew, Gaby thought. It was time to go. Out across the flats the tide had turned under the moon. Foam-edged laps of water slid across the worm-pocked mud, meeting, mingling, filling and covering and swelling. She swiped at night-flying midges whining around her hair. Her sweat-gland insect repellent did not work on them. Yet.

'Jude!' No sign of the stupid dog. Bec had warned that she was a nervy creature, almost anything unexpected would have her bolting back to hide under the kitchen table, tail between legs. 'Jude!' A crashing in distant undergrowth.

She had been delighted by what a good funeral it had been. A celebration of life and loves. Good and pagan. No priests, no lovers – Sonia had died some years earlier in a car crash – but many friends with poetry and punk music, who came back to the house and drank a lot and behaved with the decorous debauchery of people who know the art of funerals. Friends, and cameras. The discreet watchers had never been far, outside the funeral parlour, visiting the dead at the cemetery, fixing satellite dishes in the village. Hannah had been quietly furious in the kitchen over the vegan *vol au vents*, as if the security presence had been Gaby's hideously mistaken idea of a tribute. The family argument is another part of the art of funerals. But her nieces, after hovering and muttering and shooting occasional shy glances at Gaby over their disposable plates and snap-together champagne glasses, plucked up the courage to talk to their strangely young new aunt five minutes before leaving.

'So, our cousin, your girl.'

'Serena.'

'Has she really gone into space?'

'Really. And come back.'

She could so easily have missed the e-mail. She had not gone into the Weather Room since the death. But this morning an urging called her into the room that was full of early light, and there it was, among the condolences. Many computers and networks had bounced it around; some of them intelligence services, she did not doubt. Its point of origin was listed as the United Nations in New York, but it came from a place more distant and exotic. *From: A.O. Rananatsoa. To: Gaby McAslan. To inform you that the Merina orbiter* Iles Glorieuses *made a normal and safe landing at our Réunion facility this morning at oh six twenty-two local time. All aboard are in good health, though tired. Your daughter is resting and recovering in the medical centre. I will keep you updated as to her progress.*

She went into space. She came back.

The tide was running fast. The sun had set behind the hills across the lough. Tidewater and twilight were filling up the land. Flocks of orange-billed oyster catchers came whispering in on the still air, whistling to each other. A curlew called, a painful, plaintive, yearning cry. The BDO rose. At geostationary orbit, it was half the size of the moon, recognizably a cylinder. It cast a soft green light.

You were there, she thought. You went beyond all I knew of it, into unknown regions. Did you find him, Serena? Did you tell him who you were? Did he ask about me? Or did he walk out on you like he walked out on me? The higher, nobler call? A singular man. And if he did go on, wherever he is, whatever he has become, does he think of me, as I think of him, often, and with a clench in the heart that never fails? But that's too much of a question to ask you, Serena.

You went, you came back and the world is a different place because of it. While they stick needles in you and read your blood and sniff your shit and give you sugars to suck, the planet is reeling. Already the North is calling for a new summit. The United States is re-evaluating its policy. The EU is rushing through the vote recognizing the Southern states. Embassies are being hurriedly prepared to Kirinya and Ambositra.

Funny how they find respect when you have something they need.

The Freedom Tree. She liked the name. It was a grown thing, organic. An African name for what it was, the navel cord of the planet. The oldest names in the world, in Africa.

The light was almost gone now, ebbing as the tide was flowing. The stars of the northern hemisphere were growing brighter; across the lough, the lights of the seaside towns were going on, district by district. Down the coast on the Copeland Islands, across at the mouth of the lough, over the sea in

Galloway, the lighthouses were speaking to each other in coded flashes.

'Jude!'

A rustle of dry bracken and brown gorse quills; a darting shadow. Black dog on a dark night. Across the rising tide, lights went on in the windows of the Watchhouse.

A little last mystery. In boxes in the attic, the McAslan sisters had at last solved the question of how their father had made his money. They sat on the dusty boards, each with a pile of manuscripts, reading in the light that beamed in through the chinks in the roof. Gasps and laughter.

'This is a bit spicy!'

'It's supposed to be.'

'Read this one, this page here . . .'

Guffaws.

'"He came over m'lady's pursed lips. She sucked it down as if it were finest caviar. 'More,' she whispered."'

'"'You shall be transformed into the image of my fantasies, perfectly compliant in every way, the eternal sex toy.' 'Yes, master, it will be beautiful.'"'

They both laughed at that one.

'Actually, it's pretty, you know, good.'

'For porn.'

'For porn, it's James Joyce.'

'I wonder what he did with the copies of the books?'

'I don't think we'll tell Hannah, do you?'

'No, I don't think so.'

Gaby stood by the edge of the water. The dark was almost complete. She could feel the stars above her as if they were fixed to her skin by fine wires of circumstance and ambition, dragging her through space and time.

No. I've been led too far too long by you. You have brought me back to the place where I began, and if it begins again, it will be because I choose it, not because of the powers in the sky. I unbind myself. Here, I begin myself again. I will not stay here for ever, though it may be a long exile. I will go back to Africa, because that is where the new world is being born, and Serena is there, and there is old love, and as he once said to me, no one who has been there is ever really free of it.

Venus flared on the edge of the world. Three hundred and seven to go. There are mysteries still to be discovered. There is story still to be told.

She called her black dog to her and turned towards the lighted windows of the house beyond the water.